# THE KILLING GAME

DI SIMON WISE BOOK 2

MICHAEL DYLAN

# Wednesday 16th November

# 1

It was The Dream again.

Somewhere deep in Detective Inspector Simon Wise's subconscious, he knew that. It didn't stop what he was experiencing from feeling all too real, though. And the emotions it stirred up — the panic, the fear, the desperation — well, they felt as bad as they ever did. Maybe worse. Because Wise knew how the nightmare ended. He knew it so well because he'd been having The Dream every night since that little red dot found his best friend's head. He knew that, no matter what he did or said, there was nothing he could do to stop Detective Sergeant Andy Davidson from dying.

Nothing at all.

Still, it didn't stop him from trying. Like he did every goddamn night.

*He's on that rooftop in Peckham, his hand outstretched as always. 'Please, mate. I don't know why you're doing this, but we can sort it out. We can fix it — whatever it is — if you give me the gun. You're not a murderer.'*

*'You don't know what I am!' Andy screams, his eyes wide, burning bright from all the wrong kind of chemicals. 'I have to do this.'*

*A red dot appears, as it always does, and dances across Andy's shoulders, seeking his head, finding its spot, stopping on his temple, dead still.*

*'No!' Wise shouts. He thrusts both hands up in the air, turning, trying to see where the sniper is, trying to block his line of sight. 'Don't shoot! Don't shoot.'*

*He turns back to his friend. 'The AROs have got you in their sights, Andy. Please give me the gun before it's too late. Think of Debs. Think of Katie and Mark. Please, mate.'*

*'If I don't do this,' Andy says, 'he told me he'd kill them.'*

*'Who did?' Wise takes another step forward, knowing he won't get there in time. 'If someone's threatening you or your family, we can stop them. You just have to trust me and give me the gun.'*

*Andy shakes his head. 'I'm sorry, Si. I'm sorry for ev—'*

*The bullet takes the top of Andy's skull off a heartbeat before Wise hears the crack of the gun. Time slows as Andy tumbles forward, red mist leading the way, his brains and blood already splattered across the rooftop. He lands on the concrete with a wet thud and lies unmoving, his eyes open and fixed on Wise, accusing him. 'Why did you let them kill me again, Si?' Andy says. 'Why?'*

*'I'm sorry,' Wise says. 'I tried. I tried. I tried.' He wants to scream. He wants to cry. His best friend is dead, and he doesn't understand why.*

*'Bastard deserved it,' a man says with a chuckle. His voice is so familiar. It's like Wise has known it all his life. South London accent. Wise turns, horrified, and sees a man lurking in the shadows, a smoking gun in his hand. He's tall and broad-shouldered. The same height and build as Wise.*

*Wise can't make out the man's face, though. It's too dark. Hidden.*

*Wise takes a step towards him, trying to see the man's identity, terrified that he knows exactly who it is. 'Who are you?' he shouts.*

*The man points the gun at Wise as he retreats further into the shadows. 'I'm coming for you next.'*

*'Who are you?' Wise screams. 'Who are you?'*

*The man doesn't answer. He just walks backwards, gun in hand, away from Wise, away from Andy's corpse, until he's lost in the shadows.*

*Wise begins to run. He has to catch the man. Stop him. Bring him to justice. He picks up speed, running faster and faster, heart racing.*

*'Who are you?' he cries.*

'Simon. Wake up.'

*'Who are you?' Wise is lost in the darkness, running, running, running. The man's gone, but Wise can't stop running. He has to find him. Find the killer.*

'Simon. Wake up. You're having a bad dream.'

*Wise hears the voice in the darkness calling him. He knows it. Loves it. It's his wife's voice. Jean's voice.*

'Simon, wake up.'

*He's having The Dream. All he has to do is open his eyes and it'll be over. He'll be safe.*

'Wake up.'

Wise opened his eyes and didn't know where he was.

He blinked furiously in the darkness, aware only of his heart pounding, the sweat on his skin and the fear still coursing through him still. Slowly, other shapes formed out of the shadows, each one anchoring him back into the real world. Into the present. Into his home.

Jean was next to him in their bed, her hand on his forehead, soft and caring, eyes wide with worry. 'Hey,' she said with a smile.

Thank God.

'Jean,' Wise said with relief. 'Jean.'

'Hello, you,' his wife replied, full of love and everything good in his life. 'You were dreaming again.'

'I'm sorry,' Wise said. His mouth was so dry, it hurt to talk.

'Don't apologise. It's not your fault.'

'But I woke you up ...'

'Still not your fault.'

Wise sat up and took a couple of deep breaths, trying to settle his heart back down to a normal rate. It was still dark, the only light coming from the street lamps outside sneaking through a gap in the curtains. Sweat soaked his t-shirt, so he pulled it off and threw it on the floor. 'What time is it?'

'4 a.m.' Jean replied.

'God, I'm sorry.'

'Simon, it's okay,' Jean said. 'Was it The Dream?'

'Yeah.' Wise didn't need to go into more details. They both knew what The Dream was. After all, the basics hadn't changed since August, when his partner was shot dead on the rooftop of the Maywood estate in Peckham.

Just after it first happened, though, Wise didn't even need to be asleep to relive the moment the Armed Response Officers shot Andy. Back then, he'd see it over and over again, twenty-four hours a bloody day.

The truth was that Andy's betrayal and his death nearly broke Wise, almost destroying his marriage and career in the process. It was only thanks to the hard work of his police-appointed psychiatrist, Doctor Shaw, and the understanding and support of Jean that he pulled himself together in time before he screwed everything up. God, at one point he'd even thought about driving his car into the river and ending it all.

Now The Dream was an infrequent visitor, a painful reminder that Wise might be getting better, but he wasn't actually better. Not by a long way.

The man in the shadows was a recent addition to the dream, though. Something extra to add to the pain.

He was the man who'd ordered Andy to kill the witness. The mastermind behind Andy's corruption. A man Wise had sworn to catch.

Wise picked up the glass of water from his bedside table and drained it in four gulps.

Jean was still watching him. 'You feeling better?'

Wise nodded but said nothing. He hated lying to his wife. 'You should go back to sleep. The kids will be up soon enough.'

'So should you.'

'I'm okay. I'm going to get up and get a run in before work,' Wise said.

Jean gave him a look that said she knew how he was really feeling. 'Go easy on yourself, eh?'

'I will — now, go back to sleep.' He did his best to smile.

'I love you.'

Wise leaned over and kissed Jean. 'I love you too.'

Leaving his wife to sleep, Wise got out of bed, padded over to the chest of drawers, and grabbed his running gear.

Ten minutes later, Wise was outside, wondering why he hadn't gone straight back to sleep when he'd had the chance. It was so cold, it almost hurt to breathe. The frost coating the ground suggested that there was more than a good chance Wise would slip and break his neck at some point. A sensible person would've turned back towards their warm house. Wise, though, jogged on, down empty streets and past dark houses, heading towards Clapham Common. He was desperate to shake the lingering effects of The Dream from his mind and this was the best way he knew.

The common was a triangular patch of land, covering two hundred odd acres of parkland. It connected Clapham and Battersea together and was one of Wise's favourite places. During the day, there was always something going on, no matter the weather: from dog walking to exercise classes to kickabouts with footballs and coats as goal posts to kids playing hide and seek. At 4:30 a.m., though, it was deserted. Just the way Wise liked it.

He ran along the main path that clung to the edge of the park, heading north up Windmill Drive, past the allotments and around one of the ponds. The darkness cloaked the landscape with shadows, but Wise didn't care. He knew the route like the back of his hand and there was a comfort in feeling like he was the only person awake in the world.

Wise kept a steady pace, enjoying the sensation of his body warming up. He could feel the lingering aftereffects of the nightmare slowly fading with each yard he covered.

Not that he didn't think about the dream as he ran. He went over it again and again. Or rather, he thought about the man in the shadows. The mastermind.

Specialist Crime and Operations 10, or SCO10 for short, was running the official enquiry into Andy's case and hunting for the man behind it all. Wise had tried through friends of friends to find out what they'd discovered so far, but every approach had been rebuked.

However, the day after Wise and his team had arrested David Smythe for the Motorbike Killings, DCI Rena Heer and DS Brendan Murray turned up at Kennington to see Wise. Apparently, a new gang was trying to take over London's criminal underworld. Using a covert operative, they'd managed to get hold of a photo of the gang's leader and wanted to show it to Wise.

It was a picture of a Caucasian man, early forties, short blonde hair, well-built. A man identical in every way to Wise himself. In fact, the detectives had wanted to know if it was him.

It wasn't, of course. Wise had a cast-iron alibi that proved it was impossible for him to be the man in the picture. He'd been on a surveillance job with other police officers.

The trouble was, Wise knew who the man in the picture was.

It was his brother. His twin.

Tom Wise.

However, at the meeting three weeks ago, Wise didn't tell Heer and Murray about Tom. Instead, he claimed that he didn't know who the man was and that he couldn't help them with their inquiries.

He still didn't know why he'd done that. Why he'd lied. It was instinctive. Foolish. Insane.

Every day since, Wise had picked up the phone to call Heer to tell her the truth. Each time, though, he put the phone down without calling and kept his secret to himself for another day.

Wise told himself it was because he hoped this was all one big mistake, that his brother wasn't a murdering gangster, but even he didn't believe that lie. It felt all too real.

Of course, it didn't help that he couldn't ask Tom about the accusations. The Wise brothers didn't speak to each other. They hadn't for twenty years. Not since a fight in a pub that had left a man dead and Tom sentenced to eighteen years in prison.

Since his release, Tom had rekindled his relationship with their father, but refused any approaches from Wise himself. Wise had been with Tom when he killed a Spurs fan called Brian Sellers in a pub fight. Wise, though, had done a runner before the police got there but Tom hadn't been so quick. He'd been too busy stomping the victim's head in.

There was also another reason Wise had kept quiet about Tom. He'd not declared that he had a brother on his police application forms all those years ago. He certainly hadn't mentioned a brother who was, at that time, in prison for manslaughter. Another foolish spur-of-the-moment decision that haunted him still.

Something else he didn't know how to fix.

It was all one big bloody mess.

Wise continued to run as he went over and over it all in his mind. He followed the route that ran parallel to the South Circular Road. There was just enough light for Wise to dodge around the puddles that covered the track as he continued anticlockwise around the common. He kept his head low to avoid the gnarled branches that dangled out over the path, eager to snatch at anyone foolish enough to get too close.

By the time Wise had finished his normal two-mile circuit, he didn't have any answers. He wasn't ready to go home either, so he started the loop again, the cold long forgotten, his mind racing.

For all of Wise's mistakes, there was one thing he was sure of. Brother or not, if Tom was guilty, there was no way he was going to let him get away with what he had done to Andy. He'd make sure Tom went down.

First, though, he had to know whether it was Tom behind it all.

He needed evidence, and by God, he was going to find it.

# 2

Jack Springer was in his usual spot down the Charing Cross underpass. He was sitting on top of his sleeping bag with a bit of old cardboard underneath to keep the cold out, doing a bit of begging, when the bloke wandered over. He didn't look like anything special. Certainly not like someone Jack should be weary of, in his green anorak and Sports Direct baseball cap pulled down low over his face. He was too stick-thin to be one of those pricks that liked to liven up their day by beating up some poor homeless kid.

For a moment, Jack thought he was a cop come to nick him, but he dismissed that thought pretty quick too. Cops didn't look all guilty like this man did and they didn't hide their faces like that.

His next thought was that the man was a God botherer wanting to save Jack's soul, because he had that prim and proper air about him, but again, he dismissed the idea. Happy Clappers came in groups, wanting safety in numbers and all that when they mixed with the grim and dirty.

Nah, Jack knew what this bloke wanted. He was a poofter after a cheeky blow job in his lunch hour. He had that nervous look that those sorts had, like he was trying to pluck up his courage to speak to one of the great unwashed. No doubt, he was dealing with the guilt of wanting to have his dick given a good seeing to. He probably had a nice little wife at home too, just to add to his shame.

Anyway, Jack knew the sort, so he gave him a smile that let him know he was up for it, whatever it was.

'Hello,' the man said, his voice all posh. Definitely a poofter, after a bit of rough, because that's what all posh blokes want. Nothing turns them on more than a naughty fumble with someone they wouldn't normally trust to clean their toilets.

Jack wasn't gay himself but if he could get a tenner for a quick nosh of the bloke's knob then, as far as he was concerned, that was a good bit of business. For an extra fiver, he'd happily stick his finger up the bloke's arse too. 'Hello,' he said back.

The man hunched down in front of Jack. 'Do you want to play a game?'

Jack gave him his best little-boy-lost look. 'It depends.'

The bloke produced a handful of cash next and let Jack get a good eyeful. They were all crisp twenty-pound notes. 'There's a hundred pounds in it for you.'

Fucking hell, that made things a damn sight more interesting. A hundred quid was serious cash, and Jack knew he'd have to do a lot more than gobble the bloke off. Still, a hundred quid was a hundred quid. That would buy a burger or two and a shitload of smack. For a hundred quid, the bloke could do what he wanted, even get rough with his bit of rough. He knew it wouldn't be quick either but, maybe Jack would get a bath out of it and a soft bed for the night.

'I'll play,' Jack said. Of course, he would. He could barely keep his eyes off all that money.

The bloke leaned forward and made sure Jack looked him in the eye. 'Let me tell you what the game is first, before you agree.'

'Sure. You're the boss.' Jack had to look away, though. There was something in the man's eyes he didn't like. Something wrong. They were as dark as night.

'All you have to do is avoid me for the rest of the day and night. If you make it back here tomorrow without me catching you, then you win.'

'That's it?'

'Like a game of hide and seek.' The man's smile was cold and cruel, and Jack knew he should tell him to fuck off, but he couldn't keep his eyes off that money.

'If you want to play,' the man said, 'I'll give you all this money now and, if you succeed, I'll give you another hundred tomorrow.'

Jack needed no more convincing. 'Deal.' His hand shot out for the money.

Now, Jack was quick, but the bloke was quicker. He caught Jack's wrist with his free hand, squeezing till it fucking hurt and Jack gasped with pain. For a thin bloke, the man was bloody strong. 'There's a catch ... if I catch you.'

Of course, there was. 'What's that then?'

'If I catch you, I get to hurt you and there'll be no more money.' The man said it all so matter-of-fact like. So cold, he was practically frozen. Another red flag. Jack should've bailed then. Told him to shove his hundred quid. The strength in the man's grip was enough of a warning that he was bad news, but Jack wanted the money. Anyway, he could handle a bit of pain. When you sleep on the streets, someone's going to give you a kicking at some point, so you had best get used to it.

'I get to keep this hundred though?' Jack asked.

'Absolutely.'

'You're on, then,' Jack said, and the man let go of his wrist. A second later, he had the cash in his hand. 'When do you want to start?'

'Right now,' the bloke said. 'I'll count to a hundred.'

He hadn't even got to five before Jack was off, money in his pocket, sleeping bag tucked under his arm and a grin on his face. He ran as fast as he could down the tunnel and up the steps, out into the grey daylight of the London street. People gawped as he raced past, probably wondering who he'd robbed, not realising the dickhead had given his cash away.

A game of hide and seek? Stay out of the bloke's way for a day and night? It was going to be the easiest hundred quid Jack ever earned.

He crossed over The Strand, nearly taking out a bicycle courier, then legged it past Nelson's Column, scaring the crap out of a load of pigeons on his way. He stopped running after he passed the Canadian embassy, though, and not just because a copper gave him a nasty look, thinking he was up to no good.

The truth was, he was already out of breath. Unsurprisingly, a steady diet of intravenous drug use didn't make Jack fit enough to run a marathon. Instead, he tucked his head down and walked as fast as he could up Haymarket and then cut back towards Leicester Square. He stopped long enough in a doorway to dig out his phone, a shitty pay-as-you go thing, and tapped out a text to Mad Donnie, his dealer.

*You in?*

What with the running and the hundred quid burning a hole in his pocket, Jack's heart was going like the clappers while he waited for a reply. Thankfully, he didn't have to wait long.

*Yeah but don't come around if you don't have no cheddar.*

That got Jack grinning. *I got cheddar. You got KFC?*

The reply pinged back even quicker this time. *How much you want?*

*A family bucket.* That was five bags at twenty quid a bag. He could just imagine Donnie's face when he read that.

*Cash only or no chicken.* Donnie had every right to doubt he had money. Jack didn't know how many times he'd turned up at Donnie's squat without a pot to piss in and trying to beg some gear on credit. But not this time. Not now he was quids in.

*Be there in 20*, Jack typed and hit send. He was virtually skipping down into the Tube station again. It was like Christmas day. He was going to get so high, he'd not come down for a year.

He jumped the ticket barrier, ignoring the guard's shouts, and took the escalator down to the Northern Line. Jack looked around a few times, looking for the man in a green anorak just in case he was following, but there was no sign of the bloke.

He howled with laughter at the thought of the geezer realising he'd already lost Jack and his money. And if he thought Jack was going to be at Charing Cross the next day, he was going to be disappointed. Another ton would be nice, but Jack wasn't greedy. The money in his pocket was more than enough.

Jack took the Tube all the way up to Camden. He took his time making his way out of the station, feeling so pleased with himself as he stepped back onto the street. Five minutes later, he crossed the canal by St. Michael's, giving the church the finger on the way like he always did. After all, he bloody hated churches.

His father had dragged him to their local one every Sunday, making him bow his head in prayer, while his old man begged forgiveness for his sins. He'd be all contrite until he got Jack home, and then he'd be only too happy to rack up his sins again. The way Jack saw it, if God was on his old man's side, then God could go fuck himself. One day, when he was older, Jack promised he'd go looking for his father with a big sharp knife. He'd cut that bastard's cock off, then shove it up his arse and his dad could see for himself how much fun it was.

No wonder Jack needed his fried chicken to keep him happy.

It would've been faster to keep going straight up Camden Road, then turn down Royal College Street to get to Mad Donnie's gaff on Randolph Street, but Jack cut down the canal instead. It was getting dark and there were no streetlights on the towpath. Fewer people too. Somehow, that felt safer than being surrounded by the crowds. Halfway along, he stopped and had a gander to see if the bloke was about, but, of course, he wasn't. How could he be?

'Easy money,' Jack said to the wind and set off again, pausing only to pick up a half-smoked cigarette that someone had tossed aside and stamped out. He carefully pressed the sides until it looked like a fag again, stuck it in his mouth and lit it. Jack took a long, hard drag as he walked along the path, enjoying the nicotine hit while thinking about the heroin hit he was going to have in a few minutes.

Sometimes, it was the simple pleasures in life that made it all worthwhile.

So caught up in his little bubble of happiness, Jack didn't even see the bloke step out of the shadows in front of him until they were almost on top of each other.

Jack jumped back with a start. The man wasn't wearing his green coat anymore. It looked the same style, but this one was a dark blue and Jack thought that was weird. Why change?

Then, he saw the blade in the man's hand. Glinting, despite the dark sky. Long and curved. More like a sword than a knife.

'Gotcha,' the man said.

'No.' The cigarette fell from Jack's fingers.

He should've known there was no such thing as easy money.

# 3

Wise cursed as rain splattered across the windshield of his battered Mondeo. Someone had murdered a kid on a canal towpath and rain was the last thing they needed. Any evidence left by the killer or killers was going to get washed away, making his job that much more difficult. Unless, of course, Forensics were already at the scene and had a tent up over everything.

Still, it was good he'd been called out on a job. He'd spent far too much of the day thinking about Tom — as he had ever since the visit from SCO10.

He drove down St Pancras Way towards the railway bridge, changing the speed of his window wipers to compensate for the ever-increasing rainfall. Bruges Place was just up ahead on the right, running underneath the bridge. A police car half-blocked the road, its blue lights warning Joe Public to stay away.

Wise slowed and wound down his window just enough to show his warrant card to the uniform on duty. Immediately, the rain found its way inside his car, onto his face and jacket. It was worse for the uniform, of course. He looked positively miserable as he bent down to check Wise's identification, rain running off his hat like a waterfall.

The moment he'd noted Wise's rank, he waved Wise through and slunk back under the shelter of the bridge as quick as he could.

There were already a number of police vehicles parked further on down the road, closer to the intersection with Royal College Street. Wise headed straight for them, passing a gated housing estate, its spiked black railings hoping to keep out its less affluent neighbours, of which there were a lot. That was the trouble with living somewhere 'up-and-coming.' It still had more than its fair share of 'down-and-outs.'

Of course, it wouldn't be the case for much longer. Camden was yet another one of those areas of London that was undergoing gentrification at an incredible pace. For now though, there were million-pound houses jostling for space next to squats. Ultra-modern apartment buildings rubbed shoulders with council housing. No doubt, the media darlings and finance whizzes living in the new enclave wouldn't be happy with a murder taking place on their doorstep.

As Wise drew nearer to the scene, he was glad, at least, to see the Forensics van was there. Maybe his luck was in and they'd got the area covered before the heavens opened up. Maybe they'd already found a truckload of evidence that would make solving the case a piece of cake.

Yeah, right.

Wise had been a police officer long enough to know how often that happened.

Wise parked behind the Forensics van and grabbed his phone from the passenger seat. It beeped before he could slip it into his pocket. It was a WhatsApp message from Jean. *What time will you be back? Kids want to have dinner with you. X*

As always, Wise felt a stab of guilt because he knew he'd not be joining them for pizza or whatever Jean had rustled up. With a sigh, he quickly typed a reply. *Just been called to an incident. Will probably be late. Sorry. X.* He hit send, but then added another message. *Love you. Give the kids a kiss X.*

His phone pinged again. *You big softy X.*

With a smile on his face, Wise got out of the car and slipped his phone into his overcoat pocket. The rain did its best to ruin his good mood though, stinging his face with cold, wet kisses of its own. He turned his collar up, but it offered little protection, instead giving the rain a helping hand to run down his neck. As he trudged along to find the others, he thought about his umbrella by the front door of his house, all nice and dry. Maybe a good soaking was what he needed to make him remember to bring it with him in the future.

He passed Detective Sergeant Roy Hicks' car and then spotted Detective Sergeant Hannah Markham's red Ducati Monster. It was a beautiful motorbike, but not the sort of thing anyone without a death wish would want to ride in a rainstorm.

Two more uniforms waited by the steps down to the canal. One of them must've recognised Wise because she moved aside without asking for his identification. 'Just down the steps, sir, and turn right.'

'Thank you,' Wise replied and followed her instructions, pausing only to wipe the rain from his face, for all the good it did him. He trudged down the steps to the towpath, doing his best to avoid the growing puddles, aware that his shoes were totally inadequate for the weather and the trousers of his suit were already soaked and covered in mud.

Blue and white police tape stretched across the towpath fifty yards on, stopping anyone hoping to walk along it. Hicksy was standing to one side, sheltering under an umbrella, head slouched forward, in a beige raincoat that looked like he'd slept in it. Hannah stood on the other side of the path, a waxed motorbike jacket done up tight to the top of her neck, with her arms crossed and getting dumped on by the rain. Neither looked too happy.

Two white forensic tents, connected to each other, blocked off the path completely about another hundred yards on. They stood in stark contrast to the dark, overhanging trees and the green slime that covered the surface of the canal.

Scene Of Crime Officers bustled about in their blue suits, hoods pulled up and masks on, going in and out of the tent.

There were no boats moored on their side of the river thankfully, but there were plenty lined up on the opposite bank. The weather kept their inhabitants inside, but Wise could see a fair few faces at windows watching the goings on. With any luck, there'd be a witness or two among them.

'Guv,' Hannah said as he approached his two officers.

Wise gave her a nod. 'Hannah, Hicksy.'

'Alright,' Hicksy grunted back.

'What have we got?' Wise asked.

'Young lad had his throat cut,' Hannah said.

'His throat?' Wise stared at the forensics tent, imaging the body inside. 'Any other wounds?'

'No. Just the one from ear to ear.'

'And it was a cut, not a stabbing?'

'Definitely not a stabbing.'

'Okay. That's different.' Knife crimes were increasing year on year, with London recording over eleven thousand offences the previous year. A couple of hundred of those were murders, but nearly all of them were fights gone wrong or muggings that got out of hand, perpetrated by teenagers trying to act tough.

Just like Wise and his brother back in the day.

'I don't think a flick knife did this, Guv,' Hicksy said. 'It's bloody nasty.'

'Has the Home Office pathologist turned up yet?' Wise asked.

'Not yet,' Hicksy said. 'But I heard it's Dodson who's coming. So we could be waiting awhile.'

'Great.' Wise looked at his watch. It was gone 4 p.m. The man was probably already in a pub somewhere and wouldn't be in a hurry to leave. God only knew what state he'd be in when he did finally turn up. 'Let's have a look ourselves, then.'

'I'll leave you to it,' Hicksy said. 'I've already had a gander.'

'Have we got anyone talking to the people in the boats opposite?' Wise asked.

Hicksy nodded. 'School Boy's over there with some uniforms.'

School Boy was the nickname for trainee detective constable

Callum Chabolah. A good lad and a hard worker, he was still green around the ears.

'Why don't you go give him a hand, Hicksy? Give him some of your experience, eh?' Wise said.

Hicksy scowled at Hannah, then nodded. 'Sure.'

As he trudged off to find Callum, Wise and Hannah signed in with the scene of crime officer. They then entered the first tent where they got kitted out with the one-size-fits-all forensic suits.

Because Wise was a big man at six foot one, with a boxer's build, the suits were awkward to get into at the best of times. Now it was especially difficult when he was all but soaked through to the skin. Even when he had it done up, the material was stretched so tight that any movement had the potential to become a disaster.

'I wouldn't bend down if I were you,' Hannah said with a smile as she pulled the hood over her head.

'Don't jinx me,' Wise said as he hobbled on one foot so he could put a covering over his other shoe. Swapping feet, he repeated the process, cursing all the while. The damned suits had always been a bane in his career.

A SOCO had placed metal treads along the ground from the first tent through to the second, where the body was, to protect the crime scene from being marred by people moving back and forth. Wise was glad to see the gravel path underneath wasn't too waterlogged, either.

Using the treads, Wise and Hannah entered the second tent, and Wise got his first view of the victim.

The body lay in the middle of the tented off area; a boy, Caucasian, muddy blond hair, staring upwards, a surprised expression on his face, a bloody red gash under his chin, cut so deep that Wise could see the severed windpipe and got a good glimpse of bone.

The bright light from the halogen lamps made the kid look like some macabre work of art lying in a pool of his own blood, the front of his clothes all stained red.

'How old do you think he is?' Hannah asked. She might've seen the body already, but there was no hiding the sadness on her face.

'Fifteen? Sixteen?' Wise replied. 'Maybe younger. Certainly no age to die.' He ran his eyes over the boy's clothes. Duct tape held one of his trainers together. His black puffer jacket had rips and holes a plenty as well. 'Any ID on him?'

'Nothing. No money either. The only things he had with him were a sleeping bag and a cheap phone,' Hannah said, 'but the SOCOs have already bagged and tagged those.'

'Okay. That tells us something. You don't take your sleeping bag for a walk unless you're homeless.'

'Yeah. Poor kid.'

Wise crouched down to look closer at the fatal wound and felt his forensic suit pull even tighter. 'I've not seen a cut like this before. A bit more effort and the killer would've severed the head.'

'The killer could've come up behind him and taken him by surprise,' Hannah said.

'Yeah, maybe. I can't imagine you'd stand still and let someone cut your throat without putting up a fight.' Wise peered closer. The wound itself looked very clean. 'Whatever knife the killer used must've been extremely sharp, to cut that deep.'

'Why can't these oiks get murdered when it's not bloody raining?' a man's voice said from behind them in the first tent.

Wise straightened up as they listened to the man clamber into a forensic suit.

'Shit. Bugger,' the newcomer said. 'Fuck.'

Wise glanced over at Hannah and raised his eyebrows. It would appear that Doctor Harold Dodson had arrived.

# 4

'Shit. Bugger. Damn,' Dodson continued to mutter.

Wise would've laughed if it wasn't for the dread growing inside him. The pathologist had been on the job for a long time. He'd been one of the best once, but the years had taken their toll. It was well known that Dodson now liked to drink a little too much and his standards had slipped. Not enough to get himself disciplined, but that wouldn't be far off if he kept going the way he was. Wise wasn't a gambling man, but he'd give good odds that Dodson was going to be in a terrible state.

Finally suited, Dodson struggled through the tent flaps. He wasn't a tall man, around five feet six, most of his weight packed around his gut. The blue hood made the redness of his face and his bulbous nose stand out all the more. He wasn't happy to see Wise and Hannah with the body. 'What are you bloody well doing here?'

'Just trying to do some detective work, Doctor,' Wise said. 'I'm DI Wise and this is DS Markham.'

'Well, I hope you haven't been interfering with the body,' Dodson said. His voice was thick and beer soaked. He stumbled forward but caught himself and, somehow, made it look like it was intentional as he bent down beside the boy. 'Another bloody statistic to add to the knife epidemic.'

'He's a boy, not a number,' Wise said, wondering how much the pathologist had to drink. The man wasn't slurring his words, but that didn't mean much. He'd met too many functioning alcoholics in his time.

Dodson looked up at Wise, showing the redness in his eyes. 'Not by the time I see them. Anyway, all these ... kids seem to be determined to get themselves killed these days. We're just here to clean up their mess.'

Wise bit back a retort, even though he vehemently disagreed with what Dodson had said.

The pathologist turned his attention back to the body. 'I'd say the "boy" has been dead for no more than a couple of hours.'

'The 999 call came in at 3:15 p.m.,' Hannah said.

'So, I'm right,' Dodson said, not looking up. 'Thank God for that. My ego needed your affirmation.'

'I take it there's no need to ask you for the cause of death,' Wise said, still trying to be nice.

'Well, I'm willing to rule out a heart attack for now,' Dodson said. 'And drowning.'

Wise exchanged looks with Hannah again and shook his head. 'Right,' he said. 'We'll leave you to it. We'll be in touch.'

'Lucky me,' Dodson said. 'I'll count the minutes.'

Ignoring the man, Wise left the pathologist to work and returned to the first tent, where he removed his forensic suit and retrieved his overcoat. Hannah did likewise. The rain was still chucking it down by the sounds of the battering the tent was getting, just to add to the mood.

'Let's find Hicksy,' Wise said, pulling his collar up, wincing as the wet material touched his neck. Hannah's waxed motorbike jacket looked much more effective than his own coat. Then again, he wouldn't fancy riding a bike in this sort of downpour, no matter what he was wearing. His Mondeo might be falling apart, but at least it kept him dry.

Neither spoke until they were outside again. The rain was coming down in sheets, pounding the life out of everything and turning the towpath into a quagmire. It had gotten dark too while they were in the tent, and there was no street lighting along the pathway, adding to the sense of misery.

'What do you think?' Wise asked as he and Hannah trudged over to the stairs back up to Bruges Place.

'About what?' Hannah said. 'The kid or Mister Happy back there?'

Wise smiled, despite the water running off his nose. 'The kid.'

'If this was a mugging or a fight that went too far, I would've expected the stab wound to be around his chest, some panicked thrust to the main body mass,' Hannah said. 'Maybe some other cuts where he fended off the first jabs. But this? It doesn't feel right.'

'I agree,' Wise said. 'There was no serration around the wound that you'd get if someone had carved his throat open with a sawing motion.'

'But why kill him?' Hannah said. 'The kid had nothing worth stealing, and he didn't look big enough to worry anyone.'

'Maybe it was an argument over drugs? Or maybe he was begging on the wrong patch?' Not that Wise thought either option was right. He glanced over to the forensic tents, feeling the unease in his gut. His copper's instinct refused to accept that this was just another knife fight gone wrong. Something wasn't right. 'We need to find out who the kid was and start piecing his life together. See what turns up. And I want to know what was used to cut his throat like that. I doubt it was your run-of-the-mill kitchen knife.'

'I'll chase up getting the kid's details once he's in the morgue. He might be in the system already.'

'He probably will be. If he's been living on the streets, there's more than a good chance our lot has picked him up for something or other.'

They climbed the stairs back to the main road. Wise walked over to the uniforms guarding the entrance to the towpath.

The female officer gave him a nod. 'Hello, Inspector.'

'Hi,' Wise said. The officer's face was definitely familiar, but he couldn't place where he knew her from. 'Did Doctor Dodson drive here?'

'Yes, sir,' the officer replied, exchanging looks with her colleague. She pointed to a Renault Megane that looked about twenty years old and in worse condition than Wise's car. 'That's his.'

'When he comes back, I want you to breathalyse him before you let him drive home,' Wise said. 'The man smells like he's just fallen out of a pub.'

'Yes, sir,' the officer replied. 'He did look a bit unsteady when he checked in with us.'

'He might not like that, sir,' the other officer said.

'If he gets nasty, threaten to arrest him,' Wise replied.

'Yes, sir.'

'Cheers,' Wise said. He turned back to Hannah. 'Come on.' They crossed over the canal and then descended the steps on the other side.

'I think the good doctor might get a bit pissed off if he has to blow in a bag,' Hannah said.

'Yeah? Well, he should get drunk on his own time, then, not ours. Maybe it'll make him realise he's got a problem.' Dodson's attitude and his complete lack of sympathy for the dead boy had pissed Wise off. He hoped he never stopped caring about the victims of the crimes he investigated.

Down on the other bank, boats lined the side of the canal all the way down towards Camden Town itself, each one painted in a different colour of the rainbow. The canal itself ran all the way through Paddington, Maida Vale, Regent's Park and London Zoo right up into the heart of Camden Town and King's Cross. Back in the days of the Industrial Revolution, it played a vital role in transporting goods in and out of the country, right until the railways changed everything yet again.

Now, though, the canal was a strip of tranquillity in the middle of the bustling city. Even in the rain, Wise could appreciate the appeal of living on the water, still a part of society, but not really. It said something about a person who lived that sort of life, to be a bohemian in a city that only cared about what you could afford. Then again, maybe he was being romantic. The truth was more likely that living on a canal boat was the only way some people could live in one of the most expensive cities in the world.

Up ahead, Hicksy and Callum climbed out of one of the boats. Hicksy spotted Wise and Hannah approaching and waved them over before opening up his umbrella again.

'Hi, Guv,' Callum said. Even the rain didn't seem able to dampen his good mood. Wise tried to remember if he'd been that constantly enthusiastic back when he was a trainee. Somehow, he doubted it.

'You two found anything?' Wise asked.

'Yeah,' Hicksy replied. 'We just spoke to the lady inside this boat and she says she saw it all. Wanna have a chat with her?'

'Sure.'

'Good. I told her you would. Her name's Doreen McGuin.'

Wise climbed onto the small deck at the front of the boat. Hannah went to follow, but Hicksy put up a hand. 'It's pretty cramped in there, Diversity. Probably best if just me and the governor go in.'

'No problem,' Hannah said, her face impassive, despite Hicky using his nickname for her. Wise had asked him not to call her that, but the man was a stubborn bastard. 'Let me look after your umbrella for you while you're inside. Least I can do.'

Hicksy didn't look too keen, but he handed over the umbrella all the same before clambering onto the boat. He knocked on a set of double doors.

'Come in,' a frail voice called out.

Hicksy opened the door and motioned for Wise to go in first. Ducking his head, Wise stepped inside. He found himself in what must have been the boat's dining area, with banquette seating running along one side, and a table just big enough for four people to squeeze around. Past that was a kitchen and then a living area, where a white-haired lady, sitting in a small armchair, waved at him. 'Come through, luv.'

'I'll just take my coat off,' Wise called back, making room for

Hicksy to enter the cabin. 'I don't want to drip water all over your nice home.'

'There's a hook behind you,' Doreen said, with a slight Irish twang. Wise couldn't help but notice the thickness of the woman's glasses. He could already imagine a defence counsel attacking her eyesight if she was ever called as a witness.

'Give us your coat,' Hicksy said. 'I'll hang it up.'

Wise shrugged off his overcoat. 'Cheers.'

'Don't be fooled by the old lady schtick,' Hicksy whispered as he took the coat. 'She's fucking razor sharp.'

'Noted,' Wise said and made his way over to the old girl.

Hicksy hadn't been exaggerating when he'd said the space was cramped. It certainly wasn't made for someone Wise's size. He had to stoop his head and half-turn sideways as he made his way towards Doreen, taking great care not to knock anything over on the way. She had a collection of Toby jugs running along the window ledges. The line of faces, gurning away, only added to the uncomfortableness of the cabin.

Wise had always hated small spaces, even before he'd grown as big as he was. He didn't know why — certainly no one else in his family suffered with claustrophobia — but he had never shaken it. In fact, after his twin brother, Tom, went to prison, it had only gotten worse. Most of the time, though, all he had to do was avoid things like lifts and the Tube and he could almost pretend he didn't have a problem. However, the small boat with its slightly swaying floor was already starting to affect him. It didn't help that Doreen had a small electric fire humming away that made the interior sweltering hot. The fog of cigarette smoke hanging over her head wasn't great either.

'How are you, Doreen?' Wise asked when he finally made it to the living area. 'I'm Detective Inspector Simon Wise.'

Doreen, who had a white corgi on her lap, looked him up and down. 'Jesus Christ, what do they feed you? Little children? Look at the size of you!'

'I'm partial to the odd plate of scrambled eggs,' Wise replied.

'I'm not sure all the eggs in London could keep you satisfied. Not to mention what your poor wife must have to deal with, eh?' Doreen chuckled. She had a china cup full of tea on a saucer next to her on a side table, and an ashtray that had seen plenty of use already. She waved at the empty seat opposite her. 'Sit down before I hurt my neck looking up at you.'

'That's very kind,' Wise said, perching on the edge of the armchair. Like everything else in the boat, it wasn't designed for someone like Wise, and he only hoped his weight wouldn't break the damn thing. 'This is all very nice. How long have you lived here?'

'Too bloody long. My husband, Sean, was the one who thought it was a good idea to sell up and buy the boat. "We'll be free," he said, the daft sod. Back then, though, the wife had to go along with whatever the man decided. I hated it at first, but now? I have everything I need and Mitzi likes it.'

'Mitzi?'

Doreen pointed to the dog on her lap. 'Mitzi.'

'Ah. What about Sean?'

'He died ten years back, so it doesn't matter what he thinks. He was right though — almost.' Doreen's face creased up in a smile, deepening the wrinkles on her face and making her glasses slide up her nose. 'I am free, but it wasn't the boat that made it happen. It took him dying. I've been as happy as Larry since that miserable git popped his clogs.'

Wise returned the smile. He liked Doreen. She reminded him of his own grandmother. 'DS Hicks tells me you saw the incident on the other bank?'

'Oh, my good God. Didn't I just! I wish I hadn't. Awful, it was. Truly awful. I'll be having nightmares about it for the rest of my life.'

Wise knew how that felt. 'Do you mind going over it once more with me?'

'Well,' Doreen said, 'as I told your young man over there. I was just having a cup of tea and a cheeky fag, just watching the world go by and minding my own business, as you do, when I saw the boy walking along the path over the way there.' She waved towards the window opposite her.

'And you were sitting where you are now?' Wise asked.

'To start with, but then I got up and went over to the window.'

'Why was that?'

'I wasn't being nosey, but the boy had this big thing under his arm and I wondered what it was.' She leaned forward and lowered her voice. 'You get a lot of toe rags down here, dumping stuff in the canal. I must admit, I thought the boy was going to chuck something in the water and I wasn't going to have any of that.'

Wise nodded. 'What time was this?'

'Just after three. I'd already taken Mitzi out for her afternoon walk and picked up a pack of Dunhill's from the corner shop, so I was pretty settled for the afternoon.'

'Then what happened?'

'The boy stops just where your tent is now and looks back behind him, like he was looking for a friend or something. He's moving his head around as you do when you're trying to have a good butcher's. He even had me looking too, but there was no one behind him. Then he sets off again, but he only made it another step or two when this other man appears out of nowhere.'

'You didn't see where he came from?' Wise asked.

'No. He must've been hiding in the bushes or something but up he pops, and the kid stops like he's been frightened silly,' Doreen said. 'Next thing I know, the man has this sword thing in his hand and he cuts the young lad across the throat.' She shivered at the memory. 'I tell you, it's not like it is on TV. I didn't think someone had that much blood in them. It came out like a fountain, it did.'

'The man with the sword,' Wise said, keeping his voice soft. 'What did he look like?'

'He had on a blue coat and black baseball cap, but that's all I can tell you.'

'Short? Tall? Fat? Thin?'

Doreen shrugged. 'About average, I suppose.'

'Skin colour?'

'Ooh.' Doreen sucked in a deep breath. 'If I had to guess, I'd say white, but I'm not betting my life savings on that — not that I've got a lot to put down if I did.'

'You're doing great, Doreen,' Wise said. 'This is really helpful.'

'Ah, you're just saying that to make me feel good.'

'Not at all. Now, you said he was holding a sword — can you describe that to me?'

'I say a sword, but it wasn't like one of those things you'd see on *Game of Thrones*,' Doreen said. 'But it weren't no knife either. You'd definitely not use it to cut your veggies up.'

'How long was the blade?'

'About the length of your forearm, I'd say. Yeah, about that.'

Wise glanced down at his arm. 'About forty-five centimetres, then?'

'You tell me. I still convert everything to shillings and tuppences.'

'And was it straight or curved?'

'Curved. Definitely curved. In fact, it looked a bit like a big metal banana, if that makes sense.'

Wise nodded as if it did. 'It certainly sounds like a sword, Doreen.'

The old girl looked happy with that.

'Did you see where the man in the baseball cap went afterwards?'

'I'm sorry. After he killed the boy, I ducked my head down and went looking for my phone to call you lot. I mean, if he thought I'd seen him like, he could've come over to get me with that sword of his, eh?'

'You did the right thing, Doreen,' Wise said. 'And you've been a massive help. Thank you for your time.'

'I hope you catch the bugger,' Doreen said.

'We'll do our best. Look after yourself, eh?' Wise stood and had to take a second to find his balance. He wasn't sure if the boat was actually moving, but he felt uncomfortable all the same as he edged his way back to Hicksy and the way out. Each to their own, but he'd be more than happy to get off Doreen's boat.

Hicksy passed him his wet coat, and he shrugged it back on, feeling the dampness of it adding to his discomfort.

'Told you she was sharp,' Hicksy said as they stepped outside.

Wise didn't reply. He just needed to get back outside. He was through the double doors in an instant and gulping fresh London air as soon as he was outside. Even the cold and rain felt like an improvement.

'How did you get on, Guv?' Hannah asked from under Hicksy's umbrella.

'Apparently, we're looking for a man with a sword,' Wise replied.

'Nothing unusual then,' Hannah replied.

'It's London,' Hicksy replied. 'We don't do ordinary here.'

# 5

After leaving the crime scene, Wise headed back to Kennington Police Station. It was gone 6 p.m. by the time he reached the station.

Wise parked his car, buzzed himself into the building, and headed up to the third floor. His team operated out of Major Incident Room-One and Wise had a shoebox of an office at the back of that.

As he climbed the stairs, he was aware of how quiet the station was after the hustle and bustle of the day. It'd gone from bursting at the seams with bodies to a ghost town. No uniforms were stationed at Kennington anymore, and apart from the Murder Investigation Teams that called it home, most of the people working out of the station now were backroom support staff — people who balanced books and project managed stuff — and they had the luxury of clocking off at a normal time every day.

That just left the detectives wandering around like lost souls as they dealt with things that couldn't wait about until the clock ticked around to 9 a.m. the next day. Like murdered boys on canal paths.

When Wise entered MIR-One, Sarah Choi was on her own, beavering away at her desk. Despite being small for a police officer, she didn't take any crap from anyone and she was damn good at running the incident room. She looked up and smiled when she saw Wise. 'Hello. I hear we caught a bad one.'

'A teenage boy had his throat cut from ear to ear,' Wise said. 'A witness said the killer used a sword.'

'Ow.' Sarah shook her head. 'A sword?'

'A banana shaped sword, apparently.'

She smiled. 'That's a new one on me.'

'Me too.'

'School Boy said the victim was homeless,' Sarah said.

'Looks that way.'

'Poor chap.'

'Yeah. Life certainly hadn't done him any favours.'

'I've already put in the request for all the CCTV in the area,' Sarah said. 'We should have it first thing in the morning.'

'Can you let everyone know we'll have the DMM at 8:30 a.m.?' Wise asked.

'Already done,' Sarah said.

Of course it was. Sarah was damn organised and she knew how Wise operated. He considered the Daily Management Meeting the heart of any investigation. It was where he and his team shared all their discoveries and discussed any theories as they tried to solve some of the most heinous crimes there were.

The information went up on three connected whiteboards at the end of the room. Like the rest of the station, they'd seen better days and were more a murky grey in colour than white. One said, "What do we know?" The second said, "What do we think?" and the third, "What can we prove?" For Wise, these were the essential questions that needed answering in every investigation. What were the facts, what were the theories, and what was the evidence that tied everything together?

Somehow, seeing everything scribbled on those knackered old boards always helped Wise see patterns others didn't. They'd gradually point him in the right direction, to the point where he trusted those boards almost as much as he trusted his team. He even liked the faded notes from past investigations that still lingered upon their surfaces, stubbornly refusing to be rubbed completely away — as if to say, 'don't forget about me.'

Next to the whiteboards, a forty-inch TV was fixed to the wall. Newer by a good decade than most of the Murder Team's equipment, the TV was linked to all the news networks, as well as the team's computers. The team could broadcast any information on the TV for the entire team to see.

His office was to the left of the whiteboards. There was barely enough room for his desk, a chair, and a filing cabinet. It could get like a sauna in there during the summer, and naturally, to compensate, it got cold enough to freeze the balls off a brass monkey during the winter. But it had a door, and Wise enjoyed his privacy when he could.

Entering it now, Wise took off his coat and hung it on the hook fixed to the back of the door. His suit jacket was creased but at least it was still more or less dry. He couldn't quite say the same about his trousers. They were soaked and covered in mud.

Still, he'd not stay for long. It would be good to get back in time to at least put the kids to bed, maybe read Claire a story — if she'd still let him. His daughter was only seven, but she was becoming more and more independent by the day and happy to boss the rest of the family around, especially her brother. Ed might've been two years older, but he seemed happy to run around at his sister's beck and call if it meant he had a quiet life.

It always amazed him how different his two kids were from each other — Little Mister Sensible and Little Miss Chaos. Wise and his wife raised them both in exactly the same way, but they were like night and day in their personalities.

But why was he surprised? The same could be said about Wise and his own brother — especially now.

He'd not noticed it when they were kids so much. Identical in looks, he and Tom were like one growing up, or so he'd thought. Looking back now, though, it was Tom who was always pushing Wise into doing some bad. They pinched sweets from the local shop when they were five or six, then they were fighting every Saturday night when they were teenagers. That said, Wise had always been happy to go along with it. Happy to follow Tom, his big brother, by all of two minutes and thirty seconds.

And now? If what he feared was true, Tom was literally the complete opposite of Wise. The gangster and the detective. Night and bloody day.

Wise sat down behind his desk, opened the bottom drawer and took out a grey folder. He placed it on his desk and started going through the notes it contained, even though he knew its contents back to front, and had lived a good part of its brutal story first-hand.

It was the sad tale of the downfall of Wise's former partner, Detective Sergeant Andy Davidson. The file contained a picture of Andy in happier times. The Geordie showing off his crooked smile, eyes gleaming with mischief, flirting with the camera in the same way he flirted with any woman who had a heartbeat. Andy used to say his smile had got him laid more times than Mick Jagger and that probably wasn't far from the truth.

Wise and Andy had worked together for almost all their careers and had become fast friends, despite the fact Wise was a committed family man and Andy a serial adulterer. The man had been Wise's best man at his wedding and godfather to his children.

So, to say it was a shock when Wise found out that Andy was bent was probably as much of an understatement as it could get.

And it wasn't just that Andy was taking a few backhanders. After he had died on that Peckham rooftop, other crimes soon came to light, including the murder of a prostitute who was blackmailing the officer. Everywhere they looked, more shit popped up. Drugs, gambling, assault, witness tampering — Andy had been a one-man crime wave.

Now, every case Andy had been involved in was being looked at. Every conviction examined. All Wise's good work was being torn apart, looking for any lies or crimes that might've put innocent people away. And more than a few eyes were on Wise and his team as well. After all, where there was one rotten apple, there were normally more. Even Wise had his doubts about the others, and he hated Andy for making him think like that. He hated the fact they were all tarred with Andy's guilt.

Next, Wise pulled out a mugshot of Elrit Selmani. He was an Albanian gangster who'd murdered a prostitute in front of a witness called Derrick Morris. Heavily bearded, Selmani scowled at the camera, his eyes in shadow under a unibrow. The man was now serving a life sentence in Belmarsh Prison, because Andy had failed to kill Derrick Morris that night in August.

Whoever Andy was working for had wanted Morris dead so Selmani could go free. Therefore, it stood to reason that Selmani would know who that person was.

Selmani would know if it was Tom.

Staring at the man's picture, Wise made a note to arrange a visit.

There was a knock on Wise's door, interrupting his thoughts.

'Yes?' he called out.

The door opened, and Sarah stuck her head through the gap. 'I've got an ID on the dead kid.'

Wise stood up. 'Show me.'

He followed Sarah back to her desk in the main room. There was a mugshot on her screen. 'This is Jack Springer,' Sarah said. 'Our dead boy. Fifteen years old.'

Wise looked at the picture. Grown up eyes sat uncomfortably in the face of the child. 'What's his story?'

'Born in Brighton, an only child,' Sarah said. 'His mother left when he was seven and he was raised by his father, a Terry Springer. Jack was a bit of a handful by the looks of it though. There's some shoplifting charges, truancy issues and a few cautions about antisocial behaviour. Then, when he was twelve, he made allegations that his father was sexually abusing him. Social services investigated at the time but found no proof that he was telling the truth, so they left him in the care of his father. So Jack ran away from home. They found him and returned him home. This went on several more times until, finally, he scarpered one day and made it up to London two and a half years ago.'

Listening to Jack's history, Wise could feel his heart breaking bit by bit. He couldn't imagine what it must've been like for Jack, living in a home where one of the two people who should care for him more than life itself abandoned him and the other abused him. To make it worse, when he asked for help, no doubt mustering all the courage he could, no one believed him.

Wise shook his head. 'The kid never had a chance.'

'Yeah, well, he was determined not to go back. He got arrested a few times up here — the usual stuff; shoplifting, possession, even one time for soliciting — but he always did a runner after social services came to pick him up.'

'Those arrests — were they in any particular area of the city?'

Sarah tapped away at her keyboard, then peered at her screen. 'Possession was in Camden, the others were all in and around Charing Cross.'

'Okay,' Wise said. 'So, Camden to score, Charing Cross to work.'

'Looks like it,' Sarah said.

'Pull the CCTV from earlier today at Charing Cross as well,' Wise said. 'Maybe we'll pick Jack up there. He had no money on him when we found him, but I can't imagine he'd have gone over to his dealer with no cash, especially not in the middle of the day.'

'That's a lot of film to go through.'

'Don't worry. I'll get people to help you.'

'I'd appreciate it,' Sarah said.

'Yeah, well, everyone let this kid down while he was alive,' Wise said. 'We need to do alright by him now he's dead.'

# Thursday 17th November

# 6

It was a full house in MIR-One for the Daily Management Meeting when Wise walked in clutching his coffee from Luigi's. Jono and Hicksy were sitting together, whispering to each other. DC Ian 'Donut' Vollers was at his desk in the middle of the room, a little circle of space around him. Perhaps if the man worked a bit harder on his personal hygiene, he might find his popularity improved, but for now, his body odour was enough of a barrier to stop a bullet. DC Alan 'Brains' Park was tapping away at his computer, his face white from the glow of the screen. Wise passed Sarah as she chatted to Callum, an energy drink clutched tightly in his hand. Sarah had already added pictures of Jack Springer to the whiteboard, under the "What do we know?" section, along with his name and date of birth.

Hannah sat on the edge of her desk by Wise's office, her motorbike helmet next to her. 'Morning, Guv.'

'Morning, Hannah,' Wise replied.

'I've got a bit of news for you,' she said.

'Good, I hope.'

'Well, that depends.'

'Go on,' Wise said, not sure if he wanted to know.

'Dodson got arrested last night for refusing a breathalyser.'

'You're joking.'

Hannah shook her head. 'Apparently, the officers guarding the scene did as you asked when he returned to his car and asked him to take a test. He refused and got quite nasty about it. Both officers believed him to be over the limit, so they took him to Holborn nick where he still refused to blow into a bag.'

'Christ. What happened then?'

'They charged him with refusing to provide a sample, then let him go home. I would imagine there'll be some more fallout today.'

Wise sighed. That wasn't what he'd wanted to happen. 'Hopefully, this will be a wakeup call for the man and he can get some help.'

Hannah raised an eyebrow. 'Always the optimist.'

'I try my best.' Wise gave her a wink and headed into his office, where he dumped his coat. He then headed back out to the main room and stood in front of the whiteboard. Putting his coffee down on a table, he turned to face his team. 'Right, everyone. Let's have your attention.'

Silence fell on the room.

'Yesterday afternoon, Jack Springer, aged fifteen, was murdered on the towpath of the Camden canal by having his throat cut from ear to ear,' Wise said. 'As you can see from the mugshot, Jack had more than his fair share of run-ins with us, despite his young age. Judging by the state of his clothes and the fact he was carrying a sleeping bag, it would suggest that he was also homeless. Hicksy, can you fill everyone in on yesterday's events, please?'

The big man stood up and walked over to join Wise at the front of the room. His zig-zag of a nose gave him the look of a bouncer who'd taken a few too many knocks along the way. 'We received a 999 call yesterday at 3:15 p.m. from a Mrs Doreen McGuin, a resident in one of the canal boats, to say she'd witnessed the young lad being murdered. She described his killer as a man in a blue coat and black baseball cap, armed with a sword.'

'Maybe it was one of Brains' *Dungeons and Dragons* mates,' Jono said. A few people chuckled at that.

'At least I've got friends,' Brains shot back, getting more laughs.

'Any you've met in real life?' Jono replied.

'Enough. Pay attention,' Wise said, and the room fell silent once more.

'When Doreen first noticed the lad, she said he was looking around as if to see if anyone was following him. Then, the killer appeared in front of him "out of nowhere" and cut the lad's throat with a single cut. We interviewed the other boat residents, but no one else saw anything — or wouldn't admit they had,' Hicksy continued.

'It's interesting that the witness said Jack was looking around as if he were being followed,' Wise said. 'Had something happened earlier to make him think that, or was he just looking around for a friend to join him? The fact that the attacker "appeared out of nowhere" might indicate they knew Jack would be travelling along that route and they were, therefore, lying in wait for him. Or they could've just been waiting for anyone to attack and Jack was the unlucky person who was in the wrong place at the wrong time.'

'Unlucky doesn't quite cover it, eh?' Hicksy said. 'The kid's throat got cut down to the bone.'

'We obviously need to piece together the victim's life,' Wise said. 'Sarah, can you fill everyone in on what you've found out about Jack's background so far?'

Sarah stood up as Hicksy returned to his seat. She didn't bother joining Wise at the front, but looked around the room as she spoke, her eyes glinting under her severe fringe. She ran through Jack's history, from running away from home amid allegations of sexual abuse to his more recent arrests.

'Why didn't social services take his complaints about his father seriously?' Hannah asked. 'Surely the fact he kept running away should've told them he wasn't lying.'

'We don't know,' Sarah said. 'They're probably just as overworked and understaffed as we are and someone messed up.'

'We need to notify the father of his son's death,' Wise said. 'Can someone get on to Brighton plod to deliver the death notice?'

'I'll do that, Guv,' Callum said.

'Cheers. Ask them to report back on how he reacts. After that, you and Donut can help Sarah go through the CCTV footage. Let's trace what we can of his movements and see what turns up.'

'Sure thing, Guv,' Donut said.

'Brains, can you see if you can find out what the weapon is?' Wise asked. 'The witness described it as sword-like and forty-five centimetres long. She also said it was shaped like a banana.'

'I'm on it,' Brains said. If there was anything, the man would find it. They didn't nickname him 'Brains' just because of his black-framed glasses that were too big for his face. Somehow, he managed to coax information out of the knackered computers that no one else on Wise's team could. 'I have a bit of info as well, by the way.'

'What's that?' Wise asked.

'The victim had a pay-as-you go mobile with him. It's an old Nokia that didn't have any password protection, so we've had a look at who he's called and texted,' Brains said.

'And?'

'He was definitely on his way to score. There's a conversation with another burner phone where he asks if the other party is in, and then if they have any KFC.'

'That's heroin, isn't it?' Callum said.

Brains nodded. 'Yeah. The other party — the dealer — says they've got it but it's cash only and the victim then puts in an order for "a family bucket."'

'I'm a bit out of touch on drug dealing takeaway orders,' Wise said. 'How much is that?'

'That depends,' Jono said, scratching the stubble on his chin. 'Maybe four or five bags at twenty quid each.'

'So Jack had at least eighty pounds on him when he put the order in,' Wise said.

'And he had nothing on him when we found him,' Hannah said.

'Maybe the dealer didn't have anything to sell, but he wants the money all the same,' Hicksy said. 'If the kid's a regular, he'd know what way Jack would come, so he lies in wait with his samurai sword and job's a good 'un.'

'Brains, can we find out who the dealer is by their number?' Wise asked.

'I'm afraid not, Guv. It's a burner, so there's no contract,' Brains said. 'Best we can do is get a rough idea of the phone's location — if it's still on. Of course, there's a good chance they'd already have dumped it if they are the killer.'

'Why don't we put an order in and see what happens?' Hannah suggested.

The room turned their heads as one towards her. 'What are you suggesting, Hannah?' Wise asked.

'They're a drug dealer, right?' she said. 'So, we text them, say we're a friend of Johnnie's or whoever and they gave us the number, put in an order for some KFC and then get the address to collect. If they're the murderer, they'll have dumped the phone as Brains said, and we won't hear anything back. But, if they do reply ...' She shrugged.

Wise chuckled. He really did like the way Hannah's mind worked. 'Okay. Let's do it. Jono, Hicksy — can I leave that with you?'

Neither of the detectives looked too happy with the assignment, but both grunted their agreement.

Wise glanced over at Hannah. 'Can you find out when the postmortem is? Maybe that will tell us more about the type of knife or sword used. With any luck, it'll be some sort of exotic weapon that will be easy for us to track down.'

'Guv?' It was Jono. The man's hair was long and grey, swept back from his forehead with the help of a good dollop of grease by the looks of it. His grey suit, stained with ash and coffee, made Hicksy's crumpled attire look like something out of GQ in comparison. 'As much as I love doing drug deals, isn't this all a bit of a waste of time? I mean, there were over two hundred fatal stabbings in London last year alone, and how many of those got solved? Every teenage lad is carrying a blade these days. Trying to find one teenager in London who was wearing a blue anorak and a black baseball cap is going to be impossible.'

'So we should just forget it, then?' Wise said. 'Let whoever killed Jack off because trying to find them is going to be too difficult for us?'

Jono squirmed under Wise's gaze. 'I didn't mean that. It's just we're short staffed and we've got a shitload on our plates already. We should just be prioritising other stuff.'

'How do we pick who or what's a priority, then?' Wise replied. 'Postcodes? Age? Wealth? Ethnicity? Or maybe we just pick the easy ones, get our crime stats up, make the top brass proud?'

Jono sunk lower into his seat and dropped his eyes to the floor. 'Of course not. It's just …'

Hicksy leaned over to his friend. 'I'd shut it if I were you.'

Jono held up a hand. 'Fucking hell. It was just a suggestion.'

'It's alright,' Wise said. 'I do understand. Every day, there are more cutbacks, making our jobs harder than ever but, every day, life gets more and more difficult for everyone out there too. No one's got any money. We've got kids dropping out of school with no prospects, pissed off with the world, acting like gangsters for a bit of respect. Others, like Jack, get let down by the very systems that should be protecting them and they end up alone on the streets, just trying to survive. The truth is that the easiest thing to do for all of us is to just give up, go for the easy cases or the ones where we don't have to get our hands dirty, but I don't want to be that sort of police officer. I hope no one else here does either.'

Wise waited, looking at his crew, checking out their expressions, waiting for someone to say they disagreed, but no one did, thank God.

Wise walked over to Jack's picture on the whiteboard. 'This is the fifteen-year-old boy who needs us now. Let's not let him down like everyone else has.'

'We won't, Guv,' Sarah said. 'You can count on us.'

'Yeah, you can,' Jono said.

'Good,' Wise said. 'Let's get to it then. We've got a killer to catch.'

# 7

Hannah watched the world crawl by through rain-smeared windows as she and Wise drove to the mortuary in St Pancras. The November weather made everything look miserable. People walked all hunched up with their heads down. They looked desperate to get wherever they were going as quickly as possible, doing their best not to get their eyes taken out by the lucky sods who had umbrellas to keep the slashing rain away.

But it was more than just the rain that got Hannah — and probably everyone else — down. It was the fact that this was just the beginning of the long, dark, cold, wet months ahead of them. Daylight was going to become something that might appear around lunchtime for an hour or two, and that was it. Clothing became a battle of practical layers rather than any thought of what looked good. Normally there was, at least, Christmas to look forward to help get over that midwinter hump. However, this year for Hannah and many other people, all her spare cash was going to pay the bloody electricity bills. The way things were looking, she was going to be giving her girlfriend a can of baked beans for a Christmas present.

The traffic wasn't helping her mood, either. It was as congested and slow-moving as London got. Wise's knackered Mondeo inched along the road in stops and starts, with only the rare empty stretch to give false hope that they'd actually be able to get their speed above ten miles an hour.

Wise seemed little happier than she did, his bulk of a body all scrunched up behind the wheel, cursing every car in front of him.

'We'd be there by now if we'd taken the Tube,' Hannah said, as they struggled up York Way.

'I told you, I don't do the Tube if I can help it,' Wise said, scowling at the road as the windscreen wipers were run ragged trying to clear the rain away.

'How can you be a Londoner and not "do the Tube?"' she asked. 'It's impossible.'

'It is if you work hard enough at it,' Wise replied. 'There's cars, taxis, buses and even Boris bikes to get you around.'

'I can't imagine you on a Boris bike. You'd break the bloody thing.'

'Yeah, well, they're still an option.'

'So, what have you got against the Tube? If you don't mind me asking, that is.'

'I don't know. I just don't enjoy being squashed up with someone's armpit in my face. It makes it hard to breathe.'

'You do know you're bigger than most people?' Hannah said. 'I think it'd be your armpit in their faces, not the other way around.'

'I'm still not getting on the Tube,' Wise growled.

'Okay. You're the boss.' Hannah said with a smile. The truth was, she did kind of get where Wise was coming from. He was a big man, and it was easy to imagine how badly he'd fit in small spaces. She'd only joined Wise's Murder Investigation Team two months before, and she was still surprised at the size of the man.

Over six feet tall, Wise had a boxer's build and hands that looked like great big slabs of meat. If it wasn't for the fact that he dressed meticulously in well-cut suits and starched shirts, he'd look quite the thug. When she'd first met him, she'd thought he looked elegantly dangerous and had decided there and then that she'd never want to be on the wrong side of his temper — especially after she'd seen him nearly lose it a few times.

During the first few weeks with the team, while they were investigating the motorbike killings, there'd been occasions when she thought he was about to do serious harm to people, but he'd been a lot mellower since they'd arrested David Smythe for the murders.

'How are things between you and Hicksy?' Wise asked as they passed Farringdon Tube station.

The question took Hannah by surprise, coming out of the blue like it did. 'It's all good,' she lied. It wasn't good. Far from it, in fact, but Hannah had learned early on in the Met that some things were best kept to herself. No matter what anyone said about diversity, equality and inclusion, Hannah was only too aware that she worked in a police service that was institutionally racist, sexist and homophobic. None of which was good for her career considering she was a black, female, and gay officer. She didn't need to be labelled a troublemaker on top of that.

'Yeah?'

She could hear the disbelief in Wise's voice. 'Yeah.'

'It didn't look good yesterday,' Wise said, not giving up.

'It was raining.' She glanced over at her boss. He was a good man. A decent man. She knew he'd already spoken to Hicksy about his attitude towards her, but all that had done was make the man even more resentful. Anyway, she could deal with her own crap. She didn't need anyone coming to rescue her. 'Any word on when David Smythe's trial is going to happen?'

Wise grinned. 'Nice change of subject.'

'I was just curious. Last I heard, his solicitor was trying to get him out on bail.'

'What a weasel that man is! Mr Paul bloody Trelford of Trelford, Mayers and Jenkins, solicitors to the wealthy. He'd defend Hitler if he was around today and had enough money to pay for it.'

'They're not going to get Smythe out, are they?'

'No,' Wise replied. 'The man's the very definition of a flight risk. Who knows what money he has squirrelled away that we don't know about? Or if he's got hidden passports? We still don't even know where he got his gun from. There's no way anyone's going to risk him doing a bunk.'

'It still makes me smile, thinking about the look on his face when we nicked him,' Hannah said. 'He was so outraged.'

'Yeah, that memory keeps me warm at night,' Wise said.

Smythe had murdered four billionaires back in September, making it look like the work of a random serial killer. In the end, Wise and Hannah had found him hiding in a secret room in a house he owned, but only after the man had everyone running around in circles and Wise himself had been taken off the case. For Hannah's first outing with the Murder Team, it had been quite the baptism of fire.

The traffic crawled on, past King's Cross. They turned left into Goods Way, then right onto Camley Street, following alongside the route of the old canal. As she gazed out over the water, Hannah's mind drifted back to the previous day, thinking about Jack lying on the towpath.

That kid should've been safe at home, worrying about exams and having crushes on other kids his own age. If only someone had listened to him when he'd made the complaints about his father and believed him, he might've had a chance. But no, they kept putting a vulnerable kid back into the hands of his abuser.

And now he was in the bloody morgue.

Suddenly, the pounding rain stopped, and the world went dark as Wise drove through the Camley Street underpass, breaking Hannah from her thoughts. The peace lasted while they passed under the train tracks leading to St Pancras Station, then the rain returned with a fury as they popped out the other side.

'There's the mortuary,' Wise said, slowing down and then pulling into a space next to some grey garage doors.

The building wasn't what Hannah was expecting. In fact, the front of the building looked more like a fancy office building or a hotel. Brown vertical panelling framed a white entrance and cedar doors. 'There's obviously money in dead bodies. This all looks new.'

Wise turned off the engine. 'Well, they're never going to run out of customers.'

Hannah arched an eyebrow. 'True.'

'Come on. Let's see what sort of welcome we get from Dodson.' He grabbed his overcoat from the back seat. 'Hopefully, he won't come at me with a scalpel.'

'It's never boring around you,' Hannah said, opening her own door. The rain immediately found her, cold and cruel, but she ignored it as she climbed out of Wise's battered Mondeo. She had her Belstaff waterproof wax motorbike jacket on, and that would keep most of her dry and warm. Anyway, Hannah had never been the sort of person who feared a little rain. It wasn't as if she'd melt just because her hair got wet. She had it pulled tight against her head anyway and tied in a bun at the back, so she certainly didn't have to worry about looking a mess.

Wise half-jogged over to the main entrance, his coat held over his head like an umbrella. Hannah walked as if she didn't have a care in the world. Her only concession to the weather was to give her face a wipe before she entered the mortuary.

The inside was just as well-designed as the outside; all discreet lighting, and smooth concrete walls, floors, and furniture. A wooden bench ran along one wall next to a rubber plant and there was an abstract piece of art on the wall behind the reception desk. Muzak played through hidden speakers to add to the sense of calm. The place was definitely more like a hotel than a mortuary. It certainly couldn't be more different from the morgue at the back of King's College Hospital in Camberwell. That hadn't had money spent on it in decades and it certainly didn't worry about niceties like music.

A woman in a suit and with tastefully styled hair smiled at them from behind the long concrete desk. 'Hello.'

Wise introduced himself and Hannah. 'We're here for the Jack Springer autopsy.'

'One moment,' the woman said and picked up a phone.

Half a minute later, an orderly appeared, dressed in a green scrubs, gown and green wellington boots. 'This way, please.'

Hannah and Wise followed her through a set of double doors and into the working part of the mortuary. Immediately, Hannah felt the chill as the air-conditioning drove down the temperature to a level more suitable for keeping dead bodies from rotting. She shivered as her wet skin tingled at the sudden change.

The orderly led them down a long corridor to another set of doors. 'The viewing suite is through here.'

'Thank you,' Wise said. Hannah noticed that his voice seemed tighter than normal, as if he were controlling some sort of emotional response of his own.

She nearly asked him if anything was wrong as they entered the suite, but the sight of Jack's naked body stopped her. He lay on the other side of the floor-to-ceiling windows that overlooked the examination room, on a steel table that made him look even younger than he was. As well as the cut across his neck, black and ugly as hell, he'd been opened from his collarbone down to his navel, so the pathologist could remove, examine and weigh his internal organs.

Someone had washed his body, removing the ground-in dirt and the blood. Clean, she could see a mess of tattoos that covered his arms and some of his chest, already faded and blurred despite his young age. They mingled with a multitude of bruises, track marks and other scars, all telling their own tales of a lifetime of pain.

'He looks so small,' Hannah said, almost to herself, as she peered through the window. 'You can see all his bones through his skin.'

'I wonder where Dodson is,' Wise said, looking from one end of the room to the other but the examination room was deserted apart from the body.

'Doctor Dodson's on stress leave,' a woman said from behind them. They both turned and found Harmet Singh standing by the door. The small Indian woman smiled. 'Apparently, there was a little ruckus last night and the good doctor has requested time to recover. Until then, I'm afraid you're stuck with me instead.'

'It's good to see you again, Doctor,' Wise said, immediately looking like a weight had been lifted off his shoulders.

'Is it?' Singh replied. 'I thought you were avoiding me.'

'Why would I do that?' Wise said.

'Well, you still owe me that drink from the Motorbike Killer case,' Singh said. 'In fact, I think you said you'd buy me several if you got a result.'

'I must admit I'd forgotten about that,' Wise said. 'It wasn't personal.'

Singh arched an eyebrow. 'No? I would've thought being forgotten about was as personal as it gets.'

'That's not what I meant ...' Wise said, and Hannah could've sworn the man was blushing. 'Er ... How are you?'

'Oh, I'm fine, Detective,' Singh replied. 'Fine and dandy. And you?'

'Good. I'm good. I ... Er ...' Wise was looking as flustered as a fourteen-year-old boy on a first date. There was something about the way the small pathologist chatted with the large detective that always seemed to push Wise off-step. In fact, it bordered on the flirtatious. So much so that it made Hannah feel like she was intruding by being there. It was a feeling she didn't like.

'Have you had a chance to look at the body, Doctor?' Hannah asked, wanting to get things back on track.

Singh walked over and joined them at the window. 'I have, and it's all terribly sad. Even if he hadn't had his throat cut, the boy was in a terrible state. We found track marks on both arms and between his toes that indicate a long-term, intravenous drug habit.'

'How long-term?' Wise asked.

'Hard to be certain, but I'd say he's been using heavily for at least a couple of years,' Singh said.

Hannah shook her head. 'He's only fifteen.'

'Then he started very young,' Singh replied. 'Unsurprisingly, he has malnutrition, as you can tell by the visibility of his bones through the body, and his body is covered in bruises. Some recent, some less so. At some point, he had his arm broken, but it wasn't set properly before it was allowed to heal. We found signs also of other fractures — the right humerus, right and left radius, left ulna, right tibia and fibula and so on.

These are very old injuries, but they suggest a history of physical abuse.'

'The lad made accusations against his father of sexual abuse,' Wise said, 'but there was nothing in the reports that he was being beaten as well.'

'These things tend to go together, unfortunately,' Singh said.

'What about the fatal injury?' Wise asked.

'That was a single cut with a very sharp blade. It goes from left to right that would suggest the killer was right-handed.'

'When you say it was a "very sharp blade," Doctor,' Wise said, 'how sharp are we talking?'

'Scalpel sharp,' Singh replied. 'But this wasn't a scalpel. The blade was approximately one centimetre thick at its widest part. It reminds me of the type of cut a meat cleaver would make — except that knife has a straight edge, whereas the murder weapon has a curve at one end.'

'A witness described it as a sword,' Hannah said. 'About the length of someone's forearm.'

Singh shrugged. 'Perhaps it was — but we're not looking for a weapon with a pointy end. This blade had a curved tip.'

'Like a samurai sword?' Wise asked.

'I'm not a sword expert,' Singh said. 'All I can tell you is that the blade went in and out in one motion, cutting eight centimetres into the neck at the deepest point.'

'How strong would you have to be to do that?' Hannah asked. 'I mean, even with a sharp blade, it can't be easy to cut through that amount of flesh.'

'That's hard to say. If you know what you're doing and you have the right amount of momentum, etcetera, then muscle doesn't really come into it.' Singh looked down at the boy on the metal slab. 'And look at him. He's all skin and bone. There's not that much of him to cut through.'

'So, you can't tell us anything about the person who did this, then?' Wise asked.

'Not really — apart from the fact that they are probably right-handed as the cut goes from left to right

. I can't tell you that you're looking for a man, six foot two, two hundred and fifty pounds or anything like that.'

'That's a shame,' Hannah muttered.

'But, as I said, you have to know what you're doing,' Singh said. 'That takes practice.'

'How do you practice cutting someone's throat?' Hannah said.

Singh gave her a look that suggested she thought Hannah was quite stupid for asking that question. 'I would imagine they started on something small — like cats or dogs — and then worked their way up to bigger things before they got this good.'

'You sound like you admire them,' Hannah said.

'No, I don't admire them,' Singh replied. 'But I spend my days cutting bodies open and I know you don't make an incision like that by sheer luck. It takes hard work.'

Hannah glanced over at Wise. The detective was still looking down at the boy's corpse.

'If they've worked this hard to get this good,' Wise said eventually, 'they're not going to stop with just this one, are they?'

'No,' Singh said. 'And I doubt this was their first murder, either.'

'Wonderful,' Wise said. 'The boss won't like that.'

'Well, I've not had a chance to look over my records,' Singh said, 'but I do remember another case like this; a homeless teenager had his throat cut back in June or July, I think it was.'

'Do you recall the name?' Wise asked.

Singh screwed up her face as she thought. 'I think ... I think it was Kareem or something like that. Maybe Khalid. He was killed over Shepherd's Bush way.'

Hannah made a note. 'I'll get Brains to look into it.'

'I'll check my own records when I get back to the office,' Singh said.

Wise shook his head. 'I can't tell you how much I hope you're wrong about this, Doc.'

Singh smiled. 'I can't remember the last time I was wrong about anything.'

# 8

'What a shit hole,' Hicksy said when he saw the block of flats where the victim's drug dealer lived.

'It is certainly that,' Jono said, looking the decrepit building up and down. It sat on the corner of Randolph Street and St Pancras Way, made of shit-brown brick and looking about as unloved as a place could get. The fence that encircled it was made of more rust than metal and leaned this way and that, as if it wasn't sure which direction it should collapse in. There were only four floors, thankfully, and each one had a balcony overlooking the main entrance. Once they'd been painted white and had, perhaps, looked half-decent for about five minutes, but the few flecks of paint that remained on them now were stained by dirt, rain and pollution. In fact, Jono wouldn't have been surprised if he'd found a bulldozer outside, ready to tear the place down.

They had School Boy with them and the kid wasn't too happy about being press-ganged into coming along. 'I don't know why I'm here. I'm supposed to be checking CCTV with Sarah and Donut,' he said for the umpteenth time.

'Ow, give it a rest,' Hicksy said. 'The Guv won't mind you helping us.'

'But he told you to do this,' School Boy said. 'Not me.'

'We look like cops,' Hicksy said. 'You don't. Now you've changed out of your school uniform, you look like someone who'd buy drugs.'

School Boy stopped dead in the street. 'Why? Because I'm black?'

'No,' Hicksy said. 'Not because you're black — but that helps.'

School Boy looked at Jono as if he couldn't believe what he'd just heard. Jono, on the other hand, could. He'd heard much worse from his partner over the years. He coughed, then spat out whatever muck had come up from his lungs. His mother would've disapproved but, going by the crap on the ground around his feet, no one around here would notice and, if they did, they wouldn't give two monkeys.

'What Hicksy meant,' Jono said, 'was that him and me look like a couple of sad, middle-aged police officers and I doubt the person we're about to visit would even open the door once he clocked us. But you, being young, don't have that look yet. Our drug dealer will talk to you. Colour has nothing to do with it.'

'Alright,' School Boy said, not sounding convinced.

'I still can't believe fucking Diversity's idea worked,' Hicksy muttered, just to make things worse. Diversity was his partner's nickname for DS Hannah Markham, whom he was convinced only had a job to satisfy some sort of government inflicted quota. No one ever had a good nick name — School Boy's was a good case in point — but this one was particularly insensitive and no one else on the team used it.

'He's a drug dealer,' Jono said as they walked up to the main entrance to the block of flats. He took care to step over the steaming turd someone's pet had left on the pavement. 'So, giving out his address to a complete stranger who wants to buy drugs is probably an everyday occurrence. It's just a shame that, today, he's got some visitors who are only pretending that they want an armful of smack.'

'What if he's got a weapon?' School Boy said. The main doors to the flats groaned as Jono pushed them open and the stench of something very rotten indeed hit them all around the face.

'He won't open the door with a weapon,' Jono said, trying not to gag. 'But he'll open the door. Once he does that, then we'll bulldoze in after you. If he's not that welcoming, we'll still bulldoze our way in — just get your boot in the way so he can't slam the door shut on us before we have a chance to move.'

The worst kind of graffiti covered the walls. None of it was imaginative or even remotely artistic. In fact, Jono didn't want to look too closely, as some of it looked like someone had hand-smeared some of it with shit. He noted that "Phil took it up the arse" and "If you want a good time, call Tina on ..." She was, apparently, according to another piece of art, also "a whore."

Of course, there was no bloody lift, and the stairs were also acting as a rubbish tip and toilet for the residents and their guests. 'Watch out for needles,' Jono said as they made their way up. 'This job isn't worth getting hepatitis or AIDS over.'

'What a shit hole,' Hicksy said again.

'What did you expect?' Jono said. 'You saw the outside. Did you think that the place would've had some sort of glam makeover inside?'

School Boy laughed. 'Yeah. Like that posh bloke with the hair and funny beard had worked his magic on the place for Changing Rooms or something?'

Hicksy didn't like that. The looks he threw about were as dirty as the floors and walls, but Jono had told him loads of times that the man had to learn how to take a joke himself. 'What floor's the dealer on?' he said instead, stomping up the stairs.

'Second floor,' School Boy replied, giving Jono an 'Oh dear' look.

Jono winked back. He liked School Boy. The lad had a good heart and was a grafter. He was also very glad the dealer was only one more flight up. He was already out of breath and starting to sweat. It was no surprise all things considered, but still, it pissed him off. Getting old sucked — not that he was going to get the chance to get much older. That sucked even more.

He had to pause for breath when they reached the second floor, which was just as disgusting as the ground floor. The smell didn't seem quite so bad, though, so that was something at least. Hicksy and School Boy had stopped halfway down the corridor.

'Something tells me this is the one,' Hicksy said. When Jono caught up with them, he saw why. Instead of a normal door, this one was made of steel with six locks running down one side and a spyhole in the middle.

'Where'd he get that?' Jono said. 'Drug Dealers-R-Us?'

'Good job we got an invite,' Hicksy said. 'Even the Big Red Key wouldn't get that open.' The Big Red Key was a steel battering ram the police used to break doors down. Not much could withstand it, but Hicksy was right about this one. Whoever the dealer was, he didn't want any unwelcome visitors.

'Alright,' Jono said. 'As we planned it.' He stepped to the right of the door and Hicksy went left, while School Boy got the prime spot in front of the spyhole.

School Boy gave Jono a nervous look. 'I just knock?'

'You just knock,' Jono confirmed.

The kid gave his body a little jiggle to shake out the nerves, then did as he was told and knocked. Somewhere, a dog barked in answer, but it didn't seem to come from within the dealer's flat, so that was something. The last thing Jono needed was to get bitten by some rabies-infested mutt.

School Boy had to knock again before there was movement inside.

'Who is it?' a man's voice called out, sounding like he'd been gargling broken glass.

'My name's Max,' School Boy called out. 'Johnnie's mate.'

'Hold your money up so I can see it,' the man said, sounding like an extra from Trainspotting.

School Boy held up some crumpled twenties to the spyhole. 'Open sesame.'

'Hold on, smart arse.' Locks turned, bolts scraped free, and the door opened wide. 'Come in,' Glass Voice said.

'Cheers, man,' School Boy said, stepping forward, and then Jono and Hicksy were moving. They were still pretty fast for a pair of sad old men, long past their best. They were in and past School Boy in a flash and both of them had Glass Voice face first up against the wall before he even had a clue what was going on.

'Oi, you fuckers,' the man rasped. 'What yeez doing?'

Jono let the man's head back just far enough to get a look at his warrant card. 'Under the Misuse of Drugs Act 1972, we believe you are in possession of controlled drugs, and are intending to supply those drugs to persons unknown.'

'I ain't got nothing,' the man said as Hicksy yanked one arm behind his back and slapped a handcuff on his wrist. Keeping the man's head against the wall, Jono manoeuvred the other arm behind his back so Hicksy could cuff that too.

'Is there anyone else here?' Hicksy asked as School Boy shut the front door.

'Fuck off,' Glass Voice said. His breath was enough to sap all of Jono's patience.

He banged the dealer's head just hard enough against the wall. 'You're not being very helpful.'

'That hurt,' the dealer moaned.

'Yeah? Well, I'm only just getting warmed up,' Jono said as the others went off to check the other rooms. 'Next time, I'll see if I can put your head through the wall into next door's living room.'

'You can't do that if you're a copper. There's rules.'

'You could go see my boss and tell him I was a naughty boy. Somehow, I don't think he's going to believe you — and it's not like you've got any witnesses here to back you up.'

Hicksy reappeared. 'He's alone, but that's not surprising. The place is disgusting.' He gave the dealer a pat on the cheek. 'You ever thought about buying a Hoover and doing a bit of housework? Maybe throw some rubbish out?'

'What's the point?' Glass Voice said. 'It'll only get dirty again.'

'Fucking hell,' Jono said. 'If you said that to my missus, she'd cut your balls off. Now, where can we go for a friendly chat?'

'You're not arresting me?' Glass Voice said.

'Not yet.' Jono let go of the dealer.

The man tried giving Jono the eyeball as if he wasn't intimidated by anything, but it was a laughable attempt, and even he knew it. In the end, he shrugged and then walked through to what was, in a past life, a sitting room.

Jono wasn't sure what he'd call the space now. Granted, there was a sofa and an armchair, but both looked like they'd had the stuffing ripped from them long ago and it was only the dirt holding them together. They were covered in fag burns, piss stains and God only knew what else.

There was a coffee table too, but its surface was buried under overflowing ashtrays, old pizza boxes, take-out containers, a few wank mags and all the paraphernalia that a junkie needed to shoot up. Jono counted at least a dozen needles lying around, all used. The only thing that hadn't been trashed was the big wide-screen TV stuck to the wall and the Sky box beneath it.

'You going to uncuff me?' Glass Voice said.

Jono laughed. 'Not yet.'

The dealer plonked himself down on the edge of the armchair. 'Make yourself at home then.'

'I think we'll stand,' Jono said, wrinkling his nose.

Hicksy peered at the magazines on the coffee table. 'Bloody hell, I didn't think they made those anymore. Not since they invented the internet.'

'I ain't got a computer,' Glass Voice said.

School Boy reappeared from a doorway. He held a bag in his blue gloved hands. 'There's more than a family bucket of KFC in here.'

'Ooh, you naughty boy,' Hicksy said. 'Naughty, naughty, naughty.'

'I've never seen that bag before,' Glass Voice said.

Jono held up a finger. 'Let that be the last lie you tell. Let's start with something simple — what's your name?'

'Donnie,' Glass Voice said.

'Nice to meet you, Donnie,' Jono said. 'Now, what can you tell us about Jack Springer?'

# 9

Sarah waved at Wise the moment he walked through the doors of MIR-One with Hannah, her face bright with excitement. Donut was with her at her desk and he, too, shared the same bright-eyed look that Wise knew only too well came with progress.

'What have you got?' he said, walking over. He glanced over at Brains as he passed. The man had his head down, staring at his own monitor, the glow of the screen making him look paler than normal. Only Jono and Hicksy were still out and about.

Sarah leaned back in her chair and blew her fringe with the bottom of her lip. 'We've almost got the lot.'

'You have?' Wise came to her side of the desk, feeling the buzz himself, so he could see her monitor as Donut made way for both Wise and Hannah.

'Well, don't get too excited,' Sarah said. 'I've not got a name and address for you.'

'What have you got then?' Wise asked.

Sarah taped at her keyboard and a video player appeared on her screen, with an image of a pedestrian tunnel. The time stamp in the corner said *0830HRS*. 'Instead of going through all the footage from around the murder scene hoping to spot the kid, I thought I'd check

Charing Cross. I thought the lad might've gone there to earn some money first.'

'It's a prime begging spot,' Donut added. 'Forty-odd thousand commuters go through there during peak hours.'

'But there are some areas that are better than others,' Sarah added. 'The main station itself isn't great because station staff and uniforms move any beggars or homeless people on pretty quickly. But the pedestrian tunnels are rarely checked and, of course, they're warm and dry places to be compared to being out on the pavements. So, we started looking there first.' She hit play.

The video came to life with commuters bustling back and forth. Everyone was in a hurry in that London way, ignoring everything and everyone around them, heads down, moving quickly. Sarah pointed to the bottom right of the screen. 'And here comes Jack.'

Wise watched the young lad shuffle into the frame, his blond hair hanging over most of his face, sleeping bag and a patch of cardboard under one arm and something white in his other hand. Compared to everyone else around him, he was moving in slow motion, which wasn't surprising — he had no office to rush to, no business meeting to make or shop to open. Instead, he stopped halfway down the tunnel on the left-hand side, dropped the cardboard onto the ground, then placed his sleeping bag over that.

With that all sorted, Jack sat down, with his back against the tunnel wall, and held out the white thing in his other hand. Wise peered closer at the screen. 'What's that in his hand?'

'Looks like a McDonalds cup,' Sarah said. 'For people to put money in.'

Sure enough, they watched Jack rattle the cup at passersby. Most ignored him as they ignored everything else, but the odd person would slow down or stop, toss something into the cup, and then move on.

'I'll fast forward the next bit,' Sarah said. 'He doesn't move from his spot all day, eats some food he gets out of his coat pocket, that sort of stuff.' The screen sped up, and the images turned into a Benny Hill sketch with everyone rushing around at a hundred miles an hour —

except for Jack, who remained in his spot. The clock in the corner rushed through the hours until Sarah set everything back to normal speed at *1245HRS*.

Two people approached Jack on the screen, one black, one Caucasian. The Caucasian had really long, dark, matted hair, and Wise couldn't tell if they were male or female. Their layers of clothing hid their body shape well. Both looked as messed up as Jack, though.

The young lad grinned when he saw them approach and raised a hand that the black kid hi-fived. 'They know each other,' Wise said.

'Yep. Definitely friends,' Donut said.

The two arrivals sat down on either side of Jack and one produced a packet of cigarettes, sharing them out amongst themselves. The three sat and puffed away, ignoring the commuters and the no smoking signs, as the clock ticked over to *1305HRS*.

Sarah then froze the frame. 'Watch this chap, the IC1 male.' She tapped the screen over the image of a man in a green anorak and a black baseball cap before restarting the film. The man walked past the three young people but, unlike ninety-nine percent of everyone else in Charing Cross, he slowed as he did so, watching the three of them smoke their fags. He then disappeared from the screen.

'Right ...' Wise said, hoping for a bit more than just someone walking past.

'Be patient,' Sarah said as she hit fast-forward again. Jack's friends jumped up and scuttled off, leaving him alone. People shot past as before, with the odd one diverting to give Jack money. Sarah let everything return to normal again at *1345HRS*. 'Watch the top left of the screen.'

And there he was.

Anorak Man reappeared on the footage. He walked past Jack again, slowing as he did so again, clearly looking at the young beggar, but he didn't stop, didn't speak to him, and then he was gone again, off screen.

'I take it he comes back again?' Wise asked.

Sarah fast-forwarded again to *1410HRS*. Anorak Man returned, walking from right to left, again slowing, watching, but not stopping. The man definitely looked suspicious.

'I thought our witness said the killer had a dark blue coat on?' Wise said.

'She did.' Sarah clicked away and another fast-forward took the video to *1430HRS*. 'This is when they talk.'

Jack was alone in the tunnel, with hardly any other pedestrians in sight. Anorak Man returned but, this time, he headed straight towards Jack, pausing only to let people pass by. When he reached Jack, he bent down and spoke to the lad. Even over the poor quality of the CCTV footage, Wise could see the lad smiling. Then Anorak Man offered him something. Jack's hand shot out to take it, but Anorak Man caught the hand first. There was another brief conversation before the man released Jack and the kid took what the man had in his other hand. Then the lad was off and running, sleeping bag under his arm, cardboard abandoned.

Anorak Man watched him go. He waited a short while before he ran off after Jack.

'There's more,' Sarah said. 'We've pieced together footage that shows Jack legging it across Trafalgar Square. He then walks up Haymarket, before doubling back to Leicester Square Tube.'

'What about Anorak Man?' Wise asked.

'Yeah, he's following.' Sarah hit play. She edited footage from a variety of cameras, showing Jack along the route she'd described. On more than one occasion, the lad stopped and looked around before continuing.

'He knows he's being followed,' Wise said, 'or, at least, thinks he might be.'

Sarah hit pause, then opened up another screen. 'Here's Anorak Man.' The time stamp was half a minute to a minute behind Jack's clips, but there was the man in the coat and hat moving at speed along exactly the same route as Jack. 'He's definitely after him.'

'What about on the Tube?' Hannah asked.

Sarah turned in her chair to look at Hannah. 'We've not got all the footage in, but it's the same — except the kid's pretty chilled out.' She moved her mouse, clicked, and a still image appeared on the screen. It was of Jack sitting on the Tube, sleeping bag on his lap and a big grin on his face.

'He looks like Christmas came early,' Donut said.

'What did Anorak Man give him earlier?' Wise asked.

'Probably money. Maybe drugs,' Sarah said. 'Whatever it was, it was worth more to Jack than what he had in his McDonalds cup.'

'Did he leave that behind?' Wise hadn't noticed when he'd watched the earlier clip.

'Yeah,' Sarah replied. 'He only grabbed his sleeping bag when he legged it.'

'I can't see Anorak Man in the Tube image,' Hannah said.

Sarah smiled. 'That's because his coat's not green anymore.' She tapped the screen again, on the head of a man in a black Sports Direct baseball cap and a dark blue anorak.

Wise grinned. 'As per our witness. When did he change coats, though?'

'I think it's the same coat, Guv — just turned inside out,' Sarah said.

'And if Jack's looking for a bloke in a green anorak, he's not going to give someone in a blue one a second glance,' Hannah said. 'Simple but clever.'

Wise stared at the man in the now blue coat. He'd pulled the hat down enough to hide most of his face. 'Do you know if there are any shots of him where we can see what he looks like clearly?'

'No. He knows there's cameras everywhere, so he keeps his head down and the cap on from what we've seen so far,' Sarah said. 'Maybe a shop camera might've caught him once they get out in Camden. I'll get bodies looking tomorrow.'

'He does get out in Camden?' Wise said.

'They both do.' Sarah hit play on her main video again, and Wise watched the Tube stop. Jack got up from his seat and left. The next camera showed him strolling along the platform, with the mystery man following on just behind. The final CCTV footage was from the

World's End exit from Camden Tube Station; Jack passed by the camera, then the man.

Wise nodded. 'Good. This is really good. Let's keep calling him Anorak Man for now, just so we all know who we're talking about.'

'Thought you'd be pleased,' Sarah said.

'Print off some screen grabs of both Jack and Anorak Man and get them up on the whiteboard, along with a map showing the journey from Charing Cross to the murder site,' Wise said.

'I'll get on it now,' Donut said.

'How tall do you reckon he is?' Wise asked.

'I'd say a bit under average height,' Sarah said. 'Maybe five feet eight or nine. Maybe a bit less. He's certainly not a big bloke.'

'Probably why he picked Jack,' Hannah said. 'A malnourished teenager is an easier victim than someone his own size.'

'That makes sense,' Wise agreed. 'Good work, everyone.'

He glanced over at Brains again, still beavering away behind his screen. Singh had said that it was more than likely this wasn't the killer's first murder. If anyone could find more cases, it'd be Brains.

Leaving Sarah and the others, Wise walked over to Brains' desk. The man looked up as Wise approached, peering over the top of his glasses and smiled.

'Brains,' Wise said.

'Guv.'

'Any luck with the weapon?'

'Sorry. I've been having a trawl around, but no joy yet. I rang Hendon and asked them to have a look through their collection for us and send us any pictures of knives or swords that match the description.'

Hendon was where the Met trained its new recruits. As part of the facilities, they had a room that was a cross between a museum and armoury. It stored every type of weapon a police officer might face going about their day-today duty.

The cadets got regular tours for two reasons. First, it was to help them identify weapons used by criminals while committing an offence. The second reason was to warn them of what they faced every day when they put on their uniform and went to work. It was designed to make every cadet realise they weren't playing some sort of game of cops and robbers. It was a serious business and they could die if they weren't careful.

'Keep me informed on what they turn up,' Wise said. 'Also, can you have a nosey around on HOLMES for me? I was just at the PM with Hannah and Doctor Singh reckons our killer's done this before. She mentioned a similar case she saw back in June or July. A lad killed over Shepherd's Bush way. She thought his name was Kareem or Khalid. And there might be others. She reckons the killer didn't get this good at cutting throats without practice.'

The Home Office Large Major Enquiry System was the national database used on all murder investigations and one of its primary functions was to link similar cases across the various police services across the UK and Brains was a magician when it came to digging out the information stored in it.

'We would've heard about others like this if that was the case, wouldn't we?' Brains asked.

'I hope so,' Wise said, but he wouldn't bet on it. For all the technology and advancements made in police investigations, he also knew that the thirty-five thousand police officers in the Met were run ragged trying to keep on top of their caseloads. Things easily could slip through the gaps.

The doors to MIR-One opened and Jono and Hicksy walked through, with Callum trailing behind. They looked cold and bedraggled, and Jono had a scowl that would curdle milk.

'How was your drug deal?' Wise asked.

'Eventful,' Jono replied. 'We miss anything here?'

Wise pointed to the picture of Anorak Man that Donut had already stuck up on the whiteboard. 'Meet our killer.'

# 10

Jono, Hicksy, and Callum went up to the whiteboard and stared at the picture of Anorak Man. 'So, this geezer is the killer?' Hicksy said. 'How'd you find him?'

Wise glanced at his watch. It was just gone 7 p.m. 'I think we all need to get up to speed before tomorrow.' He headed to the whiteboards and then turned to face his team. He clapped his hands. 'Everyone! Can I have your attention, please? I know it's late, but I'd rather go through everything that's been uncovered today while it's still fresh in everyone's minds, so we can hit the ground running tomorrow.'

Wise waited until everyone faced the whiteboards. Once they were settled, he turned to Sarah. 'Can you show everyone the footage you've put together?'

Sarah tapped away at her computer and the CCTV footage she'd discovered appeared on the big screen by the whiteboards. She played the film while Donut stuck more still shots of Anorak Man up on the board.

'Shame we haven't got a decent picture of his face,' Brains said.

'He's really aware of the cameras,' Sarah replied.

'Can you have a look at the CCTV at Charing Cross for the days leading up to the murder?' Wise said. 'Anorak Man checked out Jack a few times before he spoke to the lad, but maybe this wasn't the first time he did that. Maybe he'd done a few recons of the area. If that's the case, there might be a shot of him without the hat.'

'Will do,' Sarah said.

'Jono? Hicksy? How did you get on?' Wise asked the older detectives.

'We had fun this afternoon,' Hicksy said. 'We went and had a chat with the victim's toe rag of a dealer.'

'And?'

'Young Jack was a regular punter,' Jono said. 'He'd buy a bag most days, paying in shrapnel that he got through begging. When he didn't have enough cash, he'd beg for some gear on credit, but "Mad" Donnie Parsons isn't, apparently, a charity. No cheddar, no class A cheese.'

'Yesterday, though,' Hicksy continued. 'As we saw with his text messages, he gets in touch with Donnie. Wants the family bucket. That's five bags of smack at twenty quid a pop, but with a ten quid discount for buying in bulk.'

'Now, we've seen the footage from Charing Cross, I'm thinking that Anorak Man gives Jack ninety or a hundred big ones,' Jono said. 'Right before he sprints off, and that's where Jack got the cash to buy his gear.'

Wise turned back to Sarah. 'Can you run that meeting again?'

Sarah tapped away at her keyboard and they all watched again as Anorak Man approached Jack in the tunnel and the two chatted. Anorak Man held out something that Jack went to take, but the man grabbed his arm.

'Stop it there,' Wise said.

The images on the screen froze.

'That's the money being passed over,' Wise said.

'But why the hand grab before giving it over?' Sarah asked. 'It's not like Jack was trying to steal it.'

'It looks like he's threatening him or something,' Hannah said, peering at the screen.

'Maybe,' Wise said. 'Or bargaining maybe? The kid doesn't look scared.'

'He certainly can't take his eyes off the money,' Jono said.

'A hundred quid is a lot of money for a kid begging for change,' Hannah said.

'If they're doing a deal, what's Anorak Man get in return?' Sarah said.

Hicksy tutted. 'Probably sex. A quick blow job or a bunk in the station toilets. The kid agrees, then does a runner when he gets the money. Anorak Man goes after him, all pissed off and, when he catches him, he gets his knife out instead of his cock.'

'Yeah ... but Anorak Man doesn't rush after him at first. If Jack had ripped him off, he would've gone after him straight away,' Wise said.

'Not if the kid caught him by surprise,' Donut said. 'Maybe he's just shocked at being robbed instead of getting his blowjob?'

Wise wasn't so sure. 'Sarah, hit play again.' The film jerked to life. They watched Anorak Man release Jack and then Jack legging it. Anorak Man didn't follow for a good while, then he was off like a lightning bolt too. 'There's a delay — a significant delay — before he sets off after Jack.'

'Can you play that again?' Hannah asked, stepping closer to the screen, eyes fixed on the image.

Sarah did as she was asked, and the entire team watched the events again.

'What is it?' Wise asked Hannah when the film ended.

Hannah still had her eyes on the frozen screen. 'I'm not sure ... Can I see it one more time?'

Once more, they all watched the events play out again. This time, when it finished, Hannah turned to look at Wise. 'This is going to sound daft.'

'There are no daft ideas here,' Wise said.

Hannah chewed on her lip for a second, then grimaced. 'I think he's counting to a hundred.'

'He's doing what?' Wise asked.

'Well, maybe he's not, but he waits for exactly the time it takes to count to a hundred — you know, like you used to do when you were kids.'

'Play it again,' Wise said and this time, as they all watched, he too counted while Anorak Man waited to go off after Jack. It was, as Hannah said, exactly the time it took to count to a hundred. 'I think you're right.'

'Bloody hell,' Jono said. 'It can't be. That's what you do when you play hide 'n' seek — count to a hundred, then "I'm coming, ready or not."'

Wise looked over at the old police officer. 'Maybe this is exactly that — a game. A killing game.'

Wise's words rippled through the team. He could see the shock on their faces as they thought through the implications of what he'd said.

'A game?' Jono said. 'You sure? That would be pretty fucked up.'

'Anorak Man goes looking for a young, vulnerable person. He spots Jack and offers him money for something. Tells him it's a game — hence the counting to a hundred to give him a head start. Then, when he catches Jack, he kills him and takes his money back.'

'Fuuuuuuuuuuuck,' Hicksy said.

'Makes sense to me,' Hannah said. 'Even though I wish it didn't.'

'No wonder Doctor Singh thinks there might be others,' Brains said. 'He certainly doesn't look like this is the first time he's played this game.'

'The big question remains though,' Wise said. 'Who is he?'

Everyone stared at the picture of the man in the black Sports Direct cap, his head angled oh so carefully away from the camera.

'Finding him has to be our chief priority,' Wise continued. 'Sarah, let's hammer the CCTV. No one's perfect. He must pop up somewhere where we can see his face better. Jono, Hicksy — can you take pictures of Anorak Man and show it to any young homeless people around Charing Cross, Waterloo or anywhere else you can think of? If this man has been hunting amongst them, maybe someone knows something. Seen something.'

'What about putting an appeal out on TV?' Jono said, looking far from happy with the action he'd been given. 'Wouldn't that be better?'

'I'd rather keep it on the QT for now,' Wise replied. 'Who knows what he'll do if he sees himself on TV? It might make our job harder.'

'It's not bloody easy now,' Jono muttered. 'At least it'd save us a load of fucking leg work.'

'We didn't become cops for an easy life,' Wise replied.

'Just once would be nice, though,' Jono bounced back.

Wise paused, taking a breath to not get into a stupid argument in front of everyone. 'It's late now and you've all done great work today. Go home, go to the pub, go do whatever it is that's going to make you feel a little better about life, then I'll see you back here in the morning.'

There were nods and grunts as everyone got up from their desks and started collecting their things. As they did so, Wise wandered over to Jono. 'Can we have a quick chat?'

Jono nodded. 'Sure.' He turned to Hicksy. 'See you tomorrow, mate.'

'Yeah, can't wait,' Hicksy replied.

'We can talk in my office,' Wise said.

'That sort of chat, eh?' Jono replied. 'Great.'

Wise headed over to his door in the corner of MIR-One and opened it, stepping aside to let Jono go in first. The detective took the seat in front of Wise's desk while Wise made his way round to the other side.

'Is everything okay?' Wise asked, once they were settled.

'It's marvellous,' Jono replied, full of sarcasm. The man had been overweight as long as Wise had known him, with a bulbous nose that came from enjoying his whisky too much. Now, though, there was something else, a tiredness in his eyes, that made Jono look positively ancient.

'It doesn't seem that way,' Wise replied.

Jono waved the remark away. 'Look, I'm sorry if I was being a bit of a smart arse back there. I didn't mean anything by it.'

'I know.'

'Well, my mouth gets ahead of me sometimes.'

Wise smiled as if it to say it was okay, but that he knew there was more to it. He said nothing, though. Silence was often a better way of getting people to talk than asking questions.

Of course, using a cop's trick on another cop meant Jono knew exactly what he was doing. There was an awkward pause between them as they both looked at each other, then Jono sighed, pushed his hair back with both hands, then rubbed his face. 'Fuck. You don't have anything to drink tucked away in that desk of yours?'

Wise leaned back, opened a drawer, and pulled out an orange bottle. 'Gatorade?'

'Has it got vodka mixed in it?'

'Sorry. Just electrolytes.'

Jono chuckled and shook his head. 'I suppose that's why you look like you do and I look like I do.'

'Trust me, I'm a mess on the inside.'

'You can't be as fucked up as me.'

'Do you want to tell me about it?' Wise asked.

'You don't need to know my shit. You've got enough on your plate.'

'Jono, maybe it'll help to talk about it?'

'I don't normally do confessions,' Jono said. 'Or talk about feelings.'

'How's that working out so far?'

'Christ, you sound like my wife.'

'Well, we both care about you.'

'I'm not sure she'd agree with you. She thinks I'm an idiot,' Jono said. He fidgeted in his seat, twisting his fingers together for want of something to do. For a moment, Wise thought he was going to get up and leave, but then Jono sagged in his seat and let out a big puff of air. 'I had to see the doctor the other week.'

'I didn't know you weren't feeling well,' Wise said.

'You get to my age and sometimes you can forget what it feels like to feel good,' Jono said, 'but I was feeling worse than normal. Tired all the time, bones aching, that sort of shit.' He paused and pursed his lips. 'And I've started coughing up blood.'

'Ah,' Wise said. He didn't need to be a doctor to know that wasn't good.

'Ah in-fucking-deed.'

'What did the doctor say?'

'Fucking cancer. In my lungs. Turns out that shit they put on the front of fag packets is true — smoking kills.' Jono held up both his hands as if to say, 'What can I do?'

'Shit,' Wise said. 'How far along is it?'

'I'm not going to die tomorrow, but it's far enough along,' Jono said. 'Far enough for it to be serious.'

'Have the doctors got a treatment plan for you?'

'Yeah.' Jono shrugged. 'The usual. Radiation therapy and chemotherapy and all that bollocks, but I don't know. Maybe I should just accept it for what it is. I've had a good run. The kids are grown up, and the wife doesn't need the hassle of looking after me for too long. And the police may pay shit, but the pension will see her alright once I'm gone.'

'Have they given you any timeframes?'

'If I have the treatment, then maybe they can cure it and its happy ever after. If I don't ... six months or something like that and adios muchachos.'

'I'm so sorry, mate,' Wise said. 'If you need to take some time off, it's okay. There are more important things than The Job.'

'Yeah, well, for now, I'd rather keep working. At least then I can pretend everything's normal for a few hours a day,' Jono said.

'Have you told anyone else?'

'Just Hicksy — and that was only because he'd noticed I'd stopped smoking.'

'Bloody hell. Maybe he'll make a decent detective, after all,' Wise said with a smile.

'I know, right? Bloody amazed me, he did, with that bit of observation.' Jono sighed. 'Anyway, you asked. That's all my shit. Sorry to dump it on you.'

'You don't have to apologise for anything,' Wise replied. 'I'm glad you told me and, for what it's worth, I hope you decide to fight this thing. Life would be pretty boring around here without you.'

Jono got up and rolled his neck. 'Well, not everyone's got my sparkling personality.' He patted his jacket pockets as if looking for something, then stopped himself. 'I forgot. No fags. I don't smoke anymore. You'd think, what with the bastard things killing me, I'd not want one but, for some reason, I want them more now than ever.'

'It'll get better,' Wise said. 'The giving up smoking, I mean.'

Jono smiled, but it didn't reach his eyes. 'I wouldn't want to bet on that if I were you.'

'Good night, mate.'

'Yeah. You too.'

Wise watched Jono head back into MIR-One, feeling nothing but sadness for the man. Jono was only in his fifties. No matter what brave face Jono tried to put on it, that was only half a life and the man deserved more than that.

But cancer was a bastard. It didn't care. It'd killed Wise's own mother back when he was a teenager, despite everything the hospital did for her. It'd been horrible watching her die bit by bit each day, seeing the light in his life fading as the cancer grew.

Shit.

He stood up and walked back into the incident room. The face of Jack Springer stared back at him from the whiteboard. There was someone else who'd known how unfair life could be. Someone else who'd not deserved his fate.

Well, Wise was going to do his damnedest to make sure no one else ended up like Jack.

He stopped in front of the picture of Anorak Man and stared at the blurry image, the Sports Direct cap, the half-hidden face, feeling the old familiar rage boil within him. 'Playtime's over. We're onto you now.'

# Friday 18th November

# 11

Wise hadn't slept well. The Dream had seen to that. He'd woken up screaming at just gone 5 that morning, frightening Jean in the process and piling more guilt onto his shoulders. It was bad enough that he was still suffering from the fallout of Andy's death, but his wife didn't deserve to suffer, too. He'd suggested moving back into the spare room, but she'd told him not to.

'You're making progress,' Jean said.

'Not enough,' Wise replied. 'Not fast enough.'

'You're the only one setting a timetable for everything. Go easy on yourself for once, eh?' Jean lay back, her eyes already half-closing. 'What did Doctor Shaw say?'

'It'll take time.' Doctor Shaw was his police-appointed psychiatrist. He'd been seeing her since Andy's death and, he had to admit, she'd stopped him from doing something stupid more than once.

'There you go. Give yourself time.' The words were all but mumbled as his wife shifted in the bed, getting comfortable, then she was asleep again.

Wise watched for a few moments, jealous of how easily she could do that. Wise knew there was no point in him trying. He'd just toss and turn, getting more and more worked up that he was awake when he shouldn't be.

Instead, he slunk out of bed and got his running kit on. Ironically, the one good thing about having a messed up head and not sleeping well was that Wise was getting plenty of exercise in.

Downstairs, he drank a glass of water and looked out the window. It was dark, wet, and freezing outside. If he had half a brain, he'd give up the thought of running, put the kettle on and read the paper or something sensible like that, but he was dressed now, with his winter tights on under his shorts, a long-sleeved fleece under his top and an all-weather jacket. His dad had seen him once in all his winter kit, and laughed. Apparently, when his dad had been a kid, he had to run through snowstorms wearing nothing by a pair of shorts and a rugby shirt. Character-building, he'd called it. Wise wasn't sure he agreed with his dad about that.

After finding one of his many running playlists on his phone, Wise stuck his AirPods in, pulled a watch cap down over his ears, and slipped on his Nike running gloves.

As *Are You Gonna Be My Girl* by Jet started in his ears, Wise stepped out into the darkness. He had the music set just loud enough to drown out his thoughts as he set off down the street. He kept the pace nice and slow, giving his muscles the chance to warm up, grateful that all his expensive kit was doing its job. Only Wise's face felt the pinch of the cold.

By the time Wise reached the common, he felt good enough to put on some speed. He chose the shorter circuit but pushed the pace, feeling the sweat break out on his body despite the weather. His feet splashed through puddles and squelched in mud, but he kept going, needing the endorphins, needing the pain.

Forty minutes later, he was home and in his garage, the back of which he'd turned into a mini gym. Squeezed between the front of his wife's Escort and the door to the house, he'd set up a bench, a rack of weights and his beloved punch bag. He'd had it for over twenty years now, and the heavy-duty bag was a mess of patches where he'd had to repair splits in the leather. Weighing seventy pounds, it dangled from the garage ceiling on chains. Jean had tried to get him to throw it away plenty of times in the past, but there wasn't a chance in hell of that happening. He and that bag had been through too much for him to give up on it just because it was knackered and smelly.

Wise stripped down to the waist, despite the temperature of the garage not being much higher than it was outside. Steam came off his body and every breath he took left a trail of mist in its wake.

He knew he was tired, but he still put on his old, bashed up gloves and stepped up to the bag. Like with the run, Wise started slowly, working his shoulders, jabbing at the bag, moving his heavy feet.

He'd had a trainer once who loved making Wise spar another round and then another when he had nothing left in the tank. 'This is the real world,' he'd say. 'You can't stop a fight with someone just because you're tired. You can't tell them to wait until you've had a rest if they want to kill you. You have to dig deep, get primal, draw on your need to survive and fight!'

So now, as then, Wise pushed himself, finding strength to punch harder, doing his best to hurt his beloved bag, to burst another seam or tear another hole in that worn-out leather.

As he pounded the bag, he thought of Andy and that rooftop, of Tom and his fears, and he thought of little Jack Springer, dead on a table, long before his time.

He thought of Anorak Man and his silly game, counting to one hundred: 'Coming ready or not.' And, as he hammered his fists into the swinging bag, Singh's words echoed through his mind: 'I doubt this was their first murder.'

On and on he went, punching with all his might until the sweat ran down him in rivers once more and his knuckles screamed in pain despite the gloves. On and on he went, until he was screaming at the madness of it all. On and on he went, until exhaustion finally said enough was enough, dragging down his arms, pressing with all its weight on his shoulders, weakening his legs, until his eyes stung with perspiration, until his mouth was raw, until his fury was gone. Only then did Wise stop and sink to his knees, gulping for air, heart hammering away.

It took an effort to crawl back inside the house and slink up the stairs to the bathroom, but despite the pain, Wise felt good. He felt alive. In control. He could hear the others stirring as he climbed into the shower. Soon, they'd be up and getting ready for school. With any luck, Wise would have time to have breakfast with Jean and the kids before heading in.

There was no DMM arranged for that morning, as everyone had their actions from the night before. Instead, Wise was meeting DCI Roberts, his boss, to update her on the Anorak Man case.

He stood in the shower for a few minutes with the water scalding hot, battering his skin. Then, when his skin was stinging nicely, he lowered the temperature until it was lukewarm and scrubbed the sweat from his body and washed his hair. Finally, when he was as clean as he could get, he turned the water down one last time, to its lowest setting. Now, it was a test of endurance as the ice-cold water pummelled him, bringing his body temperature down with it. He took long, slow lungfuls of air as the tiredness washed away and his heartrate returned to normal.

Jean thought he was mad for this morning ritual — and she'd cursed him more than once when she'd gone to shower after him, and turned it on without checking the settings — but it worked for him. Even after the fitful night's sleep and the exertions of the run and the punch bag, he actually felt ready to face the day.

By the time he was all suited and booted, the rest of the family were up and about. Jean was in the kitchen making breakfast, wearing leggings and an old sweatshirt of Wise's. It dwarfed her but, somehow, she made it look stylish and comfortable. He came up behind her and gave her a kiss. 'Morning. Sorry about last night.'

'Ah, don't worry,' she replied, sliding an omelette out of the frying pan and onto a plate. 'How are you feeling now?'

'Better. The exercise helped.' He wandered over to the Nespresso machine and stuck a capsule in. It gurgled and whirred and filled a mug up halfway. Wise popped a second capsule in to fill it up to the brim.

'You know that's probably the most expensive way to make a cup of coffee,' Jean said.

Wise lifted the mug up to his nose and inhaled the aroma before taking a sip. 'But it tastes so good.'

'I wish I'd never bought you the thing. Paying for all those capsules is going to bankrupt us.'

'And it's bad for the environment,' a voice said from the doorway. It was Claire, his daughter, seven years old, going on fifteen. Her curly hair looked like it hadn't seen a brush in years and her school uniform was all over the place. The top button of her blouse was undone, the tie's knot hung halfway down her chest and somehow she'd found two black socks that clearly didn't match. Wise had to smile at the sight of her. She definitely marched to the beat of her own drum and didn't care what anyone else had to say on the subject.

She walked over to Wise. 'Did you know,' she said, 'that thirteen thousand five hundred coffee capsules are going into landfills every minute?'

Wise took another sip of his coffee. It was delicious. 'No, I didn't.'

'And,' she said, pointing a finger at her father's cup, 'it takes between one hundred and fifty to five hundred years for one capsule to breakdown in that landfill.'

'That doesn't sound good,' Wise said.

'It's not.' Claire jabbed a finger towards the cup of coffee in his hand. 'That is killing the planet.'

'That's interesting. Where did you learn that?'

'From YouTube,' his son said, entering the kitchen. Ed was nine years old and as different to his sister as a human being could be. He was a serious boy who cared about everything. And, whereas his sister liked to live in a mess, he liked to have everything in its place. Even his hair was already perfectly brushed, and his uniform was smart and tidy. 'She learns everything from YouTube.'

'No, I don't,' Claire snapped back. 'Anyway, it's better than just playing boring video games all day.'

'They're not boring,' Ed said. 'You're just too dumb to know how to play them.'

'I'm not dumb. You're dumb,' Claire shouted, rushing over to her brother, arm already cocked back to punch him.

'Hey, hey, hey,' Jean said, slipping between them in an instant. 'No fighting. Your dad's here, so let's have a nice, quiet breakfast together.'

That seemed to do it as Ed and Claire broke away from each other and took their places at the kitchen table. Jean glanced over at Wise. 'That omelette's for you. Eat it before it gets cold.'

'You're amazing,' Wise said.

'I know.' Jean gave him a wink and then busied herself getting the kids their food. Wise joined them with his omelette and his coffee and, for the next fifteen minutes, he enjoyed the mayhem of family life and listened to his kids' tales of school. Apparently, Claire's form teacher hated her as she kept giving her the most difficult maths questions to solve, while Ed had volunteered to help out in the school library three times a week.

When he couldn't put off going to work any longer, he slipped his plate and cup into the dishwasher, kissed everyone goodbye, grabbed his overcoat and headed out the door.

It took him an hour to fight his way over to Kennington but he still made it with a few minutes to spare before his meeting with Roberts. There was just enough time to run over the road to Luigi's, the Italian cafe that made the best coffee for miles around. Wise had never done the sums, but he had a feeling that quite a chunk of his salary went into Luigi's pocket. Still, like the capsules at home, it was worth it.

Just walking through the door made Wise happy. There was something about the way the smell of the coffee mixed with the aroma of the wonderful food on offer that gave Wise a dopamine hit, especially when it was all topped off with the scent of fresh bread and pastries.

It was a family-run business too, and Wise enjoyed watching Luigi's crew banter amongst themselves. He was sure they had their moments and no doubt the arguments were ferocious but, for the most part, there was genuine affection for each other on display. Luigi, red-faced and his dark curly hair greased back, took the orders, while his daughters, Sofia and Elena, made the coffees and teas in a fog of steam behind him. Luigi's wife, stern-faced Maria, worked the till.

'Detective Inspector!' Luigi said as he walked through the doors. 'You're looking well today.'

'Thank you, my friend,' Wise replied. 'How's things?'

'Oh, I can't complain,' Luigi said.

'Ha! All he does is complain,' Maria muttered, with a shake of her head.

Wise smiled at Luigi's wife. 'And how are you, Maria?'

'The till is broken. That is how I am,' she said, curling her lip in distaste. 'You must pay cash or there is no coffee for you.'

'No problem,' Wise said. He didn't mention the till seemed to be broken more and more often these days. Maria had never been too keen on people paying by card but, since Lockdown, she appeared to be on a one-woman crusade to get people paying with cash again. She'd rather risk the germs if it meant she could keep some of her income hidden from the taxman.

Wise turned back to Luigi. 'I'll have a triple espresso and two flat whites to go, please.'

'Coming right up,' the owner said.

While his daughters busied themselves making the order, Wise moved along to Maria to pay. She held out a hand. 'Nine pounds, ninety-seven.'

Wise shook his head and dug a tenner out of his pocket. Somehow, it seemed cheaper when he paid by card and just tapped the payment through. 'Here you go.'

Maria looked at the money. 'No tip?'

They stared at each for a heartbeat or two before Wise caved and stuck his hand back in his pocket. He only had one coin on him and he showed Maria the fifty pence piece before placing it on the counter. 'That's all I've got.'

She gave him a look of utter disgust, as if he'd insulted her, her mother, her grandmother and the whole of Italy by offering such a paltry sum, but she had it in the till in a blink of an eye.

Sofia passed Wise his coffees with a smile of sympathy. 'Here you go.'

'Thanks.' Wise took the lid off the triple espresso, and knocked the drink down in one, wincing as the hot coffee scorched his throat. However, the immediate caffeine kick more than made up for the discomfort.

Leaving the empty cup on the counter, Wise carried the other two back to the nick.

Roberts' office was on the second floor. It was bigger than Wise's but not by much, and she always seemed to be drowning in paperwork of one sort or another. So much so that she complained often that she was more of an administrator now than an actual detective who solved crimes.

Wise had always been an ambitious officer, but he wasn't sure he wanted to be promoted up to a DCI if it meant he'd be stuck in the same position as Roberts. The change in responsibilities hadn't made his boss a happier person, that was for sure.

Roberts had never been much of a smiler but, these days, she never seemed to lose the grim set to her mouth and her silver hair, always cut short, was getting whiter by the day.

'Morning, Boss,' Wise said on entering. He placed one of the coffees in front of her. 'That's for you.'

'Cheers, Simon. Take a seat,' Roberts said, barely looking up from the paper she was reading.

Wise settled into one of the guest chairs and took a sip of coffee while he waited for Roberts to finish whatever she was doing. Finally, she scrawled her name across the bottom of the paper and looked up. 'Sorry about that.'

'I heard a rumour that the Met was going to try to go paperless,' Wise said. 'To save the trees.'

'I wish,' his boss said. 'All they've done is add a mountain of emails and instant messages to the dead forests they send my way every day.' She sighed. 'Anyway, tell me about your latest.'

Wise ran through the latest on the Jack Springer case and their theories on the killer's game.

'Are you sure, Simon?' Roberts said when he was finished. 'Just because he hung around for a little while before going after the kid, it doesn't mean he was counting to a hundred.'

'It seems very plausible to me, especially with the handover of the money.'

'Or we could look for someone who just got pissed off that the kid nicked his money without giving him a blowjob.'

'There's more to it than that,' Wise said. 'And Doctor Singh reckons there'll be other murders that we don't know about.'

Roberts sat back in her chair. 'Don't go over complicating things, Simon. I don't want a load of unsolved murders suddenly dropping onto our books, screwing our stats up. We've got enough on our plates as it is — and not enough bodies to deal with it.'

'We'll go where the evidence leads us, boss,' Wise said. 'That's all.'

'All I'm saying is that if it looks like a duck, quacks like a duck and walks like a duck, don't go looking for a bloody herd of cows to go with it. We haven't got the budget anymore for taking on the world.'

'Are you telling me not to investigate this?' Wise said. 'Because if you are, I want you to be very clear about it.'

'Jesus, Simon. Of course I'm not telling you that.' Roberts' eyes narrowed to slits. 'Just don't fuck things up.'

'I'll do my best.' Wise stood, suddenly very keen to be out of there. 'Enjoy your coffee.'

'Keep me updated,' Roberts said, already picking up another piece of paper.

Wise left her office, even more determined not to ever become a DCI. At least, not Roberts' version of one. And she could stick her suggestions. He was going to pursue the leads wherever they may go.

## 12

MIR-One was bustling with activity when Wise walked through the doors. Sarah and her team were already going through more CCTV footage, looking for other sightings of the Anorak Man. Brains was there too, hiding behind his monitor, beavering away as he looked for other cases. And Hannah was at her desk, talking on her phone.

Wise nodded hellos as he walked past his team and headed into his office, still pissed off by Roberts' attitude. Wise hung his overcoat over the hook on the back of his door and squeezed in behind his desk. Taking another sip of coffee, he had to admit he could see her point to a certain extent. She was right when she said they were overworked and understaffed, but he didn't believe in picking and choosing what got investigated or not.

The trouble was that, now the Met was overrun by bean counters and politicians, success was measured in quantifiable terms via the Police Reported Crimes stats. As a result, there was considerable pressure to keep the numbers down on everything. The logic being that, if fewer crimes were reported, it meant less crimes were being committed and the Met could say it was doing its job properly. He'd heard of officers logging some robberies under 'lost property,' because they knew they'd never find the perpetrators and didn't want an unsolved case on their books. Attempted burglaries became 'criminal damage' and so on. It was all subtle stuff, massaging the labelling of what was reported so that serious incidents looked like they were going down.

There were also stories about someone, caught for one crime, being persuaded to "confess" to other crimes that they didn't do in exchange for a reduced sentence, so the officers got to improve their detection rates.

It was all madness and it didn't help anyone. What's more, it destroyed the trust in the police just so the higher-ups and the politicians could claim they were succeeding in the war against crime when the reality was quite the opposite. Even worse, it made the police stop caring about what really mattered: getting criminals off the street and getting justice for the victims.

There was a knock at his door.

'Yeah?' Wise called out.

Hannah popped her head around the door. 'Hendon has sent over some pictures of possible murder weapons. Do you want to have a look?'

Wise stood up from his desk. 'Anything interesting?'

'If by interesting, you mean vicious and nasty, then yeah.'

Wise followed Hannah back into the incident room. She'd laid out a load of printouts across two desks, each with a picture of a different weapon.

'Most of these are variations of machetes,' Hannah said. 'They match Doctor Singh's description of the murder weapon — long blade, curved tip — as well as Mrs McGuin's statement that the blade was some forty centimetres long. The Rambo knives amongst this lot look too short for what we're after, though.'

Wise quickly ran his eyes over them. The Rambo knives were easy to spot, with the serrated edges on one side. 'Yeah, I agree,' Wise said. 'They're nasty, but no one's going to mistake them for a sword. The machetes, though ...' They came in a variety of shapes with single-hand grips and long blades. He could definitely see some of them being mistaken for a sword. 'Mrs McGuin did say the weapon was banana-shaped as well.'

He turned over the pictures of weapons that weren't immediately right, starting with the Rambo knives and moving onto the machetes that had straight-edges on both sides. That left four pictures of weapons that looked possible.

Wise and Hannah leaned over the pictures, looking closely at each one. 'How do you carry something this size around without drawing attention to yourself?' Hannah asked. 'You can hardly stick it in your back pocket or tuck it into your belt.'

Wise stopped by one image. Whereas the other machetes had curves to them, the picture in front of him was the only one that had more of a banana shape to it. It almost looked like a boomerang, except it had a grip at one end and a sharp blade at the other. 'This looks a good fit,' Wise said, tapping the picture.

'Hold on a minute,' Hannah said. She jogged back to her desk, picked up some notes she'd scrawled down, and returned to Wise. 'That is a kukri knife, apparently,' she said, reading from the paper. 'Made famous by the Gurkhas.'

'The Gurkhas, eh?' Wise said. 'They'd have the skills to cut someone's throat in one go.'

'The person we're looking for isn't Nepalese, though,' Hannah said. She pointed to the picture of Anorak Man on the board. 'He's as white as they come.'

'From what I remember, the regiment recruits officers from the UK and the Commonwealth, though. Our man could be among them.'

'Gurkhas are elite warriors, aren't they? One of them gone rogue could do some serious damage.'

'Yeah — but let's not get ahead of ourselves just yet. Make some calls. Find out where they are based in the UK and where they are right now. Who knows, they might be out of the country somewhere?' Wise said. 'And look into where Joe Public could get hold of one of these kukri knives. I doubt they sell them in B&Q. Maybe there's just one place in London you can buy one. If that's the case, then we need to find out who's picked up one recently.'

Hannah nodded. 'Alright. I'll hit the phones.'

'Shout when you have something,' Wise said. Leaving Hannah, he headed over to Brains' desk. 'How are you getting on?'

'I've found the doctor's other victim, Guv,' Brains replied, looking up from his monitor. 'Or I think I have. Have a look at this.' He moved his chair back so Wise could see his screen. 'This is Kareem Abdul. He was fourteen years old.'

The picture showed a serious-looking lad with knitted brows and dark eyes, wearing a white shirt and a badly knotted school tie that reminded Wise of his daughter's that morning.

'He was murdered in Shepherd's Bush on Thirtieth of June this year,' Brains said. 'Throat cut from ear to ear.'

'Just like Jack,' Wise said.

'I've read Doctor Singh's PM notes. It's more or less identical to the report on our victim.'

'Where did he die?'

'They found the body on Shepherd's Bush Green by the playground,' Brains said. 'No cameras and it was late — time of death was put at somewhere between 10:30 p.m. and 11:30 p.m. — so not that many people around on the park itself. No eyewitnesses came forward either, despite it being kicking out time at the nearby pubs.'

'Who investigated it?' Wise asked.

'Hammersmith but, by the looks of it — and this is only my opinion — they didn't put much effort into it. It wasn't assigned to a murder team and I can't find any more entries into the case book after the first couple of days.'

'Two days? Seriously?'

Brains nodded.

'Who was the SIO?' Wise asked.

'A DCI John Hollins.'

Wise shook his head. 'Give him a call and tell him I'd like to have a chat.'

Brains' eyebrows popped up above his glasses. 'You're not

planning on telling him off, are you, Guv? What with him being a senior officer and all?'

'Who? Me?' Wise said. 'I'd never do anything as foolish as that.'

Brains sighed. 'I'll make the call.'

'Good man,' Wise said. He only hoped he could keep his word. The way he felt, he wasn't so sure.

## 13

'How come it's always you and me that have to trudge through the streets, freezing our knackers off, asking people questions?' Hicksy said.

Jono tried not to roll his eyes. 'It's because we've got such winning personalities.'

'Fuck off,' Hicksy replied. 'I may be a right charmer, but you? A pint of sour milk's more appealing.' The man didn't look like he had a neck at the best of times, but now he had his chin tucked as tight as he could against his chest, his head appeared to be attached to his collarbone.

'I think someone's been telling you porkies if you believe that,' Jono laughed. 'Everyone knows I'm the popular one.'

'Are you, though?'

Jono didn't reply. He was starting to think the man might have a point. They'd only been out and about for just over an hour and his feet were already killing him. It didn't help either that there was a bastard of a wind blowing off the Thames that cut through his overcoat as if it wasn't there.

They were walking along the South Bank, down by Waterloo Bridge, armed with pictures of Anorak Man to show around. It was that post rush hour time of day when the commuters were already at their desks, shop counters and restaurant kitchens. Normally, the day-trippers would surface around about now, but the weather was doing its best to keep the crowds away. The people Jono and Hicksy needed to talk to were still around though, sheltering from the wind in the doorways or tucked away down alleyways. So far, though, it had been pretty fruitless. When they'd asked questions, all they'd got back were blank stares, abuse or ignorance. Sometimes, it was a combination of all three. One thing was certain, London's homeless didn't like the police much, and Jono couldn't really blame them for that.

'I gotta admit, sometimes I feel like a fucking dinosaur,' Hicksy said, sniffing as he looked around. 'The world I knew doesn't exist anymore. I mean, look at this place.' He pointed to the fenced off area underneath the South Bank Centre, and the graffiti-covered concrete. 'That used to be one scary place to walk through, but now it's been closed off so someone can turn it into a bunch of tofu restaurants soon. The way things are going, there won't be any dirt left in this city. Everything will be all sanitised and disinfected like some bloody theme park. You'll be able to buy a fucking falafel tortilla wrap, but not a bacon and egg sandwich.'

'It'll still be here. We'll just have to look harder for it. The billionaires might try to turn London into some sort of financial Disneyland, but the real London will be tucked away behind the scenes.'

'Still doesn't sound like a place I want to live in,' Hicksy said.

Jono paused. 'Be grateful you get the choice. Some of us aren't so lucky.'

That stopped Hicksy dead in his tracks. His mate went white-faced. 'Shit. I didn't mean ... fuck. Sorry. I wasn't thinking. You know me — always sticking my big foot in my mouth.'

Jono squeezed his friend's shoulder. 'It's alright, mate. Sometimes, I forget about it too. Unfortunately, it all comes back to me pretty quickly.'

'Have you thought anymore about what you're going to do?'

'Not yet,' Jono said. The two men started walking again, heading up the steps towards the Royal Festival Hall. 'None of the bloody options are that thrilling, are they? I kinda feel like if I don't make a decision, I can put off the whole dying thing for a bit longer.'

'I don't think sticking your head in the sand is going to help this time, mate.'

Jono puffed his cheeks out. 'I know, I know. But it's hard enough agreeing not to have a fag today, let alone saying I'll let them pump me full of chemicals and radiation.'

'Who knows? Maybe you'll get superpowers like the Incredible Hulk.'

'Or all my hair will fall out and my balls will shrink to the size of peanuts.'

Hicksy looked him up and down. 'First off, going bald's got to be better than that mess you call a hairstyle. As for your balls, your missus told me that peanuts would be an improvement on what you've presently got tucked away in your jockstrap.'

Jono chuckled. 'She's not normally so complimentary about what I've got down there. You must've caught her in a good mood.'

'Oh, she was in a good mood, alright. She told me I was the best shag she'd had in years.'

'Don't let it go to your head — she tells everyone that.'

Both men laughed as they walked past the main entrance to the Festival Hall, then silence fell between them as the wind whipped their good humour away.

'I'm not going to get all soppy on you, mate,' Hicksy said, 'but being a selfish git, I don't want you to die. Go start the treatment before it's too late. Some hope's got to be better than none.'

Jono smiled at his friend. 'You just don't want to be partnered with Princess Diversity if I die.'

'Fuck me. I hadn't even thought about that possibility. That settles it — you have to get the chemo. For my sake.'

'Well, if you put it like that, I'll call the doctor on Monday.' They passed a dim sum restaurant that looked completely chocker inside, next to a brasserie that was completely empty.

'Good man,' Hicksy said.

They headed back down more steps to the street level on Belvedere Road. Jono looked left and right. 'Which way do you want to go?'

'Anywhere we can get a decent coffee without being asked if we want soy or oat milk,' Hicksy said.

Jono pointed left. 'Let's go this way. We can check out Leake Street Arches, then go to the hole in the wall cafe just past that. They do coffee that'll keep you awake for days.'

'I'll be happy with hot and wet,' Hicksy said, pulling his coat tighter, before halting. He tapped Jono on the arm and pointed to an alley between buildings. There were two human shapes wrapped up in blankets, using a wheelie bin as a windshield. 'Let's have a chat with them.'

'I hope they don't smell of piss,' Jono muttered.

The two men wandered over. As they approached, the human shapes turned to look their way, dirty faces poking out from under blankets, eyes going wide as they no doubt recognised the two men as coppers.

Jono waved. 'You doing alright?'

The two faces just stared back.

'Pretty cold out here, isn't it?' Jono tried again, trying to sound cheerful.

Silence.

Bloody hell, this was turning out to be one special morning. 'Look, we're not going to cause any trouble. We just want to ask you a couple of questions.'

'If they bolt, I'm not legging it after them,' Hicksy muttered and Jono didn't disagree. He'd never been much of a runner, but now his lungs were screwed up, he definitely wouldn't give Linford Christie any sleepless nights. Thankfully though, the two under the blankets remained tensed up but stayed where they were.

'I just want to show you a picture and see if you recognise someone. That's all.'

'You couldn't lend us a fiver, could you?' the one on the left, a lad, said. His voice, somehow, sounded young and old at the same time. 'For a cup of tea, like, or something to eat?'

'Lend you a fiver?' Jono said, raising his eyebrows in disbelief.

The lad nodded. 'Yeah.'

'How are you going to pay it back if I lend it to you?'

There was a wobble of the blanket as the lad shrugged.

Jono sighed, dug into his pocket and pulled out some shrapnel, and walked over to the kid. He might not have smelled of piss, but the aroma coming off him wasn't anything special. 'This is all I've got.'

The lad held out a grubby hand, and Jono deposited his change into it. 'Cheers, man.'

The money disappeared pretty damn quick. 'What do you want?'

Doing his best not to breathe in through his nose, Jono pulled out a picture of Anorak Man, bent down and showed it to the lad. 'Just wanted to know if you've seen this bloke around?'

'Could be anyone,' the lad said. 'What's he done?'

'He's a very dangerous man,' Jono said. 'He's been hurting people like you.'

The lad shrugged. 'I ain't seen him.'

'What about your friend?' Jono moved the picture towards the second person, but they dropped their eyes down to the ground.

'She ain't seen him either,' the lad said.

'I'd still like her to have a look,' Jono replied, not moving the picture.

The girl kept her head down. 'I ain't seen him.'

'Can you just have a proper look at the picture?' Jono kept his voice calm and fatherly.

Slowly, the girl lifted her head up. Her eyes flicked to the picture for the briefest of moments, then they went up to look at Jono. 'Nah. I ain't seen him.'

For a moment, Jono thought about asking for his change back, but there was no point. It was probably already germ-infested and what could you buy for one pound twenty these days, anyway? You couldn't even get a cup of tea. Not even half a cup.

'Look after yourself,' Jono said instead, not sounding like he meant it, and straightened up. He rejoined Hicksy and the two men resumed walking. 'I notice you stayed a healthy distance away.'

'Just covering your back,' Hicksy said. 'Keeping you safe.'

'Yeah? How about next time you do the talking and I'll stay downwind for a change?'

'But you're all charm. They like you. If I did the talking, we'd all end up having a ruck.'

'Have you ever thought about not pissing everyone off?' Jono asked.

'Why would I do that?' Hicksy said, and Jono wasn't sure if his friend was joking or not.

They walked on. The wind whipped off the river and cut straight through them with such a ferocity that it brought tears to Jono's eyes. 'This is a waste of time.'

'At least it's better than doing chores for the missus,' Hicksy said.

'Not much better,' Jono replied.

Five minutes later, they reached Leake Street Arches. Like everywhere in London, what was once a long, dark tunnel running under Waterloo station had been turned into yet another gentrified attraction; the arches were now home to a Vietnamese restaurant, a cafe and an art gallery. Tables and benches ran along one side, with drought and chess boards painted onto the tabletops. There were a few people sitting around with coffees and snacks.

Every inch of the tunnel walls and the roof were covered in graffiti of every description. There were the usual tags and indecipherable squiggles but there were also some pretty impressive portraits of people, cartoon characters and, in one place, a giant ape scowled over one of the restaurants. A large sign near the start of the arches declared it 'the world's largest legal street art site.'

'Fucking hell,' Hicksy said. 'They're even making vandalism a tourist attraction now. I used to spend half my days chasing Herberts around for doing this when I was in uniform.'

'I'm amazed you can remember that far back,' Jono replied. 'Next, you'll be telling me about nicking a horse and carriage for speeding.'

Hicksy nodded towards the restaurant tables. 'What have we got here?'

A woman with a small child on her hip walked between tables, begging for cash from the customers. However, it was the two lads loitering around some people taking selfies by the graffiti wall that had got Hicky's attention. They looked like they were after a handbag or a phone to snatch. 'Let's talk to them first, before we have to nick them for doing something stupid.'

'And I'm definitely not running after them if they leg it,' Jono said.

'Let's just take that as a given, eh?' Hicksy said. He headed towards the lads. 'Oi, you two. A word, please.'

'Feds!' one of them shouted and then they were off, sprinting as fast as they could in the opposite direction to Hicksy and Jono.

Everyone else in the tunnel looked their way, trying to see what the fuss was about. Jono gave a wave of acknowledgement while Hicksy just laughed. 'Maybe we should've dressed more casually.'

Jono looked him up and down. 'That's not possible. You already look like a tramp.'

'I do? Have you looked in the mirror lately?'

'Not if I can help it. I'm depressed enough as it is.'

'Let's try the woman with the kid,' Hicksy said. 'I don't think she'll be able to scarper too quickly.'

The woman in question stood frozen in between two tables, watching Jono and Hicksy approach. She looked maybe Middle Eastern, but it was hard to tell what was just dirt and what was natural. Her black hair was tied back off her face with a headscarf. Her baby, bundled up in a blue romper suit and hood, sucked fiercely on a dummy.

Jono held up both hands. 'We just want to ask you some questions. No one's in trouble and we're not going to arrest anyone.'

'We'll even buy you a coffee,' Hicksy said.

'A coffee and a sandwich,' the woman replied.

Jono glanced over at Hicksy. 'I'll have a black coffee too.'

'Why am I getting it?' Hicksy said, sounding outraged.

'Because you offered.'

'Fabulous,' Hicksy replied. 'I'll be right back with your order, sir.'

As Hicksy stomped off to the cafe, the woman slid onto a bench at an empty table. Jono sat opposite her and smiled. 'Thank you for talking to us.'

'What do you want?' she replied, her accent confirming Middle Eastern origins.

'I'm Detective Sergeant Jonathan Gray,' Jono said, keeping the smile, but he wasn't sure if it was helping. His wife had told him on many an occasion that it made him look constipated. 'What's your name?'

'Why do you want to know?' Her dark eyes glared with hostility, however Jono had stopped being bothered by such things long ago. He'd been married thirty years, after all.

'It's just easier talking if I know your name.'

The woman shook her head. 'It's Fatima.'

Jono nodded. 'It's nice to meet you, Fatima. How old is your baby?'

'She is one year old.'

'And does she have a name?'

'Esme.'

'A beautiful name,' Jono said, not that he had an opinion either way. It just seemed the right thing to say.

'So? What you want?' Fatima said, apparently immune to Jono's charms — something she shared with most women.

Jono looked around and spotted Hicksy returning, a tray in hand. 'Ah, here comes our waiter.'

Hicksy sat down, plonking the tray on the table. 'Help yourselves.'

'Thanks,' Jono said and passed a coffee and the lone sandwich on the tray to Fatima. 'This is my colleague, DS Roy Hicks. Hicksy, this is Fatima.'

'Nice to meet you, Fatima,' Hicksy said, his smile even more frightening than Jono's.

Fatima said nothing.

Jono took the picture of Anorak Man out of his pocket and placed it on the table in front of Fatima as she bit a chunk off the sandwich.

'We're investigating several murders within the homeless community, Fatima, and we're looking for this man.'

She peered at the picture as she chewed. 'This the killer?'

'He's a person of interest,' Hicksy said.

Fatima looked up. 'The killer.'

Jono smiled. 'Have you seen him around? Maybe talking to others like you? Maybe offering them money or drugs?'

Fatima looked at the picture again. 'This picture. It's no good. You can't see his face.'

'It's the best we have, unfortunately.'

Fatima's mouth turned down in disapproval. Jono knew Americans called that look frowning, but he had no idea what the proper name for it was. It definitely wasn't frowning though — that was an eyebrow thing. 'It could be anyone,' she said.

'Have you seen a man, though, hanging around, maybe talking to people, looking suspicious?'

'Everyone who talks to people like me is suspicious.' Fatima took another bite of her sandwich, nearly finishing it. 'You want to arrest us, to hurt us, to beat us, to fuck us. Some ...' She nodded at the picture. 'Want to cut us.'

Both Jono and Hicksy perked up. They'd not mentioned knives or cuts or anything like that. 'So, you do know who I'm talking about?' Jono said.

Fatima shrugged. 'It depends. You got money to pay me?'

Jono glanced at Hicksy.

'Don't look at me. I just bought the bloody coffees,' Hicksy said.

With a sigh, Jono reached into his coat pocket and pulled out his wallet. Of course, it was sod's law that he only had a twenty on him. He pulled the note out. 'I don't suppose you have any change?'

Fatima snatched the note from his hand. 'You need to speak to a girl called Katie. She meet this man. He hurt her.'

Now, that was something. It might even be worth twenty quid. 'Sounds like we do indeed need to speak to her. Can you take us to this Katie?'

'You find her okay without me,' Fatima said. 'She's normally up at Waterloo. She begs near the flower shop.'

'Waterloo is a pretty busy place, Fatima,' Jono said. 'How will we know who Katie is?'

'You'll know.' Fatima tapped the picture. 'This man cut her face open.'

# 14

Hammersmith Police Station was just past the Flyover on the Fulham Palace Road. The street was barely wide enough for the two-way traffic that kept it chock-a-block twenty-four hours a day. Originally built in 1939, the squat Grade II listed building was renovated and expanded to drag the place kicking and screaming into the 21st century. Naturally, as with every government project, it took far longer than planned and cost at least twice as much as they thought it would, finally reopening in 2020.

The first sign of modernity were the steel anti-crash bollards that ran along the kerb outside, ensuring that anyone with a van and intent to do harm would have no luck trying to drive into the station. The main entrance was in the old building, with the Met's crest of arms standing proudly above the doors, however the bulk of the station was in the new addition next door. And, unlike Kennington, everything in Hammersmith was as cutting edge as it could get. Even the stables for the horses looked better than anything Wise's team had to put up with.

The coffee, too, was decent — much to Wise's surprise. It made waiting for DCI John Hollins to turn up a bit more bearable. However, the man was now running thirty minutes late for their meeting, and Wise's patience was running out despite the excellent coffee.

'Looking at your watch every two minutes won't speed things up,' Hannah said. They were sitting in a small meeting room that overlooked the library opposite. Wise had taken Hannah with him to Hammersmith as she had a knack of stopping him from making a fool of himself and, somehow, he thought that might be useful.

'If I was a suspicious person, I'd think the DCI was trying to avoid us,' Wise said.

'He's probably just refreshing himself with the case files.'

'From what we've seen, that should have taken no more than a couple of minutes. There's hardly a mountain of information to go through.' Wise took another sip of coffee. 'If he's pissed off somewhere, I'll ...'

The door to the meeting room opened. Both Wise and Hannah looked up to see a tired man with a large white beard walk in, a folder clutched to his chest. 'Sorry to keep you waiting. It's a bloody madhouse today. I've not even had time to pee.'

'If you need to go, we can wait another five minutes,' Wise said, unimpressed.

The man dropped his file on the table. 'It's alright. This won't take long.'

Wise exchanged a glance with Hannah. This wasn't getting off to a very good start. 'We might need a bit more time than that.' He held out a hand. 'I'm DI Simon Wise and this is DS Hannah Markham.'

The man ignored Wise's hand and sat down. 'I hear you want to know about the Kareem Abdul murder.'

Wise put his hand down. 'You are DCI Hollins?'

The man looked at Wise like he was an idiot. 'No, I'm the bloody Queen of England.' He looked down at the folder as he opened it. 'Now, what do you want to know?'

Wise was about to say something about the man's rudeness when Hannah lightly tapped his foot and gave him a slight shake of her head. Wise took a breath instead. 'Could you talk us through the case, please?'

Hollins let out a sigh of his own. 'There's not much to tell you. Kareem Abdul was found dead on Shepherd's Bush Green, by the playground, on the thirtieth of June, his throat cut. There were no witnesses. No forensics. No CCTV. Nothing, in fact, to work with. His father said Kareem was involved with a gang in Hackney, where he grew up, so we believe his death was connected to that but, with nothing to go on, the case is a non-starter.'

'Did you find where Kareem had been earlier in the day?' Wise asked.

'What's that got to do with him getting his throat cut in Shepherd's Bush?' Hollins replied.

'We're investigating a very similar murder,' Hannah said before Wise could be a bit more blunt about things. 'A homeless boy was murdered in Camden, throat cut just like Kareem.'

'Must be the same gang then,' Hollins said.

'We don't think it is a gang,' Wise said. 'We've got CCTV footage of an IC1 male having an interaction with our victim and then following him as he headed from Charing Cross to Camden. We believe he's the killer.'

'A gang member,' Hollins said, sounding as bored as he could.

'No.'

The way Wise said it made Hollins look up. 'I'm sorry, Inspector — what did you say?' Hollins' boredom was gone. Now he sounded as pissed off as Wise felt.

'What the inspector meant was that our suspect doesn't fit any sort of gang profile,' Hannah said, smiling. 'We think he's hunting homeless people and murdering them — that's why we were curious if you'd tracked Kareem's movements earlier in the day. Perhaps he met our suspect?'

'I don't know what it's like in Kennington, but we don't have the resources to check every CCTV camera in London to find some gang member.' Hollins pushed the folder across the table to Wise and Hannah. 'Anyway, I've spoken to my boss, and he's very happy for me to pass the Kareem Abdul case over to you. So, there you go. Enjoy.'

Wise looked down at the folder. There had to be only five sheets of paper in it. The man had done sod all in trying to find out who'd killed Kareem.

Hollins stood up. 'Now, if you'll excuse me, I have to go and have that slash. Have a good trip back to your nick.' Hollins didn't wait for Wise or Hannah to say anything. He just walked out of the room.

'He was something special,' Hannah said. 'Bet he came top in his class at charm school.'

Wise was seething. 'He does nothing and then comes in acting like he's king of the world. I've got a good mind to go back and have a word with him.'

'And what good would that get us?'

'Not a thing, but I'd feel better.'

'Right up until they suspended you.'

Wise pinched the bridge of his nose. 'You're right. But Kareem was killed back in June. We're not going to find a thing to help us now.'

Hannah picked up the folder and stood up. 'You did the right thing. Kareem deserves justice just as much as Jack.'

Wise got to his feet as well, still shaking his head. 'People like him …'

'Yeah, well,' Hannah said. 'The world's full of dickheads.'

'The Met especially. I just can't get over how much he didn't give a monkey's about any of it.' Wise stood up and downed the rest of his drink. 'At least the coffee was good.'

'That's something, eh?'

Wise looked at Hannah. 'Sometimes it feels like that's the only thing.'

They took the lift down to the car park, the Kareem Abdul case folder tucked under Hannah's arm. It was only a short ride — no more than six floors — and that was the only reason Wise didn't go hunting for some stairs to take instead. Even so, being in the small space still had Wise squirming inside, especially when more people got in two floors down. He glanced over at the maximum capacity sign that claimed the lift could hold twelve people comfortably, and yet it felt way too crowded with six. Even the air felt in short supply and Wise dug a finger into his shirt collar, trying to find a bit more wiggle room to stop himself choking. He took a step back to give himself some more space away from the press of bodies and clunked against the back of the lift, adding to his sense of entrapment.

The lift stopped on the ground floor and the other passengers all got out, leaving Wise and Hannah alone to continue to the car park.

As Wise let out a sigh of relief, Hannah gave him a quizzical look. 'Are you claustrophobic or something?'

The question made him jump. 'No. Why do you say that?'

The lift stopped. The doors opened and Wise all but fell out into the car park, leaving Hannah laughing behind him. 'No reason,' she said. 'But I get why you don't enjoy travelling on the Tube now.'

Wise shot her a look. 'I'm not claustrophobic — I just don't like confined spaces that much. They make me feel uncomfortable.'

'I think you'll find that's the very definition of claustrophobia,' Hannah replied, still smiling.

They walked over to the Mondeo, and Wise unlocked the doors. 'I'm not scared of confined spaces,' he said over the roof of the car. 'I just don't like them.'

They both got in the car. Hannah kept quiet as she buckled her seatbelt, and Wise felt guilty for snapping at her. It wasn't her fault the damn lift had put him on edge. Still, he didn't say anything until they were out of the car park and in the traffic on the Fulham Palace Road, then turned left onto the A3219. 'Sorry about the lift thing.'

'That's alright,' Hannah said. 'Don't worry about it.'

'I shouldn't have got short with you. That dickhead of a DCI just rubbed me up the wrong way.'

Hannah flicked through the folder. 'He was probably being an arse because he knew he'd done no work on the case and didn't want to get called on it. I mean, there's nothing in this apart from the basics.'

Her phone rang before Wise could say any more.

'DS Markham,' she said on answering. 'Oh yes, thank you for getting back to me. Can you hold on one second?' She moved the phone away from her ear and pressed the button for the speaker phone. 'Sorry about that. I just wanted to put you on speaker so my boss can hear you as well.'

'That's no problem,' a man said. His accent was so polished, Wise could almost hear it sparkle over the phone.

'Can you tell me your name again?'

'I'm Major Kenneth Dixon, with the Royal Gurkha Rifles,' the man said. 'I'm calling from our barracks in Shorncliffe.'

'And I have DI Simon Wise with me,' Hannah said.

'Hello,' Wise said.

'Good to meet you both,' Dixon said. 'Now, how can I help you?'

'We're investigating a murder of a young boy on Wednesday afternoon,' Hannah said. 'And we think the killer may have used a kukri knife.'

'Hmm,' Dixon said. 'That's not good. And I suppose you want to know if one of our lads could have done it?'

'It's quite an unusual weapon for someone to have.'

'Well, it can't be someone in the Rifles,' the major said. 'Not anyone serving presently, at least. Everyone's in Kosovo at the moment, dealing with Afghan refugees. They've been there for a month or so already.'

'That's good to know,' Hannah said. 'We didn't fancy going up against one of your lot.'

'Very sensible of you.'

'Is there anything you can tell us about the kukri knife?'

'Well, it's probably the most effective knife being used by any military force in the world today. And by effective, I mean deadly,' Dixon said. 'The Gurkhas have been using them, of course, since forever. It started off as a farming tool because it's perfect for cutting, chopping or slicing anything that grows in the ground or walks upon it. And it's perfect for fighting with. During the Second World War, there was the old joke that the Gurkhas didn't need ammunition as long as they had their kukri knives.'

'What makes them so good?'

'Well, first of all, it's like fighting someone with an axe more than a knife. The cutting edge is on the inner curve so most of the weight of the weapon is on the upper part of the blade. That gives you extra momentum as you cut down, allowing the blade to cut deeper than a normal knife.'

'Ah.'

'Indeed,' Dixon said. 'Not many people walk away alive if they are facing someone with a kukri knife.'

'You wouldn't know if they are easy to get hold of outside the regiment?' Hannah asked.

'The genuine article isn't,' Dixon replied. 'Unfortunately, though, you can buy imitations at any survivalist store. The weekend warriors love them. They think holding a blunt knock-off kukri knife makes them an elite soldier. If they ever had to go into battle, though, they'd be in for a shock.'

'Would you still be able to kill someone with one of these knock-offs?' Wise asked.

'Of course,' Dixon said. 'But you could kill someone with just about anything. The genuine article — one of ours — would be like using a surgeon's scalpel, whereas a fake would be a lot more brutal in the damage it did.'

Wise exchanged glances with Markham. 'Our pathologist said it was one of the cleanest cuts she'd ever seen.'

'Hmmm. That's not good, is it?' Dixon said. 'That sounds like it could be the real thing you're after.'

'How would someone get hold of the genuine article, Major?' Wise asked.

'Well, our soldiers get to keep their knives when they leave the regiment, but ninety-nine percent of them go back to Nepal. Of course, that doesn't mean they can't sell their knives or give them away if they want to, but that doesn't happen very often. Then you've got ex-officers who'd have one, but officers' knives are more ceremonial than anything.'

'But they'd still be scalpel sharp?' Wise asked.

'Very much so. Even so, I can't imagine one of our chaps would go around killing random people.' There was a pause.

'That's good to know,' Hannah said. 'Is there anything else you can tell us?'

The major laughed. 'Do you know who the most famous victim of a kukri knife is?'

'No, we don't,' Hannah said.

'It's Dracula,' Dixon replied.

'I thought he was staked through the heart.'

'That was only in the movies. In the book, Jonathan Harker cut Dracula's throat from ear to ear with a kukri knife, then someone else stabbed him through the heart with a Bowie knife.'

Wise stared at the phone in Hannah's hand. 'What did you say?'

'They used one to kill Dracula. Apparently, kukri knives have been used to kill monsters and demons since 1897.'

Wise looked up from the phone and immediately slammed on the brakes to avoid hitting a cyclist who'd cut in front of him. 'Wanker.'

'Sorry, what was that?' Dixon said. 'I didn't hear you.'

Thank God for that. 'It was nothing, Major. Thank you for your time,' Wise said.

Hannah disconnected the call. 'Well, that was something. You don't think we're looking for Buffy the Vampire Slayer, do you?'

'As much as I'd like to meet Sarah Michelle Gellar, I don't think it's her,' Wise said. 'But there is an element of the crazies about these two murders.'

This time it was Wise's phone that interrupted them. Brains' name appeared on the screen.

'Tell me you've got some good news for me,' Wise said on answering.

'I don't think I have, Guv,' Brains replied. 'You on your way back to the nick?'

'Yeah,' Wise said. 'About twenty minutes out. What's up?'

'I'm sorry, Guv,' Brains replied. 'I found more murders that fit our guy's MO.'

'Shit. How many more?'

'I think I've found five more cases, Guv,' Brains said.

# 15

Wise blue-lighted it all the way back to Kennington, through the slashing rain, the windscreen wipers going as fast as his heart. Brains' words went over and over in his mind. Five more cases. Five more deaths. Five more kids. Dear God. What had they stumbled upon?

He slammed the Mondeo into an empty spot by the station's front door. Without waiting for Hannah, he hustled up the stairs to the third floor, and Wise all but ran to MIR-One. Everyone was there, bar Hicksy and Jono, but Wise went straight over to Brains. 'Tell me.'

'I've spent all day trawling through HOLMES, checking and double checking everything,' Brains said. 'There's five other possibles to go with Jack and Kareem. All homeless teenagers. All fatal knife wounds. Most had their throats cut from ear to ear.'

'Five?' Wise repeated, still not believing his ears. 'You sure?'

'HOLMES is,' Brains replied.

Hannah came through the doors of the incident room. Wise motioned to her to give him a minute alone with Brains. He needed a bit of time to process this new information before sharing with everyone else. 'How far back do they go?'

'Just over eighteen months,' Brains said. He shuffled through the papers on his desk and pulled out one clipped together section. 'This is the first one. Sasha Moore. Sixteen. She was murdered down by Waterloo Bridge on the South Bank.' Brains placed a picture of a young Caucasian girl down on the table. She had long brown hair, large eyes and she was wearing a blouse, tie and school blazer. 'Sasha grew up in Weybridge in Surrey, but got in with the wrong crowd, according to her parents. She ran away from home and came up to London.' Brains put another picture down to the first one. This was taken on a mortuary table. The girl's eyes were closed, but that was the only peaceful thing about the image. Her face and neck were covered in a myriad of cuts, some deeper than others. The neck wound was the worst of them all.

'Christ,' Wise said, staring at the injuries. 'He really hacked at her.'

'The postmortem counted fifteen cuts in total. Eight were fatal.'

'And there are four others like this?'

Brains nodded. 'Not as hacked up as Sasha, but yeah.'

Just then, Hicksy and Jono came through the doors, looking wet and bedraggled.

'Alright, Guv,' Jono said. He shook his head like a wet dog. 'We missed anything?'

'Yeah, quite a bit,' Wise replied. 'Dry yourselves off and then we'll go through it all.' Wise turned back to Brains. 'Show me the others.'

One by one, the detective showed the pictures of the lost souls who'd been horrifically murdered. Listening to how they'd died, seeing their injuries, Wise knew they'd all died at the hands of the same person — Anorak Man.

Looking up, he saw everyone else was watching. 'Thanks for being patient, everyone. I know it's late, but I think you all need to hear what Brains has uncovered — and, unfortunately, I'm going to need you to come in tomorrow to crack on with everything.'

There were groans at the thought of working on a Saturday, but Wise held up his hand and silence fell over the room.

'I don't want to lose my weekend either but, once you've heard what Brains has to say, you'll understand why it's necessary,' Wise said. 'Brains, over to you.'

'Right. Okay.' Brains stood up, pushed his glasses back up to the top of his nose, and headed to the whiteboards, armed with his stack of paper. He placed the notes on a desk near the boards and quickly shuffled through them, his cheeks colouring as everyone else watched him.

He took the picture of Sasha and taped it to the board. 'Sasha Moore. Sixteen. Murdered by Waterloo Bridge on twenty-third of March, 2020.' He collected another picture and stuck that to the board as well, keeping his back to the room as he did so. 'Leroy Jenkins. Sixteen. Murdered in King's Cross on fifth of August, 2020.' Another picture went up. 'Mark Stay. Eighteen. Murdered down by Smithfield Market on twelfth December 2020.'

The team watched in silence as Brains added another two pictures to the board. 'Alice Kuang. Seventeen. Murdered by St. Pancreas Station on fourth of March, 2021. And finally, Ben Trills, sixteen. Murdered on the corner of Oxford Street and Tottenham Court Road on the sixteenth of August. These kids were all living on the streets. Some were drug addicts. Some weren't. All five were killed with a bladed weapon, described as a 'meat cleaver,' a 'carving knife,' a 'butcher's knife' and a 'sword.'

The pictures of the victims were all taken before life had forced the kids out onto the streets. Back when they were children with families and homes. Some were in school uniforms, some were in normal clothes, all trying to smile for the camera, some more successfully than others.

'The first, Sasha, was cut fifteen times until she finally succumbed to the killer's attack,' Brains continued. 'Most of the others, though, were killed like Jack, with a single cut to the throat.'

'Have you found any attacks where the victim survived?' Wise asked.

'I've only just started trawling through those,' Brains said. 'Unfortunately, there's a lot to look through, what with knife crime being what it is. Plus, there's a good chance some attacks might've gone unreported. These kids aren't the sort to go running to the police.'

'Bloody hell,' Donut said. 'How many more cases do you think we'll end up with?'

'I can't say,' Brains replied. 'It could be none, or it could be dozens.'

That bit of information swept around MIR-One like a shockwave.

'About that,' Jono said, pushing his lank hair back from his face. He looked pale and worn out, even more so than usual. 'We might have an attack survivor to look for.'

'We spoke to a woman called Fatima down Leake Street Arches,' Hicksy said. 'She told us about this girl, Katie, who was apparently attacked by Anorak Man, except she lived — just. She said this Katie had her face cut open by him.'

'When was this?' Wise asked.

'The woman we spoke to didn't know dates, but it must've been a while ago. Katie is back on the streets.'

'So, she might be able to identify Anorak Man?' Wise said.

'Hopefully,' Jono said, then coughed. 'We've just got to find her first. That's where it gets tricky.'

'Fatima said Katie normally begs up by the flower stall at Waterloo station,' Hicksy said. 'But there was no sign of her when we went to look just now.'

'Make finding her a priority,' Wise said. 'Hopefully, she can come in and do a photofit for us.'

'We'll look again tomorrow,' Jono said. 'But it could be she only works Waterloo during the week when all the commuters are about.'

'Or she's dead,' Donut said.

'Alright,' Wise said. 'Let's keep it positive. Let's hope she's still alive and willing to talk. We've made really good progress over the last few days. Let's keep the pace going and, all being well, we can put this to bed sooner rather than later.' He walked over to the picture of Anorak Man. 'It looks like this man has killed seven teenagers in eighteen months. Let's make sure no one else falls victim to him.'

There was a chorus of, 'Yes, Guv,' from the team.

'Now, go get some sleep,' Wise said. 'We've got to put in some hard yards tomorrow.'

As everyone left, Wise stared at the faces of the dead on the whiteboard. People like Dodson with his 'another bloody statistic' viewpoint, Roberts with her 'don't go over-complicating things' commands and Harris and his 'we don't have the resources' attitudes had allowed Anorak Man to get away with things for too long.

Well, no more.

# 16

'Hannah? Hannah?'

Hannah jerked upright from where she'd been lying on the sofa. Her girlfriend, Emma, was staring at her with a strange look on her face.

'Sorry, what did you say?' Hannah asked.

'Did you hear a single word of what I've been saying?' Emma asked.

Hannah winced. 'Sorry. I ... I was a million miles away.'

Emma pointed to the TV, where Netflix counted down to another episode. 'I asked if you wanted to watch another one?'

Shit. Hannah didn't even know what they were watching, let alone if it was any good. 'Er ... If you want.'

'Do you even like the show?'

'It's okay,' Hannah replied, trying to sound as nonchalant as she could.

Emma laughed. 'It's a good job you're a copper and not a criminal. You're a terrible liar. Do you even know what the show is?'

Earlier, they'd been watching some series about a beautiful young thing having a wonderful life in Paris, but Hannah had stopped paying attention about five minutes after it had started. Her thoughts had drifted back to the poor young things on the whiteboards who'd had an awful life in London. But Emma had turned that show on after dinner and it was closer to midnight now. She could've put anything on since then. She winced again. 'No. Sorry.'

Emma sat up, picked up the remote and turned the TV off, giving her full attention to Hannah. 'What's up? You've been in a weird mood all night.'

'Have I?' Hannah tried to sound surprised, but she knew it was true. She'd been trapped in her own mind all night long, full of fears and worries. She wasn't even sure if she'd asked Emma how her day had gone and, if she had, she certainly hadn't paid any attention to the answer.

'You know you have.'

'It's nothing.'

'Hannah …' Emma fixed her big, brown eyes on Hannah. 'You can talk to me.'

Hannah shook her head. 'It's nothing, really. I just keep thinking about the case we've got on. It's …'

'Hold on for a sec,' Emma said, getting up from her chair.

The sudden movement threw Hannah. It was hard for her to open up about things at the best of times, and Emma had interrupted her without a second thought. Trying not to be annoyed, she watched her girlfriend go over to the kitchen part of their living room/kitchen combo and open up the fridge. A second later, she had a cold bottle of white wine in her hand, quickly adding two clean glasses to the other.

'Everything's better with wine,' Emma said with a big grin, and Hannah forced a smile back in return. She joined Hannah on the sofa, passed her both glasses and then unscrewed the bottle top.

'I shouldn't really drink,' Hannah said. 'I've got to work tomorrow.'

'One glass isn't going to kill you,' Emma said, filling both up to near the brim.

'Trying to fit two glasses into one might,' Hannah said, her frustration building.

'I promise to resuscitate you if it all goes horribly wrong.' Emma pressed herself against Hannah, moulding her body somehow, so it felt like the two of them just fitted perfectly together. 'Now, tell me what's what.'

'You really don't want to know.'

'I do, H. If something's bothering you, then I want you to tell me about it.' She took a sip of wine, still smiling. Like it was all fun and games. Like Hannah's worries were over something trivial. Like a bad haircut or the size of her bum — the sort of thing Emma fretted over.

Well, it wasn't trivial. Far from it.

'Someone's has been killing homeless kids,' Hannah said matter-of-factly and just a little cruelly. 'Seven of them so far. The lucky ones had their throats cut from ear to ear. The less fortunate were hacked to death.'

'Shit.' Emma's mouth fell open. The wine glass wavered in her hand.

'Yeah. Shit.' Hannah knew she should shut up, certainly not say anything else, but she wasn't in the mood to let Emma off so lightly. Maybe she needed to learn that there were more important things in life than binge watching a load of crap on Netflix. 'We've got all the dead kids' pictures stuck up on these whiteboards at work. Some of them were taken at school or at their homes, all happy and smiley, before whatever made them run away and go live on the streets. They all look so young in them, so innocent, and yet they're all dead. All murdered. And I can't help thinking about what sort of sick bastard could do such a thing to people who are so helpless, so lost.'

'Shit.' The smile was long gone from Emma's face and her wine glass looked forgotten in her hand. Apparently, being slapped in the face by real life wasn't what she'd been expecting.

Immediately, a surge of guilt shot through Hannah. She'd gone too far. Been too mean. And why? Emma's heart was in the right place. It certainly wasn't her fault that Hannah felt like crap. Emma had only been meaning to help. 'I'm sorry. I shouldn't have told you.'

'It's alright,' Emma replied, making Hannah feel even worse. 'If you can't talk to me, who can you talk to?'

'Thank you.' Hannah took a sip of wine, but the alcohol was bitter on her tongue. She knew she shouldn't say anymore, despite what Emma had said. Her girlfriend was a schoolteacher. She led a normal life, doing normal things. She didn't need to hear about the darkness Hannah had to deal with day in, day out. But Hannah did need to talk and Emma was right, there was no one else she could turn to. Especially since it wasn't really the case itself that was bothering her. Not really.

Hannah took a deep breath. She hated opening up about things and talking about her feelings. No one in her family talked about the stuff that went on inside each of them. Still, Emma deserved to know the truth — especially since Hannah had just been a bitch to her. 'The thing is, the governor is all fired up about it — quite rightly, too. We need to stop this bastard. It's just ...' Hannah's voice trailed off, unsure of what to say, scared somehow that speaking of her worries would somehow make it even more of a problem.

Emma squeezed her hand. 'It's okay.'

Hannah saw the love in Emma's eyes and felt more guilt for being the way she was. She'd spent her whole life building walls to protect herself, and it was difficult to let anyone past them. Even Emma. God, why was she like that?

'It's okay,' Emma said again.

'What if I'm not good enough to catch him?' Hannah forced the words out in a whisper.

Emma let out an awkward half-chuckle. Surprised, not amused. 'What do you mean by that?'

'You'll think I'm crazy.'

'I won't. I promise.'

'I don't think I'm any good at my job.'

'That is crazy,' Emma said. 'You're a brilliant police officer.'

'Or maybe I'm just good at faking it?' Hannah said. 'When I was at Brixton, I was investigating robberies and rapes and all sorts, but somehow, they never felt as difficult as the cases I'm working on at Kennington. Or as important. I mean, there's a kid out there, living on the streets right now whose life is as shit as it gets and yet, if I don't find this psychopath in time, they're going to end up victim number eight. And I keep thinking they need someone really good working on this and yet they've got me.'

'But it's not down to you on your own, is it?' Emma said. 'You're part of a team. You have to solve this together. That's what happened with the last big case you had — that Motorbike Killer chap.'

Hannah had to smile when Emma called David Smythe "that motorbike killer chap." The man was a monster. A stuck up, rich boy, who was too clever for his own good and lacking any sort of empathy or emotion. Even after being arrested, the man had shown no remorse for what he'd done.

'What if that was just luck?' Hannah said. 'I mean, me and the governor went completely rogue, running around, chasing desperate theories. It could have just as easily gone the other way. We could've solved nothing and I would've been out of a job.'

Emma put her wineglass down on a side table, took Hannah's glass, and placed it next to hers. 'Come here.' She pulled Hannah into an embrace and kissed her gently on the lips. 'You need to be kinder to yourself. Was it luck catching that creep or two very smart people using their talent to see what everyone else was missing? Didn't you tell me that your boss liked the way you made him think? That they wouldn't have caught that bloke if not for you?'

'What if he was just telling me that to make me feel good?'

Emma sat back but held onto both of Hannah's hands. 'From what you've told me of him, he's not the sort of bloke to bullshit anyone. He wouldn't partner up with you all the time if he thought you weren't up to it.'

'Or he thinks I need watching. That he can't trust me with anyone else.'

Emma shook her head. 'You do know this all in your head? It's classic imposter syndrome. You've worked damn hard to get here, to be on this team. Don't put yourself down.'

Hannah nodded. She knew what Emma was saying was true but, somehow, she couldn't bring herself to believe it. The doubts in her mind were too loud to be ignored or dismissed by facts and logic.

'You are listening to me, aren't you?' Emma said, moving her head to find Hannah's eyes.

'Of course I am,' Hannah lied and leaned in to kiss her girlfriend, regretting saying anything and keen to change the subject.

She'd spent her whole life not fitting in, whether that was at school, university or in the police. It seemed like 'uncomfortable' was her default life setting. Hannah knew she covered up her insecurity and doubts with perfectionism and a 'take no shit' personality.

Sometimes, she could pretend she had her life in order so well that she almost believed it. Then something stupid would happen and her illusions would come crashing down, making it harder than ever to rebuild them.

Even Hicksy's bloody jibes about her being on the team as a diversity hire hurt. After all, she'd applied to join Wise's team because she knew no one else wanted the gig. She'd told herself that she was being ambitious and driven by doing so, but maybe she'd just been taking an easy option?

As she and Emma kissed, she hoped Emma wouldn't think less of her about what she'd just said. Even though they'd been together five years and living together for three, she knew Emma liked Hannah being in charge and being the strong one, while her girlfriend got to be emotional and all sensitive.

If only Emma realised how fucking tiring it was trying to live up to that perception. The truth was, it wasn't only at work where Hannah felt like an imposter.

# Saturday 19th November

# 17

It felt strange driving into work without a suit on, but Wise had decided that, in acknowledgement that it was the weekend, he'd dress down for a change. It was something he didn't do too often and Jean had done a double take when he'd come downstairs in jeans and a black roll-neck.

'I thought you were going to work?' she'd said.

'I am,' Wise replied.

'Fair enough,' Jean said, trying not to laugh. The kids weren't so restrained. Ed, his eldest, howled as he asked if Wise was going undercover as a spy while Claire, his youngest, pretended not to recognise him.

No doubt the piss-taking would continue when he got into Kennington, but if it lifted the mood, that was a good thing. His team spent every minute of the working day dealing with the worst humanity had to offer. Anything that raised a smile was worth it, even if it was at Wise's own expense.

Jono's news still played on his mind as well. He'd not known what to say the night before when Jono had told him the news. What could he say? Nothing that would change anything. Nothing that could make the situation better.

Fucking cancer. What a bastard evil thing it was.

It'd killed his own mum back when Wise was thirteen. A heavy smoker like Jono, she'd withered away over long, hard months, enduring treatments that seemed to make her worse, not better. She'd stayed optimistic, though, always smiling and joking with her lads, acting as if she didn't care that she was dying. Looking back now, Wise had to wonder how much of that had been a front to stop Tom and him from worrying when she must've been in so much pain.

In the end, though, there'd been no hiding it. Especially not in the hospice when she was all skin and bone and covered in sores. She'd cried then and begged to be put out of her misery, not understanding why, in a civilised world, she had to continue to suffer when death was waiting for her, anyway.

Wise had got angry seeing her like that, selfishly wanting her to stay alive as long as possible, and hating the fact he was going to lose her. An anger that still lurked inside him, waiting for an opportunity to rear its ugly face.

He'd gone off the rails after his mum had died. Both he and Tom took their pain out on anyone unfortunate enough to cross their paths. They caused trouble at school and around the neighbourhood, thinking they were big and clever when they were just scared and lost.

Wise switched the radio on, wanting to shake his mood. A sports talk show was on and Chelsea was the main topic of discussion. There were having a nightmare of a season after sacking their Champions League winning manager, Thomas Tuchel, and replacing him with the bloke from Brighton. Since then, the team couldn't buy a win and every match was a humiliation. It was heart-breaking to see.

Of course, Chelsea always got Wise thinking about his dad and he realised he'd not spoken to him for a while. Wise turned off the radio and dialled his old man. It might've only been 8:30 a.m. on a Saturday, but he knew his father would be up and about, probably armed with a hundred things to do that day.

The ring tone echoed around the Mondeo's interior via the car's

Bluetooth speaker. On and on it chirped, so long in fact that Wise was about to hang up when his father finally answered.

'Simon! Everything alright?' His dad sounded out of breath.

'Just ringing to say hello,' Wise replied. 'I haven't interrupted anything, have I?'

'God, no,' his dad said. 'I was just outside, tidying up the paddock when I heard the phone ring.'

Wise smiled. "The paddock," as his dad put it, was a tiny patch of grass out the back of the house that made up the old man's garden. 'I'm amazed you made it in time. Do you want me to call back after you've caught your breath, or do you need to have a lie down?'

'Cheeky bugger. What are you up to? Sounds like you're in the car.'

'Yeah. Just driving into work. We picked up a nasty new case this week.'

'I bet Jean loved that.'

'She was alright about it, actually,' Wise said. 'Things have been better recently between us.'

'That's good to hear. You did well with that one.'

'Yeah, I did. How's things with you?'

'Oh, can't complain. My knee doesn't like this weather but, then again, the rest of me isn't that keen on it either.'

Wise glanced up at the grey clouds rolling across the sky. 'It looks like there's more rain on the way. You better hurry if you've got more to do in the garden.'

'Nah, I've got it all bagged up and ready to take down to the tip,' his dad said. 'Actually, I'd better get a move on. The place shuts at midday and I'm meeting Tom down the pub after that.'

'You're meeting Tom?' A chill ran through Wise.

'Yeah. We're going down to the Grapes. They've got the Chelsea - Newcastle game on. Apparently, they're showing it via some illegal satellite feed from the Middle East or something like that — not that you heard that from me.'

'Don't worry, Dad. I'm not about to dob in the pub.' Wise took a breath. 'How's Tom?'

'I've not seen him for a while,' his dad said. 'He's been busy — or so he says.'

'Has he told you what he's doing for work these days?' Wise was doing his best to sound casual, but no doubt failing miserably.

'No,' his dad chuckled. 'Last time I asked, he just tapped his nose and said, "Don't ask."'

'He still driving the Beamer?' The last time Wise had run into Tom outside his dad's place, Tom had driven off in a brand-new BMW 5 series.

'Of course he is. You don't get rid of a motor like that, do you? Bloody lovely it is.'

'Yeah, it is,' Wise said, thinking that he wouldn't mind getting hold of the license plate number and doing a check on it. It'd be interesting to see who it was registered to and under what address. He'd already done a PNC check under the name of Tom Wise, but found nothing.

'How are the kids?' his dad asked.

'What?' The question threw Wise, his mind still on his brother.

'The kids,' his dad repeated. 'How are they?'

'They're good. Doing really well, actually. Ed's working hard at school, getting good marks, and Claire's Claire. She lives on her iPad most of the time, but she seems to be happy enough.'

'Well, give them a kiss from their old grandad, eh?'

'I will do.'

'Right. I best be off,' his dad said. 'Let me know when you get some time off. It'd be good to get together and see the little ones.'

'I'll sort out some dates with Jean,' Wise said. 'Enjoy the game.'

'Ta-ta, son,' his dad said and ended the call.

The Sour Grapes was a pub on Streatham High Street, about a ten-minute walk from his dad's place. There was no parking outside, so it was more than likely that Tom would park at their dad's and walk over to the pub with him. That would give Wise a good two hours to pop around and grab the reg number of Tom's Beamer and his brother would be none the wiser.

With any luck, he could make a start on proving his brother wasn't a murdering gangster.

He had one more call to make before he got into Kennington. He dialled his boss, DCI Anne Roberts.

Unlike his father, the phone barely had time to ring before she answered. 'Why are you calling me on a Saturday?'

Wise smiled. So much for "hello," then. 'You know that murder we picked up on Wednesday afternoon?'

'The fatal stabbing?' There were the sounds of pots being clunked about in the background. For some reason, though, Wise couldn't imagine his boss being much of a cook.

'It was a bit more than a stabbing,' he said. 'Anyway, Brains has found six other similar murders, all carried out within the last two years.'

A pot was slammed down on a counter. 'Please tell me you're joking.'

'Afraid not, boss.'

'Oh, Simon.' It was amazing how much disappointment she managed to fit into his name. 'Where are you now?'

'I'm driving into the nick. I've got everyone working today. Tomorrow too, most likely.'

Roberts let out an almighty sigh. 'I'll meet you there.'

# 18

Wise had just finished quickly going over everyone's actions points when Detective Chief Inspector Anne Roberts walked into MIR-One. His boss signalled for Wise to carry on before parking herself on top of one of the desks at the side of the room.

Wise turned his attention back to his troops. 'Alright everyone, you know what to do. Let's put in some hard graft this morning and, hopefully, we can all go back to our lives while there's still some of the weekend left.'

Hicksy held up his hand like he was in school.

'Yes, Hicksy,' Wise said.

'I was just wondering why you're dressed like the Milk Tray Man? You doing a bit of moonlighting after this?' Hicksy's crack got a few laughs, but not as many as he'd been expecting, judging by the look on his face.

'You're dating yourself a bit with that reference, mate,' Wise replied. 'I don't think most of the team were alive the last time that ad was on TV.' The Milk Tray Man had been a series of TV commercials in the seventies and eighties, advertising a box of chocolates "for the ladies." It featured a James Bond-like hero in a black roll-neck doing James Bond-like things.

Hicksy waved the comment off. 'Kids these days wouldn't know quality advertising if it slapped them in the face. It's all bloody TikTok dances and influencers.'

'Please tell me you're not on TikTok, mate,' Jono said.

'Oh, fuck off,' Hicksy replied. 'You're the only sad bastard around here.'

'Okay. Let's get to it,' Wise said. Everyone got up and broke off into their action groups, so Wise headed over to Roberts.

She, too, had dressed down for the day, wearing a dark green hoodie that swamped her petite figure but seemed to do little to contain her mood.

'Sorry to drag you in,' Wise said.

Roberts glanced over at the whiteboards. 'I still can't believe you've turned a simple stabbing into something more.'

'I'm not sure a fifteen-year-old boy getting his throat opened from ear-to-ear can be classified as "a simple stabbing" but yeah, Brains found these others while he was doing a trawl through HOLMES.'

Wise followed Roberts as she walked over to the boards, her eyes fixed on the victims' faces. 'Another serial killer, so soon after Smythe? Not really what we needed.'

'We don't get to pick the crimes, unfortunately.'

Roberts arched an eyebrow. 'Well, I'm sure the Super will be happy at the news.' The Super was Detective Chief Superintendent Walling, a master at dealing with the politics within the Met. He'd never been one of Wise's biggest fans, though. 'How far back do these go?'

Wise pointed to the picture of Sasha Moore. 'We believe she's the first victim. Sasha was murdered by Waterloo Bridge on the twenty-third of March last year.'

'Eighteen months ago? And no one spotted this until now?'

'Apparently not.'

She stopped by a blurry picture of Anorak Man, his face all but hidden by his baseball cap. 'Who's this?'

'We've got him on CCTV talking to the last victim and then following him across town. He matches the description of the killer given to us by an eyewitness.'

'There's not a better shot of his face?'

Wise shook his head. 'Not yet. He's aware of where the cameras are and keeps his head down and the cap on at all times. We're digging up the CCTV from the other cases to see if he's there as well.'

'That's going to be a lot of footage,' Roberts said.

'I was going to ask you, actually, if we could get some more bodies in to help go through it all. I've got Sarah, Callum and Donut on it at the moment, but some more eyes would speed everything up.'

Roberts sighed. 'I'll have to have a look and see what the budget allows. The higher-ups have tightened all the purse strings so much that I don't think we even have a pot to piss in anymore.'

'But surely ... We've got seven murders here ... that has to merit more support?'

'Simon, you've got seven dead homeless kids — most of whom were probably drug addicts, thieves, and prostitutes. The Brass won't get too worked up about them, not enough to go opening up their wallets.'

'What?' Wise couldn't believe what he'd just heard. 'They're people. They had lives, hopes and dreams. The world might've given them a shitty deal, but that doesn't make them fair game for some sicko to kill. They deserve our best — just like everyone else.'

'I'm not disagreeing with you,' Roberts said. 'I'm just being honest. But I will ask. Fingers crossed, the accountants will say yes.'

'It feels like their jobs are more important than ours these days.'

'According to the Home Secretary, they are.'

Wise stopped himself from saying what he thought about that particular politician. However, he had another card up his sleeve to play. 'When you do speak to the bean counters, maybe mention we don't want another Stephen Port PR disaster. If the public hears of these murders, they'll think we did nothing about them because we don't care about homeless people.'

Stephen Port drugged, raped and murdered four men before

dumping their bodies near his flat in Barking, between June 2014 and September 2015. However, investigating officers failed to link the deaths, despite the obvious similarities between the murders. That mistake allowed Port to carry on killing longer than he should've. A report on the investigation also implied that, because all the victims were gay, the police didn't prioritise the investigations in the first place. Even now, some six years later, there were ongoing enquiries into how the Met handled the investigation. When they were finished, no one expected them to be anything but damning in their findings.

'Christ. That's all we need,' Roberts said. 'We certainly don't need another bloody mess on our doorstep. It was bad enough with the Smythe fiasco.'

Walling had removed Wise from the investigation into the Motorbike Killer and had DCI Riddleton take over. The new man declared on nationwide TV that the murders were being carried out by an unemployed, possibly homeless, motorbike messenger. He couldn't have been more wrong.

'That's why I don't think we can drag our feet on this investigation,' Wise said, trying not to smile at Roberts' discomfort. 'The press will eat us up if they found out.'

'Yes, quite. Now, I've got a mountain of paperwork I might as well tackle now I'm here. Keep me informed about how you get on with this lot,' Roberts said. 'Hopefully we can catch your Anorak Man before he kills again.'

Wise nodded. 'Will do.'

Roberts went to leave, then stopped. 'By the way, have you heard anything else from SCO10?' she said.

The question was like a slap in the face, but Wise did his best not to let it show. 'I've not heard a Dicky Bird from them since we met in your office.'

'Let's hope it stays that way,' Roberts said. 'Right. I'd better get on. You know where I am if you need me.'

'Cheers, boss.' Wise watched her go, wondering if SCO10 had shown Roberts the picture of his brother and, if they had, what she thought of it. It was a good job he had a cast-iron alibi for where he was when the picture was taken, otherwise he knew they'd have arrested him there and then.

He headed over to his office. Thinking about it now, it was strange he'd not heard anything from DCI Heer or DS Murray since the meeting. What did that mean? Had they lost all interest in him, or was there a reason they were keeping what they were up to so covert?

Once he was in his office with the door closed, Wise went over to the small window and looked out over Kennington Road and The Four Rams gastropub opposite. It'd been a good boozer once, before a chain had taken it over and turned everything on their menu into an 'experience' and charged twice as much for half the amount.

The main high street was quiet for a Saturday, but there were still a few people walking with grim determination to get wherever they were going. It wasn't raining for once, but the miserable November weather wouldn't really tempt anyone to go for an idle wander.

Wise scanned the parked cars, checking out who was out and about. He half expected to see squads of undercover police officers watching the station, waiting for Wise to reappear.

And, of course, there was Tom himself. According to SCO10, their covert operative who'd infiltrated the gang was murdered because of the picture he'd taken of Tom. The last thing Wise wanted to do was warn his brother that he was looking into his activities. If Tom was as dangerous as SCO10 made out, Wise didn't want to risk any ramifications from his little investigation. It wasn't as if he was Tom's favourite person to begin with.

Leaving the window, he sat down behind his desk and logged into his laptop. Roberts wasn't the only one with admin work. Opening his email, he saw there was a message from Belmarsh Prison. It was a response to his request to see Elrit Selmani.

Holding his breath, he opened the email.

The request was approved.

He had a visit in the books for Tuesday, 10 a.m.

Maybe Wise could start getting some answers then.

# 19

Hannah stared at the victims' pictures on the whiteboard and the seven teenagers stared back. If only they could speak to her, let her know what had happened and why they'd died. All she could feel, though, was their pain and helplessness. Whatever had happened to them in their lives, they didn't deserve to end up dead like this.

'What are you thinking?'

Hannah jumped in shock. She'd not noticed Wise come out of his office. She put her hand against her chest. 'Bloody hell, Guv. You startled me there.'

'Sorry,' Wise said with a smile.

'It's okay. It's my fault,' Hannah said, feeling foolish. 'My mind was ...' She waved at the board. 'I haven't been able to stop thinking about these kids all night.'

'You're not the only one,' Wise said. 'It's another horrible case we've found for ourselves.'

'What I don't understand, though, is why Anorak Man is doing it. Why go after these kids? They have nothing. They're not hurting anyone. It can't just be for some sort of sick kicks. To play a game.'

Wise nodded. 'Alright. Let's think about that.' He walked over to the whiteboard and picked up a marker pen. 'The main motives for killing someone are money, power, sex and vengeance.'

'Right,' Hannah said as Wise wrote the four categories on the board under the "What do we think?" section. 'I think we can scratch off "money" though. These kids had none and, if the CCTV is anything to go by, Anorak Man gave Jack something before he legged it.'

'I agree,' Wise said, putting a line through the word "money." 'We can probably discard "vengeance" too. Maybe one of these kids hurt him somehow, but not all of them.' He crossed that off as well.

'That leaves sex and power.'

'The good ones.'

'But none of these kids were sexually assaulted in the attacks,' Hannah said. 'And the victims are a mix of boys and girls. If the attacks were sexual in motive, wouldn't Anorak Man pick one gender over the other?'

'Well, he could be bisexual, but that's about as rare as snow in April in serial killing terms,' Wise said. 'That leaves us with power.'

'They're all young. Broke. Homeless. Physically weak. Some were drug addicts, too,' Hannah said. 'It'd be easy to feel superior to them.'

'So, Anorak Man goes hunting around the train and Tube stations of London, looking for someone young and desperate — like these kids,' Wise continued. 'He goes over to talk to them, offers them something that they want or need — drugs, money, whatever it is — and, straight away, establishes control of them. We saw Jack run off. Maybe he thinks he's got one over on Anorak Man, like he's the one in charge, and yet the whole time Anorak Man is following him, knowing he's going to kill the kid. That's power.'

'Like some sort of God complex,' Hannah said. 'Deciding if someone lives or dies.'

'Yeah. I could imagine that would be quite intoxicating. Addictive.' Wise stared at the faces on the board. 'He won't give up that power unless we stop him.'

'How do we do that?' Hannah asked. It was the question that had been plaguing her all night. The question she wished she had an answer to.

Wise pointed at the picture of Sasha Moore. 'She's the first victim we know of.'

'That's right.'

'Her attack was more vicious than the others. The killer hacked at her.' Wise suddenly looked around the incident room, then spotted who he was looking for. 'Brains!'

Brains' head popped up from behind his monitor. 'Yeah, Guv?'

'Can you come and join us for a minute?'

Brains got up from his desk and walked over to the boards.

'We were just talking about the first victim,' Wise said.

Brains nodded. 'Sasha.'

'How many times was she cut or stabbed?'

'Fifteen times,' Brains said.

'Do you have a diagram of where those cuts were?'

'Yeah. It's in the PM report.'

'Can you grab everything you've got on Sasha so we can have a look?'

Brains darted back to his desk and then returned with a folder in his hands. He placed it on a desk, shuffled through and then pulled out a cream piece of paper. 'Here you go.'

Hannah and Wise looked down at the sheet of paper. There were black and white outlines of the human body, front and back. The pathologist had marked with red lines where the cuts had been. There were several over Sasha's hands and arms, some on her face and neck, her chest and then more on her back and neck. Brains pointed to one cut on the back of her neck to the right. 'This was the final one — the killing cut. It was also the deepest, with an incision depth of four inches.'

'So, it's a frenzied attack,' Wise said. 'He starts off attacking Sasha face on. The cuts on her hands and arms are defensive wounds — she's trying to fend him off, but he keeps on cutting away. She goes down and he continues slashing at her. The final cut ...' Wise hefted an imaginary knife in his right hand. 'She's lying down, bleeding, dying, and he chops down into her neck, finishing her.' He hacked down with his imaginary weapon.

'That takes serious effort,' Hannah said.

'Yeah. There's a lot of anger in that. Maybe hate,' Wise said.

'Hold on a sec,' Brains said. He went back to his desk, picked up another sheet of paper, and returned. 'I've noted down how many cuts each victim had.' He picked up one of the whiteboard pens. He wrote fifteen cuts under Sasha's picture, four cuts under Leroy's, two under Mark's, then one under the remaining victims.

'Even with Doctor Singh's theory about the killer practising to get good enough to kill someone with a single cut, there's a big difference between the fifteen wounds Sasha suffered and the four Leroy endured,' Wise said.

'Leroy had one massive slash across his chest,' Brains said. 'From his left collarbone down to his right hip, two to right forearm, then the last cut across his throat.'

Hannah glanced at Wise, trying to follow the way he thought. 'Anorak Man comes at him with the knife. Leroy puts his right arm up, gets cut, drops his arm. The killer then cuts him across the chest before finishing with the neck.'

'Sounds about right,' Wise said. 'But the frenzy has gone. He might not be skilled at what he's doing, but he's in control.'

'No anger,' Brains said.

'And the killings after Leroy follow the same pattern,' Hannah said. 'He's in control. He's got the power.'

'Agreed,' Wise said.

'So why is Sasha different?' Hannah asked.

'She's the first,' Brains said. 'He has to get up the nerve to do it. Once he's lost his virginity — as it were — by killing Sasha, he's not anxious about the next one. He knows what he's doing. Then he gets more and more confident with everyone after that.'

'The timeline is speeding up between killings too,' Wise said. 'There's four months between Sasha and Leroy, then a gap of another four months. Then it shortens to a gap of three months for the next few killings before shortening to two months between the murders of Ben and Jack.'

'Unless there are other attacks that we don't know about, as I said yesterday,' Brains said. 'Victims who survived or murders that we haven't picked up in the system for whatever reason. I mean, HOLMES 2 is good, but it's not perfect. And, if any survivors didn't bother reporting the attacks, we'll not know about them at all.'

'Like this girl, Katie, that Hicksy and Jono are looking for,' Wise said.

Hannah felt her gut lurch. 'That means either Anorak Man is enjoying killing these kids more and more and can't wait to get his next thrill, or he's at it all the time and there could be loads of other murders and attacks that we don't know about?'

'Yeah,' Brains said. 'That's about the long and the short of it.'

If Hannah had felt overwhelmed before, the realisation that the victims on the board could merely be the tip of the iceberg took her anxiety up to another level.

'Alright. That's good to know, but let's not get distracted by that for now,' Wise said. For a horrible moment, Hannah worried that he'd noticed something on her face that made him say that. 'Let's assume Sasha is the one he loses his virginity with — as Brains so eloquently put it. Why her? Was it premeditated or a spur-of-the-moment thing? He's out of control with her — did she do something that set him off? Something that sparked his anger? Made him lash out?'

'If the other murders are about power,' Hannah said, 'what if this one's different?'

Wise nodded. 'Go on.'

'The other murders are almost emotionless, right? He's playing his game, chasing after them, killing them with a single cut. But this one is full of emotion. It's frenzied. Angry. There's no control whatsoever.'

'Agreed,' Wise said.

Hannah took a deep breath, hoping she wasn't making a fool of herself. 'What if Sasha's murder is about vengeance or sex instead?

Or maybe it was about regaining control somehow, reclaiming his power.'

'She'd taken it from him somehow?' Wise walked closer to Sasha's picture. 'Sasha was a good-looking kid. Maybe she turned him down for sex? Or he had sex with her, and he blamed her for seducing him or something?'

'We should probably speak to the officers who investigated it,' Hannah said. 'See what they dug up? Maybe there's stuff they didn't put in the system.'

'Okay. You look into that. Hopefully, they did a better job of it than Hollins did with Kareem,' Wise said. 'Check out when and where she was murdered, too. If this wasn't planned, maybe Anorak Man wasn't as careful in avoiding the CCTV.'

'Surely the investigating officers would've checked all that?' Brains said.

'If they did, it'll make things easier for us,' Wise said. He glanced at his watch. 'I have to do something right now, if that's all right with you both. We can catch up later.'

'Sure,' Hannah said. 'No problem.'

'I'll help you if you want, Hannah,' Brains said.

'Cheers,' Hannah replied as she watched Wise leave. She couldn't help but wonder where he was going, and why alone? He didn't normally go off by himself. Why hadn't he asked her to go with him? Had she done something wrong?

Hannah shook the thoughts from her head. She was being stupid. She knew she was.

Hannah smiled at Brains. 'Let's get to work.'

## 20

Wise felt bad about leaving the station. The conversation with Hannah and Brains had been really constructive, and he felt like they were getting a feel for the case. And Brains was right — there could be a lot more victims out there to uncover. A hell of a lot more. Roberts would lose the plot if there were.

The traffic had picked up and, while the roads weren't weekday busy, Wise still had to fight his way down to the A3 to get to his dad's place in Streatham. As he drove, he watched everyone else go about their lives, untouched by the darkness that ran through the city they called home.

Of course, they had their problems. Who didn't? But, all being well, they didn't have to deal with the crime and the violence that lurked just beneath the surface of the city. They avoided the odd neighbourhood here and there or crossed the road when they spotted a gang of kids out for trouble. They had their triple locks on their front doors and their alarms on their cars. They stayed away from the flat-roofed pubs and minded their own business — no matter what was going on around them. They all just lived in little bubbles that kept them safe in their own little bit of London.

And, God willing, that's how they'll remain for the rest of their lives, living in peace, growing old, just dealing with the everyday crap that came their way. What most people thought of as bad wasn't really anything to worry about in the grand scheme of things.

Because, for an unfortunate few, when the really bad times came along, when the darkness invaded their lives, it destroyed everything they held dear. Violence didn't just hurt the victim, after all. It sent ripples of misery out to everyone else in that person's life, ripples that could go on and on forever.

In his time in the police, Wise had seen it all: the mugging victim who could never walk outside again without being petrified, the abused numbing themselves with drink or drugs, the grieving parent unable to accept their child could no longer walk through the front door.

At best, people would say they'd move on, that they had accepted what had happened, and made peace with whatever horrible event that occurred in their lives — but they were lying to themselves as much as anyone else. He'd learned long ago that, once the darkness had left its stain on someone's life, there was no getting rid of it, no matter how hard they tried. Some days they might forget the pain was there, only for it to reappear like a tsunami some time later, drowning everything it its path. On other days, it would breeze in like the wind, barely noticeable but impossible to ignore.

This knowledge wasn't just gained from all his time as a police officer. Wise had learned the truth the hard way, back on that fateful night when his brother had killed Brian Sellers in a pub fight that went too far.

It lingered in the background of every conversation with his father since. It lurked in the empty space next to him where, for the first sixteen years of his life, his brother had stood. And now, after the visit by SCO10, it reared up every time the phone rang or when he went to sleep.

Sometimes, he just wished there was a pill he could take that would just make him forget it all, wipe the memories from his mind, erase the guilt and the shame.

Maybe then, he wouldn't be on his way to spy on his brother.

His father lived on a road near Streatham High Street, in a terrace house originally built to house the working class that kept the city running. It had cost three grand back in the day when his father had bought it. Now houses in the street sold for silly money to people forced out of inner London by foreign buyers and property conglomerates.

It was 3:10 p.m. when Wise turned onto his father's road. Unsurprisingly for a Saturday, both sides of the street were chock-a-block with parked cars, all proudly displaying their residents' passes. On one hand, it gave Wise an excuse to drive slowly, especially when vehicles approached from the opposite direction, each driver holding their breath as they squeezed past the other. However, as he made his way along the street, Wise couldn't see his brother's car parked anywhere. The Beamer wasn't there.

Shit. So much for Wise's perfect plan.

He turned right at the end of the road, driving around the block, scanning both sides of the street, looking for the black BMW 5 series. Wise turned right again, driving on instinct, going up roads he knew like the back of his hand, past houses where old school friends had lived. He saw the home of his first girlfriend, and then spotted her father coming out the front door, bent double with age. He was a shadow of the man who'd once chased Wise away when he'd caught Wise and his daughter snogging in the front room.

But Wise hadn't come to Streatham to awaken old memories. He's come to find his brother's car. He turned out on to Streatham High Street itself, drove up past the Sour Grapes, the inside of which was packed to the rafters by the looks of things.

He then took the first left and made his way around the immediate roads near the pub. Maybe Tom parked nearby and went straight to the boozer instead of going via their dad's.

Wise's frustration grew with each turn he took, though, with each road he explored. There was no sign of the car.

What a waste of time.

Why had he come down here when he should've been back at

Kennington with the troops, doing the job he was supposed to be doing?

It was madness.

Wise glanced at the clock. It was 4 p.m. The second half was just about to start and enough was enough. Maybe his brother hadn't brought his car, choosing a taxi or an Uber or maybe even the bloody bus so he could drink while watching the game. Maybe Tom had cancelled on their old man and not shown up at all. Whatever the reason, Wise was wasting his time. It was time to head back to Kennington. Time to go back to work.

He turned into Polworth Road. It ran parallel to the high street and led into Hopton Road. All being well, he'd bypass most of the Saturday traffic before cutting back across the A3.

Wise drove past houses with their front gardens long paved over, their owners gaining a guaranteed parking spot for a loss of grass. There was an alley up ahead on the left that cut through to the high street, spilling people out right by the Sour Grapes. After closing time, it had been the venue for many a drunken fight or illicit snog for Wise and his friends back when they were teenagers, drunk on snakebite and black and stinking of fags.

Wise smiled at the memory. They were such innocent days before that night took it all away.

So caught up in the past, he almost missed the BMW on the other side of the street, spotting it only as he drove past. He looked in the rear-view mirror, trying to work out if it was a 5 series, if it was Tom's, but it was already too far back, just the shape of the car and the colour still visible.

But somehow, he knew it was.

Spotting an empty converted driveway, he swung the Mondeo in, parked and was out on the street a second later. He didn't bother doing up his coat as he walked back, trying to look just like everyone else, keeping his pace steady despite every instinct crying out for him to run.

With his eyes locked on the car, Wise slipped his phone out of his pocket, unlocked the screen, and opened the camera app. Taking a sly picture would be easier and quicker than stopping to write the number plate down.

It was definitely a 5 series too. Excellent.

Then, when he was ten or so yards away, he spotted someone in the car, sitting in the driver's seat. The sight stopped Wise in his tracks. If it was Tom, he couldn't just walk past like he had planned, cross the street and double back to where he'd parked the Mondeo.

Wise adjusted his approach so that he was all but hidden from the driver's point-of-view, even if he looked in the mirror. When he had a clear view of the number plate, he stopped, aimed his phone and took a couple of quick pictures.

As he did so, the driver's door opened, and a man got out.

It wasn't Tom. He was about six inches shorter for a start and as bald as a coot, with a neck that was as thick as a car tyre. Sticking a cigarette into his mouth, he walked around the car to the pavement and lit it. With only ten yards separating them, Wise got a good look at the man's face. He looked like an extra from a Guy Ritchie movie, all scowls and scars, with a heavy gold sovereign ring on his right hand.

Wise turned around and headed back towards the Mondeo.

'Tom!' a gruff voice called out. It was the smoker. 'Tom — the motor's over here.'

Wise didn't stop. He didn't turn around. He picked up the pace instead, head down, a man in a hurry.

The smoker didn't call out again, and he didn't come after Wise. Hopefully, he'd forget all about it and not mention to Tom that he'd seen someone who looked just like him — because that wouldn't be a good bit of information to pass on.

Not at all.

# 21

Hannah and Brains had made plenty of calls to find out more about Sasha Moore's murder, but people were slow in getting back to her as it was a Saturday. In the end, they'd decided to go and see Sasha Moore's parents and speak to them in person. Weybridge was only an hour's drive away, after all.

After calling the parents and arranging to see them, they'd jumped into Brains' Astra and headed out to the suburbs.

Hannah hadn't been to the small Surrey town before. The moment they'd turned off the A3, it was like entering a different world. They drove along winding roads with leafless trees clawing at each other overhead. The darkening sky gave everything a rather creepy appearance as they headed further into suburbia. They passed gated driveways that hinted at hidden mansions on one side, while the immaculate golf course on the other side of the road did little to lift the gloom.

'The Beatles used to live there,' Brains said, pointing to a sign that said St George's Hill. 'It used to be the most expensive place to live in the UK.' Judging by the closed gate blocking off the road and the security, it hadn't fallen far from the top of that pedestal since then. 'There's a superb car museum near here too,' Brains continued. 'If you're into that sort of thing. It's built at an old racetrack called Brooklands. They've got old racing cars, buses and planes. My kids love it.'

Judging by the enthusiasm in his voice, his kids weren't the only one. 'How many do you have?' Hannah asked. 'Kids, that is.'

'Four. Three girls and a boy.'

'Four? Bloody hell. Your poor wife.'

'Yeah, they're a handful,' Brains said as he drove around a tiny roundabout. 'I was happy with two, but my wife wanted a boy, so we kept rolling the dice until we got one. He's a right little terror, but it's good having someone else who farts in the house.'

'Brains, please!' Hannah said. 'Too much information, eh?'

'It is what it is.' He shrugged. 'You got any kids yourself?'

'Nah. Not me.'

'You're married though, aren't you?'

Hannah felt herself tense up. She hated those sorts of questions. She wasn't ashamed of being gay or her relationship with Emma, but she'd met enough homophobic dickheads in the Met to know some things were best kept to herself. 'Where do the Moores live?' she asked instead.

'Just up ahead,' Brains said. 'Near the station.'

The train station was a tiny thing in what appeared to be the middle of nowhere, with a massive car park next to it. 'What's the point of a train station if you have to drive to get to it?' Hannah said. 'Sort of defeats the whole point of getting a train, doesn't it?'

'Easier to drive to here than drive into town, I suppose,' Brains said. 'And cheaper too.'

Hannah gazed at some more massive houses. 'I don't think people here need to worry about what's cheaper.'

Brains turned down a small lane, slowing to go over some speed bumps, before finally stopping in a gravel driveway in front of a large, dark house. It didn't have a number but a name: "*Godshome.*"

'This is it,' Brains said.

Hannah peered at the imposing building. 'It doesn't look like a fun place to live.' A single light illuminated the front door, but no light shone from within. In fact, the place looked deserted. 'Maybe they saved the sunshine and flowers for the inside.'

'Only one way to find out,' Brains said, pressing the doorbell.

The sound of church bells chimed through the house. 'Blimey,' Hannah said. 'I'm starting to sense a bit of a theme here.'

They didn't have to wait long before the door opened. A woman, with long dark hair that fell down either side of her face like curtains, stood facing them. She could've been good-looking if she'd tried, but the woman had put zero effort into her appearance. In fact, Hannah got the impression she'd worked very hard to look as drab as possible. 'Are you the police?'

'Hi, I'm Detective Sergeant Markham and this is Detective Constable Park,' Hannah said. 'Are you Sasha's mother?'

The woman visibly flinched at the mention of Sasha's name. 'I'm Naomi Moore. Please, come in.' She moved back from the door to let the officers enter.

'Thank you,' Hannah said. If it was gloomy outside, the interior was positively miserable. Heavy wood panelling ran along the length of the hallway and seemed to suck up what little light there was. A small side table was tucked against the wall on one side, with house and car keys plus some small change scattered across it. The only decoration, if it could be called that, was further along the wall; a large crucifix. It looked like it belonged in a church rather than a home, but it certainly matched the mood of the house.

It wasn't hard to imagine that it would have been difficult for a teenage girl to grow up in such a grim and austere environment.

'This way,' Naomi said and set off down the hallway. She wore a black dress that touched the floor, creating the impression that she was floating rather than walking.

Hannah exchanged looks with Brains before following. The DC quietly hummed the theme tune from *The Addams Family* as he walked behind her.

Naomi opened an oak door at the end of the corridor and led the two officers into the kitchen. Thankfully, there were lights on in the room and Hannah immediately felt better for it. The heat emanating from a green Aga oven helped lift the mood. The appliance was so massive that it wouldn't fit into Hannah's own kitchen at home. In fact, as Hannah looked around, she realised the kitchen was probably the same square footage as her entire flat.

There were two men sitting a long dining table at the far end of the kitchen. They both stood as the police officers entered the kitchen. They were of equal height and, at first, Hannah thought they were brothers but, as she got closer, the differences between the two men became more apparent. The man on the left had brown hair, cut short with a side parting, blue eyes and a narrow chin, whereas the other had reddish, curly hair, dark eyes and a rounder face.

'This is my husband — and Sasha's stepfather — Joseph,' Naomi said, introducing the first man. 'I also asked Pastor Christopher to join us as well. His support and guidance have been the only things that has got us through this awful ordeal.'

Of course. A bloody pastor. What God-fearing home doesn't have one?

Hannah smiled all the same and reintroduced herself and Brains.

'Have you found Sasha's killer?' her stepfather asked, eyes all hopeful.

'I'm afraid not,' Hannah replied. 'We're actually part of a new team investigating the case. We just wanted to introduce ourselves and ask you a few questions, if that's okay?'

'But we don't know anything,' Naomi said, with a slight shrill in her voice. 'We weren't there.'

Her husband put a hand on her arm and smiled at the police officers. 'Please, take a seat and we'll do our best to help you.'

'Thank you,' Hannah replied. She sat down at the head of the table between Naomi and the pastor, while Brains sat on the other side of Pastor Christopher. 'I appreciate this is all very painful for you.'

Naomi sat with her arms crossed, glaring at Hannah and Brains. Her husband raised his eyebrows in sympathy towards the detectives, but it was the pastor who spoke next. 'Sometimes, it's hard to walk the path God chooses for us.'

'Quite,' Hannah replied, but kept her focus on the parents. 'When was the last time you saw Sasha?'

'She left home in early January of last year,' Joseph said.

Hannah nodded. 'You don't know the exact date?'

'It was a Sunday,' Joseph replied. 'The seventh — no, eighth of January.'

'Did anything happen on that day that made her leave? Was there a row of some sort? Or did she just get up and leave?'

'You know teenagers,' Joseph said. 'She refused to go to church and words were said about that, but it wasn't a row, as such. And, when we came home from the service, she'd gone. We thought she'd just popped out to see some friends, or perhaps gone to the cinema. When she didn't come home that evening ... We rang around everyone we could think of and then called the police to report her missing.'

Naomi chewed on her lips as if it was an effort to stop herself from saying anything.

'When you said, "words were spoken," what exactly was said?' Brains asked.

'We just reminded Sasha of her responsibility to the church and to God,' Joseph said. 'Life isn't about our personal gratification, and that perhaps, she only found church boring because she wasn't listening to God's words.'

Or maybe she found church boring because it was boring, Hannah thought, but she kept that to herself.

'It's a common problem amongst a lot of our younger congregation, unfortunately,' Pastor Christopher added, his good humour at odds with the rest of the room. 'We always take great care to help young people navigate through those tricky, rebellious teenage years. Sometimes, though, the devil finds his way into the heart of the odd lost soul.'

'The devil?' Hannah repeated. 'Is that what happened to Sasha? The devil found her?'

Again, Naomi tightened her lips and pressed her crossed arms against her chest.

'No, not the devil, as such,' her stepfather said quickly. 'But she had friends who were a bad influence, encouraging her to dress in a manner that wasn't fitting for a godly woman. And she was drinking underage, which was also leading to unwise life choices.'

'Such as?' Hannah said, keeping her voice soft and, she hoped, sympathetic.

Pastor Christopher leaned towards Hannah. 'We expect people to dress in a modest style, and not in a way that flaunts one's body or displays vanity. We believe women have a vital role to play as mothers and caregivers in our society. God doesn't wish them to take up men's roles and duties. And we believe that there should be no intercourse outside of marriage. Some might think these are rather old-fashioned values, Detective, but we find they work for us. In fact, if more people were to follow God's will, the world would be in a much better place.'

Hannah glanced over at Naomi, still chewing her lips together, her scowl growing ever deeper. 'And how did you feel about all this, Naomi?'

'Heart-broken,' Naomi forced out.

'That Sasha ran away from home?'

'No,' Naomi said. Her husband squeezed her arm, but she pulled away from his touch. 'Heart-broken that my daughter gave herself to the devil.'

'My love,' Joseph whispered. 'We agreed ...'

'You agreed. I did not,' his wife spat back. 'Why should we all act like her death was a surprise — a shock — when we know it wasn't? We lost her long ago, and I mourned her then. But the girl that ran from here was a whore and she died a whore's death.'

'I'm sorry,' Hannah said, shocked at Sasha's mother's words. 'Are you saying that Sasha was working as a prostitute?'

Naomi snorted in derision. 'Sasha didn't have the sense to sell her body for money. She gave it away. She walked around half-naked, tempting good, godly men with her flesh and made up lies about them when they would not respond to her advances. And, when it wasn't enough acting like a harlot in our own house, she went around the village, drinking and vaping and doing God only knows what else with any faithless man to cross her path.'

'We don't know that,' Joseph said.

'We do!' Naomi spat back. 'How many times did she accuse you of molesting her? How many times did she accuse Pastor Christopher? How many times did she accuse other members of our congregation? The devil was in that girl and, when he'd had his fill of her, he took her soul to hell.'

If Hannah was shocked before, she was reeling with Naomi's outburst. 'Sasha accused both you and Pastor Christopher of molesting her?'

'It was a cry for attention,' Joseph said. 'She was wearing more outrageous clothes by the day and I asked her to cover herself. When she refused, I tried to put something more appropriate on her and that was when she said I'd touched her in ways a father shouldn't.'

Hannah turned to the pastor. 'And what happened with you?'

'We had an intervention for Sasha at the church — to cast Satan out of her soul,' Father Christopher said with a sad smile. 'Afterwards, she told her mother we'd attacked her.' He paused. 'And raped her.'

'There was no mention of this in the reports I've read,' Brains said.

'We didn't tell the police,' the pastor replied. 'We handled everything within the church. There was no need to spread Sasha's lies any further.'

'Who was at this intervention?' Hannah asked.

'I was,' Pastor Christopher said. 'With Joseph and four of the church elders.'

'Was Mrs Moore there?'

'Only men can be present at an intervention,' the pastor said.

'So, let me get this straight,' Hannah said, trying to remain calm. 'You took Sasha to an intervention at your church, attended by six men with no other woman present. After which, she said you had attacked her, along with her stepfather and the others?'

'That's correct.'

Hannah turned to Naomi. 'And what did you do when Sasha

returned, and your daughter said she'd been molested at this exorcism?'

'I beat her with a stick and locked her in her room as any God-loving woman would do,' Naomi said, sticking her chin up proudly.

'You didn't think about reporting her accusations to the police so we could investigate the validity of her claims?' Hannah said. 'Find out if they were actually true?'

'Why? It was the devil speaking though her, trying to destroy the lives of godly people,' Naomi replied.

'And how long before Sasha ran away was this intervention?' Hannah asked. Her mind reeling with the insanity of it all.

The Moores and the pastor exchanged looks and Hannah noticed the pastor gave them a slight nod to answer.

'The day before,' Joseph said.

'Christ,' Hannah said. 'No wonder she legged it.'

'Do not blaspheme in my house,' Naomi said. 'Bad enough you come here dressed like a man, but don't you dare pass judgement on those of us who follow God's will on this earth.'

'Fair enough,' Hannah said. She stood up. 'We've taken up enough of your time.'

Brains stood too, looking equally unimpressed with the people around the table. 'We'll see ourselves out.'

'Oh,' Hannah said. 'One last thing — where were you all on the day Sasha died?'

The three exchanged looks once more.

'I was at home,' Naomi said.

'I was in London,' Joseph said. 'Looking for Sasha.'

'So was I,' the pastor added.

## 22

Wise had just walked back into MIR-One when his phone rang. It was Hannah.

'Guv,' she said, sounding breathless. 'You got a minute?'

'Sure,' Wise replied. 'Where are you?'

'Me and Brains are down in Weybridge. We've just left the house of Sasha Moore's parents and there's something really dodgy about them.'

'In what way?'

'Well, they're serious God-botherers for a start. They thought their daughter was possessed by the devil.'

'The devil?'

'Yeah, but it sounds like she was just an ordinary teenager, who wanted to have some fun. Anyway, they were so convinced she was possessed that, the day before she ran away, the stepfather and the family pastor took Sasha to their church to exorcise the devil from her with the help of four other men. Afterwards, she told her mother she'd been sexually abused by the lot of them. So, the mother beat her for lying and locked her in her room.'

'Sounds a wonderful family.'

'Yeah, they're really special, but listen to this — I asked them where they were when Sasha died.'

'And?' Wise said.

'Both the stepdad and the pastor were in London. They claimed they were looking for Sasha,' Hannah said.

'And this is new information? They didn't tell the police this before?'

'No. They kept it all Secret Squirrel.'

Wise's mind was racing. 'Being accused of sexual assault is a pretty damn good motive for killing Sasha and if they were both in London ...'

'I know,' Hannah said. 'Do you want me to bring them in for proper questioning?'

'No, not yet,' Wise said. 'Tell them we'll be in touch and come back here for now. Good work, Hannah. Really good work.'

'See you in an hour,' Hannah said and hung up.

Wise walked over to the whiteboards and stared at Sasha's picture again. Was she the start of it all? Was her death the catalyst for all that followed — or were there others still undiscovered?

He could see a pastor who blamed Sasha for tempting him into assaulting her, lashing out in anger at her, keen to silence her, seeking vengeance for making him weak. Mortal.

Or a stepfather doing the same.

It certainly explained the ferocity of the first attack.

But why continue? Why kill the others? Why play the game over and over again?

What was it as Hannah had said earlier? That killing the others would give someone a sort of God complex? Was there something in that?

Wise could feel a bubble of excitement building inside him. Hannah might've really stumbled into something. Still, there was a long way to go yet. More avenues to explore.

He walked over to where Sarah, Donut, and Callum were huddled around their monitors. 'How are you getting on?'

Sarah looked up, her eyes tired under her sharp fringe. 'We've gone over the previous four days before Jack's murder and found plenty of footage of him, but we haven't spotted Anorak Man yet.'

'It's a bit of an impossible job, though,' Donut said. 'I mean, he could be any white guy walking past.'

Wise nodded, disappointed but not surprised. 'Hannah's on her way back with some interesting information. She might have two suspects that could help your search.'

'She has?' Sarah said.

'I'll let her fill you all in when she gets back, but we should prioritise any CCTV footage from Sasha Moore's murder next.'

'I've put in requests for it all,' Callum said. 'I was told we'd have it sometime on Monday.'

'Hopefully, we'll have some help for you by then as well,' Wise said.

'That would be appreciated,' Sarah said.

'Hannah reckoned she'll be back here in an hour,' Wise said. 'Can one of you order some food for us all and chase Jono and Hicksy up as well? With any luck, we can all get home at a reasonable hour tonight.'

'I'll do it right now, Guv,' Callum said.

Wise headed into his office, sat down behind his desk, and got his phone out again. Opening up the photo app, he clicked on the picture of Tom's car. There was the license plate number, clear as day. Now, the big question was, who did the car belong to?

He signed into his laptop and logged into the DVLC. With a deep breath, he typed Tom's car details in. The result popped up instantly. Wise scanned over the details.

The BMW was registered to a Melanie Hayes, with an address in Barclay Road, off Fulham Broadway. Wise had to smile. It was a five-minute walk from Stamford Bridge.

When he and Tom had been kids, they'd both agreed to live in a place near the Chelsea ground when they were older. In their minds, nothing would be better than to roll out of bed every other Saturday and stroll down to the Bridge to see the game.

Back then, of course, they'd not known how much that neck of the woods cost. It had been a bloody expensive address back then. Now, it was astronomical.

So, who was Melanie Hayes?

He ran a PNC check next but came up with nothing. Whoever she was, she was as clean as a whistle. So Wise moved on to more public search engines, trying LinkedIn next. Quite a few women with that name popped up, but he instantly dismissed any that lived outside of London. That left him with three possibles.

The first profile he looked at was a middle-aged charity worker, but Wise's gut said it wasn't her. The second, though? She was beautiful, with long blonde hair and a dazzling smile. He could imagine her being Tom's type. And when he saw what she did for a living, he knew he'd found her. She was a senior partner at Trelford, Mayers and Jenkins, no less — London's top criminal law practice.

Well, well, well.

He moved onto Facebook but found no profile for her there. Nor at Instagram or Twitter. He didn't bother with TikTok or any of the other, newer social networks. Somehow, he didn't think a criminal lawyer would do silly dances or recreate memes.

Finally, he typed her name and the name of the practice into Google. That got him a few more hits, news stories about criminal cases she'd worked on, some of which were very high profile. She'd been part of the team that had got Harold Sumner off, despite the police seizing twenty million quid's worth of heroin in a lock-up he'd owned. In fact, she'd got the Met to issue an apology for arresting Sumner in the first place, despite the fact that everyone knew he was guilty as sin.

He leaned back in his chair, staring at the news article, with a picture of Hayes standing outside the courts with Sumner, all looking very pleased with themselves.

When Wise had first seen Hayes' name and address, he'd presumed she was Tom's girlfriend, but now he wasn't so sure. Was she just fronting everything for him? Whatever the connection between them was, hanging out with one of London's top criminal solicitors didn't make Tom appear all sweet and innocent. Far from it.

Shit. Wise felt sick thinking about it. His brother rampaging through London, waging war against other gangsters? Killing his rivals?

Even now, he couldn't believe it to be true. But there was SCO10's informant's picture, and now this. He had no doubt that seeing Selmani on Tuesday would be nothing but the final nail in the coffin.

Wise would have no more straws to grasp at, and then he'd have to work out how to take Tom down, without destroying his own life in the process.

Maybe that wouldn't be possible. Maybe losing his job was the price Wise would have to pay.

The final bill for what happened in the pub that night.

He sat lost in his thoughts until Callum knocked on his door. 'Food's arrived, Guv, and everyone's back.'

'Cheers, Callum,' Wise said, trying to sound cheerful. When he walked back out into MIR-One, everyone had already descended on the boxes of pizza like starving hyenas.

As everyone ate, the teams updated each other on their progress, from the frustrations of the fruitless trawl through CCTV to Hannah's trip to Weybridge.

'On the way back, I Googled their church,' Hannah said, 'and it's about as dodgy as it gets. It's called the Universal Church of God's Children. It originated in Brazil before spreading across the world, but it's mired in controversy everywhere it goes. Apparently, its members pay a tithe to God through the church, donating the first ten percent of their gross earnings.'

'You must be fucking joking,' Hicksy said.

'Nope — and that's not all,' Hannah replied. 'Twice a year, its members must hand over their entire monthly income to the church as an offering. They believe, by doing so, that God will protect them from poverty and guarantee salvation in the next life.'

'How can anyone agree to that?' Jono said.

'A lot of people do.' Hannah glanced at her notes. 'Apparently, the church made fourteen million quid last year across the UK.'

Hicksy let out a whistle. 'Fucking robbery.'

'It's all legal,' Hannah said.

'Weybridge is a wealthy area too,' Wise said, grateful to be thinking about anything other than his brother. 'Prime stockbroker belt. A month's salary would be a hefty amount for most of the people that live there.'

'That's not all,' Hannah continued. 'They think demon possession causes mental health issues or "abnormal" sexuality. They hold special prayer sessions for anyone infected with a demon in the hope they can cast out whatever has taken them over.'

'And that's what they did with Sasha?' Wise asked.

Hannah nodded. 'Her stepfather, the pastor —Christopher Bartholomew — and four other church elders held what they called an intervention, but we'd call it an exorcism.'

'Like in the movie?' Sarah said.

'They do it quite often, it would seem,' Hannah replied. 'And Sasha's not the first, nor the last no doubt, to make complaints of sexual assault afterwards. There are eighteen active complaints being investigated across the country at the moment. All from teenagers who said they were assaulted during these interventions.

'The church claims they have to lay hands on the possessed and, sometimes, the children need to be restrained if the devil or demon fights back. However, the alleged victims say far more happens. Far worse things.'

'God's penis at work,' Hicksy said.

'Any of those complaints from the Weybridge church?' Wise asked.

'No,' Hannah replied. 'From what I can see so far, that place looks pretty free of any controversies up till now — but that doesn't mean there aren't any.'

'Yeah, if any of the other parents are like Sasha's, they wouldn't have reported it,' Brains said. 'Her dear mum beat her for lying and locked her in her room when she spoke up.'

'Poor kid,' Wise said. 'And both the pastor and the stepfather were in London when she died?'

'They said they were looking for her — to bring her home,' Brains replied.

'So, it is possible one of them or both of them found her,' Wise said. 'And when she refused to go back home with them, things got messy and they killed her — or they went looking for her with the express intent of murdering her in the first place to keep the assault allegations quiet.'

'That's what I was thinking,' Hannah said.

'But why kill the others?' Callum asked.

'I don't know,' Wise said. 'Maybe if they think it's okay to rape a teenage girl to cast out her demons, they think it's okay to kill someone who can't be saved. Killing the others allows them to justify why they killed Sasha. Maybe they just liked the feeling of having someone's life in their hands.'

'What if they're reenacting the Dracula killing?' Hannah said. 'They think they're Buffy or whatever?'

'What are you talking about?' Jono said. 'Dracula?'

Wise told them what they'd learned the day before about how the vampire was killed in the book.

'What is this?' Hicksy said. 'Bloody demons? Vampires? It's a load of crap.'

'We don't have to believe in it, but maybe our killer does,' Wise said.

Hicksy shook his head. 'Why does everyone have to be a whack job these days? What happened to normal villains?'

'I take it you didn't have any luck in finding this Katie girl?' Wise asked.

'No, Guv,' Jono said. 'There's no sign of her at the moment, but we'll keep looking.'

'Take pictures of this pastor and Sasha's stepfather with you, just in case you find her. You never know, she might identify one of them on the spot — or both.'

'Will do, Guv,' Jono replied, before having a coughing fit that doubled him over.

'You better not have Covid,' Donut called out. 'I'm not catching that again.'

'Shut your mouth,' Hicksy snarled, jabbing a finger at his colleague. 'Or I'll do it for you.'

'He shouldn't be working if he's sick,' Donut continued. 'It puts all of us at risk.'

Hicksy took a step towards him. 'I'm telling you for the last time ...'

'Alright, everyone,' Wise said. 'Calm down. Donut — Jono's not got Covid. Hicksy, no fighting. Jono, do you need anything?'

The Welshman took a bottle of water out of his coat pocket and gulped it down. When he'd finished, he looked at Wise with tears in his eyes. 'I'm okay. Just that shitty weather out there.'

Wise nodded. 'If you need to rest tomorrow, it's not a problem.'

'I'll be fine.'

'Okay. Your call. Wise turned to Hannah. 'Hannah, can you get pictures of the two men up on the boards?'

'Of course,' Hannah replied, her eyes still on Jono, a concerned look on her face.

'Sarah, let's see if they turn up anywhere in the CCTV footage as well,' Wise said. 'Go over the Springer footage first.'

'Will do,' Sarah replied.

'Thank you. Now, let's call it a night now and we go again tomorrow.' As everyone stood up and started clearing away the debris of empty pizza boxes, Wise walked over to Hannah. 'Do you fancy going to church tomorrow? I wouldn't mind seeing this pastor for myself.'

Hannah raised an eyebrow and smiled. 'Well, it is Sunday.'

## Sunday 20th November

# 23

Wise picked up Hannah from her place in Tooting and then sped down the A3 to Surrey. He was back in his suit and feeling all the better for it, like a police officer ready to work.

They were going to meet a DCI in Surrey and Sussex Major Crimes Division first, so he didn't want to go turning up looking like a bum. Hannah, on the other hand, was dressed, as usual, in jeans, her biker boots and a black leather jacket.

'We make quite the couple,' Wise said, happy to put his foot down on the three-lane highway. 'You didn't fancy putting your Sunday best on?'

'I've got a feeling that a white guy walking into the church with a black woman will get all their heads turning anyway,' Hannah said. 'That being the case, I didn't see the point of trying to blend in. Besides, the Moores and dear Pastor Christopher already know I'm a copper.'

'Well, it's been a long time since I set foot inside a church, so this will be interesting either way.'

'You're not religious then?'

'My mum was — to a certain extent, anyway. She didn't go to

church, except at Easter and Christmas, but she believed. She probably said more than her fair share of prayers for me ...' He stopped himself before he said, "and Tom." Better to keep that nugget to himself. Now more than ever. 'But she got cancer when I was thirteen and no amount of praying did her any good then. I wasn't much into God before that but, after watching my mum die so slowly and painfully, it seemed like a load of bollocks to me.'

'I can see how that would make you think that,' Hannah said.

'What about you?'

'Nah. It was never a part of our lives growing up. My parents were working all hours, so that left little time for praying or stuff like that. I don't even think we even discussed religion — there were too many other things to worry about.'

'Well, let's see what this Universal Church of God's Children is all about. Maybe we'll see the light and come away converted,' Wise said, smiling.

'I hope not,' Hannah replied. 'The more I read about them, the more I dislike everything they stand for. Did you know there's a survivors' group for people who are no longer members of the church? A survivors' group!'

'How does the church feel about them?'

'They call them the Fallen and claim everything they say is nonsense. Apparently, they've let demons and devils into their hearts and that's why they're spreading lies about what they experienced.'

'That's a bit of an easy get-out clause, isn't it? The moment someone says something you don't agree with or does something that doesn't match your values, you condemn them as possessed.'

'You should've seen how Sasha Moore's mother talked about her. She actually seemed happy she was dead. She said she deserved it.'

'For what? Being a normal teenager? I thought it was required for every child to piss off their parents when they turned thirteen.' Wise thought about his own kids. Ed might not be any trouble when he became a teenager, but he as sure as hell knew Claire would be. That girl already had a wild streak.

'I read that the church expects women to wear ankle-length skirts at all times,' Hannah said. 'Short skirts, trousers and shorts are all banned, as they tempt men into sin.'

'Is that why you're wearing jeans to their service?'

Hannah chuckled. 'As I said, we're not fooling anyone by going along.'

Surrey and Sussex Major Crimes Division were based out of Woking Police Station, a town about fifteen minutes from Weybridge. Wise exited the A3 at the Cobham exit and headed down a winding country road. Somewhere nearby, Chelsea had their training ground, but he wasn't sure exactly where. They might even be there now, warming down after the previous day's game.

Wise had caught the highlights, if you could call them that, on *Match Of The Day* before he'd gone to bed and wished he hadn't. Chelsea had lost yet again.

They drove past the turning for Weybridge and headed down the Old Woking Road, through one village, over the M25 and into another called West Byfleet. From what Wise could see, it was just a bunch of shops along what could barely be called a high street, and not much more than that.

The road continued straight on, past what looked like a posh housing estate, then down more country roads, until they reached Woking itself and the trees were replaced by concrete and more concrete.

They followed a ring road around a shopping centre, heading under some train tracks, until they reached a road imaginatively called Station Approach. The police station was on the left, a large, red brick building behind a large, red brick wall. Wise stopped the Mondeo in front of the main gates to the car park and lowered his window.

'Woking Police Station. Can I help you?' a woman's voice said through an intercom.

'DI Wise to see a DCI Charles Boldham,' Wise said.

There was a loud buzz, and the gate creaked open. Wise drove through into a spacious and near empty car park and found the visitors' spots.

'Pretty quiet here, even for a Sunday morning,' Hannah said as they got out.

Wise shook his head and smiled. 'I hope you've not gone and jinxed it. You should know that you never say the Q word out loud.'

Hannah gave him a disapproving look. 'Oh, come on. Don't tell me you believe that superstitious claptrap?'

'I'm not superstitious, but why risk it?' Wise replied as they walked to the main doors.

'You'll be telling me you've got a lucky rabbit's foot in your pocket next.'

'Who says I haven't?' Wise held the police station door open so Hannah could walk through first. 'After you.'

Hannah was still chuckling when she walked up to the front desk. A short woman behind it smiled at her. 'DI Wise?'

Hannah pointed at Wise with her thumb over her shoulder. 'He's DI Wise. I'm DS Hannah Markham. We're here to see—'

'Me.' A man came down some stairs to the left. Tall, thin, and silver hair cut very short, looking like he'd come dressed for the pub, in a blue denim shirt, jeans and blue Adidas Gazelle trainers. Maybe Wise hadn't needed to dress up after all. The man held out a hand. 'DCI Charles Boldham. You can call me Chaz.'

Wise shook his hand. 'DI Simon Wise and this is my colleague, DS Hannah Markham.'

Boldham nodded. 'Good to meet you.'

'We appreciate you taking the time to see us, especially on a Sunday.'

'No problem. Come up to my office and we can chat there,' Boldham replied. 'If you want a coffee, there's only the machine but I have to warn you it's shit.'

'We're fine,' Wise said, despite the fact that he could've murdered a decent caffeine hit right about then. Boldham headed back up the stairs, and Wise and Hannah followed. Compared to the ancient ruin of a station from the fifties that Wise called home, Woking Police Station was positively futuristic. Wise was starting to think that

Kennington was the only police station left in the country that hadn't had a fortune spent on doing it up.

Buzzing them through frosted glass doors that opened with a swish, Boldham led the way through a large, open plan workspace on the first floor. Desks with computers that looked like they were actually made in the twenty-first century stood in neat rows, facing a series of glass-walled meeting rooms that ran along the length of one side of the room.

Boldham stopped by one door. 'This is me.' He opened it and let Wise and Hannah enter first. It was at least three times the size of DCI Roberts' office back at Kennington, with floor-to-ceiling windows that overlooked the car park and the town centre. Along with the desk and two guest chairs, there was a black leather sofa, coffee table and two armchairs set up in one corner. Boldham pointed there. 'Take a load off.'

He plonked himself down in one of the armchairs, so Wise sat on the sofa and Hannah took the other armchair. 'Very impressive nick you've got here,' Wise said.

'There used to be a school here a long time ago. Then that building became a nightclub in the eighties and nineties, but we spent so much time over here breaking up fights that we kicked them out and moved in ourselves. Then, after we merged with Sussex police, the old schoolhouse was knocked down and this replaced it. Apart from the vending machines, we're pretty happy with it.' Boldham put his feet on the coffee table. 'Now, how can I help you? You said it was something to do with the girl who ran away from home in Weybridge?'

Wise ran through main aspects of the investigation and then Hannah repeated what she'd learned in her visit to the Moores the previous day.

'Bloody hell,' Boldham said. 'No wonder you've come back down for another look at this church.'

'Have you had any run-ins with the church before?' Wise asked. 'Any other complaints?'

'Not that I'm aware of,' Boldham said. 'To be honest, I'm a bit pissed off hearing all this now because the parents said none of this to me when I went to see them after Sasha's body was found.'

'You were the one who delivered the death notice?' Hannah asked.

'For my sins, yeah,' Boldham said. 'They appeared pretty cut up about it in their own strange way.'

'Nothing struck you as odd about them?' Wise asked.

'Apart from the whole extreme Christianity thing they have going on?' Boldham replied.

'Yeah, apart from that.'

'Well, there was the fact they'd not reported her missing in the first place.'

'You're joking?' Wise said.

'No, I'm afraid not. They said they thought she was going to come home soon enough and didn't want to make a big deal about it — not wanting to waste police time and so forth,' Boldham said. 'Considering she was dead, I let it go. I figured they had enough guilt to be dealing with.'

'Yeah. You were in a tough spot,' Wise said, even though he thought the man had screwed up. It'd do him no good to say that, though. Not if he needed Boldham's help.

'Hold on a minute,' Hannah said. 'You sure they didn't report her missing?'

'One hundred percent sure,' Boldham said.

'Because when I saw the Moores yesterday, he definitely said he'd reported her missing the moment they realised she wasn't at a friend's house,' Hannah said.

'Then he was lying to you.'

'I don't like that,' Wise said. 'It's never a good sign.'

'Do you think the stepdad or the pastor might've killed her?' Boldham asked.

'It's quite the coincidence that she died on the day they were both in London.'

'I don't believe in coincidences,' Boldham said.

'Me neither,' Wise agreed. 'That's why Hannah and I are going to check out the church this morning and speak to the pastor afterwards. Depending how that goes, we might need a bit of help from your lot.'

Boldham smiled. 'You worried they might give you grief?'

'If Sasha Moore was assaulted at the intervention, it happened in that church. Who knows, maybe there's some of Sasha's DNA still lurking in a floorboard crack or something.'

'You want us to take their church apart?'

'Maybe. It depends how we get on,' Wise said.

'Wonderful.' Boldham leaned forward and brushed a speck off a shoe. 'You should've warned me. I would've put on my best Adidas trainers.'

'You've still got time to change,' Hannah said.

'I might well do that,' Boldham said with a smile. 'In the meantime, I'll put the SOCOs on standby.'

Wise checked the time. 9:45 a.m. 'We better be making a move. I'll keep you updated with how we get on.'

'Yeah, you do that,' Boldham said, standing. 'Have fun at church.'

'Oh, we will,' Wise said.

# 24

Twenty minutes after leaving Woking Police Station, Wise and Hannah arrived at the Universal Church of God's Children. The building itself wasn't much to look at. Situated at the bottom of a small residential road, it was a decent size but the roof was curved, like it belonged on a village hall or a youth centre. There were certainly no spires or arches that Wise would normally associate with a church. Even the name sign was small and tucked away, easy to miss if someone wasn't looking for it specifically. All in all, it was a very unassuming building. However, the expensive cars that lined both sides of the street told of the area's wealth and indicated probably why this location was chosen. With no available parking spots, Wise had to drive on for another few minutes before he found somewhere to leave the Mondeo.

Wise looked at his beaten-up car when they got out. 'The neighbours will probably complain I'm bringing down the house prices by parking here.'

Hannah looked around at the large homes. 'I'm surprised no one's come out to tell you to move already.'

'Probably waiting for us to go before leaving a note on the windscreen,' Wise said, putting on his suit jacket, then an overcoat over the top. 'They love a bit of passive aggressiveness in places like this.'

'How do you want to play this, Guv?' Hannah asked.

'Nicely to start off with,' Wise replied. 'Who knows? It could all be above board and Sasha was just causing trouble, being a rebellious teenager to some very strict parents, and that's why she ran away. Maybe, all they did was assault her, but that doesn't mean they murdered her.'

'All they did? I think that's enough, isn't it?' Hannah said. 'She was sixteen years old.'

'I'm not excusing it or saying we let them off — but that can be something DCI Boldham and his team can take on. Our focus has to be the murders.'

Hannah nodded, looking far from happy. The woman had fire in her, and Wise appreciated that. He'd rather have someone on his team who cared too much than not at all. God only knew there were far too many coppers in the Met who had forgotten why they'd become police officers in the first place. Like DCI Hollins.

There were no pavements along the sides of the road, only grass verges, so Wise and Hannah walked down the middle of the street to the church. As they approached the front door, two men stepped out to meet them. Even though they wore suits, they looked more like bouncers than churchgoers. The larger man had a pair of cauliflower ears, while the other, thinner man had a misshapen nose that suggested neither were strangers to violence.

'Can we help you, sir?' Broken Nose said. His dark eyes looked over Hannah with disapproval. 'Ma'am?' He had the sort of accent that came from very expensive schools, and Wise reconsidered how the men had gotten their good looks. Chances were they'd once been keen rugby players and just enjoyed pushing people about. There was a faint reddish tint to his curly hair. He didn't seem intimidated by the fact that Wise was a good deal taller and broader than he was.

Wise pointed at the doors to the church. 'We've just come to listen to the service.'

Cauliflower Ears stepped forward and put up a hand. 'I'm afraid it's not open to the public, sir.'

'What do you mean?' Wise said, stopping well within Cauliflower Ears' personal space. It was always good to let hard men know they might not be as tough or as intimidating as they thought they were. 'It's a church.'

'It's a private church,' Broken Nose said, joining his friend's side and pushing his shoulders back. 'Invitation only.'

'We were invited,' Hannah said, keeping her eyes on the building and ignoring the men.

'Who by?' Cauliflower Ears grunted.

Hannah took her time turning her attention to the men, and she made sure they saw the smile on her lips when she spoke. 'God.'

'Very funny,' Broken Nose said, getting all bristly, his little feet doing the dance that always came before a punch get thrown.

'That's not very Christian of you,' Wise said. Unlike the Two Ronnies in front of him, he didn't move. He didn't need to work himself up. He never had.

His fists tightened almost without thinking as his mouth went dry. Wise knew that if he or Hannah tried to move past the two men, Cauliflower Ears and Broken Nose would try to stop them any way they could. Back when he was younger, Wise would've already waded into the two suits in front of him and shown them the error of their ways. They'd probably already be bleeding and regretting their life choices.

But he wasn't a kid anymore. Wise wasn't there to brawl. He was a police officer. He was in control. 'What time does the service end?' he said, keeping his tone friendly, even if his eyes told another story.

'In an hour — but you still aren't coming in,' Cauliflower Ears growled back.

Wise pulled out a business card from his coat pocket and handed it over to the thug. 'Tell Pastor Christopher that we're coming to see him and not to go anywhere.'

Cauliflower Ears looked down at the card, then showed it to his mate. 'He might not want to see you.'

'It'll be in his best interests to cooperate.' Wise smiled. 'I'm not in a hurry to arrest anyone today.'

'We'll tell him,' Broken Nose said. 'Now, please leave the property.'

'We will — for now.'

'Lovely meeting you both,' Hannah said.

'What sort of church needs bouncers?' Wise said as he and Hannah walked back to the car.

'Ones that are up to no good.' Hannah glanced back over her shoulder. 'They're still watching us.'

'Yeah?' Wise looked too, saw the bruisers standing, arms crossed, giving them both the big eyeballs. 'One day, they'll meet someone tougher than they are.'

'I think they just did,' Hannah said.

Wise said nothing as unlocked the Mondeo. He didn't bother taking his coat off before climbing inside. It might not be raining, but it was still November and bloody cold.

'What now?' Hannah said.

Wise pulled out a small water bottle from the side pocket of the door and took a slug, washing the dryness from his mouth. 'We'll head back just before the service ends and wait all nice and politely. Then we'll have a chat with dear Pastor Christopher.'

'I've got a feeling we might be calling DCI Boldham at Woking sooner rather than later.'

'I don't think you're wrong about that,' Wise said. He sighed. 'Oh well, what will be will be. It's all in God's hands now.'

# 25

It was just starting to spit with rain as Wise and Hannah returned to the church. Cauliflower Ears and Broken Nose were standing by the main doors, still scowling and still as intimidating to Wise as a wet fart. He gave them a grin, and Hannah waved. The greeting infuriated them further but, before they could say or do anything, the doors to the church opened and the congregation exited.

It was interesting to watch the various couples and families walk to their cars. They were all Caucasian and looked like they were related to Jacob Rees-Mogg or would have been his best friend at school. All the men were in suits and ties that failed to make them look smart and every single woman wore, as Hannah said, long dresses down to the ankle. Make up was minimal, if at all, and their hairstyles were conservative to say the least. Most had their hair tied back in buns or ponytails, and a few wore it long. There wasn't a single woman in sight, though, with short hair or colouring of any sort that Wise could make out. The children looked like mini-versions of their parents: boys in shirts with ties, worn either under a blazer or jacket or a dark, v-neck jumper, and girls in plain dresses.

No one smiled, and when they spotted Wise and Hannah, they all scowled at the strangers.

'They're not exactly happy clappers, are they?' Hannah whispered.

'I'm not sure I'd be smiling if I'd just had to hand over ten percent of my salary to God before the taxman had even taken his cut,' Wise replied.

He watched a man and a woman come out with faces that made the others look like they were beaming with joy. They both stopped suddenly when they saw Wise and Hannah, and the man put his arm protectively around the woman's shoulders.

'That's Mr and Mrs Moore,' Hannah said, then gave the couple a nod of acknowledgement. They didn't return the greeting. Instead, they scurried off to their car.

'Not even a hello?' Wise said.

'I don't think they like us,' Hannah replied.

Finally, a red-haired man came out and spoke to Broken Nose, while Cauliflower Ears lurked in the background.

'That's him, Pastor Christopher,' Hannah said. 'Is it me or do all this lot look like they are related?'

Wise watched the two men talk; they had the same tint to their hair, the same build, but there was more life to the pastor. More vibrance. 'Yeah, maybe.'

Broken Nose pointed out Hannah and Wise. The pastor met Wise's eyes, smiled, and headed over.

'Here he comes,' Hannah whispered.

'Hallelujah,' Wise replied, watched the man approach. The pastor looked like a rock star mingling with his fans, smiling at everyone, making their day with the slightest of acknowledgements. Dishing out charm by the bucket load.

Wise took an instant dislike to the man.

He stepped forward, holding out his hand. 'Pastor Christopher? I'm Detective Inspector Simon Wise. It's a pleasure to meet you.'

The pastor shook his hand. 'Is it? I gather from my colleagues that you're threatening to arrest everyone.' He kept enough of a smile on his face to imply he'd not taken the threat seriously.

'Just an old police joke,' Wise said, happy to play along. He glanced over at Cauliflower Ears and Broken Nose. 'To be honest, I was disappointed that they wouldn't let myself and DS Markham in to listen to your service.'

'I'm afraid we've had some trouble from people who misunderstand what we do here,' Pastor Christopher replied. 'As a result, we have to be careful about who we let in. We can't risk anyone getting hurt or our service being disrupted.'

'Quite,' Wise replied. 'Now we're here though, do you have some time to have a quick chat? I'd like to go over some things you discussed with DS Markham yesterday.'

'Of course. Anything to help. Sasha's horrible death has affected everyone in the community.' The pastor waved a hand towards the church. 'Shall we go to my office?'

'Thank you.'

The two police officers followed Pastor Christopher back into the church. If the outside of the church looked like a youth centre, the interior did little to change that perception. Folding chairs faced a lectern and vinyl banners on either side proclaimed: "When God speaks, we must listen," and "Give to God all that we have, for He gives everything to us." For an organisation taking ten percent of its congregation's gross income, they weren't spending the money on interior design. Far from inspirational, the hall was dour and depressing but, maybe that was the effect they were after. Maybe it was easier to fleece unhappy people out of their money, hoping the next life was going to be better.

Pastor Christopher led Wise and Hannah through a door at the rear of the hall, and they found themselves in a small but very comfortable office. A large crucifix affixed to the wall looked over the desk and computer. The laptop was closed for now, though.

'Please, take a seat,' Pastor Christopher said, indicating the chairs in front of his desk. Unlike the ones in the main hall, these were leather and looked expensive. Wise was no expert, but they looked like a Herman Miller design or something similar. From what he could remember from a catalogue his wife had shown him once, he'd seen something similar on sale for a couple of grand each. The ergonomic wonder that the pastor settled into didn't look any cheaper either, and the desk wasn't something that came from IKEA. Apparently, Pastor Christopher wasn't opposed to a few creature comforts of his own.

As Wise was about to sit down, his phone rang. Taking it out of his pocket, he saw that the number was withheld. Sending the call to voicemail, he switched his phone to silent and sat down. 'Sorry about that.'

'No problem,' Pastor Christopher said. 'I imagine, much like a pastor's, your jobs are a twenty-four-hour commitment.'

'Isn't that always the case when your job is your calling?' Wise said with a smile.

'Very much so. We can only follow the path God sets for us,' the pastor replied.

'But first we must listen to what He asks of us.'

The pastor's eyes lit up. 'Exactly! That was actually my sermon today. We live in a world where we are bombarded constantly with messages of every kind, from tweets and texts to non-stop advertising to whatever we call entertainment today, all shouting "listen to me" as they try to drown out our Father's message.' He nodded to the pocket where Wise had put his phone. 'We've even been trained to carry around devices to ensure that we can never enjoy some peace and quiet in which to listen to God.'

'Everyone is a slave to their screens these days,' Wise said.

'Except those who worship here,' Pastor Christopher said. 'We recognise and reject the devil's work in this world.'

Hannah raised an eyebrow. 'I thought Apple made smartphones, not the devil.'

Pastor Christopher beamed. 'Have you ever wondered why they are called Apple?'

'Not really,' Hannah said.

'The devil used an apple to lure Adam and Eve into a world of sin and he hasn't changed his tricks since then.'

'I don't think Steve Jobs was the devil,' Hannah said.

'Not the devil,' the pastor said. 'But one of his servants.'

'So, you do believe there is a devil?' Wise asked.

'Of course,' Pastor Christopher replied. 'How can I believe in God and not in the devil? You can't have light without dark. You can't have purity without sin. If not for the devil and all his temptations, how can we earn our place in heaven? How can there be paradise without a hell?'

'Quite,' Wise said. The pastor was certainly charming and beaming with conviction. It must be nice to believe in something with such certainty and get so much comfort from it.

That was if he really believed the nonsense he was spouting.

Wise had been taught to believe in the simple ABCs — Assume nothing; Believe nobody; Challenge everything. And sitting before him was a human being who might well have been involved in the sexual assault of a teenage girl and who certainly made a lot of money from his congregation for reassurance that they would go to heaven in the next life. That was as good a scam as any he'd ever come across. After all, it wasn't as if anyone was ever going to come back from the dead and ask for their money back if his promises proved to be false.

'I understand from DS Markham that you believed a demon possessed Sasha Moore,' Wise said, still keeping his tone light.

The pastor sighed and nodded. 'It's heart-breaking when you see one so young fall into the clutches of the unholy despite our best efforts.'

'What were the signs?'

'It often starts in the smallest of ways — disobeying one's parents, for example, or bad language. Then they start dressing in a sexualised manner as the demon starts looking for other souls to ensnare or it persuades them to experiment with drink or drugs.'

'I think that's called just being a teenager,' Hannah said.

'I know. It can seem that way,' Pastor Christopher said. 'That's because teenagers are the most vulnerable to possession, as they assert their individualism and independence. The devil tries to tell us that there is freedom in sin when the reality is quite the opposite. The fallen become slaves to their passions, addicted to their vices, and eventually they pay the price with eternal damnation.'

'That's why you held the intervention with Sasha — to save her soul from such a fate?' Wise asked.

'Yes, of course. After all, the primary function of my job is to protect the souls of my congregation — whether that is through teaching, advice or, as in Sasha's case, intervention.'

'Do mind telling me what happens during one of these interventions?'

'I'm afraid I can't, Inspector. I don't wish to be unhelpful, but I'm not sure you'd understand even if I did. It'd be like trying to explain colour to a blind man.'

'Try me.'

'I'm sorry, but my church forbids sharing that sort of information with outsiders.' He glanced at Hannah. 'Who knows what demons are listening?'

Hannah didn't rise to the bait. She just smiled and shook her head.

'Afterwards, I understand Sasha claimed you sexually assaulted her during the intervention,' Wise said.

'I know,' Pastor Christopher said. 'I honestly believed we'd been successful in casting out her demon, but it was cleverer than we gave it credit for, and more ensconced in her soul than we thought. The moment Sasha returned home, the demon made itself known again and began spouting evil lies. Thankfully, Sasha's mother, Naomi, locked Sasha away for her own safety, otherwise I dread what would've happened.'

'Naomi Moore did more than just lock her daughter up. She beat her as well,' Hannah said.

'No, that's not quite true,' Pastor Christopher replied. 'She didn't beat her daughter — she beat the demon within her.'

'I'm not sure the law will see the difference.'

'That's why we are judged by God for what we do, not man,' Pastor Christopher said.

'Well, unfortunately, until we get to the kingdom of heaven, we are under mortal jurisdiction,' Hannah said. 'That's why we're here.'

'Perhaps you were successful in your intervention, as you initially believed,' Wise said. 'If that were so, Sasha would've been telling the truth. Is it possible she was actually assaulted?'

'You're not suggesting I —' Pastor Christopher began, but Wise held up his hand.

'Of course not. But there were others there at the intervention.' Wise glanced at Hannah.

'Sasha's stepfather and the four elders you mentioned,' Hannah continued.

'That's right,' Wise said. 'Was Sasha ever left alone with any of those men? Perhaps it's one of them who's actually the possessed? One of them doing the devil's work?'

# 26

Pastor Christopher sat back in his chair, his car salesman's smile gone. Wise had seen the look before so many times. A guilty person buying time. Trying to work out what to say that wouldn't get them into further trouble.

Wise stopped himself from smiling, although he was enjoying watching the pastor squirm, even if it was just for a few seconds.

Then the pastor switched his charm back on and leaned forward again. 'I don't think we ever left Sasha alone with one person in particular, but I wasn't present for the whole time she was at the church. However, the others present are the most senior people in our congregation, the most godly. I would say it was near impossible for any of them to be ... possessed, as you say.'

'Near impossible? So, you agree there is a possibility that Sasha was telling the truth?' Wise asked.

'No. No. Not at all. What you're suggesting is impossible. Utterly, utterly impossible.'

Wise nodded. 'That's good to hear. And I take it you've not had any other similar complaints when you've conducted these ... interventions? Other girls claiming to be assaulted?'

'Of course not. When we are successful, the saved soul is very grateful and, with the demon gone, they would do not need to lie about what happened during the intervention.'

'And yet the police have eighteen active investigations underway at the moment,' Hannah said. 'Looking into complaints made by members of the Universal Church of God's Children across the country that they were assaulted and, in some cases, raped during these interventions.'

Pastor Christopher nodded. 'All lies. They are former members of the church, who have rejected our teachings and welcomed evil into their hearts. Unfortunately, when you are fighting a war against the devil, these things happen.'

'You really think you're fighting a war?' Wise asked.

'Of course. What else would you call it?'

'I'm not sure I even believe in God, let alone the devil, to be honest,' Wise said. 'I certainly don't believe we are fighting a war.'

Pastor Christopher shook his head in disappointment. 'And that is exactly why the devil is winning. No one believes anymore. Our souls are sucked into our screens. We glorify sex and violence and we're taught to accept evil as free will. We have carnivals celebrating pride for a bunch of deviants who are possessed by demons, when really we should be outraged. So yes, I do believe we are fighting a war.'

Hannah just laughed. It wasn't the first time she'd been called a deviant. Still, the pastor's homophobia rankled with Wise and his dislike of the man grew.

'Well, thank you for your time,' Wise said, forcing himself to remain pleasant. 'It's been fascinating. Obviously, we'll need to speak to each of the other men who were at Sasha's intervention ourselves. If you can give us their names and contact details, we'll leave you to get on with the rest of your Sunday.'

On cue, Hannah got out her notebook and pen, opening it up to a fresh page and sat poised, ready to write.

Pastor Christopher wasn't so keen. His cheeks flushed. 'Their names? I'm not sure I can give out that information. There is the church's agreement of confidentiality that we have to respect.'

'We're not asking you to divulge information given to you during a confessional, Pastor,' Wise said. 'But you're not protected under the law from cooperating with us.'

'Even so,' Pastor Christopher said. 'Despite all the good work we do here, there is a lot of ill-will towards our church. Our members have been attacked and vilified. That's why we don't allow just anyone to attend our services and why I can't just give out names and phone numbers of our congregation.'

This time, it was Wise's turn to sigh. He glanced over at Hannah for a moment, then looked back at the pastor. 'I hope you'll change your mind. Cooperating with us is better than not.'

'Ah, yes. Your "joke" of earlier,' Pastor Christopher said.

Wise held up his hands. 'No one wants to go down that route.'

'What I don't understand is what any of this has to do with Sasha's murder?' the pastor said. 'It's not as if she died here. It happened in London a month later.'

'The same day you and her stepfather were in London as well,' Hannah said.

'We were looking for her to bring her home.' Pastor Christopher's voice rose, his perfectly calm demeanour cracking. It was a feeling Wise knew only too well. A feeling he wasn't averse to needling some more.

'Maybe you found her,' Wise said quietly. 'Maybe you decided that bringing Sasha home with her accusations was more trouble that she was worth.'

Pastor Christopher shot up from his seat. 'I'm a man of God, for goodness' sake. How dare you suggest such a thing?'

'You're fighting a war, aren't you? People die in wars,' Wise replied, unimpressed by the pastor's dramatics.

'I want you to leave right now,' Pastor Christopher said. 'If you want to speak to me again, make an appointment and I'll have my solicitor present.'

'Oh, we can do better than that,' Wise said, getting up from his seat. He dug out his car keys from his pocket and handed them over to Hannah. 'Do you mind getting the car and bringing it around?'

'No problem,' Hannah said.

'And call Chaz on the way. We'll be needing the SOCOs.' As Hannah left, Wise turned his attention back to the pastor, who was still standing and still acting all flustered. It must be strange for the man not to have everyone jumping to his beck and call.

'I want you to leave as well,' Pastor Christopher said.

Wise smiled and took his time getting to his feet. 'Oh, I will be. The moment my colleague returns with my car.'

'Well, you can wait outside until she does. I have other things to do.'

'Unfortunately, sir, I can't do that.'

'Why not?'

Wise produced a pair of handcuffs from his coat pocket. 'Because I am arresting you, Pastor Christopher Bartholomew, for the sexual assault and murder of Sasha Moore. You do not have to say anything. But, it may harm your defence if you do not mention when questioned something which you later rely on in court. Anything you do say may be given in evidence.'

'You have got to be joking,' the pastor said, stepping away from his desk.

'I never joke about such things. Now, if you'll just put your hands together. I don't want to hurt you when I put the cuffs on.'

'You can't ... You can't do this.'

'Oh, I can. It's literally my job to do so,' Wise said, trying to hide how much he was enjoying himself.

'George!' Pastor Christopher howled. 'John! Help me!'

Wise heard footsteps rushing towards the office door. He turned to face it just as it burst open and Broken Nose and Cauliflower Ears came bundling in.

Broken Nose lunged at Wise first, but he might as well have been moving in slow motion despite his fury. Wise sidestepped the man and drove his left fist as hard as he could into Broken Nose's jaw as he passed, dropping him instantly.

Cauliflower Ears was next, arms spread wide to grab Wise in a bear hug. Wise moved forward to meet him and punched the man straight in the solar plexus. Cauliflower Ears' eyes bulged as the air rushed out of his lungs and his heart went into just enough shock to scare the crap out of him. He went down next to his fallen friend, gasping and wheezing.

Wise turned back to the pastor, who cowered in the corner. 'Now, where were we? That's right, you were about to put your wrists together so I can put the handcuffs on.'

This time, Pastor Christopher did as he was told, visibly shaking as Wise snapped the cuffs together.

'Now, sit in your nice chair while we wait for the others to arrive,' Wise said and guided the pastor back into his ergonomic chair.

'Oth ... others?' Pastor Christopher whimpered.

'Well, now I've had to arrest you,' Wise explained, 'Scene Of Crime Officers are on their way here. They are going to take this place apart bit by tiny bit to see what's what. We're also going to confiscate any computers you have and any of the devil's phones you may have hidden away. After that, they'll move onto your house and do the same again there. By the time we're finished, we'll know all your dirty little secrets.'

'You can't do that,' Pastor Christopher said. 'You need a search warrant.'

'Have you been watching too much television?' Wise said with mock indignation. 'Shame on you, Pastor. Those crime shows aren't very accurate, I'm afraid. You see, now I've arrested you here in the church, I have the legal right to search the premises and take whatever evidence I see fit without going through the hassle of getting a search warrant. And I simply need a senior officer's permission to search your house.' He leaned forward. 'You being difficult has actually saved me a lot of time and hassle.'

'You're an evil man,' Pastor Christopher spat.

Wise smiled. 'I think you'll find I'm on the side of the angels. It's you I'm worried about.'

# 27

For once, Jono was glad to be working on a Sunday. It got him out of more awkward conversations with his wife about what he was going to do about his bloody cancer. It had only been a week since he'd been given the news and he was already fed up talking about it. He couldn't even put the TV on without her chirping away in his ear. When he didn't want to talk, his wife would slink off to cry in a corner somewhere, making Jono feel guilty on top of everything else.

It wasn't as if he wasn't fretting about it twenty-fours a day. Even when he was at work and everyone else was talking about dead kids, the thought was there, niggling away at him.

*'You're going to die.'*

*'You're going to die.'*

*'You're going to die.'*

Fuck. Jono was going to go insane long before the cancer got him.

The nights were the worst, lying there, next to the wife, listening to her sleep, while that damned thought kept him wide awake. Most nights now, he just stared at the ceiling until it was time to haul his dying body out of bed and head back to work.

Jono had tried knocking himself out with melatonin tablets. He'd tried downing shots of Night Nurse. He'd tried downing half a bottle of scotch. None of it worked. None of it could shut that horrible thought up.

*'You're going to die.'*

*'You're going to die.'*

*'You're going to die.'*

Even now, walking around Waterloo Station with Hicksy, it was there, in his mind, as irritating as a bloody Chihuahua trying to hump some poor sod's leg.

*'You're going to die.'*

*'You're going to die.'*

*'You're going to die.'*

It didn't help that he was supposed to get back to the doctor in the morning and tell her what he was going to do. Common sense, his wife, and everyone else said get the treatment. After all, what was there to lose? Apart from his hair, of course, and a lot of people would say that was a good thing. It wasn't as if he'd die any quicker and, if he was being honest, there was no avoiding the pain either. Both routes pretty much guaranteed a shitload of that.

Of course, there was the third option. The shortcut straight to the end. One way to avoid the pain and the discomfort. One way to go out without losing his hair and control of his bowels.

The one way he kept coming back to. The one way that got more attractive the more he thought about it. If he did it right, it'd be pretty damn painless, too. The irony wasn't lost on him that his wife would kill him if he did it, though, if not in this life, then the next.

If there was a heaven, that is. And, if there was, who was to say he deserved a spot? He'd tried his best to do the right thing throughout his life, helping people when he could, and he'd definitely put a good share of wrong 'uns away. That had to count, right?

Not that he'd ever believed in that claptrap, but now? Christ on a bike, he was praying for a divine miracle with the best of them. Every time his phone rang, Jono hoped it was the hospital, telling him it had all been a big mistake, that they had mixed his tests results up with some other poor sod's. It never was, though. And he knew how messed up it was to think that — hoping that someone else, anyone else, deserved the death sentence that he'd been given, instead of him.

Not that the voice in his head thought that, hoped that, believed that.

It knew the truth.

*'You're going to die.'*

*'You're going to die.'*

*'You're going to die.'*

'Shut the fuck up,' Jono mumbled.

'What did you say?' Hicksy replied, stopping suddenly.

Jono dragged a tired smile to his face. 'Nothing, mate. Just talking to myself.'

'First sign of madness, that is.'

'I lost my marbles long ago. You know that. The day I signed up for this shit, they should've dragged me off to the funny farm.'

Jono and Hicksy were on their fourth lap of Waterloo Station, looking for the girl Fatima had told them about. Unfortunately, there was no sign of her by the flower shop or anywhere else. The station was busy with day-trippers instead of office workers, but there wasn't the crowded madness of the week. In fact, it felt almost civilised.

'Do you want to take a break?' Hicksy said, giving him that concerned look of his. The one Jono hated. Like he expected Jono to keel over there and then. He wished he'd said nothing about the bloody cancer to anyone. He loathed their pity.

'I'm fine,' he snapped back.

'I just thought a coffee would be nice.' Hicksy pointed to the balcony that overlooked the whole station. 'I was thinking we could perch ourselves up there and keep an eye out without looking like a right pair of tits going around in circles.'

'Sorry, mate,' Jono said, feeling another wave of guilt swell within him. 'I'm just a bit touchy these days.'

'It's okay. You've got good reasons.'

'Come on, then. My treat.'

'Fucking hell,' Hicksy said, pulling his phone out of his coat pocket. 'I better call you an ambulance. I can't remember the last time you put your hand in your pocket.'

'Piss off,' Jono laughed back. 'I got them that time we were down Streatham way.'

'That was a year ago. At least.'

'Well, there you go.' The two men trudged up the iron steps to the balcony and headed over to the Costa. A couple of tables were full; a young mum and dad, trying to wrangle their two kids into behaving and not doing a very good job of it, and two teenage girls, looking at their phones instead of speaking to each other.

Hicksy grabbed a table by the railing, with a good view of the station and well away from the kids, while Jono went over to the counter. After working together for donkey's years, he didn't need to ask what Hicksy wanted to drink — a large coffee, a splash of milk and three sugars. He thought about ordering a decaf for himself — part of his get healthy kick — but, in the end, he couldn't bring himself to pay money for a cup of muddy water with no oomph. It was bad enough he'd had to give up the fags.

Anyway, considering what was growing inside him, what difference was a bit of caffeine going to make?

*'You're going to die.'*

*'You're going to die.'*

*'You're going to die.'*

'One large coffee with a splash of milk,' he said to the barista, 'and one double expresso please.'

'No problem,' the young lad replied, Australian or Kiwi judging by his accent, all blond surfer fringe. God only knew why he'd leave somewhere sunny to sell coffee in a fucking train station in cold, wet London. 'Where are you sitting? I'll bring them over when they're ready.'

'You see that ugly bloke over there?' Jono said, pointing to Hicksy. 'The one who looks like a tramp having a bad day?'

'Got it,' the lad said. 'Give me a minute.'

Jono paid the man, grabbed a handful of sugar sachets, and headed back to Hicksy. 'Any joy?' he said, sitting down.

'Nah.' Hicksy scratched at his stubble. 'I reckon this Katie only works Monday to Friday.'

'I'm not sure begging counts as a nine-to-five job, mate.'

'Yeah? You'd be surprised. I reckon she probably makes more than you and me, just by sitting on her arse with her hand out — and she doesn't have to pay tax on any of it.'

'I'm not sure it's as lucrative as you or the Daily Mail make out,' Jono said. 'I mean, she's bloody homeless for a start. No one would want that, especially with winter coming up.'

The barista came over and placed their coffees on their table. Hicksy eyed Jono's small cup. 'That looks like an expresso.'

'Well done, detective,' Jono said. 'But it's actually a double expresso.' He picked up the cup, took a sip, and smiled. 'And it's lovely.'

'Your missus told me you're to drink bloody decaf.'

'Yeah, but that tastes like shit.'

'I'm not having her give me a bollocking just because you're weak-willed. She scares me at the best of times.'

'Well, if you won't tell, I won't.'

Hicksy shook his head. 'You'll never keep it a secret. One look from your wife and you'll be squealing. Then she'll come after me.'

But Jono wasn't really listening. Someone had caught his eye: a girl walking towards the clock from the eastern side of the station. Her oversized parka looked like it was about ten years past its best and she had a Labrador on a string lead by her side. But it wasn't her pet or her wardrobe that had caught Jono's attention. It was the vivid scar that ran down the side of her face. Still bright red and angry. A knife wound if Jono had ever seen one.

Jono tapped Hicksy and pointed. 'Katie.'

Hicksy followed the direction of Jono's finger. 'It is, isn't it?'

'It fucking is.' Both officers stood and headed to the stairs down. 'Oi, Jason Donovan,' Jono shouted to the Barista. 'Keep an eye on our coffees. We'll be back in a minute.'

They moved quickly for two middle-aged men who were more familiar with the interior of a pub than a gym, but Jono could feel himself starting to lose his breath as they made their way down the stairs to the main station level.

'You stop her,' Hicksy said. 'I'll come up from behind, in case she does a runner.'

Jono nodded, not trusting himself to have enough air for words. Then he coughed, trying to clear the muck that had suddenly blocked his throat. Hicksy didn't notice, though. He'd gone, moving around to intercept the girl.

Jono gobbed a load of mucus onto the floor, but there seemed to be another ton of the stuff working its way up from his lungs. His poor, cancer-riddled lungs.

*'You're going to die.'*

*'You're going to die.'*

*'You're going to die.'*

He didn't even try to argue with the voice in the back of his head. The way he was feeling, there was a good chance it was going to happen sooner rather than later. He spat again, then choked on more muck.

Christ. He shouldn't have had that bloody coffee.

The girl was heading straight for him, though, eyes down, not looking at anything or anyone. The big dog next to her was wagging its tail, happy as Larry, too.

Jono moved towards her, coughing into the sleeve of his coat, trying to blink away the stars popping up in the outside of his vision, aware of the sweat coating his face. It didn't help that his lungs felt like bricks in his chest, either.

'Excuse me, miss,' Jono croaked when the girl was five yards away. 'Could I—'

He didn't finish the sentence. He was too busy falling face first on the ground.

# 28

Hannah drove Wise's Mondeo up to the church, cursing it all the way. There was a reason she drove a motorbike. As far as she was concerned, four wheels were two too many. She was just glad Wise wasn't next to her, witnessing her kangaroo jump his car up the road.

At least there were plenty of parking spots outside the church, now the congregation had gone home. Not that Boldham or his SOCOs would care about parking spaces when they turned up. They'd just block the road off and go from there.

The thought made Hannah smile. That would get the local curtain twitchers going. A right proper scandal on their doorsteps. It'd keep them in gossip for months.

Entering the church, Hannah noticed the two doormen were nowhere in sight. Then she saw the door to Pastor Christopher's office was open. Panicking, she ran, hoping that the thugs hadn't gone after Wise while she was away.

The sight of what was inside stopped her in her tracks, though. Pastor Christopher was at his desk with his hands handcuffed, while the two bouncers sat on the floor, with their backs to the wall and both looking dazed and confused. The one with the broken nose and dark eyes had a bruise forming on his jawline.

Wise, on the other hand, was in one of the seats opposite the pastor, looking very pleased with himself. 'You took your time.'

'I was gone five minutes,' Hannah said, not believing what she was seeing. 'What happened here?'

Wise nodded towards Pastor Christopher. 'This idiot resisted arrest by calling in the Two Ronnies here. So, those two idiots ...' he indicated the doormen with a tilt of his chin, 'are now under arrest for assaulting a police officer and obstruction of a police officer.'

Hannah raised an eyebrow. 'So much for taking things slowly.'

Wise held up his hands as if to say, "What can you do?"

'You caution everyone?'

'Of course. You call Chaz?'

'Yeah. DCI Boldham is on his way.' There was no way she was calling Boldham "Chaz." It was a ridiculous name for a grown man. She glanced at her watch. 'Should be here any minute.'

'Great. Hopefully, we won't have to wait too long.'

'This is preposterous,' Pastor Christopher said. 'I demand you let me go.'

'Demand away,' Wise said. 'It's not going to make a jot of difference.'

'Devils,' the pastor growled.

Wise sighed. 'Sticks and stones.'

There was the sound of cars stopping outside, of doors opening and shutting. 'Sounds like the cavalry has arrived,' Hannah said.

Wise stood up. 'Let's go and introduce everyone.' He walked around to the other side of the desk and hauled the pastor up, then glanced down at the goons. 'Move it, you two.'

Hannah followed Wise and the others back out into the main hall just as Boldham walked in through the doors, with half a dozen uniforms. He'd added a black leather jacket to his look of earlier. 'What's all this, then?'

'Pastor Christopher here is under arrest for the murder of Sasha

Moore,' Wise said. 'We'll take the pastor back to Kennington with us, but can you take his goon squad to your nick?'

'What's the charge for them?' Boldham asked, looking the two men up and down.

'Assault of a police officer and obstruction.'

'You two did have fun.'

'That was all done to the governor, not me,' Hannah replied.

Boldham nodded. He turned to the uniforms. 'You heard them. Put the two big lads in the van and the pastor in the back of the DI's car.'

Hannah threw one of them the car keys. 'It's the beaten-up Mondeo out front.'

'What do you want the SOCOs to look at?' Boldham asked once the others had been taken away.

'There's a laptop in the office that I want digital forensics to have a look ASAP,' Wise said. 'Plus any other devices you find. The pastor said they don't use smart phones as they're invented by the devil, but I'm not sure I believe him.'

'The devil? Right,' Boldham said. 'What about the rest of the place?'

'I haven't looked around yet,' Wise said, 'but we need to find where they hold the interventions. Wherever that is needs to be gone over with a fine-tooth comb. It's been over a year and a half since Sasha was here, but hopefully there'll be something. Maybe even evidence of other attacks. I wouldn't bother with the main hall area, though. There were a hundred odd people in it only this morning.'

'Alright,' Boldham said. 'Best get started. We should get the magic blue suits on if we're going to poke about.'

Wise turned to Hannah. 'You concentrate on the office. I want to know who these four elders are.'

They all walked outside to organised chaos as the SOCOs prepared to search the church. Pastor Christopher glared at them from the back of the Mondeo. 'How long should we leave him stewing in the back of the car?' Hannah asked as she took a suit off a SOCO.

'No more than an hour,' Wise said. 'It is November, after all. I don't want him freezing to death before we talk to him.'

'Do you think he did it?'

'There's something about Sasha's murder. It was the first one. The most violent. I think she was killed for a reason and that unleashed whatever is making the killer carry on.' Wise pulled on the forensic suit, struggling to fit into it as ever. 'You heard him in there. They think they're fighting a war and people do awful things in wars.'

Hannah's phone rang. She pulled out of her jacket pocket and saw that it was Hicksy. What the hell did he want? She was tempted to reject the call, but something told her it might be important. After all, the man barely spoke to her at the best of times and he'd certainly never rung her before. She glanced over at Wise and mimed that she was going to take the call. The governor nodded and headed back to the church with Boldham.

'Yeah?' she said on answering.

'It's Hicksy. You with the Guv?' The man sounded scared and out of breath.

'Yeah. What's wrong?'

'I've been trying to call him. It's Jono. He collapsed.'

'He did what?' Hannah said.

'He fucking collapsed. They've taken him to Saint Thomas' Hospital.'

'You with him now?'

'Yeah, but they won't let me into see him.' Hicksy sounded like he was about to cry. 'We found the witness we were after as well, a second before it happened. The girl ran though when Jono went down.'

Hannah looked around for Wise, but he was back in the church. Shit. 'Jono'll be okay.'

'No, he won't. He's bloody dying.'

'You don't know that,' Hannah said. 'They'll sort him out in hospital.'

'Just tell the governor.' Hicksy ended the call.

Hannah slipped her phone back into her pocket and ran into the church. 'Where's the DI?' she called out to a couple of SOCOs. 'The big bloke?'

One of them pointed to a doorway to the right of the stage on the opposite side of the pastor's office. Hannah didn't need telling twice. She sprinted over and through the door, clomping down a corridor. Wise and Boldham were standing at the far end by another door, looking into the room on the other side.

'Guv!' she cried. Wise and Boldham both turned. Both looked shocked.

Hannah skidded to a halt and saw what was in the room behind them. Saw what had appalled the two detectives. A large, life-size cross was fixed to the far wall. Shackles hung from either side of the crossbeam and another pair was fixed to the base. Soundproofing covered the rest of the walls. There were no windows.

'We found the intervention room,' Wise said.

# 29

Wise hammered the Mondeo back up the A3 to London, worried about Jono and feeling guilty for having his phone on silent earlier. There had been ten missed calls from Hicksy by the time Hannah had told him what had happened. A few too from that unknown number. He'd not listened to the voice mails that Hicksy had left, though. There wasn't any need. Not yet. His imagination was doing a fine enough job of filling in the gaps of what he'd missed and running over what he should've done differently.

Why had he sent Jono out walking the streets of London again? He'd seen how knackered he looked the night before. In fact, why hadn't he made the man take some time off after he'd found out about the cancer? Or at least checked with HR what he should do? There had to be some best practices he should've followed. The Met had guidebooks on everything, after all.

He'd called St Thomas' to find out how Jono was, but they wouldn't give out any information over the phone. So, Wise had called Hicksy, apologised for being unavailable and told him to let Wise know the moment there was news. After that, all Wise could do was get on with his job, and that meant taking the pastor back up to London for questioning.

Dear old Pastor Christopher Bartholomew was handcuffed in the back, looking as miserable as sin. The charm of earlier was long gone. The man knew he was in the shit. He knew they'd seen the intervention room.

It looked like it belonged in a S&M club, not a church. A place of sin, not godliness. It wasn't hard to imagine what it must've been like for Sasha Moore — or anyone else — to be handcuffed to that cross, surrounded by the pastor and his cronies. Even if they were only praying over her, it would've been terrifying. But Wise knew more than that went on in that room. Way more.

He glanced in the rear-view mirror and caught Pastor Christopher watching him. Did the man really think he was doing God's work by torturing teenagers? Or was it all a façade? A power game to scam people out of money and molest little kids?

Was he the murderer?

A big part of Wise wished he'd given the pastor a good smack in the head along with his friends, but he was glad he hadn't. Whatever this man was up to, Wise wanted him to go to prison and not get off because Wise had lost control.

Kennington Police Station didn't have any interview rooms anymore, so they took the pastor instead to the next nearest station, where they had custody officers and holding cells.

Just off Brixton Road and a stone's throw from the Brixton Academy, Wise's favourite music venue from back in the day, Brixton Police Station was originally built in the 1850s, extended in the early 1900s and then, like Kennington, rebuilt in the fifties onwards.

Back when Wise was starting out as a copper in the early naughties, Brixton was considered a very modern and well-kitted out nick. But like the police service as a whole, the last thirteen years in particular had been cruel. Cutback after cutback after cutback had left the amount of police officers looking after London's nine million residents at wafer thin levels. Its buildings and equipment had fared no better, especially as every government contractor saw even the smallest job as a way of earning millions. Brixton, once one of the Met's best stations, now looked like it was about to fall down. In fact, he didn't feel as bad about Kennington as he had done earlier. Maybe it was just Hammersmith that had gobbled up all the Met's refurb budget.

'I haven't missed this place,' Hannah muttered as they got out of the car. The station was twice the size of Kennington, with three rows of large windows, all stacked on top of each other, overlooking the Brixton Road.

'The question is: have they missed you?' Wise asked. He opened the back door and hauled the pastor out.

'I doubt it,' Hannah replied, taking up position on the other side of Pastor Christopher. Together, they marched him into the station.

The receptionist looked up from behind a plexiglass screen as they entered the building. She smiled when she saw Hannah. 'Alright, stranger. Long time, no see. How are you?'

'Alright, Daphne. We need to book this one in with the custody sergeant,' Hannah replied with a grin of her own.

Daphne looked the pastor up and down and wasn't impressed by the looks of things. 'You know the way,' she said and buzzed them through.

Hannah led Wise and Pastor Christopher through the blue door and into the station proper. Fluorescent lighting buzzed overhead as they walked down a long white corridor to the custody suites.

As they walked, Wise's phone buzzed again. He took it out of his pocket and checked the screen. It was an unknown number again. 'I'll catch up with you,' he said to Hannah, then turned and headed back towards the reception area as he answered the phone. 'Detective Inspector Simon Wise.'

'Good of you to answer the phone at last,' a man said.

Wise stopped with his hand on the door to the reception, unable to push it open. Nausea hit his gut like a tidal wave. He knew he should say something, but he couldn't.

The man chuckled. 'Cat got your tongue, Si?'

'Hello Tom,' Wise said, forcing the words out.

'Oh, so you do know who it is,' his brother said. 'I was wondering.'

'How are you?'

'I'm tickety-boo. You?'

'I'm doing okay,' Wise replied, his mind racing. Why was his brother calling? He didn't even know Tom had his number. Had their dad given it to him? Wise doubted it. The old man would've said something.

'How's work? You busy?'

'Yeah. Just a bit.'

'I would imagine you always are,' Tom said, sounding far too cheerful. 'All those crimes happening across the city, all those murders that need solving. I don't know how you find time to do anything else.'

'It's not that bad, sometimes.'

'Well, Dad says he hardly sees you.'

'I saw him a few weeks ago,' Wise said. 'The day you went to the football with him.' The night they'd run into each other outside the family home.

'It's a shame you didn't pop in and say hello yesterday,' Tom said. 'I heard you were in the neighbourhood.'

So, that was it. The bull-necked smoker had told Tom he'd seen Wise. 'Actually, that's exactly what I did. I was just passing through, saw someone sitting in your car and thought it was you. Being brotherly, I went to say hello, but it wasn't you.'

'No. It was Gorgeous Gary, my driver.'

'Why did you need a driver?'

'I knew I was going to have a few pints with the old man so I couldn't drive, could I? Gary is my designated driver.' Tom laughed. 'You know me, I've learnt my lesson. I don't break the law anymore.'

'That's good to know,' Wise said, feeling sick. It was like it was all a game to his brother. Telling the truth with his lies.

'Anyway, I'm glad you weren't sticking your nose in where it's not wanted,' Tom said. 'I mean, I know we're not close anymore, but I still don't want to have a serious falling out with you, Si. Not more than we've had, anyway. Dad wouldn't like it.'

'Yeah, well, sometimes you can't always get what you want.'

'You don't have to tell me that. I was the one who went to prison.'

Because you were the one who killed someone, Wise thought, but he said nothing. Nor did Tom, waiting for a reaction.

The silence on the phone was painful. It was easy to imagine his brother on the other end of the line, still angry, still full of hate towards his brother. Burning with a fury that twenty years inside couldn't put out.

And things were only going to get worse between them. Far worse.

In the end, it was Tom who spoke. The false humour was gone from his voice. 'As fun as this has been, brother, I've got things to do, people to see. You know how it is.'

'Yeah, I do,' Wise said.

'Now, don't take this the wrong way, but we went twenty-odd years without running in to each other,' Tom said. 'And I think that's one tradition worth keeping. You get my meaning? No "I was just passing through" or shit like that. Even when I see the old man, I don't want you popping by either intentionally or accidentally. In fact, if I see you walking down the same street as me, I'm going to get very upset, and when I get upset, things get messy. All sorts of people can get hurt. Especially innocent bystanders.' There was a pause. 'How are the kids, by the way?'

Wise said nothing.

'Dad says they're lovely. It must be a constant worry, though, keeping them safe. There are a lot of sickos out there.'

Wise didn't know what to say. The bastard was threatening his kids.

Tom chuckled. 'I hope I made myself clear.'

'Like fucking crystal,' Wise said through gritted teeth.

'Good,' Tom said. 'Now, you have a nice life and stay the fuck out of mine.'

The line went dead.

Wise stood staring at his phone in the police station corridor, lost for words, Tom's threats echoing through his mind. The warning about his kids. His goddamn kids.

Christ.

Was there even any point in going to see Selmani during the week? Did he need any more confirmation that Tom was the top man SCO10 was after? Was he just being a glutton for punishment?

He should call DCI Heer. Come clean. Tell her everything. If it meant the end of his career, then so be it. He was only protecting Tom with his silence and, if he was the one who ruined Andy ... Wise felt sick thinking about that.

Had he picked Andy because he was Wise's partner? Was that his way of getting back at his brother?

*'If I don't do this,' Andy says, 'he told me he'd kill them.'*

*'Who did?' Wise takes another step forward. 'If someone's threatening you or your family, we can stop them. You just have to trust me and give me the gun.'*

*The two men stare at each other. Twenty years of history relives in their eyes. Their friendship. Their bond. Surely, he'll give up. Andy's no killer.*

*'Please mate.'*

*Andy shakes his head. 'I'm sorry, Si. I'm sorry for ev—'*

*Something punches Andy off his feet a heartbeat before Wise hears the crack of the gun. Time slows as Andy tumbles forward, red mist leading the way, his brains and blood already splattered across the rooftop. He lands on the concrete with a wet thud and lies unmoving, his eyes open and fixed on Wise, a hole in the side of his temple where the red dot had been.*

It was as if he was there again, on that roof, in the summer heat, the stink of burning asphalt in his nostrils. He could see the blood. See his friend. See him dead.

Dear God.

Wise ran from the corridor, banged through the doors to the reception and out into the car park, into the cold night air, trying to keep the bile in his gut down, knowing that he couldn't. He could feel it bubbling away, the heat already burning his throat as his stomach spasmed, tightening up into a knot.

He staggered to the side of a patrol car, trying to get out the way, out of sight, trying to hold it down.

*All he can see is Andy dying.*

*Andy dead.*

*And it's all Tom's fault.*

Guilt punched Wise in the stomach and the bile rushed up his throat, and there was no stopping it. He doubled over, puking all over the car park. Half-digested food splattered on the concrete as he yakked his guts up.

By the time he'd finished retching up all the contents from his stomach, Wise was shaking, and tears ran down his cheeks. He sucked in lungfuls of air, trying to steady himself. He'd not had an episode like that for weeks. He thought he was past it. Recovered.

What a damn fool he was. The darkness would never let him go.

# 30

An hour later, Wise sat next to Hannah in an interview suite in Brixton nick, a table separating them from the pastor and his solicitor, a man named Michael Theobold. Neither looked happy. Pastor Christopher had only spent two hours in a cell, but all the carefully cultivated charisma of earlier was long gone. He now looked like he was barely containing his temper at how he was being treated. The solicitor, a tall, thin man with a bald skull, stared at Wise through thick, black-framed glasses. Despite it being early Sunday evening, he wore a blue, pinstriped suit that set off his pink tie very well indeed. In different circumstances, Wise would've asked where he'd got the suit from.

They'd got as far as giving their names for the benefit of the tape recording the interview, but not much progress had been made with the interview itself.

'I'll be filing official complaints against both you and DS Markham here,' Theobold said, 'for religious persecution, Inspector, and false arrest. You'll be lucky if you'll be allowed to give out parking tickets after this.'

'Noted,' Wise said. Waiting for the pastor's solicitor to arrive had given him time to compose himself after Tom's call and tidy himself up as well. Now the shock had subsided, he was angry that he'd allowed his brother to rattle him like that. Still, it was a warning that he wasn't completely over what happened to Andy. Maybe he wouldn't be until Tom was behind bars again.

It was the same with the pastor. Wise knew the man was guilty of something, but what? He looked over at Pastor Christopher, but the man wouldn't meet his eyes. 'We found your little intervention room at the church. It didn't look like a very spiritual place. In fact, it looked like something out of an S&M club.'

'My client is here to answer questions, Inspector,' Theobold said. 'Not to listen to your opinions on things you don't understand.'

'Was that the room where you staged your intervention with Sasha Moore?' Wise asked.

'No comment,' Pastor Christopher replied, his focused on his hands on the table.

'Did you chain Sasha Moore to the cross?'

'No comment.'

'Did you sexually assault Sasha Moore when she was chained to the cross?'

'No comment.'

'How many ...'

Theobold held up a hand. 'Do you have any physical evidence that this ... Sasha Moore was even in this room that you found, let alone attacked there?'

'Not yet,' Wise replied. 'Forensics are going over everything now.'

'Right,' Theobold said. 'What about an eyewitness who saw both Sasha Moore and my client in there together or saw this alleged assault?'

'Not yet,' Wise said, not taking his eyes off the pastor. 'Who were the four other men with you at the intervention?'

'No comment,' Pastor Christopher replied.

'I'm sorry, Inspector,' Theobold said. 'I thought my client was arrested on suspicion of the murder of Sasha ...' he looked down at his notes. '... On the fifteenth of March last year. What have the events of the intervention got to do with that?'

'I'd say being accused of sexual assault by a sixteen-year-old girl is a pretty good motive for murder,' Wise said.

'Well, let's concentrate on the actual crime we're here to discuss first, shall we?' Theobold said, with a smug smile that got Wise clenching his already bruised fist. 'Do you have any proof of any sort linking my client to this poor girl's death?'

'I believe your client sexually assaulted or aided in the sexual assault of Sasha Moore under the pretence of an intervention and then murdered or aided in the murder of Sasha Moore in order to stop her making an official complaint against him and his church.'

'I didn't ask what you believed,' Theobold said. 'I asked if you had any proof. If you haven't got any, I suggest you terminate this interview, apologise to my client and let him return home to his wife and family.'

'If I've got things so wrong, Pastor,' Wise said, 'why don't you tell me what really happened? Set the record straight and all that.'

'No comment,' Pastor Christopher replied.

'If you're not going to talk to us,' Wise said, 'you're only making yourself look more guilty.'

Theobold shook his head. 'This is just a waste of time.'

'I agree,' Wise said. 'Now, you told Detective Sergeant Markham that both you and Joseph Moore were in London on the day Sasha was murdered.'

'That's right,' the pastor replied. 'We were looking for her.'

'Why?'

'Why?'

'Why were you looking for her?' Wise asked.

'She was a sixteen-year-old girl who'd run away from home,' Pastor Christopher said. 'We wanted to get her back home, where she would be safe.'

'We?' Hannah asked.

'Myself, her family, the rest of congregation,' Pastor Christopher said. 'We all cared very deeply for her.'

'Even though you believed her possessed by a demon?' Wise said.

'Especially because we knew she was. What sort of pastor would I be if I just abandoned every soul the devil took?' Pastor Christopher looked from Wise to Hannah. 'I believed if I could get her home to her loving family, then we could still have a chance to save her. Alas, we were too late.'

'Her loving family?' Hannah scoffed. 'The same people who beat her and locked her up? Who gave her up to you to be assaulted?'

'Again, you have no proof that Sasha Moore was assaulted,' Theobold said. 'Let alone by my client.'

'Was the fifteenth of March the only time you went looking for Sasha?' Wise asked.

'No,' Pastor Christopher said. 'After she ran away, her stepfather and I went at least once a week to London to look for her.'

'Just once a week?' Wise said. 'It doesn't sound like you were that worried. If my daughter was missing, I think I'd be out all day and all night until I found her.'

'Well, I can't speak for the Moores. Perhaps they were doing that — but I have other responsibilities and commitments. I went when I could. I did my best.'

'Where did you look?'

'All over, really. We used the Tube to get around, so we checked the stations, the tourist sites. A few times we checked out some squats that we heard about.'

'So you searched together?'

'Sometimes. Other times we split up.'

'What about on the fifteenth?' Wise asked.

'We got the train up after lunch, then I headed over to Islington to look around there. I don't know where Joseph looked. We met up again at Waterloo around 6 and got the train home, where we heard the awful news,' Pastor Christopher said.

'And there were just the two of you that day looking for Sasha? No one else from the church?'

The pastor shook his head.

'Did you know the Moores hadn't reported their daughter missing to the police?' Hannah asked.

Pastor Christopher gave a sad shake of his head. 'I did. We all believed we could get her home without their help.'

'Looking back now, do you think that was a mistake?' Hannah said.

'What my client thinks of things is not relevant in the slightest,' Theobold interjected. 'You arrested my client for murder and yet the only thing we all agree on is that he used his own personal time to look for a missing girl. You should be thanking him, not arresting him.'

'We all agree he was in London on the day of the murder and at the time Sasha was killed,' Wise said. 'And I think we've established your client had sufficient motive to kill Sasha Moore as well.'

'And yet you have no evidence at all, Inspector. Nothing that would convince the Crown to take these absurd charges before a judge and jury,' Theobold said. 'You're just wasting everyone's time and I've had enough.' Theobold stood up dramatically. 'We're leaving.'

The pastor got to his feet, but Wise and Hannah stayed where they were.

'I'm sorry, but your client isn't going home,' Wise said.

Theobold's cheeks flushed with anger. 'What?'

'We can hold Pastor Christopher for twenty-four hours.' Wise glanced at his watch. 'Now, I was never any good at maths but, by my reckoning, we've only used up two of those twenty-four hours.'

'You can't possibly mean to keep my client overnight,' Theobold said.

'I think I might just do that,' Wise said with his best "Fuck you," smile. He glanced over at Hannah and gave her a nod.

'Interview terminated at eighteen ten,' Hannah said and turned the tape off. Both officers got to their feet. 'Someone will be along to take you back to your cell in a minute, sir.'

'This is outrageous,' Theobold shouted after them as they left the interview suite. 'I'm going to have your jobs for this.'

'You sure about this, Guv?' Hannah said once they were alone in the corridor. 'That brief of his is something else.'

Wise sighed. 'I'm not sure of anything, except the fact the pastor has done something, and he's trying to cover whatever it is up. Whether that's our murder or just an assault is anyone's guess at the moment.'

'Do you think we should find out where he was on the dates of the other murders?'

'Yeah, we should. But let him stew for a while longer.' Wise checked his watch. 'I'm going to check in on Jono at Saint Thomas's. We can resume interviewing him at 8 p.m.'

Hannah nodded. 'I'll chase up Boldham. See if the Woking lot has found anything we can use.'

'Thank you.' Wise went to leave, then stopped. 'I know it's Sunday. If you need to be somewhere or do something, it's okay.'

Hannah laughed. 'The last time I left you by yourself, you got into a fight and beat up two people. I think I'll stay with you for now. Probably safer for all of us.'

'You might have a point. I'll see you in a bit.'

'See you, Guv.'

Wise walked away, flexing his hands, feeling the bruising and the swelling on the knuckles. He should probably ice them, but there was no time for that. He wanted to make sure Jono was okay. Still, he couldn't help but think about the fight — if it could be called that. Had the two men deserved it? Could he have stopped them some other way? Probably. Trouble was, he'd acted on instinct and his instinct always turned to violence first.

And God help him, but he'd really enjoyed knocking the two thugs down. He'd enjoyed it far too much. He flexed his fingers, trying not to think about when he'd been a kid, fighting alongside Tom. How much fun that had been, too.

# 31

It was an easy ten-minute drive from Brixton nick to Saint Thomas', especially since most sensible people were at home, making the most of the last of the weekend.

Wise headed straight up the South Lambeth Road, then took a left by Vauxhall over to the Albert Embankment, trying not to think about how much he hated hospitals. After all, as his old man used to say, hospitals were full of sick people and who wanted to be around them? God only knew he'd spent enough time in the damned things when he was a young lad, watching the NHS try everything they could to stop the cancer that was killing his mum — and failing.

If he was being honest, it had scared the shit out of him back then. There were teenage kids, teetotal health fanatics, bible-clutching old timers and everything in-between in the hospital ward with his mum. Cancer never discriminated in any way over who it visited.

A lucky few walked away and rang the bell, declaring themselves cancer free, but he could probably count those on the fingers of one hand. The rest had to make do with a trip to the pearly gates where they could ask God himself what they'd done to deserve dying like that.

No wonder he and Tom had gone off the rails, spreading their pain about with their fists, hiding their fear with rage.

And now he was going to see Jono in another ward full of sick, dying people.

He headed up Lambeth Palace Road, barely noticing the city all lit up. Pretty soon, they'd be digging out the Christmas decorations, turning the place into a winter wonderland. Now, though, it was just cold, dark and wet.

It took him a few circuits of the hospital before he found a parking spot a few minutes' walk away. Of course, as he got out of the car, Mother Nature decided to start raining again. He turned up the collar up on his overcoat and marched as quickly as he could to the monolithic building.

Named after Saint Thomas Becket, it was one of the oldest hospitals in London. Originally established in Southwark, it was moved to its current position in Lambeth, opposite the Houses of Parliament, in the late 1860s. Queen Victoria herself was said to have laid the first stone but, somehow, Wise couldn't imagine the grand old lady moving much of anything herself.

The Nazis had bombed the crap out of the place during World War Two and it had to wait until the fifties before reconstruction began. That work went on through the sixties before finally being completed in 1975. Looking up at the white concrete clad building, Wise noted that the postwar period hadn't been a golden age for architecture. In fact, it was easy to imagine that the architects of that period were competing to design the ugliest looking building. Maybe it was some joke they laughed about down at the pub as they told tales of the monstrosities they had under construction.

Wise stopped for a second outside the main entrance and wiped the rain from his face, trying to find some positivity to hide all the emotions going through him. Then, with a deep breath, he stepped inside.

It was busy inside, even for a Sunday night, as people tried to get a doctor to look at their bleeding faces, broken arms or broken minds. A few appeared to have nothing wrong with them except a desire for somewhere warm to sit. Two nurses were trying to calm down a middle-aged man who was determined to take his clothes off in the waiting area, while screaming about being ignored. Someone else, their head covered with a hood, was violently vomiting into a bucket. Wise dreaded to think what it must be like there on a Friday or Saturday evening.

Despite everything going on around him or, perhaps because of it, he found a smile for the lady working behind the reception desk. No doubt, she'd rather be at home watching Netflix. 'Hi,' he said. 'I'm here to see a Mr Jonathan Gray. He was brought in this afternoon.'

'Jonathan Gray?' the woman repeated. Even the bags under her eyes had bags. Wise hoped her shift would end soon.

'That's the one,' he replied.

The receptionist perched a pair of half-moon glasses on the end of her nose and tapped away at her keyboard, licking her lips all the while. Suddenly, her fingers stopped typing. She leaned closer to the screen until less than an inch separated her nose from the monitor. Apparently, that was the optimal distance to read the information on it with her glasses on. Wise didn't want to imagine what she was like without them.

'He's in Intensive Care,' she said, her voice suddenly softer. 'Are you immediate family?'

Shit. It was that serious? Wise held up his warrant card to save a longer and more complicated conversation, then realised she probably couldn't see what it was. 'I'm Detective Inspector Wise,' he said in the end. 'I just want to check up on how he's doing.'

'Ooh,' the woman said, her face brightening. 'Is he a witness to a crime or something?'

'I just need to see how he is,' Wise said.

Unable to get some gossip to spread, the woman sighed and directed Wise to the ICU. Head down, he sauntered off down the corridor and through the double doors. Away from the mayhem of the reception area, things were immediately quieter, soundtracked by the normal hustle and bustle of a hospital: trollies rolling past, phones ringing, machines beeping, someone coughing, lift doors opening and so on.

A sign proclaimed "Intensive Care Unit" in big, red letters above another set of double doors, as if warning everyone not to enter.

Wise, unfortunately, didn't have a choice.

Pushing through the doors, Wise found himself in ordered chaos. The doctors and nurses moved quicker, clutching clipboards, anxious looks on faces. Some beds were curtained off from sight, while others had patients on show who were connected to every type of machine going, monitoring vital signs, pumping hearts, and feeding oxygen.

He found the nurses' station easily enough, and he was soon on his way to a private room at the end of the ward. When he found it, Hicksy was sitting outside on a blue plastic chair, slouched over, his elbows on his knees and head down.

'Hicksy,' Wise said, gripping his shoulder. 'How is he?'

Hicksy looked up, his eyes red as if he'd been crying. 'Not good, Guv. Not good at all.'

Wise looked through the door's window. Jono was in bed, his upper body raised at an angle, tubes going into his arms and an oxygen mask clamped over his face. Sitting next to him and holding onto Jono's hand with both of hers was a woman with short, dark hair and tear-streaked make-up.

Jono's wife.

Wise realised he didn't know her name, despite working with Jono for nigh on seven or eight years. He'd always referred to her as 'the missus' or something similar.

'Have they told you what's wrong?' Wise asked.

'It's his lungs,' Hicksy said. 'Some sort of shit in them.'

Jono's wife must've heard the two men talking, because she looked up, face full of worry, then it quickly changed to relief when she saw it wasn't a doctor. She stood up, said something to the sleeping Jono, and headed over to the door.

'Hi,' Wise said as she stepped out into the corridor. 'I'm DI Simon Wise. I work with Jono.'

'The governor,' Jono's wife said with a sad smile. 'Jono talks about you all the time.'

'I'm sorry, I've been trying to remember your name, but it's slipped my mind.'

'I'm Pat.' She held out a hand, then all but withdrew it again. 'I'm sorry. Are we shaking hands these days or not? I get confused.'

Wise reached out and took Pat's hand. 'I think we can shake.'

Pat tried another smile. 'Bloody Covid.'

Hicksy got to his feet. 'Would you like me to get you a cup of tea, Pat?'

'That would be lovely, Roy. Thank you,' she replied.

'I'll catch up with you later, Guv,' Hicksy said, then shuffled off.

Pat watched him go. 'I think he's taken it harder than me.'

'He and Jono have been partners for a long time,' Wise said. He nodded to her husband in the other room. 'How is he?'

'Alive and asleep for now,' Pat said. 'The stupid sod's got blood clots in his lungs. The doctors say the next forty-eight hours might be a bit dicey but, if he gets through that, he'll be out of here by the end of the week. After that ...' Pat shrugged.

'He told me about the cancer.'

'He tell you he doesn't want to do the treatment?'

'Jono mentioned he was thinking about his options,' Wise said.

'He's a stubborn idiot, is what he is,' Pat said. She wrapped her arms around her chest. 'Options! What options? He either has the treatment or he doesn't. One gives him a fighting chance. The other ...' Pat shook her head.

'It must be difficult for you both,' Wise said, unsure of what else he could say. He certainly had no advice to give. There was a big part of him that wished that his mother hadn't gone through all the hell she did while the doctors were trying to cure her. After all, he'd seen how much she suffered through it all. Then the selfish part of him was glad she had endured it because he'd gotten to spend more time with her before she died. Somehow, those painful last few months became more precious to him than the thirteen good years beforehand were. Probably because he'd known there was only a finite amount of time left with his mother and he needed to savour each remaining minute as best he could.

Of course, he hated the fact that his most vivid memories were of his mum dying, racked with pain. He had a horrible feeling too that Pat was about to go through the very same experience, no matter what Jono decided.

Pat had her eyes fixed on her husband in the other room as more tears worked their way down her cheeks. 'He can be a right pain in the arse sometimes,' she said, more to herself than to Wise. 'But I wouldn't swap him for anyone.'

Wise squeezed her shoulder. 'Let him know I came in to see him and I'll be back tomorrow.'

'I will,' Pat replied, not looking away from Jono.

Wise didn't say any more. He headed back the way he'd come, trying to keep his pace nice and even, fighting the urge to run away from the sterile stink, misery and the bleeping machines.

He was glad of the cold and the rain when he made it back outside. He stood staring out across the Thames, at Parliament and Big Ben and the boats and the cars and all the lights in buildings stretching off north. It was London's life in all its glory, pushing back against the night sky with all its might. For a brief, beautiful moment, nothing else mattered. It was just him and the city he loved in all its dirty, grimy beauty.

Poor bloody Jono. He hoped the man pulled through. He hoped some miracle would get him better.

His phone rang. The caller ID said it was DCI Roberts. 'Alright, boss?' Wise said on answering.

'What the fuck have you done now?' Roberts said.

'I don't know,' Wise replied, not in the mood for a bollocking. 'I've just been to see Jono in the ICU.'

That threw her, as he knew it would. 'What? Jono? What's happened? Is he okay?'

'He's alive for now. Blood clots in his lungs, though. Next few days will be touch and go.' He paused, looking down at the river. The

London Eye was still turning, doing its tourist thing. Wise hadn't bothered visiting it, though. 'So, what have I done?'

'I suppose we can both find out tomorrow morning. Walling wants us in his office at 8 a.m.'

Shit. 'Detective Chief Superintendent Walling?'

'Is there another Walling in your life?'

'Unfortunately not,' Wise said.

Roberts sighed. 'Why is it only your cases that get out of control?'

'I'm not sure I like the implication in that remark,' Wise said.

'I warned you that you didn't want another fiasco on your hands and yet, here we are a day later, and you've got us all swimming in shit,' Roberts said.

'Hold on a minute,' Wise said. 'At what point am I responsible for what's happened?'

'Whose idea was it to go waltzing around Weybridge like Billy Big Boots?'

'I was following a lead.'

'Was it necessary to arrest a pastor and raid a church? And I understand you beat up two of the congregation, for God's sake.'

'Would you rather they beat me up instead? Because that's what they wanted to do.'

Roberts didn't say anything. She let the silence drag out over the phone. Waiting for Wise to say something. Well, he'd not done anything wrong, so he wasn't going to start apologising, if that's what she wanted. Wise could drag the silence out with the best of them.

'Do you still have the pastor in custody?' she said eventually.

'Yeah,' Wise replied.

'What about his brief?'

'Michael Theobold? Yeah, he's still there too, I think.'

'Well, it turns out Mr Theobold is a good friend and golf companion of Detective Chief Superintendent Walling,' Roberts said.

Wise closed his eyes for a moment. 'Of course he is.'

'Needless to say, they've spoken.'

'Hence the 8 a.m. bollocking tomorrow.'

Roberts nodded. 'Hence the 8 a.m. bollocking tomorrow.'

'Did Theobold tell Walling that we discovered a sex chamber in the church? That his client was refusing to cooperate with us?'

'I think he concentrated on the fact that you don't have any evidence linking his client to any of the murders,' Roberts said.

Wise sighed. 'He's not wrong, but my gut says he's tied up in it somehow.'

'Your gut won't get us a conviction, but it might land us a lawsuit,' Roberts said. 'And cost us our jobs.'

'That seems to be the case with everything we investigate these days,' Wise said. 'Look, I've got him there. Let me talk to him one more time and then we'll release him so he can have a nice night's sleep in his own bed. That way, when Walling rips me a new one in the morning, we can tell him we've already let the pastor go.'

'Sometimes, I think you've got some sort of death wish,' Roberts said.

*The bullet takes the top of Andy's skull off a heartbeat before Wise hears the crack of the gun. Time slows as Andy tumbles forward, red mist leading the way, his brains and blood already splattered across the rooftop. He lands on the concrete with a wet thud and lies unmoving, his eyes open and fixed on Wise, accusing him.*

Wise blinked. 'I haven't got a death wish. I just don't do politics.'

'I'm sorry,' Roberts said. 'Ever since Andy died, it's been one big, long bloody mess.'

'Yeah, well, you're not wrong about that.' Wise looked back at the hospital. 'I'd best head back and let the pastor go. I'll see you tomorrow. 8 a.m.'

'Try not to let anything else go tits up until then,' Roberts said.

'I'll try.' It was no guarantee, but it was the best he could do.

The line went dead, and Wise was left staring at the river. Tomorrow was going to be fun.

# 32

Hannah nursed a can of Diet Coke in the canteen at Brixton nick, wondering if she'd really messed things up. She was the one who'd gone down to see Sasha Moore's parents. She was the one who'd thought they were all hiding something. She was the one who'd got Wise focusing on Pastor Christopher and the church.

But now, alone and tired, she wasn't feeling so confident. Maybe it was just the sexual assault they were hiding. That was serious enough but, with Sasha dead and no one else talking, it'd be hard to prove a crime had been committed, no matter what samples forensics might find.

And that lawyer of the pastor's, Michael Theobold, had Hannah worried even more. He'd said he was going to file official complaints against both her and Wise in the morning, and that was the last thing she needed going on her record. The Powers-That-Be had already had words with her after the Motorbike Killer case. Despite getting a result, they'd not liked the fact she and Wise had gone rogue and conducted a side investigation. DCI Roberts had told Hannah she was worried that she wasn't a team player.

She'd not told Wise about that conversation — the man had

enough on his plate, after all — but it had stuck in Hannah's head ever since.

Maybe it was no surprise she was doubting herself. She'd thought joining a murder team would make her career. She certainly didn't want it to destroy it.

'Hello, stranger.'

Hannah looked up and saw DC Samira Sathiah standing by her table. 'Wow. Hey. Oh my God.' Hannah stumbled up from her seat and hugged her old friend. 'How are you?'

Samira gave her a big grin. 'Pissed off that you've not called. You too good for your old Brixton mates?'

Hannah shook her head. 'I'm sorry. The new job's been mad. I've not had a minute to myself.' She grimaced. 'If it helps, I've been shit towards everyone.'

'You better not be lying to me,' Samira said.

'I'm not. I really am a terrible friend to everyone.' Hannah pointed to the chair opposite her. 'You got time now?'

'I'd rather go to the pub and catch up there.'

'Sorry. I'm waiting for my governor to get back. We've got a suspect in the holding cells downstairs that we're in the middle of questioning.'

'Alright. Here it is, then. Give me a sec to get a drink.'

Hannah nodded. 'Sure.'

'You want anything?' Samira asked.

Hannah held up the Diet Coke. 'I'm good.'

She watched Samira saunter over to the drinks machine, dig some change out of her pocket, and pop it in the slot. She returned a minute later, clutching a can of her own. Samira plonked herself down on the plastic chair and cracked open the can. 'So, fancy pants, tell me everything.'

'I'm certainly not fancy,' Hannah said. 'Far from it.'

'Well, one of us is a big shot murder detective. The other is still explaining to people how unlikely it is we'll catch whoever broke into their home and nicked all their stuff,' Samira said.

'I hated that,' Hannah replied. 'Sometimes I felt like I was just filling out crime reports for insurance companies instead of solving crimes.'

'Yeah. I am the paperwork queen.' Samira took a slurp from her can. 'So, your suspect downstairs ... What's he — or she — done, then?'

'Someone's been killing homeless people,' Hannah said. 'The bloke we've got downstairs might be involved.'

'You don't sound so sure?'

'I'm not sure of anything these days. I mean, the guy's definitely dodgy, but I don't think he's a killer.'

Samira leaned on the table. 'You told your governor that?'

'No, not yet. I just don't want to make an arse of myself if I get it all wrong,' Hannah said.

'How long have I known you?' Samira asked.

'Since we were cadets in Hendon.'

'Exactly. And how many times in all those long years have you got something wrong?'

Hannah rubbed her face, feeling knackered. 'Probably more times than I know.'

'Yeah, right,' Samira said. 'They didn't call you Princess Perfect because you kept fucking up, did they?'

'I thought it was because they couldn't call me Stuck-Up Bitch to my face.'

'Well, there was that — but really, it was because you didn't screw up like the rest of us. And when we graduated, you still didn't fuck up,' Samira said. 'Why do you think those pricks upstairs picked on you so much?'

Hannah smiled. 'Because they're racist, homophobic, misogynistic pigs?'

'Yeah — but also because you made them all look bad.'

'I thought they did that by themselves.'

'Don't doubt yourself, H.' Samira reached over and squeezed Hannah's hand. 'Just remember, you're bloody good at what you do.'

Before Hannah could reply, her phone rang. It was Chas Boldham from Woking nick. 'I'm sorry. I've got to take this,' she said.

'It's good seeing you, H.' Samira gave her a wink. 'Next time, call me and take me to the pub.'

'I will.' Hannah got up and answered the phone. 'DS Markham.'

'It's Chaz,' the DCI said.

'Hello, sir,' Hannah replied as she walked to a quiet corner of the canteen. She hated senior officers trying to be all matey. It normally preceded them being all handsy.

'How are you getting on with our dashing pastor?' Boldham asked.

'He's got some jumped-up solicitor acting all high and mighty on us. Apparently, he's filing official complaints against us tomorrow for religious discrimination and a million other things,' Hannah said. 'What about you?'

'The SOCOs are having a field day with that intervention room of theirs,' Boldham said. 'Someone's taken bleach to it, but they've done a terrible job. There's semen everywhere — but without a complaint from a victim, it's not illegal. It's just unhygienic.'

'Fantastic.'

'It's not been all bad, though. You know those church elders you wanted names for?'

'You've found them?'

'In a way,' Boldham said. 'Some snooty-nosed neighbour came over to complain about us doing our jobs. Turns out he's a member of the congregation here and, after I got chatting with him and, using my incredible charm, he gave me the names of all the elders. We ran them though the system and I've now got their addresses too.'

That bit of news perked her up. 'Oh, you wonderful man. Thank you.'

'I'm emailing you the details now,' Boldham said.

The email alert on her phone pinged in her ear. 'I think that's them arriving.'

'Alright. Good luck,' Boldham said. 'Let us know how you get on and I'll keep you updated from my end.'

'Thank you, sir. Really appreciate the help,' Hannah said.

'No problem. It's not like I had anything special planned for my weekend,' Boldham said. 'Speak soon.'

The call ended, Hannah went immediately to her email app, found the message from Boldham and opened it. She ran down the list; Mark Elliot, Neil Hendry, Thomas Kind and Ray Butler.

Her phone buzzed again. It was a text from Wise: *Where are you?*

She pinged back: *Canteen*.

A minute or two later, Wise wandered in and joined her at the table. He looked exhausted.

'I wouldn't have the coffee here,' Hannah said, 'in case you were tempted. It's foul.'

'That's good. I'm trying to cut down on the caffeine, anyway,' he replied.

Normally, Hannah would've scoffed at a remark like that. No way was the governor ever going to give up his coffees. But now wasn't the time for jokes, though. 'How's Jono?'

Wise updated her with the not-so-good news.

'I'm sorry,' Hannah said. 'Jono always seemed like a nice guy.' Admittedly, that hadn't been her first impression of the man. In fact, she'd thought both him and Hicksy were relics from the past when she'd first been introduced to them, but she'd soon thought better of Jono, once she'd gotten past his garbage chic look. He might have outdated views, but he didn't have the anger and resentment that made Hicksy so difficult to be around.

'What about you? Anything happen while I was away?' Wise asked.

Hannah told Wise about the call with Boldham and showed him the list.

'That's great,' Wise said. 'First thing in the morning, I want pictures and backgrounds on these four and let's get them in for interviews.'

'What about our friend downstairs?' Hannah asked.

Wise smiled. 'Well, they've summoned me to an 8 a.m. meeting with Detective Chief Superintendent Walling. Apparently, Theobold has been making calls to complain about the pastor's arrest.'

That was the last thing Hannah wanted to hear. 'What do we do?'

'I want to run the list of murder dates past him and see what he says. If he's got nothing to hide, then he should be happy to give us his whereabouts. Once we have that information to check, he can go, but if he still wants to go no comment, then we keep him in. Maybe a night in a cell will make him want to cooperate.'

'Shall I get him brought up to an interview room now?' Hannah asked.

'Yeah. Let's get it over and done with.'

# 33

10 p.m. on a Sunday night, and Wise and Hannah were back in an interview room with Pastor Christopher and his solicitor, Michael Theobold. The tape was running, and the formalities were done once more. Everyone looked tired and ill-tempered and the room stunk of body odour and stale coffee.

Wise knew he should just release the pastor. Maybe if he did that, Walling wouldn't go full on nuclear in the morning but, the way he saw it, he was getting a bollocking no matter what he did. So, in for a penny, in for a pound and all that. Besides, he really didn't like Pastor Christopher's solicitor. The feeling was mutual as well, if the looks Theobold was throwing his way were anything to go by.

'I'm surprised you're still continuing this farce, Detective Inspector,' Theobold sneered. 'I thought you were cleverer than that.'

'Sorry to disappoint you. I'm only Wise by name, it would seem,' Wise said, before turning his attention to the pastor. 'Where were you on the afternoon of Thursday, tenth of November?'

The question seemed to throw the pastor for a moment. 'Thursday? This past Thursday?'

Theobold whispered something into his client's ear.

'No, it's okay. I'll answer if it will help sort out this terrible misunderstanding,' Pastor Christopher said. 'Thursday afternoon, we have a tea and prayer meeting at the church. It's mainly the same, small group of housewives who come along each week. I was with them until they all left around 4:30, and then I stayed on until around 6 p.m. to tidy up.'

'And will you give us the names of those who were there?' Hannah asked.

'Certainly,' Pastor Christopher said.

'But not the names of the church elders?' Wise asked.

'That information is confidential,' Pastor Christopher said.

Hannah got out a piece of paper from the file in front of her. She made a show of reading it, but kept its contents hidden from the two men opposite her. 'Is Mark Elliot one of the elders?'

Pastor Christopher looked like someone had slapped him around the face. 'No comment.'

'Neil Hendry?'

The colour continued to drain from Pastor Christopher's face. 'No comment.'

'Thomas Kind?'

'No comment.'

'Ray Butler?'

'This is nonsense,' Theobold said. 'Are you running through some random list of names? Are you going to ask my client if he knows Boris Johnson next? Or Harry Styles?'

'Does he?' Wise asked.

'No, he bloody doesn't. Now, enough's enough,' Theobold said.

Wise held up a finger. 'We're nearly done.'

'Where were you on the fourth of August last year?' Hannah asked.

'I've no idea,' the pastor replied, 'without looking at my diaries.'

'Second of December?'

'I need my diaries.'

Hannah ran through the other dates and got the same answers.

Wise didn't mind. If the pastor had rolled off a load of alibis off just like that, he'd be more suspicious.

'What have any of these dates got to do with my client?' Theobold demanded.

'Sasha Moore isn't the only teenager to be murdered recently,' Wise said. 'Six others have been killed in the same way.'

'This is ridiculous,' Theobold said. 'Are you suggesting my client is a serial killer now?'

'Is he?'

Theobold leaned forward. 'I suggest you think very carefully about what you say next, Inspector. Think very carefully indeed.'

Wise ignored the man. 'When we spoke to you earlier, you said you were fighting a war against the devil.'

'I was speaking metaphorically. You know that,' Pastor Christopher said.

'Were you?' Wise said. 'We know you believe in trying to exorcise demons from the possessed. What about those that can't be saved? Would it not be a mercy to end their lives?'

'Of course not. All life is sacred.'

'Mrs Moore seemed quite happy that her daughter was dead,' Hannah said. 'She thought it was a good thing because of what you've taught her in your church.'

'Watch yourself, Detective,' Theobold said.

'He's their shepherd,' Hannah said. 'He's teaching them this nonsense. And what he says has consequences.'

'Has my client told anyone to go on a killing spree?' Theobold asked.

Wise looked at the pastor. 'Have you?'

'Of course not,' Pastor Christopher replied.

'Well, there you go,' Theobold said. 'Now, unless you have some proof that implicates my client in any sort of wrongdoing, can you stop wasting all our time and let my client get back to his family?'

Wise glanced over at Hannah, just to eke out the moment. A part of him wanted to prolong things just out of sheer bloody-mindedness, but, as much as he hated politics, now wasn't the time to hit self-destruct. He sighed. 'You can go for now. But this isn't the end of things — no matter what connections some of you have.'

Theobold laughed. 'You keep telling yourself that if it helps, Inspector. In the meantime, we'll be going. Come on, Pastor, let's get you home.'

Pastor Christopher stood up. 'I didn't kill Sasha, Inspector. Please believe me.'

Wise gave the man his most insincere smile. 'Of course. You're a man of God. I know you wouldn't lie to me.'

'Come on,' Theobold said, taking his client by the arm. 'There's no point talking to this neanderthal. Let's get you home.'

Wise watched them leave, then turned to Hannah. 'Call Boldham in Woking. Tell him that we've let the pastor go for now, but that doesn't mean we stop putting the pressure on him. Something happened to Sasha Moore in that torture chamber of his and others, too. Of that I have no doubt, and I want the bastard to go down for whatever he's been involved in.'

Hannah nodded. 'What about the murders?'

'I don't think he's our killer, but he knows the person who is,' Wise said. 'Bring in the stepfather and the elders tomorrow and let's see what they have to say for themselves.'

'Won't that cause more problems with the Super?'

'Let me worry about that,' Wise said. 'Now, go get some sleep. It'll be another long day tomorrow.'

Hannah stood up, then paused. She looked like she wanted to say something, but wasn't sure if she could.

'Something wrong?' Wise asked.

Hannah took a deep breath. 'Are we doing the right thing, Guv? Going after these church people if they're that connected?'

'I don't care about their connections. If they've done something wrong, then we go after them. That's all that matters. I don't care if they're the bloody Prime Minister, a city banker or a road sweeper,' Wise said. He could've added "or my brother" to that list, but he kept that to himself.

'As long as you're sure,' Hannah said, not sounding convinced.

'I am. Being a police officer isn't about winning popularity contests or making people happy,' Wise said. 'We live in a world where we have to deal with the most awful things that people can do and it's our job to stop them. We may piss the odd person off along the way, but that's nothing compared to what our victims and their families go through.'

Hannah smiled. 'I suppose I better toughen up then.'

Wise got to his feet. 'Yeah, a little — but not too much. It's better to care. It's better to doubt. That's what makes us better detectives.'

'I'll remember that,' Hannah said. 'I'll see you in the morning.'

'Thanks again.' Wise watched her go, glad he had her on his team. Hannah Markham was one of the good ones.

Unlike Andy. Unlike his brother.

# Monday 21st November

# 34

Another broken night's sleep meant Wise got in early to Kennington, even if he was in a sour mood. Early enough that Luigi's was just opening as he walked through their door to get his caffeine fix for the morning. Maria must've seen something on his face, though, because for once she didn't give him any grief for wanting to pay for his drinks by card.

By the time Wise was in MIR-One, it was still only 7:15 a.m. and the incident room was blissfully empty. After leaving his overcoat in his office, Wise stood in front of the whiteboards, coffee in hand, and ran his eyes over the case so far.

Someone — Sarah, no doubt — had added pictures of the four elders, Mark Elliot, Neil Hendry, Thomas Kind and Ray Butler, to the boards, along with their dates of birth. They ranged in age from mid-forties to late-sixties.

Wise tried to remember if he'd seen their faces at the church the previous day, but none sprung to mind. It didn't help that they all had the same unassuming middle-class look about them. None of them looked like a serial killer, but that was a stupid thing to think. What killer did?

No, Anorak Man was crafty, careful, and skilled. He was no crazed madman or violent thug. He was someone who could walk down the street and no one would notice him.

Wise looked from the pictures of the six men to the CCTV screen grab of Anorak Man and back again. None of them looked like him and yet all of them did. Why couldn't one of them at least be overweight, or have a different skin colour so they could easily eliminate them from their enquiries?

Maybe today Sarah would find a better shot of Anorak Man on the CCTV footage they had coming in or place one of these men near the crime scene. Anything that would help narrow down their suspect list.

Of course, someone had seen him; the girl Katie, whom Jono and Hicksy had been searching for.

Shit. Jono. Wise had forgotten all about him. Feeling guilty, he dug out his phone and called Hicksy.

'I'm on my way in,' Hicksy said on answering, sounding like he'd just woken up.

'It's okay. There's no rush,' Wise said. 'I was just wondering if you had any news about how Jono is doing?'

'He's still alive, so that's something,' Hicksy said. 'And before I left last night, he woke up long enough to complain about being in hospital. He tried making out it was all a fuss over nothing and demanded to go home. Stupid git.'

That bit of news made Wise smile. 'I'll try to see him later.'

'He'd like that, Guv.'

'Okay. I'll see you when you get here.'

'I won't be long,' Hicksy said and ended the call.

Wise put his phone away, imagining Hicksy scrambling to get to work. Wise needed him today. Hicksy was the only one who'd seen the survivor and finding her could change everything — it didn't get much better than a living witness who could identify a killer.

The trouble was, he couldn't send Hicksy out alone to find Katie and there was only one person he could think of that he could spare to go with him. Hannah.

Dear God. Either the pair of them would either end up the best of friends by the end of the day or they'd kill each other.

The door to MIR-One opened and Sarah walked into the incident room. 'Morning, Guv.'

'Hi, Sarah,' Wise replied.

'You're in early.'

'I've got an 8 a.m. with Roberts and Walling.'

'Ah,' Sarah said. Somehow, she conveyed so much with that single short word. None of it good.

Wise gave her a smile. 'You saw the pictures of the four other men who were at Sasha's intervention?'

Sarah walked over. 'Yes, I was the one who put them up. I've not done background checks on them yet though.'

Now Sarah was standing closer to him, he could smell cigarette smoke on her, despite the flowery perfume she always wore. It was no surprise, though. She was as dedicated to smoking as Wise was to working out. No doubt she'd had one or two on the doorstep of the station before coming in. 'Can you get on that first thing?'

'Of course,' Sarah replied. She glanced at her watch. 'They should all be on their way to Brixton nick by now. We had them all picked up this morning from their homes at 6 a.m.'

'Excellent. Can you also look into the minister, too? I want to know everything about him.'

'Did you have any luck getting more help to look through the CCTV?'

Wise looked at his watch. 7:50 a.m. 'I'll find out in a minute when I see the boss.'

'Good luck.'

Wise raised an eyebrow to let her know what he thought of that. Unless Walling had a personality transplant overnight, Wise knew exactly what was going to happen when he went upstairs. Luck had nothing to do with it.

He drank the last of his coffee, regretting he'd not bought a second cup from Luigi's. Then again, going in to see the Chief Super wired on too much caffeine might not be the best idea either.

He threw the empty cup in the bin and smiled to himself. What would his daughter say if she knew how many disposable cups he threw away each day on top of his capsule usage? No doubt she'd give him another lecture about saving the planet.

Unable to delay things any longer, Wise smoothed out his suit, straightened his tie and headed up to Detective Chief Superintendent Walling's office on the top floor of Kennington nick. It was like a different world up there. The walls had been painted in the last decade and someone had hung pictures of Kennington Police Station in nice frames along both sides. Even the floor was clean and highly polished for the senior officers and administrators who had their offices on the fourth floor.

He paused outside Walling's door for a moment, wishing he could be anywhere but there, then knocked.

'Come in,' Walling's voice boomed.

Wise opened the door and entered. Roberts was already sitting in front of Walling's desk. Walling himself was on the other side, his well-fed bulk straining the buttons on his uniform.

'Good morning, sir,' Wise said, smiling. He nodded at Roberts. 'Boss.'

Walling pointed at the empty chair next to Roberts. 'Sit.'

Surprised, Wise did as he was told. Normally, Walling kept him on his feet while lecturing him. Being asked to sit had to be a good sign. He glanced over at Roberts, but her face gave nothing away.

'I understand DCI Roberts told you of my phone call with Michael Theobold yesterday,' Walling said.

'Yes, sir,' Wise said.

'He told me you raided a church and arrested a pastor with no reason to do so.'

'I had reasons, sir.'

'Tell me.'

Walling's calm demeanour had Wise perplexed. Normally, by now, the chief would be red-faced and shouting about Wise's incompetence. He ran over the details of the case, from Springer's murder, Anorak Man and the other cases Brains uncovered, and how that led them to Weybridge.

Walling remained calm as he listened, interrupting only occasionally to ask questions to clarify points. When Wise was finished, he leaned back in his chair and steepled his fingers. There was a pause as Walling seemed to think about what to say. Then he did something very strange, indeed. He smiled. 'Well done, Simon. I think you and your team have done great work on this so far and so quickly.'

'You do?' Roberts said. 'What about the complaints from the solicitor?'

'The man's a prick. I always do my best to avoid him when I'm down at the golf club but, somehow, he thinks I'm his friend. So much so that he thinks it's okay to call me on a Sunday night to complain about one of my officers doing his job. The damn cheek of the man,' Walling said. 'Just make sure you do everything by the book. If you leave even the smallest of loopholes, he'll find it and exploit it.'

'I'll be careful,' Wise said.

'This is your second serial killer in a few months, Simon,' Walling said. 'You impressed the powers-that-be with how well you handled everything last time. It would be good if you could get a quick result on this one as well. Finding that eyewitness is key.'

'Yes, sir.'

Walling gave Wise a nod. 'Good. Keep me informed and don't worry about Theobold. He's all bark and no bite. Terrible golfer too.'

'Okay.' Wise stood up, still slightly unsure of what had just happened. Still, he wouldn't look a gift horse in the mouth. 'Have a good day, sir.'

'I'll walk you down to MIR-One,' Roberts said, also getting to her feet.

Neither spoke until they were on the stairs going down and well out of earshot of anyone.

'Did I imagine that?' Wise asked.

'If you did, then we're having the same delusions,' Roberts replied. 'That was not what I was expecting.'

'It's nice having his support for once.'

'Don't let it go to your head. He'll turn on you in an instant if you make him look bad.'

'I know.' Wise glanced out the window. It was going to be another cold, wet day. 'Did you have any luck getting us any extra bodies?'

'Not yet. Everyone is maxed out. I'll try again today, but I can't promise anything.'

'We could really do with them. Especially now we're a man short.'

They stopped on the landing to the third floor. 'How is Jono?' Roberts asked.

'Holding on for now.'

'That's something, at least,' Roberts said. 'Good luck today. Call me if you have any news.'

Wise left Roberts and headed into MIR-One. Everyone was there, waiting for him. Everyone except Jono, of course. There was a big, empty spot next to Hicksy, who looked even more tired than he normally did.

'Morning, everyone,' Wise said, walking to the front of the room. 'We have a busy day with lots to do and there's just us to do it.' He ran over the events of the previous day, so everyone was up to speed.

'Uniforms are picking up Joseph Moore, Mark Elliot, Neil Hendry, Thomas Kind and Ray Butler,' Sarah said. 'I've done a basic background check on them all, but there's nothing. Not even a parking ticket or a speeding fine amongst the lot of them. They're not on social media either.'

'They probably think Facebook is run by the devil,' Hannah said.

'They might not be wrong about that,' Wise said. 'What about dear Pastor Christopher?'

'He's even more of an enigma,' Sarah said. 'From what I can tell, he doesn't even exist.'

'What do you mean?'

'I can't find anything on Christopher Bartholomew. No driving licence, no socials, no criminal records, no debts, no phone. Nothing. The man's a ghost.'

'What about his prints and DNA?' Hannah asked.

'We'll hear about those later today,' Sarah said.

'Good. Maybe there's something there,' Wise said. 'I don't believe in ghosts. People that clean are hiding normally hiding something very dirty. Hannah, call Chaz Boldham. Let's get eyes on the pastor. I don't want him doing a runner.'

Hannah nodded.

'Did you speak to the boss about more help?' Sarah asked. 'We're drowning with all we've got to do.'

'I did, but there's no joy yet. She said everyone is short on resources at the moment. We'll just have to keep struggling on until we get more bodies.'

Donut groaned, but Sarah whacked him on the arm to shut him up. 'You can count on us.'

'I appreciate that,' Wise said. 'Hicksy, I need you to go back to Waterloo and keep looking for this Katie girl. She could be the key to solving all of this.'

'Will do,' Hicksy said.

'Hannah, I want you to go along too,' Wise continued.

Hicksy's mouth fell open. 'It's alright. I can cope on my own. Probably better that way.'

'And what if the girl sees you and does a runner?' Wise said. 'I don't want you to end up in the hospital bed next to Jono because you had to sprint twenty yards.'

'That's not going to happen.'

'I know — because Hannah's going with you.'

'Fucking great,' Hicksy said.

Wise glanced over at Hannah, who didn't look too happy either.

'Katie is our best hope of identifying Anorak Man,' Wise said. 'Finding her is the most important action we have today. That's why I want you both on this. We can't afford to lose her a second time.'

'That was hardly our fault,' Hicksy muttered.

'No one said it was. But the next time will be — so let's make sure it doesn't happen,' Wise said. He looked around his team. 'Has anyone got any questions?'

No one said anything. Wise clapped his hands together. 'Right. Let's get cracking! I want to ruin someone's day today.'

## 35

It was a twelve-minute walk to Waterloo station from Kennington. A twelve-minute walk in which Hannah and Hicksy didn't say a word to each other. She'd tried, of course. Hannah had asked how Jono was as they left the nick and got a grunt back. As Hicksy had stomped off, she'd silently called him a wanker, then gone after him.

They reached Waterloo just after 9:30 a.m. It was the tail end of the Monday morning rush hour. The place was still heaving, though, as people scurried about in every direction trying to get wherever they were going. Hannah had read somewhere that over a quarter of a million people used Waterloo station every day. Looking at the crowds now, she reckoned that could be an underestimation. Wise might not like the Tube, but Hannah wasn't much of a commuter herself. She couldn't think of anything worse than dragging her arse out of bed each morning to get a train from Nowhere-On-Thames into London, paying a small fortune to be squashed in like cattle for an hour.

No wonder no one looked happy.

On top of all that, it was the start of another work week with ten days to go before payday and some bloody awful November weather to go with it. It might not have been raining for once, but everything felt damp and uncomfortable and dirty puddles covered the ground.

Of course, on top of all that, Hannah had Hicksy to deal with, so she reckoned she had more reasons than most to feel glum. She still wasn't sure why the governor had asked the two of them to pair up, knowing Hicksy hated her bloody guts.

She glanced over at the neanderthal. His chin was stuck to his chest and his eyes were just dark shadows hidden beneath his scowling monobrow as he marched through the station. His sour mood was obvious to everyone, as the crush of commuters miraculously parted like the Red Sea in front of him.

He hadn't even told her where they were going or what this Katie looked like. All she knew was that she had an obvious scar down her face.

Hannah glanced up at the electronic boards above the platform entrances, with their myriad destinations all across the South of England. Guildford, Oxshot, Milford, Walton, New Malden, Surbiton, Berrylands. It was like a list of locations from *Midsomer Murders*. Places for *Daily Mail* readers to get outraged about pesky foreigners that would never walk down their streets.

Hicksy passed the WH Smith kiosk and headed to the far right corner of the station. There was a sandwich shop full of plastic wrapped meals, chocolate, crisps and soft drinks, a bakers that pretended to be Greggs but wasn't, an off-licence that sold cans of gin and tonic alongside mini bottles of wine and large cans of lager, and a flower shop. The store was empty. Most likely its prime business hours were at the end of the working day, with people grabbing last minute bouquets on their way to romantic dates or to pretend some significant occasion hadn't been forgotten. Now, though, there was only a bored-looking girl behind the till, scrolling through her phone and totally oblivious to anyone and everything around her. She certainly didn't notice Hicksy marching towards her.

'Oi,' he said when he was a foot away from the till.

The girl looked up, surprised at Hicksy's arrival, then fear flashed across her face when she got a good look at the angry man in front of her. 'I can't open the till,' she said. 'My boss has the key and she ain't here.'

'I'm not here to rob you,' Hicksy growled.

The answer didn't put the girl at ease. 'Whatever. I don't want no trouble, man. They don't pay me enough for putting up with any shit.'

Hicksy held up his warrant card. 'I'm police.'

The girl tried not to laugh. 'Fuck off. That's fake, that is.'

Hannah had enough. She came up behind Hicksy, doing her best not to gag at his eighties aftershave, and held up her own ID. 'I know it's hard to believe, luv,' she said, 'but he really is a copper. Me too. I'm Detective Sergeant Markham and we'd like to ask you a couple of quick questions.'

The girl looked from Hannah to Hicksy and back again. 'I ain't done nothing wrong.'

'There's a girl who begs near here,' Hicksy said. 'Katie. She's got a scar.' Hicksy ran a finger down his cheek.

'What's that gotta do with me?' the girl said. 'She's not my mate.'

'Have you seen her today?' Hannah asked.

The girl shook her head. 'Nah — but I ain't been looking, have I?'

'Too busy dealing with all your millions of customers?' Hicksy said.

'It's hard work, alright?' The girl tutted. 'I'd like to see you last two minutes in here.'

The giggle came out of Hannah's mouth before she could stop it. The thought of Hicksy working in a flower shop was too much for her.

Hicksy heard and spun to face her. 'What's so bloody funny?'

Hannah held up both hands. 'Nothing.'

Hicksy turned back to the girl, angrier than before. 'When was the last time you saw her?'

The girl behind the till shrugged. 'I dunno. Last week sometime? I don't work weekends, do I? So maybe Thursday or Friday. She's here most days, though.'

Hicksy fished a crumpled business card out of his raincoat pocket and held it out to the girl. 'You see her, you call me straight away. Got it?'

The girl took the card but didn't look too happy about it. 'I ain't no snitch.'

'We're trying to find the man who hurt her,' Hannah said. 'That's all.'

'Just call me when you see her,' Hicksy said and headed off back into the station.

Hannah gave the girl a smile. 'Thanks.'

The smile she got back was as insincere as they come. The girl then made a point of making sure Hannah saw her drop Hicksy's card in the bin. Bloody wonderful.

'Cheers,' Hannah said and went after Hicksy. He was already twenty yards ahead of her. 'Hey!'

He stopped and turned to face her, face red and eyes black. 'What?'

'Look — I know we're not friends or anything, but we've got a job to do,' Hannah said. 'You ignoring me and charging around looking for agro isn't going to do any of us a favour.'

'Oh, so you're going to tell me how to do my job now?'

'I'm not telling you how to do anything. I just want us to work together as a team.'

Hicksy took a step towards her. 'We are not a team. Not now. Not ever.'

'The governor asked us to work together,' Hannah said, standing her ground. The two of them were of equal height, but Hicksy probably had forty-five kilos on her in weight. 'So can we stop dicking about and find this girl?'

'You think you're so fucking special.'

'No, I don't. I just want to do my job.'

Hicksy stared at her, and Hannah could see him shake as he tried to control the rage within him. For a moment, she thought he might strike her, so she shifted her feet in order to defend herself. Maybe she should've backed off, but she was pissed off, too. She'd had enough of the man's bullshit.

Maybe Hicksy saw something in her eyes because she saw his body visibly unclench. That didn't mean he'd calmed down, though.

'Fine.' Hicksy spat the word out, filling it with enough venom to make a cobra proud. 'You're the boss. What do you want me to do?'

'Christ, Hicksy. Why are you so bloody angry? What have I done to piss you off? Apart from breathing, that is?'

Hicksy shook his head, then rubbed his face. 'You really don't get it, do you?'

'I can't help being black or a woman, if that's what you're getting at,' Hannah said. 'You need to deal with it.'

'It's got nothing to do with that. I'm not a fucking racist or a sexist, no matter what you think.'

'Then what is it? Because you've been giving me shit since the moment I walked through the door.'

'Fuck it,' Hicksy said, waving her comment down. 'I can't be arsed. Let's find this girl and be done with it.'

'You don't get off that easy,' Hannah said. 'Let's clear the air here and now — if you've got the balls to do it.'

'The balls? You don't know the meaning of the word.'

'Yeah? I've met enough dickheads in the Met who seem to love swinging their tiny pricks around in order to feel good about themselves.'

Something odd happened to Hicksy's face when Hannah said that. His mouth twitched once, twice, then she got a glimpse of his yellow teeth, right before he started to laugh. 'Fucking hell. You've got a way with words.'

'Well,' Hannah said. 'I'm glad I amuse you.'

Hicksy took a deep breath. 'Look. It's not you. Not really. It's just ...' He looked around the station, then scratched the stubble on his chin. 'I've been a cop for nearly thirty years, right? Thirty long bloody years. In that time, I've worked my arse off, working my way up through the ranks. I've even done some good work in that time, put some real criminals behind bars and yet ...' Hicksy ground his teeth together as he stewed over what to say next.

'But to the brass, thirty years means nothing except it's a good reason for them to be whispering in my ear that I should start thinking about retiring, right? They want me to be put out to pasture like some knackered old mule. I'm the past, apparently, and people like you ... well, to them, you're the fucking future. Fast tracking your way to get what I had to slog my guts out to achieve. And that ... that is what I don't like. That's what makes my blood boil.'

Hannah nodded, amazed at the man's confession, seeing him perhaps for the first time for who he really was. All Hicksy's huff and puff was just to hide a scared man who didn't know what his place was in the world anymore. 'They can't make you retire, can they?'

'No, but they can make it hard for me to stay. No one my age wants to be told how to suck eggs by someone half their age.'

'I'm sorry. I didn't mean to give that impression ...'

'Whatever.' He sighed. 'We better get on with looking for Katie. How about we do a couple more circuits here, then check downstairs?'

Hannah nodded. 'Sure.'

They set off walking anticlockwise around the station, peering in the shops, then moving out to check out the taxi rank.

'Don't tell anyone any of that,' Hicksy said. 'I've got a reputation to protect.'

Hannah smiled. 'You can count on me. Heaven forbid anyone gets the impression you're human.'

'Anyway, I might take them up on the offer. Get out of the game. Especially if Jono ...' His voice trailed off.

'How is he?' Hannah asked.

'The boss tell you he's got cancer?'

Hannah stopped walking. 'Shit, no. Cancer?'

'Yeah. In his lungs.' Hicksy strolled on, back into the main station.

Hannah had to jog to catch up with him. 'How bad is it?'

'It's fucking cancer. It's bad no matter what.'

'Is that why he's in the hospital now?'

'No. He's got blood clots in his lungs on top of it all. The daft git. He can't just have the one killer disease, could he?'

'You must be worried,' Hannah said.

'Course I am. He's my bloody best mate. Him and me have been through everything together.' Hicksy sniffed. 'That's why I don't know if I want to carry on if he's not around. At least when Jono's around, I can pretend the world's the way it should be. A place where I'm not some dinosaur waiting for the meteor to strike.'

'It doesn't have to be like that,' Hannah said. 'You could change with the times. You know? Not be all Sweeney about everything.'

Hicksy laughed, but there was no joviality in the sound. Just bitterness. 'You don't get it. I don't want to change. It's the rest of the world I want to change. I want it all to go back to the way it was, back to when everything made sense. When I could call a spade a spade, when I didn't have to worry about someone's fucking pronouns or take into consideration someone's feelings when I arrest them.' He turned to look at Hannah. 'Life was good back then. Not shit like it is now.'

'I don't think there's any going back,' Hannah said.

'And that is why I'm always angry.'

Hannah nodded, feeling the man's pain. She'd always known he was a man out of step with the rest of the world, but she'd only thought about in terms of how that affected her. However, she knew only too well what it was like to be in the minority and what it felt like not to fit in. She understood how exhausting that was, how angry it made her.

As Hicksy set off again, she couldn't help but think that the two of them might well be chalk and cheese, but maybe they had something in common after all.

They finished another lap of the station without spotting Katie.

'Check out the Tube?' Hicksy said.

'You said Katie had a dog with her the last time you saw her?' Hannah asked.

'Yeah. A Labrador.'

'Why don't we have a look outside? Maybe she's walking the mutt now rush hour's over or gone to get something to eat before the afternoon crowd comes back?'

Hicksy sniffed. 'Makes sense.'

They walked past the escalators to the underground and headed out of Victory Arch into the cold and damp outside. Stairs led straight down to street level, where crash barriers had been set up to stop any cars from mounting the pavement. A cruel wind came off the Thames and Hannah zipped her jacket up to the neck once more.

Hicksy rubbed his hands together. 'Talk about brass monkeys.'

But Hannah had forgotten about the cold. She was staring at a girl in a beaten-up parka standing at the bottom of the steps, a white scar ran down her left cheek from the top of her forehead to her jawline. Her Labrador was beside her, on a lead made from a bit of old rope.

Hannah tapped Hicksy on the arm. 'That's Katie, right?'

Hearing her name, the girl looked up, clocked Hannah and Hicksy, and that was that. She was off like the clappers, running along Cab Road towards York Road, her dog bounding alongside her.

'Shit,' Hannah said and then she was off too, down the steps two at a time, wishing she'd worn trainers instead of her biker boots. She couldn't let Katie get away.

## 36

Wise was back at Brixton Police Station in an interview room. Brains was beside him and, looking very sad for himself, Joseph Moore was in the hot seat opposite. His solicitor wasn't from some fancy practice in the city, though. Instead, he had a legal aid brief next to him, called Charmaine Miller. She was a stocky lady who looked utterly bored with being there.

Moore looked very different from when Wise had last seen him leaving his church on Sunday. Then he'd been immaculately turned out. Now, his hair was dishevelled, his shirt was crumpled and he couldn't stop twitching in his seat as he looked all wide-eyed from Wise to Brains and back again. In short, he looked like someone who'd been dragged out of his bed by the police in the early hours and was absolutely terrified with the predicament he found himself in.

The other four church elders were also in Brixton, in individual holding cells, unable to talk to each other, and waiting their own turn with Wise.

'This is all a mistake,' Moore said. 'A mistake.'

'That's good to hear,' Wise said. 'The sooner we can clear everything up, the sooner we can get you home.'

'Thank you. Thank you,' Moore replied with a nervous smile.

'Now, you're Sasha's stepfather — not her father?' Wise asked.

'That's right. Her biological father died when she was three years old in a car crash. Naomi started attending our church shortly after that and I was introduced to her one Sunday.'

'Who by?'

'The head of church at the time. Pastor Alexander. He's moved to a different church now.'

'That was kind of him to connect you both.'

'The church likes to do that. They prefer us to meet people who share our faith and beliefs.'

'So, it was an arranged marriage, in a way?'

'I like to think of it more like match-making,' Moore said.

'How long after that were you both married?' Wise asked.

'Er ... about three months.'

'That was quick.'

Moore dropped his head. 'It felt right to us.'

'And how did you feel about being a father to Sasha?'

He looked up, tried a smile. 'I felt blessed. She was a lovely girl. I was honoured that God chose me to be her father.'

'And how did she feel about you being her stepfather?'

'Good. Good. She was so young when she lost her father that she didn't really understand what was happening. In the end, I'm the only father she's ever really known.'

Wise nodded, giving Moore his entire attention. 'And when did things start going wrong?'

'When she was fourteen, turning fifteen,' Moore replied. 'It was small things at first. Arguing with her mother, not wanting to go to church, trying to wear clothes that weren't appropriate. The more we tried to get her to behave as she should, the more she pushed back.'

'And when did you think she'd been possessed by a demon?' Wise asked.

Moore's solicitor looked up for the first time, suddenly interested in the conversation now demons had been mentioned.

'After about six months of things getting worse and worse, we spoke to Pastor Christopher about Sasha's behaviour, asking for his advice,' Moore said. 'He visited our house, saw Sasha and immediately realised what had happened.'

'That Sasha had been possessed?' Wise clarified.

'Yes. That's right.'

Moore's brief was listening open-mouthed, not even trying to hide her shock at what was being said. Wise wasn't sure how much help she was going to be to her client, but that wasn't his problem. He pushed on. 'What did you do next?'

'Pastor Christopher prayed over her, commanding the demon to leave her body,' Moore said. 'We thought that would be enough, but after a few days, Sasha was worse than ever.'

'In what way?'

'She snuck out of the house to who knows where and came back drunk. She was vaping, wearing make-up — that sort of stuff.'

'Was this when you held the intervention?'

Moore shifted in his seat. 'Pastor Christopher told us it was the only way to save her.'

'And you believed him?' Wise asked.

'Of course,' Moore replied, his voice soft, almost child-like. He had none of the bluster or confidence of the previous day. 'He guides every part of our lives.'

'How did Sasha feel about this?'

'She was no longer in control of herself. The demon had her in its grip and it fought against us. That's why we called in the others to help.'

'The others?'

'The church elders.'

Moore nodded. 'That's right.'

'When you said they helped, what did they do?'

'They just helped carry her into the church van and kept her restrained until we got to the church, where she could be secured.'

'Just to clarify what you're saying: the six of you physically carried Sasha into a van, held her down while you drove her to the church and then secured her by chaining her to the cross in the padded room we found.'

Moore's eyes widened. 'It sounds awful when you say it like that. You have to remember we were dealing with a demon, a monster who would've quite happily hurt all of us, hurt Sasha. We did it to keep everyone safe.' There was a shrill to the man's voice. Again, Wise was reminded of a child trying to justify their actions.

'What happened then?' Wise asked, keeping his own voice calm and understanding.

'We're not supposed to talk about it outside the church,' Moore said.

'I understand that,' Wise said. 'But you're all in a lot of trouble at the moment, and keeping quiet isn't helping anyone.' He glanced at the brief, expecting her to interject, but she kept quiet.

'Well, once the demon was secured, we left Pastor Christopher to deal with it. He said it wasn't safe for us to witness what happened next.'

Wise straightened up. 'You weren't in the room with her?'

'No.'

'And neither were the others?'

'No.'

'So where were you?'

'We were just outside. Waiting. Pastor Christopher said I could go home, but I wanted to be there when Sasha was freed from the demon's possession. I couldn't leave her.'

'How long was Pastor Christopher alone with her?' Wise asked.

'About two hours,' Moore replied.

'And you weren't worried? You weren't concerned about what was going on in the room?'

'Of course, I was — especially when I heard the screams,' Moore said.

'The screams?'

'Yes, the screams. But I was told it was quite normal as the demon is removed from the body.' Moore shifted again in his seat as he tugged at his shirt sleeves. 'I wasn't happy about it. Obviously my daughter was in pain, but I knew we were doing what was best for her.'

'And afterwards, when Sasha told her mother she'd been assaulted? Did it still feel like you'd done the best for her?'

'I was heartbroken that the demon was still in her, and that everything we'd done had failed,' Moore said, looking up.

'And you didn't think for a minute that she might've been telling the truth?'

'No. Of course not. Pastor Christopher was as upset as I was when we told him. He said that we would just have to try again to cast out the demon.'

Wise couldn't believe his ears. 'You were planning on submitting your daughter to that ordeal again?'

'It was for her own good,' Moore cried.

'Did Sasha know this?'

'We told the demon.'

Wise shook his head. 'No wonder she ran away.'

'The demon made her do it,' Moore said. Tears formed in the corner of his eyes.

'When my officers visited you and your wife on Saturday, you told them you reported Sasha missing to the police,' Wise said. 'But no such report was made. Why was that?'

The man genuinely looked confused by the question. 'But we did. Naomi went with Pastor Christopher to do it.'

'No, they didn't.'

'But that's impossible.'

'It would appear that they lied to you, Mr Moore,' Wise said. 'About a great many things.' He glanced over at Brains and gave him a nod.

'Interview terminated at 1005,' Brains said and turned off the tape.

Wise and Brains both stood up. 'We'll speak to you again shortly, Mr Moore,' Wise said. 'In the meantime, someone will take you back to your cell.'

'But I've not done anything. I loved Sasha,' Moore cried.

Wise looked down at the wretch of the man. 'You had a funny way of showing it.'

Wise and Brains left the interview room. 'That was something,' Brains said.

'It contradicted everything Pastor Christopher told us,' Wise replied. 'He claimed he was never left alone with the girl.'

'Do you believe Moore?'

Wise glanced back at the closed interview room door. 'I do actually.' He pulled out his phone and called Sarah back at MIR-One. She answered after two rings.

'Yes?'

'Any news on the pastor yet?'

'I was just chasing everyone. They promised to get us his results in the next half hour,' Sarah said.

'Let me know the moment you hear,' Wise said. 'Pastor Christopher is key to everything.'

# 37

'Oi! Stop!' Hannah yelled as she ran after the girl in the parka. 'Stop!'

God only knew if Katie heard her. She certainly didn't heed her. She sprinted down Yorke Road like she was being chased by the devil himself, her Labrador easily keeping pace beside her.

And, of course, there wasn't a single member of the watching public interested in helping Hannah out. They just gawped at the foot race and a few got their phones out, no doubt hoping to film something to put on Instagram.

Hannah glanced back over her shoulder, but there was no sign of Hicksy following. Not that she expected he'd join in a footrace.

No, Hannah was on her bloody own. And there'd be no one to blame but her if Katie got away.

There was a blare of a horn up ahead as Katie cut across Yorke Road and headed onto Chicheley Road. Hannah followed, just avoiding getting smeared by a black cab on one side, then had to pause while a double-decker went past in the other direction.

'Come on,' she urged, bouncing on her toes as each second seemed to last an hour. Then the bus was past and Hannah sprinted into the gap, not looking at what else might be heading towards her along the road. She got a blast of a horn herself, so close it left her ears ringing, but then she was on Chicheley Road.

Katie was nearly at the end of the street, the London Eye looming high above her. Hannah dug deep, found another burst of speed from somewhere, her boots pounding the concrete as her arms pumped back and forth.

She'd always been a runner. When she was younger, she'd excelled at long distances, but she'd never been known for speed. And, since she joined the Met, running was something she did on a very rare occasion. So now, she was slow and out of practice. Just when she needed to be at her best. Shit. She couldn't let Katie get away again again.

She had to catch Katie.

'Stop! Police!' she called out again for all the good it did her. Christ, she hoped no one was filming this. She didn't need some twat playing her humiliation over and over again for cheap laughs back at Kennington.

Up ahead, Katie and her dog cut across Belvedere Road and into the park. Was she slowing, though? Or was that wishful thinking on Hannah's part?

Hannah ran on, eyes locked on the girl and her dog. Wise had thought Katie would run, that's why he'd asked Hannah to go with Hicksy. She couldn't let him down.

The path curved through Jubilee Gardens but Hannah raced across the grass, past the barren trees, doing anything to gain another yard, another inch on Katie and slowly, oh so ever so slowly, she could see she was closing in on the girl.

Katie looked back, her scar vivid down her face, eyes wide with fear. She saw Hannah still in pursuit, but that meant she didn't see the cyclist crossing her path in front of her.

They collided with an all-mighty crash; cyclist, Katie and her dog all going down in one big heap. The dog was up first, barking madly, pulling against its lead still entangled. The cyclist was up next; a messenger in winter Lycra all torn across his knees. He shouted and cursed at Katie as he hauled his mangled bike off her, telling her he was going to call the police, get her arrested, the stupid, blind twat.

'Enough!' Hannah said when she reached them, grateful the chase was over. 'It wasn't her fault.'

'Fuck off and mind your business,' the man said. He reached into a bum bag he had strapped across his chest and pulled out a phone. 'I'm calling the police.'

'I heard you the first time,' Hannah replied and showed him her warrant card. 'Now, you fuck off.'

The man did a double take at the card, then the message sunk in and he stormed off, dragging his mangled bike with him.

Hannah looked down at Katie, still flat on her back. 'You okay, luv?'

The girl said nothing as her Labrador rushed over. Katie put her arms around the dog protectively.

'I'm sorry if I scared you earlier,' Hannah said, 'but I need your help.'

'What do you want?' Katie said, still not moving.

Hannah stuck out a hand. 'Here, let me help you up.'

Katie stared at it as if it held handcuffs, then reluctantly reached up and took it. Hannah helped her to her feet, smiling as she did so. Up close, it was obvious that, despite the big parka, Katie was a petite thing, maybe no more than five feet two in height. 'You're not arresting me?'

'I just want to find the man who gave you that scar,' Hannah said. 'And I'm hoping you can help me.'

Her eyes lit up then. 'Seriously?'

'Yeah. Seriously.'

Ten minutes later, they were sitting on a bench overlooking the Thames, with cups of tea in their hands and the Labrador curled up by their feet. Hannah had called Hicksy and told them where he could find them. When she spotted his hunched hulk lumbering towards them, she pointed him out to Katie. 'This is my colleague now. He's a bit of a grump, but he's okay, really.'

'Alright, Katie,' Hicksy said once he reached them. He nodded at their teas. 'Don't suppose you got me one?'

Hannah picked up a cup from beside the bench and offered it to Hicksy. 'Should be perfect drinking temperature now.'

'Lovely,' he said, taking it. He plucked the plastic lid off and took a gulp. 'Ah. I needed that.'

'Now we're all here, Katie, we wanted to talk to you about how you got your scar,' Hannah said.

Katie took a sip of her tea and Hannah could see her hand shake. 'It was a man.'

'When was this, Katie?' Hicksy asked, sounding surprisingly gentle.

'Last summer,' Katie replied. 'He came up to me when I was begging over in Covent Garden. Said he'd give me a hundred quid if I played a game with him.'

Hannah exchanged looks with Hicksy, a part of her very happy she'd got that guess right. 'A game?'

'Yeah.' Katie took another mouthful of tea. 'He said all I had to do was avoid him for twenty-four hours and he'd give me another hundred the next day — except if he caught me, he said he'd hurt me. For two hundred quid, though, I thought I'd take my chances.'

'What did you do?'

'I fucking legged it, didn't I? I reckoned I'd lose him Chinatown way no matter how fast he was. I mean, you seen me run, right? And I didn't have Maybell with me neither.'

'Maybell?' Hannah asked.

Katie pointed at the dog. 'Maybell.'

'Nice name,' Hicksy said. 'Where did he catch you, then?'

'Down Leicester Court,' Katie replied. 'Turns out I'm not as fast as I thought I was. Anyways, the bastard had gotten in front of me somehow and comes out of this doorway with this big fucking knife. I put my arm up and knocked him, but he still cut me. I was screaming my heart out 'cause I thought I was done for, right? But these blokes come out of the gay bar on the corner. Big blokes, they were. Built like the Hulk. Well, the bastard sees them and scarpers.'

Hannah squeezed her arm. 'Lucky for you.'

'Sometimes it doesn't feel like it,' Katie said. 'Luckily, I don't look in the mirror that often.'

'If I showed you some pictures, do you think you'd recognise this bastard?' Hicksy said.

'Yeah. Easily. I'll never forget his face. Especially his eyes.'

'What about his eyes?'

'They were cold and cruel. Like he was dead inside.'

Hicksy got out the pictures from his pocket. He started with the elders first: Mark Elliot, Neil Hendry, Thomas Kind and Ray Butler.

'No. No. No. No,' Katie said to each one.

Joseph Moore's picture was next. Katie hesitated over that one but said no to that too, in the end.

Then came the pastor's picture, and Katie visibly flinched when she saw it. She stared at the man's face, good and hard, then relaxed. 'No, it's not him. I thought it was, but the man who attacked me had a mangled nose. Maybe it'd been broken at some point.'

Hannah's mouth fell open. 'What did you say?'

# 38

The man looked up as his phone rang, saw the name on the screen and shook his head. It was Christopher. Again. The pastor had been trying to get in touch ever since he'd got home from the police station the night before, but the man hadn't bothered answering any of them. He was in no mood to put up with Christopher's panic attacks. It wasn't as if he'd had a particularly good day himself. Still, he couldn't put it off any longer. Sooner or later, his wife would notice and she'd ask why he wasn't answering Christopher's calls.

'Morning,' he said on answering.

'What have you been doing?' The man could hear the panic in Christopher's voice over the telephone. 'What have you done?'

'Wait a minute.' He walked over and closed the dining-room door that he'd used as his office since Covid. He didn't need his wife hearing any of this. She was in the kitchen nearby, faffing around. 'What are you talking about?'

'The police told me seven people have been murdered,' Christopher said.

'And?'

'It was you. You killed them all.'

The man looked around the room. The highly polished wooden table that his wife barely ever let him eat at, the drinks cabinet that she hated him making use of, the sideboard with its pictures of a fake happy life. 'Don't ask what you don't want to know.'

'But why? You promised you'd not do it again.'

'And you promised you'd keep your cock in your pants.' That made Christopher shut up, and the man smiled. Everyone had their weaknesses. Even high and mighty pastors. 'You have your games. I have mine.'

'But we agreed it was only to be Sasha.'

'Well, it wasn't.' How could it be? It felt so good to kill someone. He loved that power.

'But seven people?'

Seven, but it could've been so many more. Plenty had gotten away. That's why he loved the game. Everyone had a chance to win. 'What do you want me to say?'

'That you didn't do it?'

'Grow up, Christopher. When you begged me to find the girl, you knew what I was going to do — what you wanted me to do. You didn't care about her. Why care about the others? They were nobodies. Human waste left to rot. I did them a favour, setting them free from their misery.'

'But if you'd just done what we agreed, I wouldn't have police officers sitting outside my house watching me. For God's sake, they arrested Sasha's father this morning and the others.'

That wasn't good news — but not unexpected after yesterday. He rubbed his jaw, feeling the bruise. 'Will they talk?'

Christopher sighed. 'Who knows? I've sent our solicitor to deal with it. Hopefully, they'll keep quiet until he gets there.'

'What could they say anyway? Did they see you having your way with the girl?'

'No.'

'So stop worrying. Keep spouting your claptrap to the faithful and keep taking their money in return. This will blow over.'

'How can you say that?'

'Because it will. In fact, this might actually help us,' the man said. 'It could be a good thing.'

'How? How can that remotely be possible?'

'They're looking for Sasha's killer,' the man said. 'If someone else was to die today, when they have the others in custody and you under observation ... Well, that would prove your innocence, wouldn't it?'

'You can't be serious,' Christopher said.

'I am. Very.'

'No. Don't do anything. You're right. We can wait this out. The police have nothing to tie us to anything. Don't kill anyone.'

The man laughed. For a supposed man of God, Christopher had such little faith. 'Trust me.'

'Please, I'm begging you.'

'Like you did after you raped Sasha?'

'That was a mistake. I was weak. The devil took me for a moment.'

The man laughed. 'Sometimes, I actually think you believe that claptrap you spout.'

'I do.'

'Do me a favour. Because those idiots down at your church might not know who you really are, but I do. I know you only too well. You're still the lad that I grew up with. I was there when you raped Mary Adams. I was there when she started screaming about calling the police.'

'And I was there when you caved her head in with a brick,' Christopher said.

'It made the problem go away, didn't it? No one got arrested. You got to be a pastor,' the man said.

'And I've been paying you back ever since!'

'You've given me jobs and I'm grateful for that.' He looked around his dining room, bought on money earned working for Christopher and realised how much he much he didn't want any of it. How much he hated it all. 'Anyway, leave it with me. I'll sort it — like always.'

'George, no. Don't—'

George didn't hear the rest. He'd disconnected the call.

He didn't need to hear any more of his brother's bleating. Christopher had always been weak.

George, though? He'd always known he was the strong one. Sometimes, when he let his brother's nonsense get in his head, he thought he was The Chosen One. A god on earth, with the power of life and death in his hands. But, deep down, he knew it was just a game. The only game.

He walked over to the drinks cabinet and reached up, feeling around on the top of it until he touched the kukri's scabbard. He smiled as he brought it down from its hiding place. God, how he loved it.

He went back to the table, sat down, and partly unsheathed the knife. The machete-like weapon was eighteen inches and as sharp as the day it had been given to his father, back when he'd been an officer in the Royal Gurkha Rifles.

He still remembered the first thing he'd killed with it, a black cat in Singapore when his father had been stationed there. He'd given it food for a few days until it trusted him enough to snuggle up close. Close enough to cut its throat. There was no going back after that. He'd only stopped when people had noticed that too many pets were going missing. Stopped for a few months until he couldn't put it off any longer. After that, it was a treat he gave himself every six months, no matter what country they were in.

Then along came Mary. She was the daughter of another officer of another regiment stationed in Germany. Christopher had fallen for her the moment he set eyes on her. Embarrassingly so. He followed her around with his tongue hanging out, bought her flowers and left her notes. Unfortunately, Mary thought he was just some dumb kid to lead along, enjoying the attention but wanting no more than that.

A complete and utter prick tease.

It was no wonder Christopher raped her. In fact, George had never been more proud of his brother as he had then. For the first time, he'd stood up for himself.

Of course, Christopher had to ruin it all by getting scared. Worrying about prison. Worrying about God.

One good brick had put an end to that problem, though. It hadn't been as much fun as using the kukri, but it had been better than killing a cat. Much better. Of course, if he'd known that his brother was going to become a pastor to repent for his actions, he might've put a brick in his head as well. Then again, Christopher's piousness had paid for George's lifestyle and enabled his habit, so it wasn't all bad.

George thought about the people he'd killed since then, in all the different countries. Once he was living back in the UK, George picked his holidays around where he wanted to kill in the same way others picked places to sunbathe. Using everything from his hands to ropes to knives to do the deed. Anything that would get the job done. Anything but the kukri, the very thing he most wanted to use.

Sometimes, it had gone wrong. He'd got his nose busted in Benidorm by some tramp's boyfriend who'd come out of nowhere. He'd nearly been caught by the police in Stockholm. They were warnings to be more careful. But not to stop.

George had killed no one in Britain before, though. Not until his brother had come crying about Sasha. How he'd been weak again. Ruined everything with his little prick, his dirty desires. How he'd damned his soul, blah blah blah.

Of course, George had been happy to take care of it. More than happy. Especially since he had an opportunity to use the kukri again.

He'd never thought of killing homeless people before, but killing Sasha opened his eyes. No one cared about them. No one investigated them. In fact, it was almost too easy killing them.

That's why he'd invented the game. That made it even more fun.

And now, he could do it all over again. He'd make the next one big and splashy too. Impossible to ignore. A real statement. The police would have to let everyone go once he was finished. All their suspects would have perfect alibis after all.

George smiled. God did, indeed, move in mysterious ways.

## 39

His mouth dry and his heart racing, DCI Chaz Boldham sped towards York Road, where George Samuel Bartholomew lived with his wife. He was following an Armed Response van, full of suited and booted officers ready for any sort of trouble.

It'd been painful waiting for the AROs to get organised after he'd received the arrest orders from Wise and his team. The way he saw things, though, it was better to turn up over-prepared to arrest Bartholomew than arrive on his doorstep unequipped to deal with what they may find. If the man had killed seven people with a Gurkha knife, then there was no telling what he might do when the police came to arrest him. Boldham, for one, was in no hurry to get killed for the sake of the job. He might have a stab-proof vest on under his leather jacket, but would it stop a kukri knife from opening his guts up? He'd rather the AROs shot Bartholomew instead of putting his own equipment to the test.

DS Andrew Chapman, in the passenger seat next to him, put away his phone. 'The vicar's been picked up and is on his way to Brixton. Apparently, he wasn't too happy about it.'

'First off, he's a pastor, not a vicar. Don't ask me the difference because I don't know and I don't care. Secondly, sod his happiness,' Boldham replied. 'He can lodge a complaint with God for all I care. If half of what the London lot said is true, he deserves everything coming his way.'

'I still can't believe we're going to arrest a serial killer,' Chapman replied. 'It's like something out of a movie. Stuff like this shouldn't happen in Surrey.'

'Well, apparently, it does. Let's just hope we get him without any problems,' Boldham said, trying to unclench his jaw. 'The big bosses won't be happy when they know we had him in our cells yesterday and I just let him go with just a ticking off.' Boldham could see his bloody career sailing off into the sunset if Bartholomew got away. There was no way they could let that happen.

'They can't blame you,' Chapman said. 'You didn't know. None of us did. And it wasn't as if he really beat up that DI. In fact, from what I heard, Bartholomew had more of a case to file an assault charge against the big fella for smacking him in the face.'

'You know what the Top Brass are like — they're great at pointing fingers. Still—' A squawk from the radio receivers in their ears cut him off.

'Approaching target house,' an ARO said over the airwaves. 'Preparing to stop.'

York Road was another of Weybridge's many residential streets. Houses hidden behind large bushes, brick walls and fences, lined on both sides of the road. Bartholomew lived about two-thirds of the way down on the left. They'd checked the house out on Google Maps, as well as finding pictures of its interior on a property website. It was a five-bedroom property with three bathrooms, a living room, kitchen, dining room, utility room, and breakfast room — whatever the hell that was. It was the sort of place Boldham's wife would love to live in if only she'd married a stockbroker instead of a copper, as she so often reminded him. Once she'd made comments like that as a joke, but he'd noticed these days, the jokes had an added sharpness to them and an undercurrent of bitterness that never seemed to fade. Sometimes, he felt like he lived with a hostile flatmate rather than the love of his life, arguing over bills and whether he went out too much. The irony wasn't lost on him that, if she nagged him less, he'd stay in more. Even facing down a dangerous serial killer was more appealing than getting his wife's death stares.

Boldham stopped his car just behind the ARO van that had blocked off one half of York Road. A dozen yards on, another van full of uniforms had the other half cut off. Thankfully, the high hedges would hide the vehicles from the target's house and keep their approach as covert as possible.

'Here we go,' Boldham said, unbuckling his seat belt. 'Showtime.' He regretted saying that the moment it came out of his mouth. It made him sound like some stupid American cop show wannabe, but he was nervous and he always talked bollocks when he was nervous. And he was more than nervous. In fact, the correct term was shitting it.

He and Chapman got out the car and walked over to the ARO in charge. He was a brute of a man, all decked out in a black jumpsuit, body armour and helmet. The sight of him made Boldham feel even more of a wimp.

'Alright, Chaz?' the officer said. 'You still happy to do the knocking and get the wife out of there?'

Boldham zipped up his leather jacket so the stab vest wasn't visible and to give his hands something to do. He certainly didn't want anyone to see them shaking. 'Yeah. I'll knock, the wife opens the door, I grab her and then you steam in.'

'That's the plan,' the ARO replied. 'And I've got a team in situ around the back, in case the suspect does a runner.'

'What if the suspect opens the door?' Chapman asked.

'Apparently opening doors is women's work,' Boldham said again, a bit tetchier than he'd liked. God, he needed to pee, even though he'd been just before he'd left the station and he'd not had a drop to drink since then. It was his nerves. He knew that and didn't like it. Not one bit. He clapped his hands. 'Come on, then. Let's get it done.'

Inwardly, he groaned. He was turning into a walking cliche. He shuffled his feet and tried to shake the nerves away with no one noticing that was what he was doing.

'Is the DCI's mic working?' the ARO asked into his own radio.

'Loud and clear,' an operator replied in all their ears.

'Okay. Do it by the numbers. If, at any point, you feel something's off or you feel unsafe, just say you've knocked at the wrong address and walk away. The moment you're clear, we'll go in hard,' the ARO said.

'I know what to do,' Boldham said.

The ARO nodded. 'Is everyone in position?' he asked over the radio.

'Team One White in position,' a voice crackled back.

'Team Two Black in position,' another replied.

'Any movement?' the commander asked.

'White all quiet.'

'Black all quiet.'

The ARO looked at Boldham. 'It's all yours.'

Boldham took a deep breath and set off towards the house. The White team was in position. Two AROs, hidden by bushes, were on either side of the entrance to the property, crouched and ready to pounce, Heckler & Koch MP5 submachine guns in their hands. The weapons could fire up to 800 rounds a minute and were more than capable of ripping a knife-wielding maniac to shreds. Plus, they had Glock semi-automatic pistols holstered on their hips for even more firepower.

However, seeing their heavy kit only made Boldham feel even more empty-handed and exposed as he stepped onto Bartholomew's driveway.

The stone gravel crunched underfoot. Dark windows, surrounded by red brick walls, stared back. He scanned them all as he made his way to the white front door, looking for any sign of movement. It was unnecessary, of course. The AROs already had them all under observation and would've warned him of danger long before he had any idea it existed. Even so, he couldn't help himself.

*Be calm*, he told himself. *Act natural.*

*Don't get yourself killed.*

He thought about his wife ripping him apart when he left for work that morning, even though he couldn't remember what she was pissed off about. Why couldn't they have said something nice to each other, like they used to? He didn't want a stupid row to be the last thing they said to each other if he got killed. Why hadn't he called her to tell her he loved her before he went off doing his Billy Big Boots impression?

*Get your mind on the job.*

*Breathe.*

The twenty yards to the front door took at least a year off his life, but he reached it in the end and, with another deep breath and a clench of his bowls, Boldham rang the bell.

It chimed through the interior, so loud it almost made him jump. Shit.

'Coming,' a woman's voice called out. Boldham listened to her footsteps approach, happy that it was the wife answering and not Bartholomew himself. It was true then, what they'd heard. Opening doors was women's work. He could just imagine his own wife agreeing to that bullshit.

The door swung open and a middle-aged woman, wearing a white apron over a long, floor length floral dress. 'Hello,' she said with a smile.

Boldham held up his warrant card. 'I'm Detective Chief Inspector Chaz Boldham,' he said quietly. 'Can you step out of the house, please?' As he said it, he reached for her arm and half-pulled her out of the doorway. He was nice about it. He certainly wasn't gentle. But that was his brief. His job. *Get her out of the way.*

'What's going on?' the woman cried, stumbling towards him. Boldham could hear the AROs storming up the drive behind him. Curling his other arm around her, Boldham turned Mrs Bartholomew towards the road and frogmarched her to safety.

'ARMED POLICE! ARMED POLICE!' the officers screamed as they entered the house. 'ARMED POLICE! ARMED POLICE!'

'What's going on?' the woman said as Boldham bundled her back towards the street. 'Let go of me.' She tried to tug her arm free and slip from Boldham's grasp, but he was having none of it. He knew he must be hurting her, but he didn't care. He wanted to get them both away from that house, especially if the AROs had to open fire. Boldham fixed his eyes on the gap between the bushes, the safety of the road. There was no stopping, no going back.

'We've come to arrest your husband, Mrs Bartholomew,' Boldham said, trying to ignore the calls going back and forth over the radio in his ear. Trying to sound like he was in charge.

'No change! No change!' someone shouted over the radio. 'No change! No change!'

'My husband?' her eyes darting around the street, at the vehicles and officers so out of place in the quiet neighbourhood. 'But he's not here.'

Boldham stopped halfway to his car. 'What do you mean? Where is he?'

'George has gone up to London,' Mrs Bartholomew. 'He's doing some charity work there. He helps the homeless.'

'How long ago?' Boldham asked, feeling he wanted to puke.

'About an hour or so.'

He looked around the once quiet street, at all the vehicles and officers so out of place, the army he'd summoned to catch a man who wasn't there.

Bugger.

Boldham dug out his phone, found Wise's number, and hit dial.

'Detective Inspector Wise,' the voice said in his ear.

Boldham took a deep breath. 'It's Chaz from Woking. I've got bad news, I'm afraid.'

# 40

Wise bounded out of Brixton nick with his phone clamped to his ear and yammering instructions, cursing the fact nothing had gone to plan. But when did it ever? Brains was on his tail, fixing a radio receiver into his ear. They had to get to Waterloo Station as quick as they could.

'Take Donut and Callum over to the Force Control Room. Watch the CCTV in real time. I want to know the moment you spot him,' Wise said as he ran to the squad car, its blue lights already flashing. 'Bartholomew was on the 2:45 train from Weybridge. It arrives at Waterloo in fifteen minutes.'

'We're on our way now,' Sarah replied. There were three Control Rooms in London, where officers watched the feeds from all the millions of CCTV cameras across the capital. Sarah and her team could focus their attention on the train station. If, somehow, Bartholomew slipped past the officers on the ground, they could track him and guide Wise and the others to him. 'I've already passed his details on everywhere. We've got confirmation from Surrey that he got on the train. They spotted him on the station CCTV. He's wearing his Sports Direct baseball cap, green anorak and has a small backpack. We've got also officers at every station from Weybridge to Waterloo in case he gets off early. The whole Met is looking for him.'

'Good,' Wise said, yanking the door open to the passenger seat. That was something, at least. 'Brains and I are on our way to Waterloo. Keep me informed.'

'We'll get him,' Sarah said.

'We better.' Wise disconnected the call and slammed his door shut. Once Brains was in the back, their driver accelerated out of the car park and onto Gresham Road. Waterloo was fifteen minutes away, but, with the blues and twos going, Wise hoped they'd make it in less than ten. They had to get to the bloody station before Bartholomew arrived. He didn't want to think what would happen if they didn't.

At least the driver knew what she was doing, taking a hard left onto Brixton Road, then bouncing right onto the Stockwell Road, moving fast. 'It's a straight shot up to Waterloo,' she said, swerving around a double decker. 'I just need everyone to stay out of our way.'

'Just get us there,' Wise said through gritted teeth. 'As fast as you can.'

'Do you think he's onto us?' Brains said from the back as he handed Wise an earpiece.

'I don't think so,' Wise replied. 'Boldham said he hadn't taken anything with him. His passport was at the house, his clothes. His wife said he was acting normal.'

'What's he doing then?' Brains said.

'Maybe he's hunting.' Wise fitted the receiver into his ear and immediately heard the chatter over the airwaves. 'Maybe he really is helping out with a charity.'

'You don't really think that, do you?'

'No. No, I don't.' What copper's instincts he had were screaming at him that someone would die if they didn't catch Bartholomew in time.

The driver accelerated through the tightest of gaps down the centre of the road as cars, trucks, and taxis pulled over to the side. A skate park covered in graffiti flashed by on the right as they raced up the Stockwell Road. Pedestrians rubbernecked at them as the car sped past. Wise stared straight ahead, trying to will the road to clear in front of them, eager to see the station, eager to be on the ground.

Then the driver slammed on the brakes and yanked the steering wheel to the left to avoid a messenger on a bike. The man must've either been either deaf and not heard the sirens, or just plain dumb because he'd seen the break in the traffic as an opportunity to gain a few extra yards.

'Twat,' the driver cursed as she passed him, slamming her foot down once more.

Wise checked the time. 2:36. 'We need to go faster.'

'I know, but I'm not killing anyone in the process,' the driver said.

They reached the A3, and she took a hard right. The car squeezed through a gap between a central reservation and a bus, making a few people jump in the process as the tires protested under pressure. It was a left after that, onto the South Lambeth Road. They passed terraced houses worth several million each and council houses that looked fit for demolition.

'Guv,' Hannah said in his ear. 'Me and Hicksy are here. Train's coming in at Platform Three. We've got a dozen uniforms with us too.'

'Spread them down the platform and then get some on the train when it arrives. I don't want him hiding in the toilets to avoid us. Rip the train apart if you have to,' Wise said.

'How far out are you?' Hannah asked.

'Maybe seven or eight minutes.'

'That's cutting it close.'

'I know.'

'I'll see you when I see you.'

More homes whizzed past as they charged up the South Lambeth Road. Ahead, he could see the skyscrapers of the South Bank loom above the rooftops, still too far away. They passed Vauxhall Park and turned left onto Parry Street. Then they were on the Embankment, passing Vauxhall Station.

It was a straight run now to Waterloo. Wise checked the time.

2:42.

They weren't going to make it in time.

# 41

Despite everything, George was feeling good as he watched the world trundle past. Feeling excited. There was a part of him that knew what he was doing wasn't right. That, perhaps, there was something wrong with him. But he really didn't care.

Asking him not to kill would be like asking not to breathe. It was that important to him. That essential.

He looked around at the other passengers on the train. At the fat, grey-haired woman shovelling crisps into her mouth as fast as her chubby fingers could dig them out of the packet. At the girl with the dreadlocks and the sunglasses, who probably thought she was too beautiful to be travelling on a train. At the sad, middle-aged man asleep with his mouth open. George despised them all. He was glad he wasn't like them. Like rats trapped in cages they could never see. Living miserable lives.

They'd never have his strength. Enjoy his power.

He smiled as he imagined their fear if they knew who was sitting near them, if they knew what he had done — what he was going to do.

He slipped his hand into his rucksack and touched the hilt of the kukri knife. Part of him was tempted to pull it out now and just kill everyone around him. Fill the train with their blood. Relish their screams.

Maybe one day he'd do that. Just indulge in one long orgy of murder. The police would get him for sure if he did that. Probably shoot him dead in the process. He read somewhere that they called that 'suicide by cop.' In his mind, that wasn't a bad way to go. Better than growing old and decrepit in some old people's home.

The train pulled into Vauxhall. A few people got on and off. George watched the ebb and flow of the platform. It was quiet, as one would expect for an early Monday afternoon. A mother struggled to get her pram onboard the train and, of course, no one came to help her. Everyone else had their heads down, staring at their phones, ignoring the world. Two uniformed police officers stood watching her, their yellow high-viz jackets popping out against the grey sky behind them.

No matter what country he'd lived in, the police were all the same. Dumb thugs who thought their uniforms gave them power. But how wrong they were. They had no idea what real power was. Not like he did.

Even that brute who'd knocked him down yesterday thought he was something special, but he wasn't. He was just a dog barking at sheep. He'd like to see the detective try to knock him down today, now he had his kukri knife with him. Let Detective Inspector Simon Wise test his big fists against the sharp blade. He'd not be so cocky by the time George had finished with him. Not cocky at all.

The doors hissed shut, and the wheels creaked to life. The train lurched forward, onto its final destination. Waterloo. Then The Game could begin. George could hunt. George could kill.

The perfect Monday.

He watched the platform go past. Saw more hi-viz jackets against the grey sky. More police watching the train leave. Too many police.

George looked back over his shoulder at the platform, counting quickly as the figures became ants in the distance.

There were five or six police officers on the platform. Normally, there were none. There was no need, especially on a Monday afternoon when there were barely any passengers.

A chill ran through him.

Were they looking for him? They had fingerprinted him the day before, taken his picture, along with a swab for DNA. Had that connected him to some past crime? Had he been careless? Had Christopher betrayed him?

He reached inside his coat for his phone and dialled home. He listened to the ringtone go unanswered, despite the fact his wife should've been there. There was only one reason why his wife wouldn't answer. One reason why she wasn't home.

The police were after him.

A wave of emotion swept over him, taking him by surprise. It wasn't fear. It wasn't anger.

It was joy.

This took The Game to a whole new level. It was the ultimate test. He was the prey now. He was the one being hunted.

Well, George was always happy to play The Game. And he always played to win.

A man walked past. He had a black wool watch cap pulled down over his ears and a big, black puffa jacket, perfect for the November weather.

Perfect for George.

He got up and followed the man as he made his way down the aisle. The train wasn't busy and the man in the cap passed empty seat after empty seat. George kept his distance as he trailed after him, feeling the excitement build inside.

The man went through the carriage doors, then stopped. George hesitated for a second, thinking he'd been spotted, but the man pressed the button to open the door to the loos. So that's what he was after.

George smiled. He went through the carriage door himself and stood by the toilets. No one would think twice if they saw him. They'd think he was just waiting to use them himself. He slipped his rucksack off his back and slipped his hand inside, grasping the knife hilt.

A minute passed.

Two minutes. Three.

The toilet flushed.

George readied himself.

The door opened and George stepped forward, hacking the kukri knife into the man's gut. The victim's eyes bulged as George pushed him back into the toilet, following in after.

He reached behind him and pressed the button to close and lock the door.

# 42

Hannah waited on the platform, gazing down the tracks as the train from Weybridge rumbled in. Hicksy was by the exit gates with three uniforms, while the other officers were spaced along the platform like Wise had asked. There was a team of four uniforms at the far end of the platform — Team One — who would board and search the train once it stopped.

Of course, there was no sign of Wise himself yet. That meant the responsibility was on her to spot Bartholomew when he got off the train. Her responsibility to catch him. Her opportunity to fuck it up.

She wriggled her body, trying to find some extra breathing room, despite the stab vest she had on under her jacket. She had a collapsible baton in her pocket too. If you're going up against a man with a knife, it made sense to be prepared. Somehow, she didn't think Bartholomew was going to just put up his hands when they found him.

The train slowed as it pulled into the station. 'Here we go,' she said into her mic. 'Remember, the suspect is wearing a Sports Direct baseball cap and a green anorak with a backpack. The coat is reversible so it might be blue. If you spot him, call the rest of us in before trying to apprehend him. He is armed and very dangerous.'

The team radioed back their acknowledgements as the train stopped. All along the platform, doors hissed open and people stepped out into the chilly November day. Hannah ran her eyes across the commuters and day trippers, looking for the hat, looking for the coat. Looking for Bartholomew.

And not seeing him.

'Anyone got eyes on the suspect?' she asked across the radio.

'Negative,' someone said back.

'Negative,' another officer replied.

'Negative.'

'Negative.'

'Negative.'

Then it was the governor's voice in her ear. 'Hannah,' Wise said. 'We're here. Coming over to you now.'

Hannah could feel her anxiety go up a notch. She watched a large woman waddle pass. A girl with dreads. A businessman who looked like he needed another year's worth of sleep. A man in a watch cap, blue disposable face mask and a puffa jacket. He glanced at Hannah as he walked by, dark eyes flicking over her before he turned his attention back to the exit. Most people, though, didn't even bother checking out what the police were doing on the platform. They just wanted to be on their way. That man had had a good look, though. Must be the nervous type. Still wearing a mask while the rest of the world pretended Covid didn't exist anymore. If only he knew there were deadlier killers travelling with him.

'Team One, how are you getting on? Any sign of the suspect on the train?' she asked over the radio.

'Negative,' an officer replied. 'We're halfway down. Train empty so far. Everyone's off.'

'Hicksy?' Hannah was feeling desperate now. She glanced down the platform to the ticket barriers. Hicksy was there, all hunched up in his coat, chin against his chest.

'No fucking sign of the bastard,' the old copper growled back over the radio.

The platform was emptying now, with more police on it than the public. And there was still no sign of Bartholomew.

Hannah knew she'd blown it somehow. The man had gotten past her.

'Hannah!' Wise sprinted towards her, with Brains following on behind. 'What's happening?'

'There's no sign of him, Guv,' she replied. 'Either he got off the train before Waterloo or he's got past us somehow.'

'How's that possible?' Wise glared up and down the platform, as if he'd be able to spot Bartholomew when no one else had. When she hadn't.

'DS Markham?' an officer called over the radio. 'This is Team One. We've found something on the train you need to see.'

'Where are you?' Hannah replied, looking at the train.

'Here.' An officer stuck his head out of a door thirty yards away and waved.

Hannah, Wise, and Brains jogged over and got on the train.

'It's in the toilets,' the officer said. 'There's a body.'

'Brains, wait here. Hannah, come with me,' Wise said. They moved down to the cubicle at the end of the carriage, where another officer waited, who pointed inside.

Hannah and Wise peered around the door. A man lay in a pool of blood, his face as white as snow. A Sports Direct cap lay on top of a green anorak in the sink. A small backpack lay next to the toilet.

'Someone opened up his stomach, sir,' the officer said.

'Bartholomew's swapped clothes,' Wise said. 'That's how he got past us.'

Hannah stared at the body. At a man who'd done nothing wrong except being in the wrong place at the wrong time.

Wise was on the radio, calling Sarah at the Force Control Room. 'Find him for me,' he said. 'Find anyone who might be him.'

'We'll try but, if we don't know what he looks like, I wouldn't hold out much hope.'

'Just do your best,' Wise said. 'Work some magic. Do something!'

Hannah could feel her chest tighten. The walls of the train

pressed in on her, making it hard to breathe and even harder to think. She pushed past Wise and hurried off the train, gulping damp, cold air as she stepped out onto the platform.

Bartholomew must've walked past her. She must've seen him and not recognised him. But how? Surely she'd have recognised him even with a change of coat, maybe wearing a different hat. The man's nose might not have been as busted up as Hicksy's but it was still distinctive.

Unless he was wearing a mask. A disposable mask.

The man in the watch cap and puffa jacket. The man who'd looked at her. The man with dark eyes.

Bartholomew.

She clicked her radio. 'Guv, I know what he's wearing. He walked past me five minutes ago.'

# 43

Wise, Hannah and Brains ran across Waterloo Station as fast as they could. They'd left Hicksy to look after the crime scene on the train. The man was no sprinter, after all, and speed was what was needed now.

'He's at the bottom of the escalator,' Sarah said in Wise's ear. 'Heading towards the ticket barriers to the Tube.' She'd been able to spot Bartholomew easily enough after Hannah had told her what to look for. Now the team at the Control Room had eyes on their suspect. CCTV covered nearly every inch of the underground, so Wise was feeling good about catching Bartholomew. They just had to reach him in time before he could disappear into a blind spot, and Wise had no doubt someone as canny as Bartholomew would know where they were.

'He's through the barriers,' Sarah continued. 'Walking like he hasn't got a care in the world.'

Wise and the others reached the main escalator down from the main station to the Underground. A giant poster loomed overhead, advertising the latest exhibition at the V&A. 'Get out of the way,' he shouted at the commuters in front of him. 'Police! Make room!'

People shifted to the right as Wise, Hannah, and Brains barrelled down the steps. The escalator was steep, making them slow down just enough to stop them from falling. The low ceiling, barely a foot over his head, pressed down on Wise as he stomped down the metal steps, and he could feel the old, familiar fear prickle away in his gut.

'Police! Make way!' he shouted again as a woman stepped suddenly to the left on the stairs, blocking his way. She turned, looking horrified, but not bloody moving, until another passenger grabbed her arm and hauled her back to the right just in time. Then Wise, Hannah, and Brains were on the ground and turning right towards the ticket barriers.

'He's halfway down the second escalator,' Sarah said in his ear. 'He's either going for the Northern or Bakerloo trains.'

'Any uniforms down there? Anyone who can intercept?' Wise messaged back. The ticket barriers were up ahead, a small lineup of people waiting to go through at each one. 'Out of my way! Police!' he shouted.

His cries startled almost everyone out of the way. An elderly man, though, had just tapped their Oyster card in front of him. The barriers swung open and Wise collided into him, sending both of them through the gap, before they went sprawling across the ground.

'Sorry,' he said, getting to his feet and running on. Hannah was behind him, having jumped the barriers, and he was damn glad of that.

'He's turned right,' Sarah said. 'Heading for the Northern Line. Trying to get you back up.'

'Get them to stop the bloody trains!' Wise shouted. 'We can't let him get away.'

They reached the next escalator that seemed twice as steep and twice as long as the first one. Wise was tempted to try to slide down the middle between the up and down stairs, but adverts jutted up every few metres. He could just see him doing himself an injury trying the James Bond stunt, so he stuck with the stairs, his enormous bulk totally out of place in the confined space. At least there were fewer passengers in his way this time and he had a clearer run down.

'Train's at the platform,' Sarah said. 'He's got on, but I've got them to hold the train there. He's not going anywhere.'

'Thank God for that.'

'It's packed though. Maybe three hundred people on board.'

Shit. Bartholomew could do a lot of damage before Wise got there. He could hurt a lot of people. 'What about backup?'

'Got some ... on their ... you.' Sarah's voice faded in and out as Wise reached the bottom of the stairs.

'Can you repeat that?' Wise said, but he got only static back. Great. Now they'd lost radio contact with Sarah.

'The Northern Line's to the right,' Hannah called as she caught up with him.

Following her directions, they ran together down another tight tunnel, the echoes of their footsteps chasing after them. They passed the Southbound staircase, then turned left and bounced down the stone staircase to the Northbound platform. As Sarah had promised, the Tube train was still at the platform, its doors open.

Faces peered out of the six carriages of the train, no doubt wondering what the hold-up was. Wise scanned them quickly, hoping to spot Bartholomew.

'What do we do?' Hannah said. 'How do we find him?

'We go down the platform together, each covering a set of doors to each carriage and look for him through the windows,' Wise said, only too aware of how deep underground they were. Without the movement of trains, it felt like there was no air on the platform. No space.

Damn, he hated the Tube.

'You cover the front door. I'll cover the rear,' Hannah said, pulling a retractable baton out of her pocket and flicking it to its full length. Wise wished he had one of his own, then he saw her stab-proof vest and he wished he'd grabbed one of those, too. All he had was a useless radio.

It was too late to fix that now, though, as they moved down the platform, peering through the Tube windows, looking at faces, looking for a killer.

# 44

When the Tube had pulled into the platform, George got in the first carriage at the far end of the platform and quickly slipped into a seat. He'd done it. He'd gotten away. Killing the man on the train had been a masterstroke. George had loved walking past the black bitch and her idiotic colleagues when he'd gotten off the train. He'd waltzed straight past the lot of them while they all gawped around. He'd strolled through Waterloo, down the escalators and into the Tube. And any minute now, the doors would shut and he'd be whisked away and off into London.

The trouble was, he wasn't sure of what to do after that or where to go.

George didn't have a passport on him. He had hardly any money — just enough to play The Game but not enough to go on the run. He couldn't get any more cash because the police would already be onto his bank, demanding to be notified the moment he used his debit card or credit card. There were no friends to call on, no family to shelter with. He couldn't even ask Christopher for help. The police had him under surveillance, as it was.

So what was he going to do? Wander the streets of London

aimlessly? He was in no mood to sleep rough like the nobodies he'd been killing.

Maybe he could hitchhike down to Dover and sneak onboard a lorry going to France. That was a possibility. Customs only cared about people being smuggled into the UK, not out of it.

The more he thought about it, the more he liked the idea. He could find a nice little cottage in the country, murder the owners and see out the winter in comfort. It would give him time to work out a longer-term plan. He could—

'What's the holdup, Bruv?' a man said nearby. 'We should be gone by now.'

'It's bloody Transport For London. They're useless,' a woman said. 'It's outrageous, especially with the prices they charge.'

George looked up. He saw the irritated faces of the other passengers around him. Then he saw the doors were still open. They were still at Waterloo.

A few new passengers got onboard, unaware the train wasn't departing anytime soon. Others started discussing wild theories for the delay. They ranged from a suicide on the tracks to a bomb threat to a power shortage, even though all the lights were still on. Those near the doors stuck their heads out, trying to see the cause of the delay.

No one had a clue what was going on. No one except for George.

He knew exactly what was causing the hold-up.

It was him.

The police knew where he was and were coming for him.

He pulled the stupid face mask off, happy to breathe unhindered again, and tossed it on the floor. Some old bag gave him a dirty look for that, and he was half-tempted to cut her throat for her temerity. Luckily for her, there wasn't time for that. He needed to get off that train and get away before it was too late.

George got up from his seat and walked over to the open doors. A couple of lads with durags tied around their heads and the biggest, whitest trainers on their feet, were blocking the nearest door. 'Excuse me,' he said, keeping his head down, leading with his arm, trying to find a gap between them. His other hand was inside his jacket, wrapped tight around the hilt of his knife. It was fight-or-flight time and he was ready either way.

The men begrudgingly made room for him, and George stuck his head out the door.

That was when he saw the big detective who'd punched him in the face the day before. The copper was making his way down the platform, peering through the carriage windows. The black woman was behind him with a long metal baton in her hand. They still had three carriages to go before they reached him, though. Time enough to slip away.

Of course, Wise had to look up then. 'Bartholomew!' he shouted. The other detective looked his way as well as Wise sprinted towards him.

George pulled the kukri knife out of his jacket. He slashed the man to his right across the neck. Blood jetted out as he turned and hacked the man's friend in the gut, opening him up. The man stumbled forward, all but dead, and George pushed his bleeding body out of the Tube, onto the platform and into Wise's path.

As the detective tripped over the bleeding man, George darted out of the train and ran the last few yards of the platform and down the slope into the tunnel. Into the darkness.

# 45

Wise went sprawling, his legs caught up with some poor sod whom Bartholomew had pushed in his way. He hit the platform hard, knocking the air from his lungs. For a moment, he couldn't breathe, and the body he was tangled up with only added to his sense of claustrophobia, of panic. He kicked out, pushing the man away, desperate to be free as he tried to force his lungs to work again, to gulp down air. As Bartholomew ran from the train and down into the tunnel.

Hannah grabbed him and helped haul him to his feet. 'Shit,' she said. 'Are you hurt?'

Wise looked down and saw the blood covering his hands and clothes. 'It's not mine.' They both looked down then, saw the blood pouring from the young lad on the ground, and heard the screaming from the train. There another man lay, clutching a wound on his neck as a passenger tried to stem the bleeding with a scarf.

'Oh my God,' Hannah said.

'Sarah,' Wise gasped into his radio. 'Can you hear me?'

Static crackled in his ear.

'What shall we do?' Hannah asked, her eyes wide at the sight of all the blood.

'You stay here and help,' Wise said. 'I'll go after Bartholomew.'

They both looked down the tunnel, into the dark.

'You sure?' Hannah said.

'Yes,' Wise replied, even though it was the last thing he wanted to do. 'Give me your baton.'

Hannah handed over the fifty-centimetre steel stick. 'Be careful.'

'I'll do my best,' Wise said and ran after Bartholomew.

The moment Wise was off the platform and in the tunnel, he could feel the darkness closing in around him. He had to take his time, too. The Tube ran on four rails, the second and fourth of which were electrified, with six hundred and thirty volts running through them. That was enough to burn Wise to a crisp if he wasn't careful.

Overhead, knackered and flickering fluorescent lights provided just enough light to see by as Wise made his way down the tunnel. The sound of other trains running through the Underground echoed around him and thrummed through the walls. Gasping stale air into his battered lungs, Wise squinted into the shadows, looking for any sign of his quarry and finding none. Sweat broke out across his brow and ran down his back. His hands were sticky with a dead man's blood, the metal baton heavy in his grasp. He could feel his heart racing as stone gravel crunched under foot.

Suddenly, following Bartholomew into that tunnel seemed like the stupidest thing Wise had ever done in his life.

'I could die down here,' he muttered to himself. How far away was the Embankment station? It was years since he'd last travelled anywhere by Tube and he could only remember praying for the journey to be over, not where he'd gone. He was certainly no expert on distances between stations. He might be walking for minutes or hours for all he knew.

As the tunnel curved around to the right, Wise had to walk sideways, leading the way with the baton in front of him, glancing down regularly to make sure his leg didn't touch the second live rail. There was more than enough room, but he felt like he was walking a tightrope down there in the dark, death crackling mere inches away from his feet.

He kept looking back to the Tube platform he'd just left, its bright lights shrinking with every step he took further into the tunnel. Still, there was comfort knowing it was there. It was a place to run back to if need be. A place from which help would come. Sarah had promised backup, after all. They had to be on their way — unless they were too busy with the carnage Bartholomew had left behind.

His eyes searched the dark and the shadows ahead of him, looking for anything that didn't belong in that deep, damp tunnel. A human shape. A knife. He strained his ears, trying to hear anything that would let him know where Bartholomew might be lurking. Was he waiting for Wise or running for his life?

Looking around, it was easy to believe the tunnel had been dug well over a hundred years ago. Wise could practically feel the age of the bricks around him, the history he walked along. What must've it been like back then, digging deep under London, using machines that would've felt like something out of an H.G. Wells novel?

Another train rumbled through another tunnel, and dirt fell from the roof like rain. Wise froze for a moment, his mind full of a thousand irrational fears. *Go back*, a voice in the back of his head told him. *Go back. Go back. Go back.*

But Wise was never one for listening to good advice. He was as stubborn as a mule, as his old man so often told him. Wise by name, dumb by nature. So, on he went. Deeper and deeper. Following the tunnel around. The station behind grew smaller and smaller until the curve of the walls hid it completely from sight. Its small anchor of security gone. Wise took a deep breath. Now he was truly alone.

He walked on, blinking the fear from his eyes, listening to distant trains rumble like thunder. His radio was silent in his ear. No support. No backup. And every shadow held a potential ambush.

Time lost all meaning as Wise went deeper into the tunnel, a tunnel that seemed to get narrower with every step he took. He knew it was his imagination fooling him, but that didn't quieten the voice in his head telling him go back, give up, don't be a fool. Others could stop Bartholomew. It didn't have to be him. Not down there. Not alone.

But it did. There was no one else. Just Wise down there in the dark.

And then he saw him. Two metres ahead. Illuminated by a flickering light. Standing in the middle of the tunnel. Waiting for Wise, with the big knife that was almost a sword in his hand. The knife he knew how to use so well. In comparison, the baton in his own hand now seemed totally inadequate. How could something so thin stop something so big? There wasn't much difference in length either. The knife was forty centimetres long. The baton was fifty. No real advantage but would it be the difference between life and death?

'Bartholomew,' Wise said.

'Inspector,' Bartholomew replied.

'Drop the knife.' Wise hoped he sounded confident and calm, but he felt anything but that. He'd never backed down from a fight in his life before but, in that narrow tunnel next to a rail track that could fry him, facing that knife? He didn't feel that old familiar urge to charge in with clenched fists. Far from it. For the first time in his life, Wise wanted to run. 'Drop it now.'

Bartholomew chuckled. 'I don't think so.'

'Don't be a fool. You've got nowhere to go. Officers are coming from the Embankment. More are following me from Waterloo. You're just delaying the inevitable. So, just drop the knife. It'll be better for you.'

'Do you know I was thinking about you earlier?' Bartholomew said, ignoring Wise's words. 'Back on the train from Weybridge? Before I knew you were after me? I was thinking about how you'd hit me yesterday and how much I didn't like it.'

'Few people do.' Maybe Wise could just keep him talking until backup arrived. It had to be on its way, just like he'd told Bartholomew. It had to be. Hannah wouldn't let him down.

'I thought then about how much I wanted to meet you again — but this time with my knife in my hand. To see how good you really are,' Bartholomew said. 'And now we're here. Just the two of us. It's almost as if God intended it to happen.'

'Really? Do you believe that crap?' Wise said. The gap between them really didn't seem that much. All Bartholomew had to do was take two steps and Wise would be within reach of that knife. 'Somehow, I don't think God would approve of you killing malnourished drug addicts.'

'They were nobodies. A waste of life. I did them a favour by killing them.'

'Sasha wasn't a nobody. She was just a kid running away from abuse.' Wise's hand ached from gripping the baton so tightly. Maybe if he was quick, he could knock the knife from Bartholomew's hand. How long had it been since he'd had any baton training? 'Running from your brother and his church.'

'I think you'll find it was his dick that upset her the most. Christopher could never keep it under control.'

'He raped her?'

'Her and others.'

'But not you. You just killed her.'

'Her and others.' By God, Bartholomew sounded so proud. Like it was all so easy.

For the first time in that tunnel, Wise could feel his anger rising and, with it, his fear retreated. 'Leroy Jenkins. Mark Stay. Alice Kuang. Ben Trills. Kareem Abdul. Jack Springer.'

The man shrugged. 'If you say so. I never asked their names. It never mattered. They were happy to play The Game and take their chances.'

'The game?'

'Everything's a game. Even this. Here we are, one against one. My knife. Your stick. The question is, are you ready to play?'

'I'm not here to play games,' Wise said. 'Not when you've confessed to multiple murders.'

'Those kids are just the tip of the iceberg. I've been killing people all my life. It's what I do. It's who I am.'

Wise looked over Bartholomew's shoulder. 'You get all that?'

Bartholomew turned, bringing his knife up, expecting to find someone behind him. But there was just the darkness. However, the moment he moved, Wise moved too. Leaping forward, he swung the baton with all his might, aiming for the back of Bartholomew's neck.

Wise was quick, but Bartholomew was quicker.

He ducked under the baton and slashed back with the knife as he turned to face Wise once more. It was an awkward move, but Wise still felt the kukri blade flash past, cutting a slice through his jacket. He shuffled back quickly, aware that he'd been less than a centimetre away from having his stomach opened from side to side.

Bartholomew faced him, his teeth glinting in the fluorescent light. 'So, you want to play after all. Excellent.'

Wise said nothing, his eyes fixed on the kukri knife in Bartholomew's hand. Even though his baton had a slightly longer reach, they had taught him long ago that the advantage was always with the knife man. Wise had few targets on Bartholomew that would do any real damage; basically the head, neck, and groin. A strike on the joints could work too, especially if he hit Bartholomew's wrists with enough force or got a knee, but striking anywhere else was a waste of time. A bruised arm wouldn't stop Bartholomew from killing him. Especially when Wise's whole body was a viable target for a knife. A cut anywhere would hurt Wise and slow him down, if not kill him.

Wise took a step back, then another, aware of the narrow gap he had to work in, aware of the electric rail next to his left foot.

But Bartholomew wasn't going to let him get away that easily. He slashed at Wise again, the curved blade arcing down, cutting the air in front of his face.

Wise retreated, holding his baton in front of him, watching Bartholomew. As he did so, Major Dixon's words came back to him. 'It's like fighting someone with an axe more than a knife,' the officer had said, and it was true. There was no point for Bartholomew to stab Wise with. He couldn't thrust the knife into him. He had to chop down or slash across. Every time Bartholomew missed, he had to bring the weapon up and hack down again.

There was an opportunity to strike back then — if he didn't miss-time things.

Wise took another step back, watching, waiting.

Bartholomew pulled his arm back, the blade all but horizontal to the ground and in line with his hip. He was going for Wise's gut again, cutting from right to left.

Wise pulled his baton hand back, opening up his body just a little bit more, offering more of a target. 'Come on, Bartholomew,' he said. 'You're running out of time. The whole Met's going to be here in a minute. Just give up. You're useless against anyone over the age of eighteen.'

'Go to hell,' Bartholomew snarled back, and he lashed out. The kukri blade flashed from left to right, aiming for Wise's stomach, all its weight in the top of the blade, giving it momentum, giving it cutting power.

Wise pulled his gut in, felt the blade go past, and then he brought the baton down as hard as he could, putting all his strength into the blow. The baton cracked into Bartholomew's arm, knocking it down, knocking Bartholomew off-balance.

That was when Wise drove his left fist into Bartholomew's face for the second time in two days. And, for the second time in two days, Bartholomew went down hard, falling over the first rail of four, the one that ran nearest the platforms. The one for the wheels. The unelectrified one. Lucky him.

Wise moved quickly and stamped on the wrist of Bartholomew's knife hand. It broke his grip on the weapon as well and, quite possibly, a bone or two in the process.

Wise snatched up the weapon and threw it far from Bartholomew, then pulled the wrist back behind his wrist, cuffed it and then did the same with the other.

'You're nicked,' he said with great pleasure. 'You're bloody nicked.'

# 46

Jono was no longer in the private room in St Thomas' Intensive Care Unit. He wasn't even in Intensive Care. They'd moved him to the William Gull ward on the tenth floor. When Wise arrived, he found Jono sitting upright and looking better than he had done in a long time.

'You're not dead, then?' Wise said, plonking a bunch of grapes on the small side table.

'Not yet,' Jono said, smiling. He glanced down at the grapes. 'I don't suppose you've got a small bottle of whisky with you as well? I was never too keen on grapes.'

'Sorry, mate,' Wise replied. 'Maybe next time.'

'Yeah, yeah. That's what they all say.'

'How you are doing? You look ... well.' Wise picked a grape and popped it in his mouth.

'The blood clots are all cleared up, so that's something,' Jono said. 'They've said I can go home tomorrow.'

'Pat must be pleased.'

'Yeah. She is.'

'You did well with her.'

'A real diamond.'

'Must be, to put up with you.'

'Ain't that the truth,' Jono said.

'What about the cancer?' Wise said, hating the sound of the word and all the horrible memories it carried.

'Well, the one good thing about being in a hospital full of people who are dying is that it made me realise that maybe I'm not quite ready to join them,' Jono said. 'I've agreed to have the treatment. After all, Pat's said she'll still love me if I go bald.'

Wise grinned. 'That's the best news I've heard all day.'

'How's work?' Jono asked. 'You getting anywhere with the case?'

'You've missed a lot while you've been away,' Wise said and told him about everything that had happened. 'We've charged Joshua Moore, Mark Elliot, Neil Hendry, Thomas Kind and Ray Butler with the kidnapping of Sasha Moore, and her unlawful imprisonment. The pastor too, along with the rape of Sasha Moore and accessory to her murder. His brother, though, is the big one. We've nicked George Bartholomew for the murders of Sasha Moore, Leroy Jenkins, Mark Stay, Alice Kuang, Ben Trills, Kareem Abdul and Jack Springer, as well as the attempted murder of Katie Jones.'

'Jesus,' Jono said. 'You really have been busy.'

'We've got a long way to go yet,' Wise said. 'When I was with him in the tunnels, Bartholomew said those murders were just the tip of the iceberg. I think we're going to find he's killed a lot more people over the years.'

'Well done, Guv.' The smile fell from Jono's face. 'I'm sorry I wasn't there to help.'

Wise squeezed Jono's shoulder. 'Don't even think about it. You just need to get well.'

'I'll do my best.' Then the smile was back, and Jono chuckled. 'Did you really partner up Hicksy with Markham?'

'That I did. And they didn't kill each other, but I think Hicksy would rather you were back at work sooner rather and later,' Wise said.

'Him and me both,' Jono said.

Wise stood up. 'Enjoy your grapes. I'll see you soon.'

'Good work, Guv. Damn good work.'

## Tuesday 22nd November

# 47

Wise had nearly cancelled his visit to Belmarsh Prison a dozen times that morning. After all, with all the arrests his team had made the day before, there was plenty to be getting on without wasting time with his own private investigation. Especially since he didn't have any doubts about Tom's innocence anymore. Not after his threats against Wise's family.

Despite all that, Wise still found himself making the hour-long drive from Kennington over to Thamesmead, where the category A prison was located. Built in the early nineties, Belmarsh was home to only the most violent and dangerous prisoners. Its guests at the moment included Michael Adebolajo, who murdered British soldier Lee Rigby, David Copeland, the man who bombed Brixton Market and Brick Lane, and Delroy Grant, the infamous Night Stalker and serial rapist.

But even in Belmarsh, there was an area reserved for the worst of the worst. It was a prison within the prison. The High Security Unit, known as The Box, was hidden behind twenty-foot concrete walls and access in and out granted by the prison's central command. It was where Elrit Selmani had his cell.

As a prison guard led Wise to the visiting room, he couldn't help but think what it must've been like for his brother all those years ago. Tom has spent the first part of his sentence in Feltham Prison for Young Offenders before going to Wormwood Scrubs Prison once he turned eighteen. The Scrubs was a category B prison, but that didn't mean it was a good place to do time.

Walking through The Box, Wise himself could feel his claustrophobia ratchet up another notch every time another door slammed shut and a lock engaged. It was different from being in the tunnel, though. There it had been all darkness and shadows, the smell of dirt filling his nose. Now, everywhere he looked were white walls, concrete floors, and metal doors. Daylight was something to be glimpsed through thick glass windows. The prisoners spent at least fourteen hours a day locked up in cells twelve feet by eight feet, sharing that space with one or two other prisoners. For Wise, it was the very definition of hell.

Eventually, the prison guard stopped in front of a steel door, painted white. 'Here you go.' He used his lanyard to disengage the locks and opened the door, then stepped back to let Wise enter.

Wise walked into the visiting room, then stopped dead when he saw who was waiting for him.

It wasn't Elrit Selmani.

Instead, DCI Rena Heer from Specialist Crime and Operations 10, and her colleague, DS Brendan Murray, were sitting on one side of the small table.

'Hello Inspector,' said Heer. 'Fancy meeting you here.'

The door slammed shut behind Wise. The lock engaged.

Murray placed a photograph on the table. It was the one they'd shown him back in September. Taken by a covert operative, they had thought the man in the picture was Wise. 'Before we discuss why you're so keen to see Elrit Selmani, we'd like to talk to you about your brother, Tom.'

Heer pointed at the chair opposite them. 'Take a seat.'

# Wednesday 23rd November

# 48

'Fucking hell, it's absolutely freezing up here,' Tom Wise said, slapping his gloved hands together. 'Good job I've got my North Face on, eh?'

Clarence Wu didn't reply. He just stared back at Tom, trying to pretend he didn't give a shit, while doing his best not to shiver as the wind ripped past, full of ice and spite, with nothing to stand in its way.

They were twenty-five floors off the ground, after all, on the rooftop of a new office building. It was just off the Westway, and still a good six months of hard graft away from being anywhere near finished. Right then, it was more concrete than anything else. There were no walls or windows to keep the weather out. Nothing, in fact, to provide any sort of shelter from the November night.

It was perfect for what Tom wanted — which was a nice bit of peace, quiet, and privacy. Perfect for when there were tough conversations to be had. The fact it was three in the morning, without even a star in the sky to brighten the mood, added to the ambience.

Tom wasn't alone with Clarence, though. He had a half dozen of his lads with him. Good lads who enjoyed doing the wet work when needed.

Clarence, on the other hand, was on his Jack Jones and, unlike Tom and his lads, the Chinky wasn't dressed for a night out. Not since Tom and the lads had stripped him of his fancy overcoat, suit, shirt, sock and shoes. They'd left him his silky underpants, though, because they weren't monsters. And who wanted to see a fat old bastard's shrivelled dick? Tom certainly didn't.

And he certainly was a fat fuck. The wind had plenty of spots to nip away at Clarence, sucking the heat from his skin with its cruel kisses. But maybe all that blubber around his gut had to be good for something. Maybe he was as warm as a whale, for all Tom knew.

Probably not, though. Not if those dirty looks he was throwing Tom's way were any indication of how he felt. Of course, the fact he was on his knees with his hands tied behind his back couldn't be helping his mood. And that he had to know his life expectancy was being measured in minutes.

If Tom was in his position, he'd be well pissed off.

But Tom wasn't, and that's why he was as happy as fucking Larry.

He smiled. 'Anyway, I bet you're wondering why I wanted to have this little chat with you, Clarence, old chap.'

Clarence said nothing.

'When I was younger,' Tom continued, 'I went to prison. Now, I know that's not unusual, especially in our game. I mean, everyone here's done some time — even you, I'd imagine. Even so, I was young, and I have to admit, I was scared. I'd been a tough kid growing up, handy with my fists, liked a ruck and all, but prison was different. It was full of hard men with nothing to lose and some of them saw a pretty young lad who they thought they could have some fun with.'

In the distance, a siren wailed, off on its way to help someone else somewhere far away.

'So, the first day I was there, I went in the canteen to get my scram, when the biggest, hardest motherfucker I'd ever seen comes over to me. He was a bloke called Mark Taylor. He was in there for life for killing a copper. He really did look mean too — shitty tattoos all over his face, his neck, his arms, his hands — all done with prison ink —with muscles popping out his muscles.' Tom wandered over to the edge of the building. As well as no walls and windows, there were no barriers of any sort separating the edge of the floor from the night sky. One step too far and it was long, long way down to Splatsville. Still, the view was amazing. London was all lit up and looking magnificent. God, he loved this city. Always had. He could feel the city in his blood, in his soul. No wonder he wanted it for himself.

'There I was, sitting with my metal tray, trying to eat my mash potato, beef stew and carrots, and this fucker is acting like I was his pudding. A pudding he wanted to stuff. I didn't even have to look around to know that every eye in that place was watching and waiting to see me get fucking destroyed by this bastard.

'Mark Taylor looms over me, holding out his hands like he was going to give me a big, warm hug,' Tom said. 'And invites me back to his cell to suck his cock.'

'That wasn't very nice of him,' one of Tom's lads said.

'No, it wasn't. I didn't like it one bit,' Tom said. 'And I knew that if I sucked that twat's cock, I'd spend the rest of my years inside doing a brisk trade for everyone else who felt a bit horny.' Tom bent down to look Clarence in the eye. The Chinaman didn't look away either. He gave Tom the full evil eye while he kept his mouth shut. The cold was getting to him, though. He was shivering and shaking despite his best efforts to look tough. 'So, I picked up my metal tray and rammed it in that fucker's throat as hard as I could instead. Fucked up his Adam's apple good and proper and dropped him to his knees, just like that. Then I smashed the tray into his mouth so he could suck on that instead. By the time the screws hauled me away, even dear old Mark's mum wouldn't have recognised him. The poor sod spent six months drinking out of a straw after that. I wouldn't be surprised if he still couldn't eat solid food to this day.'

'Serves him right,' Gorgeous Gary said. 'He shouldn't have tried to take liberties.'

'Exactly,' Tom said, wagging a finger at his driver. He turned back to Clarence. 'Now, why am I telling you this? Well, first, I still don't like people thinking I'm just a punk that will happily get fucked over just because someone else thinks they are the hardest bastard in town. And, secondly, I definitely won't suck anyone's cock, no matter how nicely they ask. And you, Clarence, didn't ask nicely at all.'

Tom patted Clarence on the cheek and stood up once more. 'We could've been partners, you and me. London's a big town, after all. There's plenty of money to go around. Enough for us all to be rich. But you, my son, are a greedy motherfucker. You don't want to share, do you? And then you had to hurt my lads when they wouldn't give you my money.' He laughed. 'That was very bad of you.'

Clarence looked up, curled his lip. 'Fuck you.'

'Wow, you do speak English!' Tom said. 'For a minute there, I was starting to think I'd been wasting my time, waffling away here, telling my little story. That maybe I should've brought someone with me who could speak the old kung fu.'

'You are the greedy motherfucker,' Clarence said. 'Your men took over my place. You were stealing my money. I was just taking back what was mine.'

Tom had to admit he was impressed. Plenty of people in Clarence's position would've been shitting themselves, but not this fat bastard.

'Mine. Yours. It's an old-fashioned way of looking at things, Clarence,' Tom said. 'What is it they teach you in school? "Sharing is caring?" And, as I said, all I wanted to do was share in your riches. We could've been partners.'

'Partners where I have nothing and you have everything!'

'No, you would've still had something. Just not as much as you had before. But look, if you don't want to play together, who am I to argue? Life's too short.' That got a good few laughs from the men. 'Which brings me back to my story.' He grinned, enjoying the moment, looking forward to what was coming next. 'You see, after the other lags saw me fuck up big Mark, they knew I was the business. They knew not to try their luck with me. And life outside, it turns out, is pretty much the same as life inside. So, here we are, Clarence — time to make an example out of you, so others don't think I'm some pussy out for a pounding.'

'Do what you will. I don't care,' Clarence spat back. 'All you are doing is declaring war. My people will come after you for this.'

'Good. Bring it on, We like a good ruck,' Tom said. He nodded at the two lads standing behind the gangster. Luke and Big Tony hauled Clarence to his feet. They marched him to the edge of the roof. Tom followed, aware that the wind was picking up, blowing harder, faster, colder, crueller. He could even feel its bite through his North Face jacket. It was definitely time to be off.

The lads held Clarence so that he was still facing Tom, his back to the drop and the big, beautiful city. There was fear in his eyes now, his bravado gone into the night. Standing on your tiptoes with a twenty-five floor drop behind would scare even the hardest of men. 'You let me go and we won't come after you. You have my—'

Tom pushed the fat bastard out into the night.

Clarence might've screamed on the way down, but Tom wouldn't have heard it over the wind. He turned around to look at his boys. 'Anyone hungry? My treat?'

'I'm starving,' Big Tony said, but that wasn't news to anyone. That lad always had a hunger on him.

'Come on, then.' Tom headed to the lift. 'Let's get some sweet and sour prawn balls and special fried rice. That Chinky over in Ladbroke Grove should still be open.'

'Wok and Rolls?' Gorgeous said.

'That's the one.' Tom rubbed his hands together. 'Lovely.'

All in all, it'd not been a bad night's work.

# THANK YOU

Thank you for reading *The Killing Game,* the second Detective Inspector Simon Wise thriller. It means the world to me that you have given your time to read my tales. It's your support that makes it possible for me to do this for a living, after all.

So, please spare a moment if you can to either write a review or simply rate *The Killing Game* on Amazon. Your honest opinion will help future readers decide if they want to take a chance on a new-to-them author. Leaving a review is one of the greatest things you can do for an author and it really helps our books stand out amongst all the rest.

I've been thrilled by the reception Simon Wise has received so far. It's been an exciting journey for me too so far. I'm learning lots and having fun in the process.

**DI Wise will be back in TALKING OF THE DEAD.**

Thank you once again!

Michael (Keep reading to get a free book)

GET A FREE BOOK TODAY

Sign up for my mailing list at www.michaeldylanwrites.com and get a free copy of Dead Man Running, and discover exactly how DS Andy Davidson ended up on that rooftop in Peckham with a gun in his hand.

Plus by signing up, you'll be the first to hear about the next books in the series and special deals.

# THE DI SIMON WISE SERIES

*Out Now:*

Dead Man Running

Rich Men, Dead Men

The Killing Game

Talking Of The Dead

Printed in Great Britain
by Amazon